# POSSESSED BY AN ANGEL

the man named Rebuck came out of nowhere—a maverick, a rebel, to found the Church of Michael, which threatened to destroy the foundations of organized religion, plunging the earth into chaos, terror, and religious war.

Adored by multitudes, loved by two women, Rebuck sets out on a road of passion and agony paved with betrayal that will end either in the salvation—or the damnation—of

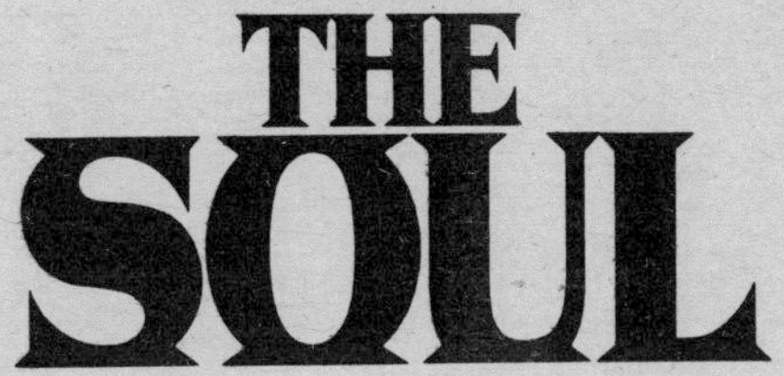

# THE SOUL

BY RON GORTON

ZEBRA BOOKS

KENSINGTON PUBLISHING CORP.

*To those all too few*
*free souls—*
*and especially to Jessie,*
*who quietly understood mine*

**ZEBRA BOOKS**

**are published by**

**KENSINGTON PUBLISHING CORP.**
**521 Fifth Avenue**
**New York, N. Y. 10017**



First Printing: December, 1977

**Printed in the United States of America**

# The Inspiration

# Preface
# October, 1945

ON A LATE October afternoon, a black DeSoto moved under a pale sun, flanked by the flame-colored trees of an upper New York State autumn. Turning off the two-lane rural highway, the bulky car passed through an open black wrought-iron gate onto a private road lined by old trees and neatly barbered lawns. From the half-open driver's window crackled a disembodied voice selling war bonds, with the strains of "praise the Lord and pass the ammunition" tinkling in the background.

The car rolled to a full stop in front of a gray Victorian building of three tall stories with an encircling porch. The radio announcer's voice was abruptly stilled. Seconds later, a slender woman stepped from the car, followed hesitantly by a young boy of seven or eight in brown knickers and brown and white checkered socks.

The woman started up the wooden steps, then stopped and looked back at the boy, who stared suspiciously at a large red brick building that sat arrogantly on a hilly plateau some two hundred yards away.

She followed his eyes as they took in another building beyond – a wooden structure, a bell tower that seemed to reach all the way up to the sky.

"Ronnie."

His eyes shifted back to the building in front of them, to the sober bronze plaque by the door that read: ALL SOULS SCHOOL and then, reluctantly back to the raven-haired woman.

"Ronnie, come on," she said softly, just above a whisper. Still the boy didn't budge. All the way from Stamford he'd sat stubbornly, not uttering a word. And now this . . .

Swallowing her anger, she walked back to him, then stopped, caught by his eyes, those strange tricolored eyes – brown, yellow with a flick of green. For a moment she felt as she had several times before, as though a key had turned and she was locked, helpless, imprisoned by those eyes. For thirty seconds he held her there, then suddenly released her, turning away with a contemptuous toss of his head. She reached down gently for his hand, but he thrust his little paws into the knicker pockets. She reached for his arm but the creaking of a door and the sound of firm footsteps on the porch brought her to a halt.

"Mrs. Rebuck? . . ."

The boy stared in astonishment at the short, baldheaded man clad in what looked like a black dress, with beads for a belt. The woman smiled faintly and led the distracted boy up the steps.

"I'm Father Deleo." His smile revealed a glint of gold. "And this . . . must be Ronald. Won't you please come in?"

The administrator's office was small, austere, smelling of incense. A statue of the Virgin Mary and Child stood in a corner. A large crucifix hung on the dark oak-paneled wall, flanked by a picture of Pope Pius XII and a portrait of the founding father with a halo about his head. Father Deleo gestured for the woman to be seated, ignoring the boy who stood close to his mother's side. The priest settled himself into a chair behind a hand-hewn oak desk. He looked with the eye of an expert appraiser at the young woman in front of him, fidgeting nervously with her purse. Her lips trembled. She was unable to find the appropriate words. How to explain why she would part with a son? Her only son.

"Father . . . I . . . I only hope I'm doing what's right." The slender hands plucked at the purse. "It hasn't been an easy decision . . . Ronnie needs the guidance of a man. With Lew gone, . . . I simply can't handle him."

Father Deleo nodded impartially and waited until she broke her silence again. "Don't get me wrong, Father, Ronnie's not a bad boy . . . it's just . . . just that he has too much energy, I can't control him. My daughter, Ronnie's sister, she's only twelve and . . . "

"Mrs. Rebuck, I understand."

"You do, Father? " The strain in her voice had eased.

"Of course. Your situation isn't at all unusual. Most of our boys *are* fatherless, or come from broken homes. I sympathize with you, Mrs. Rebuck. Truly I do. However, you've made a wise choice in placing Ronald in All Souls."

"Father," her voice trembled, "my faith is all I have left to fall back on."

He resisted the temptation to question why her faith hadn't impelled her to see to the boy's early religious education. At this point, with the interview going smoothly, nothing was to be gained . . .

"Be assured," he said, leaning forward and clasping his hands on the desk, "Ronald will find our school to be one happy family. Here, he'll have *many* fathers to help him along."

"Father, I prayed so hard . . ."

"Mrs. Rebuck," he said, pausing for maximum effect, "your prayers have been answered."

She opened her purse, took out a check and handed it to him in a swift, nervous motion. "Is the amount correct, Father?"

"Exactly, Mrs. Rebuck." He placed the check on the desk, then rose. "I hope it doesn't appear I'm rushing you but if you're to get home before dark..." He came around the desk. "Is Ronald's trunk in the car?"

She nodded as he placed his hand solicitously on her arm, and ushered her to the door. Young Ronnie darted ahead, keeping a cautious distance from the robed man.

On the porch, he summoned two older boys to remove the footlocker from the DeSoto. Veteran of countless tearful farewells, the priest took pride in orchestrating these affairs with a minimum of muss and fuss.

Standing close to his nother, Ronnie exchanged hostile glances with the two boys lugging his trunk, then looked in wonder at a man in a long, hooded robe, walking nearby, totally oblivious of the world, head bent over a small black book. Ronnie felt a trembling in his knees at the strangeness of this place, then his mother's hand came to rest lightly on his shoulder, and all at once the *knowing* she was leaving came home to him in a small inner storm of sorrow.

Josephine Rebuck drew the boy to her, pressing him to herself. She wanted to tell him so many things, but all she could do was run her fingers through his coal black hair and avoid the pleading face, yearning for her not to leave. She hugged him one more time then quickly broke away – running to the car without looking back. She couldn't look back. Not at her little boy with tears streaming down his cheeks, who sorrowfully watched the black DeSoto pull away through the iron gate, then disappear into the autumn afternoon.

HIS FIRST NIGHT away from his mother, his little body charged with anxiety. He'd bed down in an army-type cot in a large dormitory that slept the fifth and sixth grades. No room to himself, but some sixty bunk buddies. Kids from New York, New Jersey, and parts elsewhere he never knew existed. His only consolation was the privacy he had because his bed was located in the far corner of the large room, where instead of another bed to his left, a life-sized statue, mounted on a three foot pedestal, hovered over his particular area. A statue of a man with a sword upraised as if to strike down on the other man, who crouched at his feet.

Brother Anthony, a rugged looking, iron jawed individual, concluded the night prayers, and the lights went out. All but the night light that produced a glowy effect upon the statue above him. He had been informed by Brother Anthony that "Boys are forbidden to sleep on their stomachs," but he couldn't understand why. And so he gazed upon the dim, awesome figure of the man with the sword, his foot pressed on the fallen man's chest. In the eerie blue light, he realized for the first time that both of these creatures had wings.

Once asleep, he tossed and turned, restlessly dreaming of a place to hide from the huge winged things that swooped at him from overhead. His face beaded with sweat, he moaned in the night, until awakened by strong hands shaking him. Brother Anthony had heard his groans.

BEFORE BREAKFAST the entire school attended Morning Mass. A Catholic by heredity, he was not altogether unfamiliar with the service. Having taken his first Communion, he understood the meaning of the small round wafer the priest put on his tongue. It represented the body and blood of Christ. Scary, mysterious. But what sent a quiver of true terror through him was the thought of the confessional. Tell all and be absolved of your sins or else live with *mortal sin* and be condemned to burn in the fires of eternal hell. His feet moved on the rough wooden floor of the chapel as if sensing the licking flames that lurked below.

As the priest droned on in Latin from the small marble altar, Ronnie's eyes roamed about the chapel, taking in the life-sized statues, the stations of the Cross, the stained-glass windows depicting their religious scenes. Then, at the large mural on the ceiling, his eyes stopped, transfixed. There again, in bold detail, was the man with the sword and the other at his feet.

AFTER A SIMPLE breakfast, it was back up the hill to the main building, where Ronnie would attend his first class. Assigned a seat – a chair with a wide arm for a desk, located in the back row next to the windows – he would not start his classwork off with the usual reading, writing, and arithmetic, instead, there was a period in religion. A tall thin priest, who hardly spoke above a whisper, droned on about the reasons why Jesus came into the world. And when the priest went to the blackboard to explain the Trinity, Ronnie's eyes drifted toward the windows. Within seconds his thoughts were far from God the Father, the Son and the Holy Ghost. Wondering about his friends back in Stamford, he didn't hear his name. It was only when the red-headed kid seated next to him gently tapped his elbow that he realized the priest had been talking directly to him.

"Stand up, young man." The priest's whispery voise had suddenly turned to a growl. In a hastened effort to rise, Ronnie banged his knee on the desk. Half aware of the snickers fron the kids around him, he stood in the aisle, quaking, facing the thin man in the black cassock.

"Come closer, young man."

A cautious Ronnie Rebuck made his way down the aisle, stopping a few feet from the priest, who gazed over his head at the class.

"Master Rebuck, who is already quite behind in school, was daydreaming." He glared down at the boy before him. "You *were* daydreaming, were you not? Come closer."

Ronnie eased forward.

"Closer," said the priest.

The blow was quick, precise. Ronnie never saw the cupped fingers that clipped him under the chin. He looked up through a blur at the face staring down at him. He shook his head, then slowly got to his hands and knees, jaw aching, tasting the sticky-sweet blood that trickled from his mouth where he'd bitten his tongue.

At recess, Ronnie forgot his troubles in a game of marbles. Crouched down, ready to shoot, an older boy made a grab for his shooter. Struggling with the bully, Ronnie never heard the bell signaling the end of recess. Something hard and bony struck him across his ear, sending him sprawling to the concrete. He opened his eyes and looked up at the storm-cloud face of Brother Anthony.

HALLOWEEN EVE, the dorm's lights were out and he stirred on the bunk bed, unable to sleep. The bruises, how they ached. Especially his ears. And he still found difficulty swallowing, the result of that punishing uppercut. He could hear the distant sound of a train chugging along in the night. Its haunting, lonesome sound brought tears to his eyes. How he wished to be on that train. Going away, far away from this school. This strange school. The prayers, the prayers, so many prayers. And these man in black cassocks. These religious men with their devastating hands. He looked up at the shadowy statue touched by a dim beam of moonlight – at the man on his knees – and wondered what *he* had done.

The idea began as a small ripple in his mind, then grew until it became a compulsive urge. He'd run away. Tonight. Quietly he slipped out of bed, put on his underwear, socks, pants, laced up his sneakers, struggled with a sweater, collected a few articles, including a box of matches he'd picked up somewhere, a toothbrush, a ball of kite string, and stuffed them into his pillowcase.

He sat on the footlocker, his ears tuned to the natural night sounds of the dormitory. The chorus of breathing, the occasional creaking of a bed, and the soft hissing from the radiators. There was no light under the door of Brother Anthony's cubicle. As he carefully looked about, hoping no one would awaken, his eyes fell on the dimly lit statue, and for a fleeting moment he was sure the man with the sword was smiling at him.

He tiptoed past the row of beds, past the sinks and lavatory, stopping at the dormitory's entrance. With the movement of a cat, he was beyond Brother Anthony's room, down the stairs, and out of the building. Now his legs pumped like pistons as a stiff breeze snapped at his face. This night, the night of witches and goblins, illuminated by a full moon, with the wind whistling through the pines, presented a story-book setting as his little feet seemed to sail across the sloping field in the direction of the black iron gate. Suddenly he tripped, somersaulting to the ground . . . skinning both knees through his corduroy knickers. He jumped to his feet, then sprinted alongside the road. Breathless, his face gleamed in the moonlight for the gate was only fifty yards away. Catching his second wind he sprinted on, when from the shadows a massive figure in black cassock blocked his path. His young heart beat like a roll of drums as the man towered over him with eyes seemingly fire-red. The school's night watchman, a lay brother, prevented his escape.

The vengeance of All Souls had been swift. Brother Anthony, surly with sleep, had applied the razor strap mercilessly to the naked buttocks of the runaway. Of painful necessity, Ronnie Rebuck slept the rest of the night on his stomach.

THE MORNING, All Saints' Day, and Brother Anthony awakened him by clanging the dreaded bell in his ear, then proceeded to overturn the bed, sending boy and mattress to the floor. In sleep, the sinner had sinned.

That night – the night of All Saints' – an extraordinary event disrupted the showing of *Pinocchio* in the school's gym. The entire student body milled outside in the schoolyard to witness the town's fire department attempt to put out a fire. The tower on the hill, the Holy bell tower that rung out the Angelus, was ablaze. Missing from the spectators, confined to the upstairs study hall as punishment, Ronnie Rebuck pressed his nose against the window pane. Wide-eyed, he watched the kids below bubbling with excitement over the spectacle before them – firemen passing hoses and the police restraining local residents from straying too close to the flame-spitting tower. Its blazing wood lit up the hilly area, and the smoke sped like a rocket toward the clear evening sky.

Amid the shouting of frenzied voices, the swarm of humanity drew back. Firemen dropped their hoses and retreated from the hill.

A gleam came into the eyes at the window. A faint smile curved the corners of Ronnie Rebuck's mouth, as the fiery tower crashed to the ground, the great bell clanging on impact.

The Holy Tower, gutted by flames, lay in a humble heap, breathing out its final death rattle, as the slight smile on the boy's face at the window spread and spread and spread, until it glowed like a Halloween pumpkin in the reflected light.

# Book 1
# The Guiding Angel

# 1

A RED BUICK RIVIERA snailed its way under a bright-hot Florida sun that shed its golden rays impartially on the just and the unjust, on the lean Canadian in plaid swim trunks, on the plump Chicago matron with her pink beach umbrella, on the gaggle of bikini-clad girls strolling up and down the white-white sand.

Behind the dark sunglasses, the man driving the Riviera took it all in without flickering an eye. The only sign of his impatience was the knotting of powerful hands on the wheel. This was the way it went in Clearwater at tourist time – the Christmas Holidays, when the snow birds came south. The roads and beaches were jammed, and you just couldn't let it get under your skin, even if you were a high-energy, fast-action man.

The car turned onto the causeway that linked Clearwater and Clearwater Beach, a palm-lined stretch of road flanked by an inlet that flowed from the Gulf of Mexico. Up ahead, the blue-hulled daysailer circled, letting out two blasts from her air horn – the signal to the drawbridge attendant perched in a tower, looking like the warden of the waters, to unlock the bridges' steel jaws and allow Captain Weekend passage through.

The car's driver rapped the wheel with a hard hand; another five-minute wait, and all this for a copy of *Tampa Times and Tribune!* He drew a cigarette from a half-empty pack and lit up. Tossing the match out the window, he took note of a sign on a van that had drawn up alongside him. The white lettering on the shiny black surface read: THE DAY OF JUDGMENT IS NEAR. A beefy man with short-cropped sandy hair leaned out from the passenger side of the van. He smiled, a friendly grin, but the face remained expressionless – the dark glasses fixed on the doomful message.

The fellow in the van tried an even broader smile, then leaned on a fleshy arm and said: "Like it says, brother, it's later'n you think."

The face behind the sunglasses slowly shifted until it looked straight at the speaker, whose smile quickly faded.

A steady hand brought a lighted cigarette to grim lips. The man in the dark glasses drew deeply, then blew a cloud of smoke into a bewildered face.

The red Rivy rambled off the causeway entering Island Isles, a stylish waterfront community of low-slung stucco houses as multicolored as a flock of tropical birds. The car nosed into the driveway of a compact house of red brick and white stucco. Ron Rebuck emerged from the car. The metal frames of his dark glasses glittered from a reflecting sun. His once coal-black hair had turned a distinguished fox-gray that complemented a youthful face. He had a certain air about him. The trim body of a light heavyweight, the high-voltage aura of a Hollywood superagent, and the strange, tricolored eyes of a saint or a devil.

He entered the house and walked into the kitchen, where an auburn-haired, fair-skinned woman, with pool-blue eyes and the long, lithe legs of a teenager, was checking over the shopping list for Sunday's Christmas dinner.

"Rufus Manning didn't call, did he?"

"You mean your crystal ball didn't tell you?"

Ron Rebuck tossed the sunglasses onto the kitchen table, revealing the same strange light which had shone in a small boy's eyes long ago at All Souls. "Why the hostility?"

She dropped the list on the gleaming counter and went to the sink. Rinsing her hands, then drying them on a paper towel, she could feel those eyes upon her. But June Rebuck was one person who was immune to his eye magic.

"What's bothering you?" he asked.

She looked at him icily. "You really don't know . . . You're so obsessed with that book, you haven't time to think about anything else."

His face tensed. "That *book* . . . is the most important thing in my life."

"Is it, Ron? Is it really?" She looked at him, long and hard, meeting his eyes.

"Are you in some kind of bitching mood today?"

"A concerned mood, Ron. Concerned."

He looked at her in surprise. It was unlike June to come on so strong. And he could tell from the frost in those blue eyes that she was ready for all-out combat.

"You've got nothing to be concerned about."

"Well it so happens I disagree."

His look grew heavy with tension. "Disagree on what?"

"You really want to know? You'll take the time to listen and find out? Not run into that damn room?"

His eyes followed her as she went to the kitchen table. She turned, faced him fully. She deliberated, wondered if it would do any good, whether he'd truly listen. Deciding to try, she spoke on. "Since we've been married I've never interfered with whatever you wanted to do. I've simply sat around and watched you throw away career after career. Big league baseball wasn't good enough for you. Football, boxing, you lost interest. Advertising – the different ideas, creative ideas that others got rich on while you just got bored. And let's not forget when you walked off that movie set. Another potential Garfield or Bogart, they said, but you didn't want to be a big movie star. Ron, Ron, you've tossed away more careers than they have in the yellow pages."

"June – "

"Let me finish." Her eyes began to fill with tears. "I've never even asked why. If you told me we're going on a camping trip in the Sahara, all I'd ask was enough time to pack. But, now – this damn book . . . you – the way you've changed. Ir's scary . . . .This book, it's not like the rest of your ventures. You don't know it, but there's a deadliness about you!"

"Are you finished?"

"I could go on and on – "

"Don't!"

"Of course not. I'm intruding on Ron Rebuck's private world. Rufus Manning's different."

"Rufus Manning's essential. Nothing more!"

"What about us? Your son, your mother, who can't stop having nightmares over your book."

He moved toward her. That combative spirit raged in his eyes. "That was one stupid thing to say."

"Truthful!" She slammed down on the table with the palm of her hand.

He stepped back like a grizzly bothered by a bee – staring at the woman whom many believed had earned the congressional medal of patience. For ten full seconds they dueled in silent confrontation, with June finally succumbing. Easing into a chair, she said in a tone of surrender, "What's the use. You're no longer among us mortals."

His face was pitying. Secretly he yearned to tell her everything – but couldn't. Even she wouldn't understand. Could anyone? "Where's Ronnie?" he asked.

"The beach."

"Probably checking out what type of bikinis are in for the Christmas season, right?"

She nursed a smile. Then to feel his strong hands on her shoulders. Always before, whenever he touched her, she found it futile to pursue the subject of his book and the great change that had come over him, but her fears would not be dowsed by the fire of his touch. She had to know. "Ron, this book . . . why you? You of all people."

His hands slipped from her shoulders as she turned looking up at him. "You're the most unlikely man to ever write a book about religion. And what's even more peculiar is that you, a man who could hardly sit long enough to read the headlines of a paper would somehow hole up in a room for over a year – it's incredible."

"June, it happened. It was destined to happen."

"One thing," She replied, searching his face before continuing, "do you honestly feel that you've written a burning message for the world?"

His nodding wasn't good enough. She pressed

further. "Ron, you're a man who has tasted more than his share of sin."

He laughed.

"What's funny?"

"June, who is to say what is good and what is evil? Billy Hale? Norville Riggins? The Catholic church?"

"They've been doing it for a long time."

"They're ministers of myth, who through their own tongues have made God a monster of unlimited wrath."

"And your book is going to set them all straight? My husband, Ron Rebuck, the Messiah the world has been waiting for, will enlighten us all."

Angered, he moved away.

For a moment she took on those forceful eyes, the face grim with determination. The unearthly power there! She became frightened. Frightened by the very man who shared her bed, ate the meals she cooked, and fathered their child. Forced to look away, the words came painfully.

"Ron, would it matter, honestly matter, if I begged you to end this – this obsession of yours?"

He moved toward the kitchen window and looked out at the bright sunshine – a mind bothered. She'd never pressed him like this. Not once during their marrage had she rebelled. Not that it mattered, for he'd do what he wanted to do. But now the months she'd been living with this private agony of seeing him change, so totally obsessed in doing battle against the rich and powerful religious leaders of the land, found her taking a bold stand. A righteous stand. And he groped for a quick reply.

"June, how many times must I tell you there was

a reason for my not continuing in sports, the movies, and *everything* else?'

"I know. The book," she moaned.

"Yes, the book. The only book that clearly defends God."

Brimming with enthusiasm, he moved from the window to her side, as she stood in disbelief.

"When I was a boy at All Souls, the five years I slept under that statue, little did I realize my destiny was then being chosen."

"By whom, Ron? By *God*?"

"By Michael, June. No one else."

"An angel," she muttered, disenchanted.

"By a soul who lived with God. By a member of an order of beings conceived and created by God." His face tightened, the eyes gleaming.

"With the publication of my book, I will have declared open war on all those religious leaders who perpetuate the existense of a wrathful God. Every damn minister, priest, rabbi, sucking evangelist, faith healer, and those righteous reverends who pick your pockets and hold you prisoner with their pistols of fear! My book will denounce the Bible whenever it speaks of God being a murderer. The truth as it was revealed to me by Michael will bring down the Billy Hales and the rest of those religious merchants who've been using God to amass fortunes."

"Stop, Ron, stop," she pleaded.

She looked up, through teary eyes, her body shaking, the voice choked. "What about us, your family, the people who love you, depend on you — does this angel, this soul, this Michael, care how we feel?"

"June, don't you understand? Of all the people

in the entire world *I* have been chosen. Michael has delegated me to be his messenger."

"To do what, defy the Bible? Do you know what you're saying, Ron?"

"All too well."

"Ron, be sensible. You're only one man. One man against those religious leaders you keep talking about. They're organized, powerful men and once they read your book you'll become a marked man."

"I'm not so all alone, June. The force behind me is far greater than theirs."

"Michael?"

"Man's true champion."

The bitterness she felt for that name, Michael, now flamed in her eyes. "I don't give a damn about Michael. I care about you. What will happen to you. Ron . . . please . . . please stop what you're doing. Stop before it's too late. Before the religion men know what you're doing.

He did'nt answer. Instead, an eerie gleam shone in his eyes. A confident grin spawned on his lips, as a silence came to be, then he was gone. The cannonshot slam of a door told her where he was – in a room neither she nor Ron Junior dared to enter. His den, his sanctuary. The strange things that went on in that room while he was writing his book – *The Lawyers of Hell!*

THE CITY'S great buildings, their peaks hidden behind a descending veil of gray, stood ghostly quiet – a quiet that promised snow this Christmas Eve.

Cardinal Thomas Timothy Spellissy belched delicately from behind the protective cover of the *New York Times*. He'd eaten his customary breakfast – three poached eggs, ten strips of bacon, four slices of toast with marmalade, a half grapefruit, and three cups of cafe' au lait to wash it all down – and now, his personal maid, the Irish Biddy Maude O'Shea, was discreetly removing the empty plates. There had been talk regarding His Eminence's appetite. Of course *never* to his face. But he occasionally got word of backstairs gossip about his eating enough for Europe, and then his scowl could freeze the kitchen brigade into a row of statues. Whenever food was the topic of conversation, he'd insist and *dare any to disagree that a bountiful breakfast*, lavish lunch and ducal dinner enabled the body to fight off the devil's doings. His few critics thought it odd that he considered obesity to be a vital deterrent against the devil; how gluttony is *his* particular case *somehow* became so sacred.

Today, Cardinal Spellissy was in one of his better morning moods. This meant merely that from 6:00 A.M. when he arose until the saying of Morning Mass, his silence would be punctuated by an occasional grunt of approval rather than his feared frown of wrath. This was, on the whole, his favorite time of day; only a Papal summons could interrupt this cherished period of solitude.

Maude O'Shea clipped the end of the Cuban-made cigar, and handed it to him. He held it steady in one plump white hand as she lit it for him. He drew in the first puff. Bliss. The cigar was the best money could buy; he had a vault full of them. Vatican sources kept him *well* supplied.

"Tis a bleak mornin', yer warship. Looks like snow."

"Most fitting for the day before Christmas." He exhaled a cloud of pearly smoke.

"Tis almost eight o'clock, yer warship."

"Ah, yes . . . yes, thank you, Maude." He rose majestically from the chair, all two hundred and fifty pounds of him. At five-feet-ten, the Archbishop of New York was, fat, incredibly fat. But what amazed his doctors was his ability to walk without wobbling, for underneath his princely robe were a pair of spindly legs that could barely be expected to support a ninety-pound Indian fakir. Cardinal Spellissy was built like a giant top. And once you got past that tremendous tummy, you had to look hard for the cardinal's neck. Yet for years he'd confounded his doctors' dire prognostications. Although he was almost seventy-one, aside from a minor gastric condition, he'd never felt better in his life. And that smooth, round potato-face was that of a man in his fifties.

And once in his company, one soon forgot about the grotesque physique, for those round twinkling eyes sent out charisma like laser beams. And that blessed baritone had the mellow power to drown out a Wagnerian opera at the Met.

MONSIGNOR JOHN GALLOGLY was waiting for his boss, standing by one of the heavy medieval chairs in the large office on the main floor of the mansion, wondering at the Cardinal's lateness. Almost without fail, he'd be seated behind his desk at eight *sharp*, to go over the day's schedule with his youthful adjutant. The man was a bear for punctuality. But today, the clock showed ten minutes past the hour when the Cardinal came barreling in.

"Morning, John. Let's get on with the Lord's work."

The raw-boned John Gallogly, with the lean and intelligent horse-face, waited until the Cardinal seated himself, then said: "I trust you had a comfortable night, Your Eminence."

The Cardinal rasped a reply, then reached across the vast Carrara marble desk for the list of the day's appointments the Monsignor had meticulously prepared. The Cardinal's stubby fingers groped for his reading glasses, wiped them, then he looked at the appointment book opened before him. A slight frown crossed his face.

"I certainly hope those television people are more discreet than last year's bunch."

"I've been so assured, Your Eminence."

". . . cluttering up the alter with cables . . . and those lights! Do they have to be so damn bright?"

"Mr. Levine promises that everything will run smoothly this year."

The Cardinal looked up. "Levine, you say?"

"– The network's coordinator, Your Eminence."

The prelate shook his potato-shaped head in dismay. "You'd think the network would have enough sense to send us an O'Leary or a Flanagan. We're conducting Christmas Mass, not some Chanukah service."

*Strange birds, those TV people,* he said to himself, shifting his eyes from the appointment book to the yellow legal pad that contained a lengthy roster of important people who'd be attending the Midnight Mass. There were political bosses from the five New York boroughs, state and national lawmakers, a sprinkling of judges and some top-level captains of industry. Men who at one time or another were dependent on Cardinal Spellissy's powerful support.

"I see Senator Goddere heads the Washington contingent. Shame he had to get clobbered at the polls by that fishmouth of a woman. Had high hopes for him. Another JFK in the making."

"I'm afraid only a miracle can salvage his political career now, Your Eminence."

The Cardinal looked up at his number-one aide and counselor (*what did the Mafia boys call it – Consigliere?*) and a sly grin blossomed on the moon face. "We're in the business of miracles, my boy."

The Monsignor matched his smile. He was well aware of the special variety of miracle that the Cardinal performed so brilliantly.

"I don't see Congressman Laureno's name on this list."

"The Congressman's bedded down with the flu, Your Eminence. He sends deepest regrets."

The Cardinal sat back in his chair, lit up a Havana, then said dryly, "May the good Congressman have a speedy recovery . . . but, tell me, John, was his offering *regrettable* as well?"

"Substantially larger than last year, Your Eminence."

Cardinal Spellissy nodded approvingly, then closed the black-bound appointment book and looked straight ahead at his young assistant. The eyes twinkled with admiration. "Rather a light morning for such a hectic day."

John Gallogly couldn't help looking a bit pleased at the implied compliment. Knowing how much the Cardinal looked forward to conducting the annual televised Midnight Mass, he'd kept the morning schedule free. The parade of V.I.P's coming to pay homage didn't begin until late afternoon, so he had the whole A.M. to himself.

"Since you've made my morning free, we'll chat for a while."

John Gallogly appeared reluctant. In sparing the Cardinal he knew he'd turned his own day into a nightmare. Already the reception room outside his office near the entrance to the mansion was filling with people – clergy from all over the archdiocese, business people, lesser notables not part of the Cardinal's inner circle – all seeking favor. He sighed resignedly.

"Anything new on that Puerto Rican Communist, Henry Rodriguez, John?"

"I believe he's biding his time until the holidays are over."

"He'd damn well better, or his own people will hang him. How that devil's still running around loose is beyond me. In the old days they'd have slapped him in jail and thrown away the key. . . . Soft, John. This country's getting softer'n jelly."

"As the kids say, Your Eminence, the times they are a-changing. It's a new world with new thinking."

"Same world, John, more complicated, but the same world."

The Cardinal hoisted his bulk from the chair and strolled toward the great bay windows looking out on midtown Fifth Avenue.

"John, my boy, Mother Church has sailed in turbulent waters throughout the centuries, and never stuck her flag for anyone . . . nor will she ever." He turned from the windows and waved his cigar in a gesture of triumph.

The Monsignor remained silent. Yet the Cardinal couldn't help noticing his troubled expression as he waddled back to the desk.

"What ails you, Son?"

"Oh, nothing, Your Eminence."

"Nothing, you say. One might think you'd seen the Devil by the look on your face."

"Something I read, Your Eminence."

"Couldn't digest it?"

"On the contrary, Your Eminence. It was all too digestible."

"Well . . . I suppose I'd be derelict in my duty if I *didn't* alert you. . . "

His hesitation intrigued the Cardinal. It was unlike the forthright priest to appear nervous or balk over anything. And as for being derelict in his duties, the Cardinal thought it ridiculous . . . John Gallogly was the superman of the detail set.

"What is it, John?"

The young Monsignor rose to his feet, as if to stress the seriousness of what he was about to say. "Your Eminence, perhaps I'm speaking prematurely but . . ." he paused, as if to weigh the words, then continued, "I've just read a book, actually a manuscript, and I can't seem to get it out of my mind."

"Again?" The twinkle in the Cardinal's eye dimmed.

"– A most unusual text. It was brought to my attention by one of our . . . friends . . . in the publishing business. I've heard on good authority that McGuinness & McGuiness is seriously considering publishing the work. It's a radical and quite . . . plausible . . . challenge to Mother Church."

He searched for a reaction on the Cardinal's face. All he got was a noncommittal frown, which was his license to continue.

"The title is *The Lawyers Of Hell.* It's told in the form of what I guess you'd call a parable, and involves several – figures – from the Old Testament. But what makes it dangerously seductive is that it offers a radical new concept of Genesis. And at a time when the world is ripe for something new."

The Cardinal rubbed the large ring on his finger. "John, John. That book, like all the others, will blow away in the wind. Another fly-by-night, faddist pack of nonsense, unworthy of the slightest attention from us."

The Cardinal walked away from the desk, toward a conference table in a distant corner of the high-ceilinged room, behind which were shelved row on row of soberly bound books. "New concept of Genesis, you say?" He pointed to the books. "Something not found in any of these volumes?" the Cardinal asked, lowering himself into a nearby leather chair.

"I've taken it upon myself to find out, Your

Eminence. As a matter of fact, Father Bartley has divorced himself from all other duties and is researching this matter in its entirety."

The Cardinal looked at his aide, as if it were all a wasted effort.

"Your Eminence, the thrust of this author's theory is that he doesn't credit God with the idea of Man. Although he acknowledges the fact that God created man, he maintains that it was a soul in heaven who alone conceived the plan for Man's existence."

"Pray tell, which *soul*," asked the Cardinal, slightly amused.

"A soul we know as the Archangel Michael."

Gone was the jesting mood; a hint of concern played over the Cardinal's plump lips as he puffed deeply on his cigar, "I presume the fallen Archangel Lucifer is the other lawyer in the title of this book."

"Precisely, Your Grace."

"Does he claim direct contact with God? Have we another modern day Moses?" asked the Cardinal, voice dripping with sarcasm.

"No, Your Eminence, he doesn't," the priest replied. "But what I found interesting is his use of the Archangel Michael as Man's champion. Man's true father. Since he has made God a neutral being, it then logically follows that he also eliminates the stigma of a wrathful God, or eternal Hell. I need not add, Your Eminence, it conflicts totally with Church doctrine – not to mention every other Christian theology. Matter of fact, *all* other religious beliefs."

The Cardinal frowned, ditching the cigar into an ashtray as he clumsily vacated the chair. " I'm sure

Father Bartley will provide us with what little else we need to know. Don't trouble yourself any further. Mother Church has weathered hurricane after hurricane . . . and you're speaking of, at most, a potential rain shower."

"Not to belabor the point, but I have this strange feeling, with the right promotion behind this book, a flood is in the making."

"Do you now!" Cardinal Spellissy moved toward him, eyeing him skeptically. "How long have you been with me?"

"Almost three years, Your Grace."

"Three years. Could it be you've become overly cautious? So much so that a cockeyed notion in a book which has yet to be published causes you such great concern?"

"Your Grace, forgive my persistence in pursuing the subject of this book, but I strongly feel it has the substance to at least lay the groundwork for an alternative form of world religion."

The Cardinal seated his vast body behind the desk and stared at him. The blue in his eyes was frosty-cold. "An organized world religion?"

"The roots are there, Your Grace."

"Where, John? In a book?"

"*The Lawyers of Hell* is no ordinary book. It's different."

"Different? Poppycock! The mere fact it is a book makes it vulnerable. This author has left himself open to every critic out to slay a dragon. And you know theologians – they'll shred it up and eat it for breakfast. Let's be realistic, John; you yourself, but moments ago, stated this book challenges Genesis."

"And much more, Your Grace."

"Yet it *is* a book. And, I gather, written by a contemporary man."

"The Bible was created by men."

"Men who in time have become revered. The Bible has gained its power with age – two thousand years of it."

"Your Eminence, with communications so technically advanced, I feel that time is not all that necessary for the growing of a dangerous seed. Everything is speeded up, we're living in the age of Future Shock."

The Cardinal swelled like a rooster, but John Gallogly met his menacing stare. "From what you've told me, the only danger lies in your overly vulnerable mind. At the very most, John, this book sounds like nothing more than the organ of some movement that's in it strictly for the money. And I don't feel it's worth your precious time worrying about it – *for even one minute more*."

John Gallogly had already put a damper on the Cardinal's merry morning mood, but he wasn't prepared to risk turning the mood into one of smoldering rage. At least, he'd had his innings. And he had a sneaking suspicion that Thomas Timothy Spellissy's seeming indifference to the possible threat of *The Lawyers of Hell* was at least part put-on.

"With your permission, Your Eminence, I feel I should get back to my office."

The Cardinal, in the midst of lighting a fresh cigar, waved him on his way. The Monsignor turned on his heel to leave, but no sooner had he reached the door than the Cardinal called out to him.

"Tell me, John, who *is* the author of that work?"

"Rebuck, Your Eminence. A Ron Rebuck."

"Rebuck? Re . . . BUCK," roared the Cardinal. John Gallogly quietly left the room, the sound of mocking laughter ringing in his ears. The word, repeated, echoed wildly down the hall:

"Re . . . BUCK!"

BY THREE P.M. that afternoon the snow was falling in a dense white curtain. A short cab ride from the Cardinal's mansion, the strong face peering from an apartment window overlooking Central Park South didn't give a damn if the entire eastern seaboard caved in under an avalanche of snow. Somehow he'd claw his way out of the disaster and escape to his secret shangri-la in Montana, and the hell with *everything* – and *everyone* – east of the Rockies. Especially at this time of year. The Christmas season – and Rufus Manning hated Christmas! On top of his private reasons, he felt the whole thing was the giant of all hustles, the ultimate rip-off. A time of year when merchants got healthy – when love for one's fellow man was nothing more than a pack of religious bullshit!

Tomorrow, Rufus Manning would be fifty-two. A Russian Jew from the Bronx ghettos, he must once again share *his* birthday with the Christ of the *goyim*. Since childhood he'd carried the chip on his shoulder. A cursed chip that weighed heavily on his poor father who had had to take the brunt of his boyish queries. Why did *he* have to be born on the same day as Christianity's Son Of God? Or was it one of three Gods? The Divine Trinity, confusing for even Christians to comprehend. A man can change his name, his nose, but how in the name of Moses can he change his rightful birthday?

He stared at the lamps along the park below, glowing faintly like a row of haloes. He thought about his old man, a tough-hided immigrant, who'd toiled his life away in somebody else's delicatessen, falling dead over the counter at fifty-three. Too young – Rufus choked on the thought. God, he himself would be the same age in just one year. He'd never known his mother. She died in childbirth. His birth! What a horseshit way to come into this stinking world, he'd tell any fool who came to him with *his* sad story.

He tried to shake the mood, but the haunting lights in the park generated reflections, memories, loneliness, all fighting for first billing in his thoughts – a stormy past winning out.

The picture of a desperate man flashed in his mind – the small film distribution set-up that continually changed shingles whenever and wherever he could beat the rent, and the multitude of Manhattan phone booths that served as his base of operation for the distribution of sorry films. Rufus Manning knew all too well that portrait of a fifty-one-year-old man up to his neck in life's quicksand.

Without a salary and nothing but zeroes in the borrowing department, he was trapped in a dead-end alley with all the dogs of the world coming down on him, when a strange sort of angel appeared. Ron Rebuck.

Ron Rebuck, who seemed tuned to Rufus's troubles, once again came to his aide. When Rufus desperately needed a film salesman he could trust, it was Ron Rebuck who sold fifty straight T.V. stations, including one who had yet to show late-night movies. When the teamsters were out to settle an old score, a debt Rufus *forgot* to pay, it was Ron Rebuck who settled the dispute. Each time, Ron Rebuck came, did his job, then strangely slipped away. This time, help came in the form of five thousand dollars.

Ron Rebuck's five became ten, and Rufus was running – in one door and out the other. The foreclosure on the house was withdrawn, the family was eating again, and now he was in a footrace with a small army of creditors chasing him for the war debt.

A light came into Rufus's eyes as the picture of his past brightened. That day in November, when the same Ron Rebuck called. He remembered Rebuck's precise words. "Somebody will be looking for you, Roof. See him, everything will be fine." He'd passed off Ron Rebuck's strange prophecy merely as consoling words. After all, the only people looking for him were the parade of bill collectors that harassed his house. Yet that very day, fortune came his way—he was introduced to *Dude*.

A black writer named Jones was hunting for him. He had an idea for a script and Rufus Manning was his man to make it happen. Blacks liked Rufus, he had a pair of balls as big as a pawnbroker's. They liked the way he'd handled a black film in his distribution efforts. The flick had been a black bomb, but Rufus had got it some heavy print. He'd launched it. Hell, no one expected him to buy all the tickets. "You'll never find Rufus Manning," Jones was told. "That turkey's on an airplane that ain't *ever* comin' down. Try the Foreign Legion." Finally someone told him Manning lived in Connecticut. Maybe Westport.

E.C. Jones – the way he said it sounded like Easy Jones – was given a number in New York by a dubious Nancy. It rang at the office of Hughie Gilman, attorney-at-law. By late that afternoon, Easy Jones was having a sparse lunch with a ready Rufus Maning.

The idea for the film was sound, and Rufus took the man's first name seriously. Over a raw hamburger, he became the dominant partner – with percentage to match. He hustled the script, but smart money jerked him off, putting another lock on their bank accounts when the word was out that Rufus Manning was on the prowl.

"You need more than angels, Ron. You need the devil himself," Hughie Gilman told him. "And don't shoot those beady eyes at me; I'm handling your lawsuits. I can't take any more of your IOU's."

Finally, uneducated money went for his con, and against all conceivable odds, Rufus Manning produced the movie. A major distributor fell in love with the film, and Rufus Manning Presents' *Dude* was one of the few hits of a lean year. Rufus Manning was a RICH man, attaining that seldomly reached plateau of financial independence: he had survived in the hostile arena of the entertainment world. He was gladiator triumphant – badly scarred yet fiscally solvent.

CHIMES WOKE HIM to the present. He turned away from the window to the living room, expensively furnished in black and white, with chairs and tables of various geometric shapes. He stalked to the door and opened it.

"Merry Christmas, Mr. Manning," said the day

doorman with the bad bridgework. He took a large package from under his arm and handed it to Rufus.

"Little early with the Christmas bit, aren't you, Bud?" said Rufus, accepting the package.

"Christmas . . . Christmas Eve," the doorman shrugged.

"But Christmas isn't until tomorrow, right?"

The doorman flashed a fishy grin, wondering why the man was pushing it so. "You've got a point there, Mr. Manning. Just wanted to be a little early in wishing you a Merry Christmas."

Rufus wasn't buying his basket of verbal cheer. Not a chance in China he'd allow himself to get fished into this guy's annual Christmas net. Not this guy who for the last three months was at a loss for words, but now that it approached Christmas had suddenly become the friendliest dude in all New York. "Listen, maybe you *can* do me a small favor."

The doorman drew closer. Greed filled his eyes. "Just name it, Mr. Manning. Name it."

"That dude, the one who dresses in a red union suit, you know, the guy with the white beard . . . " The greedy gleam in the doorman's eyes vanished behind a cloud of suspicion. He backed off a step, as Rufus continued. "If you should happen to see him prowling around in the halls, or on the rooftop . . . shoot the fucker!"

The doorman in a hurried move backed away. Away from the beady eyes aiming to drill holes into his head. Rufus continued to glare, daring the man to utter so much as a word. He waited until the doorman escaped into the elevator, then re-entered the apartment, slamming the door.

He tore open the package. A large manuscript

filled his hands. He studied the title page. *The Lawyers of Hell* by Ron Rebuck. "Hmm," said Rufus, opening the book to its first page, and beginning to read. He never got past the preface. "ANGELS! . . . FUCKING ANGELS," he screamed. "He sends me . . . *me* . . . a book about *angels*?"

A RACING-GREEN TRIUMPH CONVERTIBLE braked loudly in the driveway. Ron Rebuck Junior, an eighteen-year-old prime candidate for a football scholarship – jumped from the car. He looked the part of a middle linebacker as he trotted to the door.

"Hey, Mom, I'm home." He peeked into the kitchen, which was empty. "Mom, where are you?"

A shushing sound from the hallway reached his ears. Entering the hall, he was taken aback by the sight of his mother – her ear pressed to the den's door.

"What's going on?" he asked.

She signaled him to be quiet.

"Dad in there?" he whispered.

She nodded.

"Is he talking to himself again?"

Stepping away from the door, she waved him forward.

When he reached her side, she whispered, "Tell me what you hear."

Reluctantly, the young Rebuck tiptoed to the door. He first stuck up one finger, then another, as she swallowed hard. Fear dawned on her face. She rushed him out of the corridor toward the far wing of the house.

"Ronnie, the voices – was one your father's?"

"Couldn't tell. Didn't sound like him."

"Did you hear what was said?"

"Sounded foreign. But what's the big mystery, Mom?"

"Someone, or something, is in that room with your father."

"Come on, Mom, not again."

"It's not my imagination, Ronnie. There's *someone* in that room with your father."

"He's probably watching a foreign movie on T.V."

"Ronnie . . . the T.V. is broken."

He looked at her queerly.

"And Ronnie . . . since when has your father learned to speak in a foreign language?"

# 3

MONSIGNOR GALLOGLY escorted the short, stocky man in the vicuna coat, fidgeting with the fedora in his hand, to the Cardinal's chambers. "Representative Winsky, Your Eminence."

Attired in formal dress, the Cardinal rose from his chair like a surfacing hippo, warmly greeting the man who bent to kiss his ring. Monsignor Gallogly shut the door behind him and headed for his office.

At thirty-six, John Gallogly was quite young to attain the religious rank of Monsignor. The role of administrative chief and counselor to a powerful prince of the pontifical elite was seldom placed in the hands of a man so untried. After his predecessor, Monsignor Gleason, an old war-horse and ancient comrade of the Cardinal's, vacated the position through death, John Gallogly was hand-picked by the Cardinal over many a more experienced man. It was rumored through the Church grapevine that the senior candidate, when hearing he was passed over for the post, delegated himself to a life of alcohol, ending in suicide.

Within six months after filling the position, the envious were silenced and the skeptics became believers, for John Gallogly attended to large and small matters alike with the same calm, confident manner. He gained the respect of nearly everyone. Priests throughout the great archdiocese admired him. Especially the manner in which he settled disputes without causing hard feelings toward any. Within a short period of time, the Cardinal himself relied heavily on him and was seldom disappointed. His mastery of detail, his wizardlike gift for anticipating problems with only the barest of clues, was only equalled by his monumental patience. His ability to withstand Cardinal Spellissy's outbursts of temper alone qualified him for sainthood.

He stepped into the large reception area that adjoined his office. A plain-looking woman of forty was tidying up – or at least pretending to, since the typewriters were hooded and ashtrays were clean. He looked at his Bulova Accutron. "Ellen, the staff's workday ended at three o'clock. It's quarter to four."

She opened a desk drawer and took out a gift-wrapped package. Straightening her dress, she went to his side and shyly handed it to him. "Merry Christmas, Monsignor."

He shook his head. "Thought we agreed there wouldn't be any exchange of presents this year."

"A venial sin, it's worth it." she replied, breezing

out of the room. He opened the card attached and read: *Merry Christmas to a future Cardinal.* Blushing, he wondered if Cardinal Spellissy shared this admiring secretary's sentiments.

Turning the brass doornob, he entered the moderate-sized, simply furnished office. Placing the present on a tidy desk, he lifted a small, thin cigar from a silver case, flicked fire from a matching lighter, then sauntered toward the window to look out at a snowy afternoon, already getting dark. Turning from the window he went to a small oak cabinet in an alcove. A pleased smile crossed his face. The Cardinal would be tied up with the Polish politician for at least a half hour, and the remaining day's agenda wouldn't become crowded until after six. From four-thirty till six, the Cardinal's appetite would be attended to. He took a bottle of sherry from the cabinet along with two glasses. Father Bartley would be arriving shortly. Filling the glasses with sherry, he looked up to see a round cherub face with thick horn-rimmed glasses peeking into the room. "Nobody here? Don't believe it," Father Bartley cheerfully exclaimed, entering.

From a small sofa, John Gallogly handed him the sherry. "Cheers."

"Radar. That's what your secret is," said Father Paul Bartley, finding a chair across from his host.

"To us both, Paul. May we be around for another Christmas."

They clicked their glasses and sipped.

A chain smoker, Father Bartley lit up a Winston and said, "Something I must ask you, John."

"Fire away."

"How do you stand up to all the shit thrown at you?"

"Meaning?"

"Terrible Tummy and his tantrums. *All* the bullshit. Every problem in the diocese seems to end up in your lap."

"That's my job, Paul."

"The job of a man bucking for Bishop, I'd say." He sipped more.

"You're sounding envious, Paul."

"Envious?" Paul Bartley looked at the man six years younger than himself. Once, he'd known the glow that was now in John Gallogly's eyes. But at forty-two he'd given up all hope of advancement. His yellow sheet read, "Rebel . . . Potential troublemaker" and he had only John Gallogly to thank for his comfortable position of resident theologian. Cardinal Spellissy had opposed his being a staff member from the beginning, but gave way to John Gallogly's desire, on the condition that if Bartley stepped out of line just one time he'd wind up as an assistant pastor in the Bedford-Stuyvesant ghetto.

"Speaking of problems, Paul, I hope my concern over that manuscript, *The Lawyers of Hell*, was strictly the result of an overly cautious mind."

Paul Bartley gulped the sherry and sat back; his cheerful mood withered too quickly to suit John Gallogly. But then again, Father Bartley, a frustrated actor, could be playing it to the hilt. John Gallogly knew this, and pressed on. "Have you formed an opinion yet?"

"A primary one."

"And?"

"When I first read it, I reacted like Terrible Tummy."

"And now?"

"Truthfully?"

"What else?"

"It grows on you. Too *much* so."

John Gallogly eyed him curiously. "Are you *seriously* telling me my initial reaction was warrented?"

"The hell with your reaction. I'm the expert in theology around here, and I find *myself* beginning to believe this man." He rose, empty glass in hand. "Don't look at me like I'm some kind of traitor. There's no defrocked priest in my future."

"Paul, you must admit, those *are* explosive words."

"And that's what I feel this Rebuck fellow has written . . . a time bomb." He poured himself another glass of sherry. "You know what I think, John? This Rebuck guy didn't write a book; he invented a religion." He popped the sherry. "What's more, a religion for *all*. Too *damned* logical, John."

John Gallogly put out the cigar. The smoke Father Bartley gave him to inhale was all he could handle. "The Cardinal feels the critics and fellow theologians will rip it to pieces."

"Has Terrible Tummy read it, John?"

"No."

"Let him read the book first – before making loose statements."

"Are you telling me this book might stand up under attack?"

"Strange as it sounds, it just might, and if I were you I'd start finding out who in hell this Ron Rebuck fellow is . . . *really* is."

"Spy on him, Paul? Watergate? CIA kind of stuff?"

"Christ sakes, we've got the biggest network in the whole wide world. John, right now you've got the chance to be a hero, but wait on this, and with the right *promoter,* it could spread like wild fire. My advise is to fix this Ron Rebuck's ass, *now.*"

John Gallogly stood. His face expressed dismay. "Paul, it's true you have a knack for getting to the point, but my God, man, you're talking like we're the Mafia."

"Aren't we?"

A rustling from the hall cut off further talk. The sound of the Cardinal's voice bidding the politician good-bye sent the Monsignor scurrying.

RUFUS MANNING donned his Loden stormcoat, stuffing ski gloves inside. It was time for him to perform his annual hypocritical rite – the buying of presents. He was forever waiting until the last moment, as though somehow, some way, Christmas might just be outlawed.

He left the apartment, stepping into the hall, the elevator close by – and *she* was there. He had seen her a dozen times. Tall and leggy, a brunette with a mouth like a magnet. Giving her a silent hello, he followed her into the elevator.

Fearing elevators, for the first time in his life he wished the Otis system would go on the bum. He yearned for a chance to find out if that stupendous-looking mouth with the teeth protruding just a little, could do the tricks he dreamed about. She smelled terrific. No fancy-shmancy perfume or cologne, but a fragrance from whatever soap she used. He guessed at her age. Thirty? Maybe, twenty-eight. Who the hell is she? Who's keeping her? he speculated, as she fumbled for something in her purse. Too uppity, he figured. Too prim and proper. Bullshit! He reconsidered. I'll bet she's a piranha after the introductions.

He wanted to say something, anything, but there was a certain air about her. A forbiddance. A don't-touch-me quality, as if she belonged only to power – and a producer of black films was a no-no. She was still fumbling through her purse as the elevator door opened at the lobby and Rufus stepped out, frustrated. He'd blown it. Getting old, he thought, passing her by. The doorman dodged his glare. Turning up the collar of his coat, he went into the street where the snow was mounting, already ankle-deep. And the forecast still was for a heavy drop.

A tall, trim man wearing sunglasses stood guard by a white Jaguar. Seeing Rufus, he hurriedly opened the driver's door.

"Mike, the shades, the shades," said Rufus, getting into the Jag and starting up the high-powered engine as the man called Mike entered on the passenger's side. Rufus eased out into the stream of traffic. "Mike, how many times must I tell you, the shades make you look like you're still busting heads. You're respectable now."

Mike Spenard ignored the remark, as the car rounded the corner, turned right, and moved slowly down Fifth Avenue as Rufus checked out Cartier, Saks, and other famous, expensive stores.

"Presents, what bullshit. Why should I have to buy gifts on Christmas?"

"Because it's Christmas, Mr. M."

"With my family, every day's Christmas."

"The shepherds brought gifts to the Baby Jesus."

"The who's brought what to WHO?" asked Rufus.

The Jaguar pulled up to the curb. "Let it idle, Mike. This won't take long. Just painful." He stepped out of the car, thinking about who he would buy presents for, running into a hired Santa Claus, vigorously clanging his bell.

"The dough, the dough, where does it go?" asked Rufus, unable to pass up the peeve within.

"Charity," said Santa, whose cheerfulness was regulated by an anticipated donation.

"Your own?" said Rufus, closely eyeballing Santa whose smile turned to a scowl.

Mike Spenard laughed as he witnessed Santa give the furtive finger to the vanishing Rufus.

IT WAS AFTER SIX when Rufus Manning returned to the apartment. Having made Maalox believers out of many, he was loaded down with presents. Among them, a birthday present for himself. A dapper-looking smoking jacket. Crushed velvet, blue, with a gray-silver collar and cuffs that matched. "Bitchy – real bitchy." he appraised himself before a full-sized mirror, liking what he viewed. He saw a rugged handsomeness, a man over six feet and of lean build, with the grace of a former athlete. A trait creditors agreed on, having unanimously proclaimed him the greatest long-distance runner of all time. But now he could walk at his own pace. He was no longer Rufus Manning wanted by Bills Anonymous, but rich Rufus Manning who could laugh at the world.

He put in a call to his answering service. There were three messages. Hughie Gilman had called from Acapulco; Ron Rebuck had phoned from Florida; and his wife, Nancy, had called twice. Would he *please* return her call. Nancy, whose refusal to live in Montana had caused their marital tiff. A strange sort of unofficial separation. He vowed never to set foot into Connecticut until she agreed to their moving west. She, bred in the East, refused to go farther west than western Connecticut. As a result, marital war broke out and Rufus took up temporary quarters in one of Hughie Gilman's heavyweight client's apartments. He'd surprise her and come home.

He didn't have to pack – most of his wardrobe was in Connecticut – but he'd take the smoking jacket. A fast call to his service, to let them know he'd left, and he was in the hallway.

In the lobby, the night doorman was hustling packages. Rufus was going to ask him about Wonder Woman on his floor, but changed his mind. It would cost him, and if he was going to Connecticut he'd have to move on without delay, for the snow was coming hard and the Merritt Parkway had to be rugged going.

A dutiful Mike Spenard came out of the Jaguar and held the driver's side open for his boss.

"Listen, Mike, no sense you coming to Connectcut. Take the holidays off."

"I better go to Connecticut with you."

"Mike, everything's cool. Spend the time with your mother."

"Roof, what if something happens to yah?"

"The only protection I need from my family . . . is lawyers." He started up the engine and a gleam crossed his face. "See yah, Mike. I'll call if I need you."

Mike Spenard grimmaced. "Yeah . . . yeah, Roof . . . have a merry –" he never tagged it as the Jag spit up slush, skidded, then purred away.

The drive to Connecticut was worse than Rufus had anticipated. Nancy was right, visibility was near zero. The Jag's wipers raced like a two-step in double time, and a feeling of apprehension, even fear, seized him. Maybe he had changed. He snapped on the stereo, hoping the music would strangle his thoughts while he battled the elements. Westport was still a helluva way to go.

Somehow, in this spooky mood, his thoughts wandered to Ron Rebuck. What did he want? Why was he phoning so insistently? Suddenly Rufus Manning felt a shiver of something beyond fear. He braced his hands on the wheel and stared straight ahead as though searching for the answer in the driving snow. . . .

RON REBUCK paid no heed to the red-orange glow of the Florida sunset, nor did he feel the cool breeze of the easterly wind that ruffled the palms. He sat on the dock behind the house, a troubled mind, engulfed in thought. Thinking about how it all started. And why. His mysterious introduction to the lesser known Lucifer's counterpart – *Michael*. Michael, the great archangel, *Like unto God*, the Bible said. Milton gave him more dimension in *Paradise Lost*. He remembered all too well that statue which hovered over his bed at All Souls. The sword-wielding Michael with Lucifer at his feet. That he was destined to write of Michael's and Lucifer's great struggle in a book, *The Lawyers of Hell*, now presented a rash of doubts within his agonized mind. For him, Ronald Albert Rebuck, to carry Michael's heavy sword and strike down upon centuries-old religious hypocrisy, to single-handedly take on the great religious powers of the day, found his mortal body quivering in denial of the insistent spirit. The war between body and soul raged within Ron Rebuck.

ED DOWIAT, his brother-in-law, a warm, hearty guy of Lithuanian extraction, suddenly appeared at the dock. "And how is Michael's messenger this Christmas Eve?" Dowiat sang out.

Handing him a scotch and soda, Ed Dowiat plopped down on a rattan chair across from the troubled man. A tall drink in hand, Ed Dowiat was mildly drunk. "Those kids of mine could drive the devil nuts."

"What devil?" said Ron Rebuck.

"The one with horns, pitchfork. You know, the one who possesses little kids. What's-a-matter, you never saw *The Exorcist* or *The Omen*?"

Ron Rebuck frowned and looked out over the choppy water, not finding him humorous.

"Christ, touchy, aren't we?"

Rebuck sipped on the scotch, then broke into an apologetic smile. "Sorry, Ed."

"Hey, he's smiling. Christ, I haven't seen you smile for a year."

Ron took a bigger slug of scotch. "Afraid the fun-loving days are gone for good."

Ed Dowiat paused, letting the words sink in, then said, "If it means anything, think of what you're doing as being blessed"

"Or cursed."

Dowiat set the drink aside. Ron Rebuck was primed. If ever there was a time to ask him about the strange, unexplained, mysteries surrounding the Rebuck household, now was the time. "Wanna tell me?"

"Tell you what?"

"Everything. All there is to know."

For a moment he felt Ron Rebuck would spill it

out like a running faucet, but that distant look came into his eyes. Yet Ed Dowiat was not to be denied. "You're gonna need me, Ron. Your destiny's not exclusive. Since the beginning of that book, I'm involved."

Ron Rebuck's eyes studied the sincere face. It wasn't the hootch talking. Ed Dowiat was a man earnestly hoping to hitch a ride on Ron Rebuck's religious train. "Ed, you don't know what's in store."

"Do *you*?"

It was a leading question and Rebuck almost bit. He managed to pass it off with, "You've got children. Young children."

"What a horseshit comeback! C'mon, Ron, you can do better'n that. And don't give me the 'Michael doesn't want you.' I've got far better qualifications than any Rufus Manning."

"Ed, you haven't the slightest idea of what you'd be getting yourself into."

"Tell me about it. Then let me decide. I'm tired of people telling me what's good and what's bad for me."

The tense face relaxed. He thought for a moment, then said, "All right, Ed, but the moment you want out, I'll understand."

"You're sounding like Christ Himself. Like I'm some Peter who's gunna denounce you."

He thought his remark had softened him up, but the tension returned to Rebuck's face. Still Dowiat pressed on. "Rufus Manning, why him, Ron?"

"He happens to be a vital part of what must happen."

"Ron, Rufus Manning is an atheist. He spells God, G-O-L-D."

"Ed, believe me, Rufus Manning is most essential."

"Ron, Rufus Manning is a no-good sunnuva bitch. He's a shark. Hell, he *is* Jaws."

"Eddie, he's the man. The man needed."

"Why? Why, Ron, did Michael tell you?"

"He's the man, believe me."

"Did Michael tell you?"

"Just believe me."

"Tell me, Ron. Michael, did he tell you?"

He studied the yellow-brown pupils in Rebuck's eyes. Eyes that seemed to have seen a truth unknown to any other man. "Take my word, Ed. Leave it at that."

"What does he say? Michael's voice, what does it sound like? Do you really see him? Does he have wings? What? Christ, Ron, you're blowing my mind – tell me!"

Suddenly beads of sweat rolled from Ron Rebuck's brow. His color was fading fast, turning a deathly gray. He was trying to tell Dowiat something, but words failed.

"What's *wrong*, Ron? *What's wrong*?" Ed Dowiat cried in alarm, seeing Ron Rebuck's hand grasp the chair's armrests so violently the wood splintered.

"My God," Dowiat said, aghast.

Ron Rebuck's body stiffened. His head jerked violently. Saliva spilled from the corners of his mouth. The eyes would shut, then open. Repeatedly. Rebuck's entire body jerked in shuddering spasms. He began to mumble. Suddenly, the incoherent mutterings became words of fire:

"BE GONE DECEIVER . . . FOR YOU ARE THE MASTER LIAR!

"LIAR? CAN YOU DENY YOUR PHYSICAL TORTURES? . . . DENOUNCE MAN'S EXISTENCE AND YOU SHALL BATHE YOUR EXHAUSTED BODY IN THE MIGHTIEST OF LAKES – TO COOL YOUR TONGUE IN THE MOST REFRESHING STREAMS."

Ed Dowiat dropped his drink. Stumbling from the chair, he backed away. Surely it was Ron Rebuck he looked upon, but the voices – the different voices! Unnaturally deep . . . hollow, as though looming from a great distance.

The air became thin as though a vacuum had been created. The word *help* stuck in Dowiat's throat. He felt a sudden shortness of breath. He couldn't move, as though his feet were anchors to the mysteriously swaying dock, when again the haunting voice "WHY SHOULD SUCH A BODY BE TRAMPLED BY THE WILL OF A SOUL THAT DOES NOT FEEL PHYSICAL PAIN? IT IS EASY FOR THE SOUL TO SPEAK, FOR IT TASTES NOT WATER – EXPERIENCES NOT DEATH!"

Ed Dowiat dropped to his knees, buckling under in the presence of whatever great powers had inhabited Ron Rebuck. Though the words were dimly familiar, his mind darkened. Through clouded eyes, he saw the convulsing Ron Rebuck in the night mist, then blacked out.

SOMETHING DREW June Rebuck out of the house, past the indoor pool, onto the lawn leading down to the dock. At first she saw only one indistinct shape silhouetted against the softly lapping water. Then, as her eyes adjusted to the darkness, she stopped, rooted stock-still in shock.

On the dock in his chair, Ron Rebuck writhed in some kind of seizure. Nearer to her, where the dock met the shore, lay the lifeless, oddly twisted body of Ed Dowiat.

She started forward, weeping with fear, when there came a great roaring sound. From the darkness beyond the dock, a great wave swept up over the agonized figure of Ron Rebuck, stopping just short of the inert Dowiat. June Rebuck screamed in mortal terror.

As the vast wave fell back, the words echoed ghostily in the night air: ". . . FOR THE SOUL TASTES NOT WATER – EXPERIENCES NOT DEATH!"

# 4

THE JAG'S MOTOR growled, its wire wheels spinning, peppering the new-white landscape with gravel, as it veered up the winding driveway toward the low-lying house, a house shaped like a cluster of over-sized candy boxes, tucked under a grove of spruce, draped with snow.

The mailbox, under a crust of snow, read *R. Manning*, but somehow he felt like a total stranger, an alien on his own grounds. Jocko, the family mutt, didn't help any with his staccato set of who-the-hell-are-you barks. And there was no spot for the Jag in the twin garage.

"Aw shit," he suddenly remembered. Nancy's parents were here. Worse, her entire family. On their traditional Christmas pilgrimage. How he hated it!

Already, he could picture the scene. Old man Riley in his perpetual coma – on a good night he *might* burp out three words. Mrs. Riley, a classic Catholic who'd made a thousand novenas when her darling daughter announced to the Christian world she would marry a Jew boy from the Bronx.

Those two he could tolerate, but what really gave Rufus the pip was Nancy's brother Kevin, the perennial hambone, and his pushy wife, Bea. He labeled them Mr. and Mrs. Zero. Prime candidates for the most boring couple of the century.

Some homecoming. "Fucking buzzards," he cursed, considering returning to New York – blizzard or not. He stifled the urge and went to the back door, loaded down with his packages. Should he knock? Knock on his own door! He thrust it open with his knee making the hinges shake. A pair of cold-looking eyes regarded him. Eyes that belonged to his mother-in-law, with "Oh, it's you, shit-bum," written in their glance. She gave him a noncommittal nod. A grudging "Hi" was all she got in return. Deliberately neglecting to shut the door, he brushed past her, en route to his den, wondering if that prick brother-in-law was sitting in his favorite chair.

He was cut off at the living room by Nancy, who rushed to greet him, dropping candy canes meant for the Christmas tree. She had that glint in her eyes. The glaze that comes from one too many, yet she looked lovelier than ever. The kind of woman age had a hard time catching. Tall, graceful, with the kind of sleek figure that could adorn the cover of any fashion magazine.

Rufus looked past her pretty face, taking it all in. The Christmas scene. Old man Riley, waiting dimly for someone to shake him to see if he was still alive.

Sister-in-law Bea, the Dixie darling, sizing him up as if he were a side of condemned meat. And horse-shit Kevin at the piano, destroying "Silent Night."

"No hello?" said Nancy, kissing him – sweet and eager as ever.

"How's the king of the jungle bunnies?" Kevin shouted over his strident pounding, while Bea smirked and Papa Riley stirred faintly as though someone had asked, "Where were you during World War I?" Rufus bit on his lip, riding out a raging urge, and ignored them all.

"Roof, I'm glad you're home . . . really."

"Let's go to the bedroom." He turned away, with Nancy running to catch up, slipping an arm around his waist.

"Where's Stewart?" he asked in a casual tone – not wanting to make a big deal over the absence of their one and only male heir.

"He promised to be home, but skiing in Vermont means more to him. You'd better talk with him."

"At least *he's* having a good time."

She darted in front of him, blocking the bedroom door. A lock of hair dangled over her eye.

"Roof, don't go in there. Not yet."

"*What*!"

"Surprise."

He searched her face. "Nancy, would you mind getting the surprise out of the bedroom?"

"It's not that easy."

"Nothing's easy, except for my getting out of these clothes and taking a shower. Look, I'm tired. *Hide* whatever it is you don't want me to see."

"There's too much to hide." She moved toward him, purring like a kitten.

"Nancy . . . are you shitting me?"

"Roof . . . don't spoil it. It's something I've worked awful hard on."

His face flashed disbelief. "Nancy, I'm going into that damn bedroom."

The gleam vanished in her eyes. A look of concern took its place.

"Okay . . . but no lights."

"No lights! How in hell do I see?"

"The table light next to the bed. The reading light."

He was in no mood for suspense. The hazardous ride from New York, thinking about Ron Rebuck, was enough mystery for one day. "Whatever," he conceded.

"Only the table light, Roof . . . you *promised*." She steered him toward the bed, and flicked on a table lamp which cast a tiny pool of light in the darkness.

"You promised." she warned.

"I promised, I *promised*. Enough with the promises."

She looked at him totally disbelieving, then suggested, "Why don't you get out of those clothes?"

"Do I detect sexual overtones?"

He could vaguely see her smile as she turned and stepped farther into the darkness until she became a slender blur at the bathroom door.

He promptly shed his winter gear down to his shorts while Nancy switched on the bathroom's night light only, then returned to the bed where Rufus sat smiling like a Cheshire cat. No sooner did she sit down on the edge of the bed than his hands started to disrobe her.

"Roof, wait . . . I have to talk with you."

"About what?" He groaned.

"Your living in New York, for one thing."

"What's another?"

"I haven't written *a list*."

"Would sex be on the list?" His arm locked around her waist.

"Roof . . . not . . . not now . . . *later*."

Pressing his weight against her, she was forcibly pinned; his hand fondled her breast while he did a number in her ear.

"*Roof*," she pleaded, struggling to be free. But he paid no heed, pushing her down on the bed, while she fought off his busy hand working on the button to her red woolen pants.

Somehow she managed to get her knees up against his chest.

"Hey . . . you got something against sex?"

"*With everyone in the living room*?"

"Git rid of 'em!"

"You're speaking about my family, Roof. Don't talk like that."

His face turned glum. Just thinking about her family gave him indigestion. "Nancy, if I'd remembered they'd be here . . . *your family* . . . I'd have stayed in New York."

She got off the bed and stood over him defiantly. "It just so happens *Mr*. Manning, that while you've been playing the whoremaster in New York, I've been –"

"*Whoremaster*? You know that for a fact?" he asked. "You really think I've been fooling around for the last month?"

Her lips formed a cautious smile. The anger faded from her eyes.

"Whether you believe it or not . . . *nothing*. The only woman that stepped into my apartment was the maid. And I wouldn't bang her with someone else's tool."

She looked at him incredulously. That a man who regularly substituted morning sex for orange juice would all of a sudden change his habits – this she couldn't believe. She started to laugh in his face when her mother's shrill voice rang out from the hallway. "There's a call for Roof on his private line."

"Who is it?" he asked.

"A Ron Rebuck . . . from Florida."

"That fucking guy's driving me nuts," he moaned to Nancy. "How'd he get my private number?"

"Talk to him, Roof."

"Nancy, I'm not in the mood. Tell him I'll call back. No, tell him I'm not here, " he shouted.

" . . . I'm sorry, I won't lie for you," Mrs. Riley grated.

He looked at Nancy. The beady eyes were spinning.

"Roof will call back, Mother."

" . . . And that's exactly what I'll tell the man," she declared in departure.

Rufus shook his head in dismay. "I suppose if it were a matter of life and death, especially *my* death, she still wouldn't lie, right?"

"That's a terrible thing to say, Roof. If it weren't for my mother while you were away, I don't know what I would have done. I had to lean on someone, didn't I?"

"I'm home. Cancel her services."

"Just like that!" Nancy said, clicking her fingers.

"Just like that," he clicked harder.

A dispute of this nature could only lead to a dead

end; talking about Ron Rebuck was a safer street. "Why *don't* you talk with Ron? Why are you avoiding him so? I thought you liked Ron Rebuck."

"It's got nothing to do with liking him."

"Then what? Does he remind you of a past you'd rather forget?"

"Nancy . . . later with Ron Rebuck. He's a spook. Writing a book about angels," he muttered.

"All right, Roof, but don't expect me to forget how Ron Rebuck helped us when things were terrible. When we were so broke."

"And I'm sure that's why he's calling. To remind me of *just* that." He got off the bed. "I'm taking a shower."

Quickly, she stepped in front of him. "No lights Roof. You promised."

"You know, you're really starting to sound like a broken record."

"Roof, if you put on the lights it'll ruin everything. I worked damn hard on surprising you. It's sort of your birthday present. *Please*."

He looked into the face shadowed by darkness. Gone was the starry-eyed girl who dreamed of turning the modeling world upside down. Replacing it was a grown woman who wore her beauty like a queen her crown. He liked what he saw. The high cheekbones, the flawless line of the nose, the soft yet alert eyes, the wide kiss-me mouth. His hands went to her waist. She pulled away, but the viselike grip brought her back – drawing her ever closer. In the darkness, he saw a flash of white teeth between parted lips as his fiery mouth met hers. The manly odor assailed her nostrils, a bristly day-old beard pressed against her tender face. They dueled with their tongues, and he grew hard; she could feel it throbbing along her upper thighs. His hands slipped from her hips, locking onto the cheeks of her firm buttocks; his vibrant, stiff weapon of love shot out from hiding in search of the lodging it knew so well.

Now, caught up, she could barely hear Kevin's bumbling of "White Christmas" from the living room. Rufus's mouth worked about her neck. A thrusting tongue teased her ear with in-and-out thrills that made her moan, her hand slithered into the cleft their bodies made until it reached his stiff prong. Her long fingers touched it, gently, then closed around the thick prick, throbbing thirstily in her hand.

He succeeded as if by magic in unbuttoning her white jersey blouse and unhooking her bra. Her nipples bare, he buried his face in her bosom, while his hands worked down-side, unfastening the large white button on her woolen pants. Her legs grew weak as the pants dropped to her ankles, his hands now caressing the firm rounded ass in tight black bikini panties. A sudden spasm and she felt herself falling onto the bed, with him beneath her.

He had her nylon briefs down to her thighs, when a loud knocking on the door turned her suddenly rigid.

"Nancy, I'd like to talk with you . . . it's rather important," said Mrs. Riley.

"Roof . . . it's my mother, wait!"

"You're kidding."

"*Wait*! . . . We've got all night." She rolled over, away from him.

"Nancy, are you all right?" Mrs. Riley asked.

"Are you –" Rufus couldn't finish the words, as a flood of anger swamped him. "What in fuck does she mean, 'are *you* all right'?"

"Roof, later, everything . . . everything will be fine." She freed herself from his hold and hopped off the bed. "I'll be right there, Mother . . . Give me a minute," she said in a tremulous voice.

She wouldn't look at him while dressing. Not at those spinning raging shoebutton eyes. Figuring she had all of a minute while he smouldered toward a tantrum, she went swiftly to the door, smoothing her hair, then looked back at him sitting on the bed, nude, frustrated, furious. "We've got all night, Roof. And please, don't –"

"The lights, *right*?" he jumped off the bed. "No lights, she says, don't ruin the surprise." Moving through the darkened bedroom toward the door, he bumped against a small table. "Shit, shit shit," he cursed, while rubbing his knee. Reaching the half-lit doorway where Nancy stood, he said snickeringly, "Like a neon factory." His fingers went for the familiar light switch. But it wasn't there.

*What had happened to the light switch*? Nancy wouldn't tell. He'd find it himself.

From wall to wall, he searched. Bumping into objects en route, each time letting out a volley of four-letter words. Finally frustrated, he yelled, "Where the fuck *are* the lights?"

From outside the room, through the half-opened door, Nancy bravely replied, "Find them yourself!"

He'd clear his mind. Analyze. The other side of the door. He was sure. Carefully, he returned to the doorway, and as deducted, the light panel was there. He flicked it on, and the master bedroom lit up.

His eyes wouldn't believe what they saw. Words finally formed, "That broad! That mothering broad!" Nancy's birthday present, a new design, a new face to *their* bedroom.

A decor without a touch of masculinity – ruffled spreads and flowery drapes. The walls, papered in the most feminine of colors, and his favorite reclining chair, a leather job, replaced by an Elizabethan hard-back. Only the large color TV set remained.

"Nancy! . . . Nancy!" he shouted, repeating the name like fire drill bell, until, accompanied by her mother, she stood at the bedroom door. Viewing Rufus in his shorts, Mama Riley retreated, leaving Nancy to brave it alone.

"What . . . what in shit have you done?"

"Stop shouting."

"You're kidding! You change the fuckin' bedroom and I'm supposed to whisper? This, this is the big surprise? *My* birthday present?"

"It's also a great improvement."

"You're killing me with improvements!"

"Roof, it was drab before. The room's alive now. Cheerful. Mother thinks it's sensational."

"It sucks! Can you understand that? It absolutely sucks!"

"Don't get hostile, Roof. I'm not in the mood for it."

He sat on the edge of the bed. Meeting her watery eyes, he said, "Did you get me home just to break my balls? Is this some kind of conspiracy you and your mother cooked up?"

"Damn you, Roof!" She turned on her heels and left.

The notion of an actual conspiracy against him gnawed at his mind. He sat there, weighing the possibilities. In his month-long absence, Nancy could easily have been maneuvered by her mother. The old battle-axe had sold Nancy on divorce. Now, when he had it made. Any halfway decent attorney could get Nancy half the spoils, not to mention his paying the attorney fee.

He happened to glance above the bed. At first he couldn't believe what he saw. He shook his head, rubbed his tired eyes. But what hung on the wall above the bed wouldn't vanish. The conspiracy he only suspected gained solidly in substance. A foot long wooden crucifix, centered over the bed's headboard, riveted his eyes.

Rufus became speechless, his mind seemingly mesmerized by the unthinkable sight. Until, livid with an unparalleled anger, he hopped onto the bed, yanked the crucifix off the wall and flung it to the carpeted floor. The base of the crucifix slid open on impact; two miniature candles and a small capped bottle fell out of the hidden enclosure.

"A fucking crucifix in *my* bedroom," he swore, and muttering curses, headed for the shower.

EARLY ARRIVALS for the Midnight Mass glanced casually at the two network mobile units parked in front of the great cathedral. Inside, the members of the vast choir began to assemble in the church's loft. Below, TV cameras manned by men with earphones were in the last stages of camera rehearsal.

At the mansion, the light in John Gallogly's office was on. He was seated behind his desk, engaged in a phone conversation. He looked at the Swiss clock on the wall. Eleven-fifteen P.M. He'd have to hurry. The Cardinal would be entering the vestibule to don the holy vestments in preparation for the celebrated High Mass.

Father Paul Bartley ambled into the room. He

waited for the conversation to end, then informed Gallogly, "Terrible Tummy's got the dogs out looking for you. I'm one of the dogs. You'd better move it; he's having one of his shit fits."

John Gallogly rose from the desk. He only half heard Father Bartley's warning. "That was Monsignor O'Dwyer, from Florida."

Paul Bartley smiled, "You took may advice and checked out this Ron Rebuck?"

"I did. A preliminary one. And it's between you and me, Paul. The Vicar General gets wind of this and we'll both be on the carpet." He came from around the desk. "Would you believe our Ron Rebuck's a Catholic?"

Bartley registered little surprise. "It figures. His book indicates he must have had Catholic teaching somewhere in his past. But for sure, he's no longer a Catholic."

"According to the Monsignor, the names Ron Rebuck, Ron Rebuck, Junior and a Josephine Rebuck, are in the diocese book of records."

"Josephine Rebuck, his wife?"

"Mother. Unless Ron Rebuck is sixty-five years old. Monsignor O'Dwyer is sure he met her. A stalwart Catholic he thinks. In any event, he's having the pastor in Clearwater parish, a Father Benedict, get a line on this Ron Rebuck. We'll shortly find out." Father Bartley's smile widened. Trailing the Monsignor out of the office, he sang out, "The long arm of *Mother* Church strikes again."

TWELVE FIFTEEN A.M. Not a person seated about the Manning living room said happy birthday. An ample number of Merry Christmases were exchanged but not a solitary "happy birthday, Rufus." And Kevin was now orating on the conditions of the banking world.

Such a schmuck, thought a smarting Rufus, who looked away, at the flickering lights on the large Christmas tree, at the angel on top, looking so pure, so virginal. Ron Rebuck came unbidden to his mind. Of all the people who braved entering his war-filled world, Ron Rebuck alone remained unconquerable. And now to send him, an atheist, a religious book about angels! He wouldn't touch it with Moses' staff. Ron Rebuck was insane. No doubt about it. "Spooky sunava bitch, leave him to his fucking *angels*," Rufus said aloud to himself. He'd get himself a drink.

He passed by Nancy, making a detour, to look out the window; the snow was still falling. He groaned. The Rileys would be overnight house guests – horrible thought.

The martini pitcher was dry, and Rufus cursed aloud. He did a quick count on who drank what, Mama Riley excluded. A tea-totaler. The old man carried his own flask of bourbon. Nancy couldn't have had more than two. He'd had one. Leaving Kevin and Bea. Fucking guzzlers! – using *his* bar, as *their* watering hole.

He'd had all of Kevin's motor-mouth he could take, and his teasing wife could toss her torso somewhere else. In a loud, clear voice, he said, "You're a fucking bore! Know that, Kevin? One kinda bore."

Nancy's eyelids sprang open, Mama Riley pricked her finger with the knitting needle, Papa Riley groaned like some poor sheep in a bull's world. Only Bea smiled approvingly.

"The fact that we're all faced with a coming

depression worse than the thirties – that's boring?" said Kevin.

Rufus looked at him, a puzzled wonder on his face, then shook his head. "What a dummy," he remarked.

"That was uncalled for, Rufus. Most uncalled for," Mrs. Riley spoke out. Nancy was quick to second.

"Was it?" said Rufus, looking pleased.

"What's uncalled for?" Kevin asked.

"Calling you a bore," Rufus hastily replied.

Bea started to giggle.

"What's *funny*?" Kevin asked her.

"Shut up, Kevin. You *are* a bore."

Nancy was fuming. "You just had to start it, didn't you, Roof? Ever since you came out of the bedroom, you've been itching for a fight. I don't like it, Roof. And I don't appreciate your calling my brother a bore."

"I thought I was being kind, *just* calling him a bore," said Rufus.

"Kind? You don't know the meaning of the word."

Kevin spoke up, "Hey, *truce*. It's *Christmas*."

"Not for Roof. He doesn't believe in Christ. He doesn't believe in God. He doesn't believe in anything," Nancy barked.

"That's right. And if that crucifix over the bed was supposed to play on my mind, you'll find it where it belongs – in the waste *paper* basket."

"Saints preserve us," Mama Riley grieved.

"Which ones? I hear a lot of 'em got canned."

"For an atheist, you seem to know something about saints," said Kevin.

"He knows about the devil," said Nancy.

"He *is* the devil," Bea added.

Mama Riley left and swiftly returned with the retrieved crucifix clutched to her bosom. "That was a terrible thing for you to do, Rufus. May God have mercy on your soul."

Rufus laughed. "What soul? What God?"

"The God who knows of your sacrilegious action."

"You mean the God who knows everything?"

"Before and after," said a serious Kevin.

"Are you referring to the Father, the Son, and what's his face, the Holy . . . Ghost?" Rufus asked.

"*Spirit*," Kevin corrected. "The Godhead. *Three* in one."

"And you really believe all that shit? You know, Kevin, you definitely are a prize dummy."

"There'll come a time you wished you'd have believed in God," Mama Riley warned.

"When's that?"

"When you stand before Him on Judgment Day."

"Amazing," said Rufus. "Grown people truly believing that crap."

"It's you that's missing the boat, not us," said Kevin.

"Don't waste your time, Kevin; religion to Roof has always been a dirty word," Nancy said.

"You'd really like to know what religion means to me? Horse shit! Pure unadulterated horse shit. And it's people like you who keep it alive. Make it possible for the Pope, Billy Hale, Norville Riggins and the rest of those assholes to be held in such high esteem."

"They're men of God," Mama Riley protested.

"Men of God, my ass! And don't give me that jazz, 'may God have mercy on my soul' . . . if there *was* a merciful God, there'd never have been a Hitler to kill six million Jews."

"I'm afraid the expression *free will* might be a little too deep for you," Kevin said mockingly.

"Don't waste your time explaining, Kevin," said Nancy.

"You're probably right. Anyone who could convert Roof would be making it to heaven the hard way."

Rufus zeroed in on Kevin, with that arrogant sneer on his face. "What's that supposed to mean?"

"It means you've had a chip on your shoulder since the day you were born."

"You bet I got a chip on my shoulder, and no fucking Ku Klux Klan, Nazi group, shit-eating Arab, or Christian crusader better knock it off."

"Bravo, Roof," Nancy falsely applauded. "Since when have you *ever* defended your Jewish heritage?"

"Since I was a chump kid in the Bronx, when you Christians threatened to stuff my kike ass with matzo balls . . . and call me Christ Killer."

Mama Riley spoke up, "For your information, the Ecumenical Council issued a proclamation stating Jews were not responsible for Jesus Christ's death."

"A little late for my youth, lady."

"Do you have any *true* friends?" Bea asked out of the blue. "In fact, do you have *one* single friend?"

Nancy picked it up before Rufus could answer. "He's got one. A Ron Rebuck. But not for long. Ron made the mistake of helping us when things weren't so rosy." She looked at Rufus. "When we were dead, flat *broke*."

"This Ron Rebuck, is he in the movie business?" Bea asked, hoping to stir the fires of conflict.

"He's been in *every* business," said Nancy, as Rufus grew angrier. "Seems Ron wrote a book. A religious book. And now Roof won't give him the time of day."

Rufus got up from the bar stool. "What about the bubonic plague? Cancer? Maybe good old-fashioned leprosy. You people are experts in *those* subjects too, aren't you?"

"The subject is this Ron Rebuck," Bea replied.

"Ron Rebuck haunts him," said Nancy. "Reminds Roof of those terrible days."

"Since when have they improved?" said Rufus, who started out of the room.

"Since the sheriff stopped coming to my door. Since bill collectors no longer call," Nancy said.

Kevin piped up, "You were lucky, Roof. Damn lucky. You just happened to make a black picture at the right tine."

"Lucky?" He stepped toward Kevin. "Guts, integrity, know the words? Foresight. But what would you know, Kevin, making millions is not your bag. An assistant vice president for over four years – who hates you?"

"Exploiting blacks and getting rich off them is third rate to me, " Kevin replied.

"Get rich, Kevin, then talk."

"Money isn't everything," Bea exclaimed.

"I'll say," Mama Riley added.

He looked at them all. Each of their faces. "You pack of hypocrites. Do you think I've forgotten how the bunch of you laid on Nancy? Telling her I was a bum. That I'd never amount to anything."

"Hold on, Rufus Manning!" Mama Riley lost her cool. "Not you nor anyone will prevent me from safeguarding my children's welfare. Their *happiness* is my rightful concern."

Rufus looked at her, then pointed to the slumbering old man next to her. "And what about his happiness?"

He stormed from the room, ignoring the savage comments that flew like arrows at his back.

He entered the bedroom, frustrated, wishing he'd never come home. He flicked on the master light, and blinked. Again, he took in the new decor, and moaned. He slammed the door shut, flicked off the light, and headed for the bed, shedding the smoking jacket en route.

Seated on the bed's edge, ripping the zipper to his pants in his haste to disrobe, he couldn't duck the wounding thoughts coming at him like line drives, and him without a mitt. *Religion*, a pack of *bigots* in *his* living room, *Christmas*, and *Ron Rebuck*, heavy flack. He grabbed for the table light next to the bed. Firmly in hand, he yanked it from its socket and hurled it against the bedroom wall. Suddenly, strangely, the TV set came alive.

He sat there, in the dark, startled, drawn to the set, looking at the picture of a man attired in rich silk garments, at His Eminence Cardinal Spellissy, about to bring the Midnight Mass to a close with his final blessing.

FAR FROM THE SEETHING Rufus Manning, at the very same time of the night, *another* watched his TV set in a darkened room his wife had reason to fear.

As the Cardinal rolled out the words: "In the Name of the Father, the Son, and the Holy Spirit," with the pudgy hand making the sign of the cross, the watchful eyes in the room shone brilliantly – like an animal in the night. Suddenly, their strange mixture of colors faded. Two crosses, blazing red, seemed to form where the eyes had been.

The TV picture included a youthful priest to the Cardinal's right, assisting at the ceremony. "THE YOUNG MAN, HE IS JOHN GALLOGLY," a voice boomed from somewhere in the room.

RON REBUCK'S FACE glowed from the reflected light cast from the TV. Gone were the images in his eyes. A smile, ever so slight, played over his lips.

# 5

THE SNOWFALL FIZZLED during the night, leaving about eight inches, carpeting the Connecticut woods and fields, turning the landscape white, dazzling clean, as though angels on high had cried tears of purity, cleansing the ground of man. A fresh start, a new beginning, the birth of Christ, fall to your knees and adore Him. Hallelujah, hallelujah!

*One* who wouldn't, Rufus Manning, was up. Fixing his own coffee in the presence of the mutt, Jocko, who was signaling an urgent need. Rufus ignored the animal's appeal.

Christmas morning and not a stir in the house. Just the two of them, man and beast, eyeballing each other contemptuously, while Rufus's hand found difficulty in bringing the coffee cup to his lips. *Nerves*, he thought, trying to pass it off – but the shaking concerned him more than he'd admit.

"Whatta you lookin' at?" he snarled at the mutt whose soft eyes begged for compassion. "Listen, dog, at *my* convenience. Can you understand that? . . . And don't look at me like I'm buying that man's best friend bit . . . Damn dog. Like, *I'm* to wait on *him*," Rufus ranted to himself. At that moment the lady of the house appeared, not looking her usual voguish self. The beneficiary of a martini hangover – giant size – she was holding her head, wishing the pounding would go away.

"Happy birthday," she groaned, falling into his lap as if the night before had never existed. "Roof . . . why didn't you let Jocko out?" she asked, jumping up and quickly swooshing him out the door.

"The hell with the lousy dog!" said Rufus, fixing himself another cup of coffee.

Returning to the kitchen, Nancy noticed his shaky hand. "When was your last physical?" she asked.

"Who cares?" he said combatively, switching the cup to his other hand.

"You need a checkup. I'll call Doctor Blakesley tomorrow."

"Later with the doctor bit. When what's-his-face and his snowplow clears the driveway, I'm gone."

Her eyes fired then slowly softened. She eased into a chair next to him. "Roof . . . last night . . . maybe I did say some things I shouldn't have . . . but I *was* high . . ."

He sipped the coffee and looked at her. "Bulshit yourself, not me."

"Why do you take that attitude? Why do you always knock what I say?"

"Because it's bullshit . . . and you know it. Every year the same thing, Christmas Eve, Christian catastrophy, and the Jew gets blamed. But no more. That was the last horror show for me." He rose from the kitchen table.

"Where are you going?"

"To *your* bedroom."

She quickly followed. "You can't leave, Roof."

"Can't I?" he kept walking.

"What about Leslie?"

He stopped at the bedroom door. "What about Leslie?"

"It so happens your darling daughter's bringing her fiance home."

He entered the boudoir. Nancy trailed behind him. "When?" he asked.

"Around noon."

"When's your family leaving?"

" . . . Roof, I'm having a brunch for Leslie and her fellow; *naturally*, my family's invited."

"Swell, you've got one less mouth to feed." He shucked the bathrobe onto a chair he despised, then went to the closet in search of winter clothes.

"Are you going to ruin my surprise for Leslie?"

His ears tuned to the sound of a motor from outside. A red Jeep was clearing the snow. Contentment filled his face. "Surprise? Nancy, I couldn't take another of your surprises."

"And what do I tell Daddy's precious little girl — her father wouldn't wait? He doesn't give a damn?"

"Leslie's an intelligent girl, she'll put the pieces together."

"Roof, if you leave, spoil things, I'll never speak to you again."

"Save the fucking threats, Nancy."

*"I mean it, Roof!"*

His shoulders sagged. He wanted to leave without hassling, but Nancy's tone of voice turned on the war drums within. "Do you take me for some kind of idiot? You lured me home and then you and your family proceed to break my chops. No seconds, Nancy!"

"Lure? I lured you home?"

"You called, not me." He fumbled with a white cashmere sweater.

"Why, you prideful bastard. I was doing my damnedest to make a peace treaty. Wanting you home –"

"To work on my head," he broke in. "A nitwit, I'm not. Any dummy could tell what happened last night was planned. Pretty good too. Must have taken you people some time to stage it all."

"Planned? Staged? What *are* you talking about?"

His feet wiggled into goatskin boots. Other than putting on his coat, he was ready to leave. "Okay, *I'll* amuse you." That shitty grin spread on his face. "The moment I got home, it was 'No lights, Roof.' Big surprise, and zammo, I put on the lights, *after* your mother purposely interrupts our making it, and the bedroom's turned into something out of Queen Victoria's court. And then it's Ron Rebuck. Like I owe my entire success to him. But wait; here comes the big one. The fucking crucifix over the bed. Yeah, that really blew my mind."

"Roof . . . I don't know anything about *that crucifix*, believe me."

"Nancy, stop shitting me. The game's over, it worked."

"Roof, neither my mother nor I put that crucifix in the room. We thought you did."

"Why in the fuck would *I* put a crucifix over the bed?"

"To have something to argue about. Who knows why you do things?"

"There's one thing I still haven't figured out yet. How'd you manage the TV bit?"

"What TV bit?"

"You don't know anything about that, either. Of course you don't. Just like the crucifix, right?"

"Roof, I'm wise to you. Stop trying to beat me down."

"Sure, Nancy, sure. You don't have the slightest idea how that TV came on all by itself, tuned to that fat-faced Cardinal making with some bullshit religious sign. Gotta admit, the timing was perfect. Who rigged it, Know-it-all Kevin?"

She looked at him queerly. "On second thought, you don't need an appointment with Doctor Blakesley, what you really need is a *shrink*!"

He brushed past her. "See yah, Nancy. Call me when you've fumigated the house of parasites."

She followed down the corridor, tempted to riddle him with unladylike words, but unable to get them out. He entered the kitchen, where Mama Riley was pouring orange juice into two glasses. Not a word was said as he passed by, to the garage and out onto the drive.

He cleared the snow from the Jag's window as Nancy watched, not hearing her mother calling for her to come inside out of the cold.

The Jag warmed up, he opened the window and looked out at Nancy. "Maybe if I were a billionaire, things would be different."

He barely heard Nancy's stinging reply – "You'll have to do more than rip off a lot of gullible blacks to make it in that league!"

RON REBUCK walked along the two-mile strip of beach under a drizzling rain. A subdued Ed Dowiat, wracked with thought, tagged behind as scatterings of gleeful kids romped about in the cold surf. The rain would get worse, the weather forecast warned. And an army of enraged tourists would spend Christmas Day sitting glumly in their motel rooms cursing the *Devil* for the unwelcome rain.

Since the bizarre incident on the dock, Ed Dowiat needed little convincing that Ron Rebuck was truly the Archangel Michael's ambassador. The great angel's messenger to *all* mankind. The words he'd dimly heard before his blackout on the dock had now come clear. He'd identified the passage out of Rebuck's book, *The Lawyers of Hell*. It was the desert sequence where Lucifer tortured the mortal body of Christ, and its soul, *Michael*.

He believed in the voices, and in the miracle of the great wave. If Ron Rebuck was truly guided by the mighty angel, there'd be other strange occurrences. He was sure. And now, *he'd* become a vital part of it all. Finally, he was to escape from the all-American rut, and follow Ron Rebuck, blindly, into the battle of their lives. The thought made his body shudder with a mixture of fear and anticipation.

"Mind if I walk with you?" he said, catching up.

"I'm leaving for New York, New Years's Eve," Ron Rebuck announced.

Dowiat looked into the rugged face dripping with rain. "But the publishing meeting's not till the third. Why so early? And New Year's *Eve*?"

The rain slackened some as both men walked on. "Ed, it's not too late to change your mind."

"Not again, Ron. Not again. What do I have to do, kiss your ring? Your feet? I'll kiss your *ass* if you tell me to."

Rebuck smiled, "After today there's no turning back. My course has been set and the mistakes must be few. It's a big mountain we're climbing, Ed."

"Ron . . . that mountain . . . I mean . . . what if it's insurmountable?"

Ron Rebuck walked along without replying. He

knew all too well what Ed Dowiat was saying. He'd be going head-to-head against the revered and mighty, acclaimed leaders of religion. Those distinguished guides of God. The gang of evangelists with their weekly and TV specials. Billy Hale. The *famous* Billy Hale, friend of Presidents. And the never-ending list of others. Norville Riggins, Rex Lombard, the faith healers and their host of believers. The Jive crusaders for Christ, the panhandling Jesus freaks, the Right Reverend this, or that, who blow the torn minds of the depressed and the lonely. Mormons, Protestants, Catholics, and Jews who fill the powerful ranks of organized religion. And *all* sharing one thing in common. The belief in a book deemed holy. The Bible. Its Old and New Testaments. Written words from the sacred testimonies of men with an unequaled flair for inflicting terror.

"You know, Ed, it doesn't surprise me that someone like Rufus Manning's an atheist. How could any *intelligent* person, after reading the Bible, truly believe in such a monstrous God?"

"Ron . . . doesn't it frighten you just a little?"

"That people believe in the Bible?"

"That, and the fact you've made it your greatest challenge. To change people's minds. I mean it's like you're telling everyone that ice cream's poisonous."

"Ed, We're living in a modern world, with science continuing to reach new heights, and religion's still in the dark ages. Once I get them to open their minds, deliver my message to the masses, the rest will take care of itself. I assure you."

Lightning cracked over the Gulf accompanied by a loud clap of thunder. This was the lightning capital of the nation, perhaps the world, and Ed Dowiat grew wary. He saw that even the kids were making a beeline from the surf to their motels. Yet Ron Rebuck remained totally calm as he spoke on. "Rufus Manning is the primary objective. With him as the promoter, the rest will fall into place."

"Ron . . . the lightning," said Dowiat, warily.

"Through Manning the foundation is laid. The missions of Michael will spring forth. And strike out against the army of hypocrites. They're preachers of poison . . . they're wrathmongers, and the politicos with their strong religious ties —"

Suddenly, amidst the thunder and lightning, he stopped.

Ed Dowiat saw that far-off look in his eyes, and tensed. He relaxed a second later as a smile crept onto Ron Rebuck's lips.

FATHER BENEDICT raised the cup of coffee to his lips. He directed his gaze at June Rebuck who avoided his eyes, Barbara Rebuck Dowiat, Ed's wife, noticed her discomfort and now wished she hadn't told her mother about the incident on the dock. She never dreamed her mother would bring a priest to June's house. Especially on Christmas Day.

"Is my son possessed?"

The round-faced, balding man smiled at the attractive silver-haired Mrs. Rebuck Senior, and said, "By whom, Mrs. Rebuck?"

"Satan. The Devil."

"I think we've all got a little of the devil in us."

Josephine Rebuck frowned. She expected better. From the moment she'd brought the priest into her daughter-in-law's home he'd seemed more amused than interested. And, if it weren't for Monsignor O'Dwyer's request that he check into Ron Rebuck's background, he somehow would have begged off coming.

"Father Benedict, what happened yesterday cannot simply be ignored . . . or treated lightly. Ever since my son began writing that book, he's changed. Unusual things have been happening around here."

Father Benedict drew forward. He'd heard enough. "Mrs. Rebuck, your son's written a book. Undoubtedly he's become obsessed with its subject. As for the voices, this can be a result of certain emotional states – schizophrenia for one. What we call 'split personality.' Your son more than likely was reliving a scene from the book and fell into a kind of hysteria."

"And the wave, Father? The strange wave?" Josephine Rebuck challenged.

He looked past her, at June Rebuck. "No offense intended, but your daughter-in-law could have *thought* she saw a wave. Isn't that so, Mrs. Rebuck?" he asked.

"June has never lied to me," Josephine Rebuck exclaimed.

"I'm sure that is so. However, with all due respect to your daughter-in-law, I'm inclined to believe this wave was nothing more than a figment of her imagination. Under the circumstances, I, too, might have imagined things." He made a move to rise. "Now, ladies, if you'll excuse me, I'm having Christmas dinner with friends."

"The room Father. What about the room" Josephine Rebuck said hastily.

"The room? Oh, yes, the room."

June Rebuck gave her mother-in-law a protesting look.

"June, it's best. You must let Father Benedict see the room."

"Maybe another time, when the man of the house is here," Father Benedict said appeasingly. He could see the worried expression on June Rebuck's face.

"Nonsense." Josephine Rebuck wouldn't hear of such a thing.

"Mother, don't you think Ron should be here?" Barbara Dowiat suggested.

"I've brought Father Benedict over because I fear for your brother. Something's terribly wrong. A mother knows these things." She looked at June. "My worries are for you as well. Please believe me, June." She stood up from the table. "I'll show you the room, Father." She looked back at June. "Does Ron lock it?"

"There's no lock *to* the door," June informed her.

Arriving at the den, Father Benedict had second thoughts. "Mrs. Rebuck, wouldn't it be much wiser if I questioned your son personally, rather than barging into his study?"

"Father, you must," she pleaded.

The look in her eye, that of a worried mother, moved the priest. He'd oblige her if nothing else. Without further ado, he reached for the doorknob.

Josephine Rebuck screamed as she saw the priest's eyes fill with pain. His body shaking violently, he toppled to the floor.

RON REBUCK silently and suddenly wheeled his car off the beach road and entered a church parking lot jammed with cars. The glass-encased notice board at the church door read: *Jasper Burr – World Famous Evangelist – Christmas Day Services*.

Ed Dowiat sat quietly and wondered what Ron Rebuck was up to. Why, out the blue, would he stop here? At once, Ed realized it all had something to do with the cryptic smile on Ron Rebuck's lips as they'd both hurriedly left the beach.

Ed was about to ask when Ron Rebuck left the car and walked briskly through the rain toward the church entrance.

Rebuck's ears filled with the singing from inside the as Ed Dowiat remained in the car, watching him worriedly.

The church was filled, almost to capacity, and the pastor was well into his introduction of Jasper Burr. The heavy-set evangelist, with long sideburns and bushy eyebrows, rose from his chair, gave a friendly slap to the minister's shoulder, then entered the pulpit and gazed out at the flock. His familiar voice thundered through the tiny church.

The thick-jowled guest evangelist looked out and over the crowd, consisting largely of men and women of middle age and older. His searching eyes fell on the man standing in the aisle at the rear of the church. He smiled approvingly when he saw an usher come to the man's side, offering to seat him. Ron Rebuck brushed off the usher and stood stock-still. The smile on the evangelist's face vanished and the paster, seeing him, grew restless.

"Thar's a seat up front, my good man," the evangelist boomed. Ron Rebuck did not respond, and remained where he was, his eyes fixed on the preacher.

At last, Jasper Burr turned away from this oddly behaved intruder and began to speak.

"Now, my friends in Christ, I'm going to talk about why the Lord God sent His one and only beloved Son into this sinful world of men. . . . "

For five minutes he rumbled on, quoting passage after passage from the New Testament to support his argument. The small church echoed with the words of Matthew, Mark, Luke and John. But Jasper Burr knew his message wasn't coming across with its usual impact – that fellow standing in the aisle was getting on his nerves. The pastor, seated to the right of the pulpit, sat helpless, seething inwardly. Already two ushers had tried seating Ron Rebuck to no avail. The pastor fought off a gnawing urge to leave his seat and order the man to either be seated or leave his church, although to do so would disrupt the services. He'd waited all year for this day – the presence of the great Jasper Burr at his small church on Christmas Day was the highlight of the year.

Suddenly, Burr cut short his Biblical argument and aimed his words directly at Ron Rebuck.

"My friend, the lord doesn't care whether you stand or sit . . . he doesn't care whether you lie down or kneel . . . that you heed his words and abide by his great law is all that matters."

Ron Rebuck didn't flinch – he ignored the many heads that turned and the eyes that stared. He looked straight ahead, at the man in the pulpit, unwaveringly.

The evangelist dropped his carefully prepared preliminaries and got right to the meat of his text, the fiery oratory that called upon sinners to repent – the rousing message that had sent shivers through congregations in every corner of the Sunbelt.

He bore down hard on the American merchants who sold their wares during the Christmas season, then read chapter and verse from the New Testament about how Christ handled such matters on the Temple steps. He went so fas as to call the giant advertising agencies the Devil's tool, and smacked his lips as he described the great punishment that was in store for them all.

Now, back in top form he raised his hands, his voice swelling with emotion. "I say to you that Jesus Christ came into this world over two thousand years ago this very day to show us the path, the road, to our eternal salvation."

He now pointed a warning finger toward the congregation and roared: "I say to you that they who do not follow the teachings of our Lord Jesus Christ, they who do not live their lives as prescrived in the Holy Bible, shall know the wrath of God . . . for in His almightly anger, He shall strike down those who turn their backs on the Holy Book . . . they who defy their Lord – "

"LIAR!"

Heads turned, eyes converged on Ron Rebuck who stood, pointing a threatening finger at the bewildered evangelist.

"How dare you poison the minds of these people? How dare you call God a murderer?"

The fiery-eyed Rebuck's onslaught found the evangelist stunned, at a loss for words. He could only watch mutely as the man who'd called him a liar turned to leave the church.

The pastor jumped to his feet and signaled the ushers to eject Rebuck. Slowly, the flush left the face of Jasper Burr; with trembling hands, he opened the Holy Bible before him. His fingers fumbled through the pages until he came to *Revelations*, as a shocked congregation watched him in silence. The words came from his mouth bitterly. "For I testify unto every man that heareth the words of the prophecy of this book. If any man shall add unto these things, God shall add unto him the plagues that are written in this book." He looked up, seeing with satisfaction that he'd recaptured his audience. He continued to read.

"And if any man shall take away from the words of the book of this prophecy, God shall take away his part out of the Book of Life, and out of the Holy City, and from the things which are written in the Book."

He paused momentarily, then continued, his voice bolder. "He which testifieth these things saith, surely I come quickly. Amen. Even so, come, Lord Jesus.

"The Grace of our Lord Jesus Christ be with you all. Amen."

No sooner had he finished and closed the Book, than fear gleamed in the eyes of the parishioners . . . as the pulpit where he stood went up in flames.

# 6

"HEY ADMIRAL!" Rufus Manning called out to the night doorman picking his nose in the apartment building's lobby.

"Me?" the man pointed to himself. He was a little guy with an abundant crop of hair and dark eyes, almost black, too large for his face.

"See someone else?" said Rufus, "and where's your hat?"

"No hat inside."

"And I could care," Rufus replied, eeking out a thin smile. "Do you know me?" he asked.

"You're Mr. Manding . . . twelfth floor."

"Manning!" Rufus corrected. "You Spanish? I get a little accent."

"Puerto Rican, señor." he said with pride.

"Ter – *rif*ic. Look, amigo . . . want you to do me a favor. No big thing," said Rufus as he took out a wad from his pocket, peeling off a fifty while the doorman looked on with "caramba" eyes.

"What can I *do* for you, Mr. Manding?"

Manning! And don't make me correct you again."

"Sorry, señor. Man-ning."

"This is out of my line, but scare up a girl for me. Send her up. Apartment twelve-o-five. And this fifty is for you . . . but she better be cake."

"A *girl*?"

"Yeah, a girl. One with legs, a face, the kind with a twat. Familiar with them?"

"But . . . but, Mr. Man . . . ning, Christmas Night . . . few hustlers on patrol. The ones that are . . . they're *scabs*. Why not a massage parlor, Mr. Manning?"

"Massage my ass. S'matter, Pancho, you got something against money? Wait a minute," said Rufus, spotting a familiar body entering the lobby from the street – that leggy brunette he'd seen on the elevator. "Pancho, that piece of cheesecake, who is she?"

"She lives on your floor, Mr. Manning . . . " He shook his head, "Trouble, señor," he warned.

"Trouble? What could *you* possibly know about trouble?" said the departing Rufus, making his way toward the elevator where she stood – tall and beautiful.

"The name's Rufus Manning. Your neighbor trying to be neighborly."

She gave him a frosty look, then pushed the elevator's button.

"C'mon superlady, I'm only a pussycat looking to share some loneliness," said Rufus, as the elevator door opened.

She stepped in and waited for him to push the button. He laughed, "Don't tell me I've made that little of an impression on you. We shared this thing before, remember?" He pushed the button to twelve. Her floor as well. "All alone, Christmas Night?" he asked, hoping to strike up a conversation while whiffing the fragrant aroma of her person. She looked straight ahead, as if he wasn't there. "Listen, how's this for the idea of the century? At least of the night. We both get ourselves a drink somewhere. You want dinner? We have a late dinner. Whatever."

The elevator passed seven, and Rufus was shooting craps. "Let me put it another way. Straight out. I'm lonely, you're lonely, New York's lonely, the whole world's lonely. Let's spoil it for everyone and get it on."

The door opened at twelve and she stepped briskly out into the hall.

"Wait up," said Rufus, "I got word Santa Claus's a mugger." He didn't see the hint of a smile on her face as he swung around her, blocking her path. He started making ridiculous hand signs, as the green eyes set above full perfect lips began to thaw.

"Mr. . . ."

"Manning. Rufus Manning. Call me Roof."

"Roof? Like a roof on a house?"

"Or apartment. Yours or mine."

"Look, Roofy Goofy, I hate to shake your shingles but you're working on the wrong girl."

"Am I? Well it's been a wrong day. What's the difference?"

She brushed past him, stopping at the door to her apartment.

"I'm going to give you one more chance," said Rufus, watching her fumble for a key in her purse. "Married?" he asked.

". . . No," she said softly, finding the key.

"Divorced? Engaged? Being kept? Widow? *What*?"

She looked at him, at that shitty grin. "Direct, aren't you?"

"Like bullets."

She placed the key in the door's lock and said, "You're shooting at the wrong target."

He wasn't in the mood for a battle of wits. His jaw stiffened. "I'll meet you the in Oak Bar at the Plaza Hotel, in an hour. We can zap each other with kinky insults over drinks."

She opened the door. "Awful sure of yourself, aren't you?"

"Like an Israeli raid."

"Mr. Manning, I come awfully high. Out of *your* league, I'm sure."

"Save that opinion for later. Look – really. Go out with me and you'll never have more fun with your clothes on. You're the only thing keeping me from winging it to Acapulco."

huskily, "Via con Dios."

. . . He stood there, in the hall, as the door slowly closed in his face. Shut out enough for one day, he banged on the door and called out loudly, If you're not all talk, you got a buyer. Oak Bar, one hour, *don't* be late!"

THE REBUCKS AND DOWIATS finished Christmas dinner and sat around the Rebucks' living room – attractively furnished in muted tones of green and blue. The rain had let up and the Dowiat children were casting their nets for mullet on the dock. Only Ron Rebuck Junior represented the younger set in after-dinner conversation. Conversation that had yet to bring up the incident with Father Benedict that afternoon.

June Rebuck couldn't remember the last time her husband had allowed himself the luxury of just sitting about. And if it hadn't been Christmas, with the entire family present, he would have eaten alone in his room tonight, as always.

All through dinner Josephine Rebuck said but a few words. She alone refused to raise her wine glass in the toast for the success of her son's book. And now, Barbara Dowiat saw that familiar look come into her mother's eyes.

"Ron . . . a priest was here today. A Father Benedict. I brought him."

Ed Dowiat smiled. "He knows," he said.

Josephine Rebuck glared at her daughter.

"Don't look at me, I didn't tell him."

"She didn't tell him. No one *had* to tell him," June Rebuck said.

Josephine Rebuck looked at the tense faces, then met her son's eyes. "Are you also aware of what happened to the good Father?"

"*What* happened?" an excited Ron Junior spoke out.

"The priest received a terrible shock from the door handle to your father's den," June said.

"No kidding!" He looked at his father. "You've got it rigged so no one can get in? Why, Dad?"

Ron Rebuck avoided the question; his eyes had not left his mother's. "I'm sure you brought the priest over here because you're worried about me. But, please, don't ever do anything like that again. It could be even more dangerous . . . and what happens is out of my hands."

"Whose hands, then, Ron? Whose hands?" Josephine Rebuck implored.

He didn't answer. Silence prevailed. Until Ron Junior broke the spell and said, "Do you hate priests, Dad?"

Ed Dowiat fielded the question. "Your father's at war with anybody who preaches of a wrathful God."

Josephine Rebuck slumped in her chair. "Can the writing of a book change you that much? Can you simply forget all you were taught?"

"*Taught*! – you mean *brainwashed*," Ed Dowiat said.

He was stopped short by a glare in Ron Rebuck's eyes – an allowance for his mother to continue, to get it *all* out of her system. "I can't believe a son of mine could turn his back on the best early Catholic

education, forget everything he learned at All Souls . . . it troubles me deeply. You often told me how much you loved Father Rinaldo, the principal at All Souls. Why you even played football for a Catholic University."
Catholic University."

Ron Rebuck leaned forward in his chair. "Mother, you yourself became partly responsible for the writing of my book when you sent me to All Souls. The seed was sown there."

"A bad seed," she replied.

"Bad? Hardly, Mother. My book doesn't use fear as its base. It doesn't make God the wrathful being the Bible makes Him out to be." His face tightened. "Isn't it damn time for someone to correct the centuries and centuries of harm done by so-called gospels? Gospels told by men who make God the greatest murderer of all?"

"Let someone else challenge the Bible. Experts."

"*What* experts?" Ron Rebuck snapped his reply.

Josephine Rebuck slumped deeper in her chair. She hadn't the energy or will to persevere. She looked at June and now realized the strain, the anguish she suffered. To have lived with such a carefree man for so long. A free soul, who devoured all that life had to offer. And now, *possessed*? Inhabited by some supernatural spirit? Driven by an unknown force to challenge the very heartbeat of established religion, the Holy Bible itself?

Josephine Rebuck checked her tongue. She would not bring up the matter of the mysterious room. Another time. After she'd talked to Father Benedict. Earlier, she'd called the rectory and was told that the priest was ill and had retired for the evening. Nothing

more was said.
storming through her fearful mind. "I heard some minister on TV called the President a God-fearing man. He was complimenting him, Dad."

Ron Rebuck looked at his son, his eyes stern. "Ronnie, if anyone ever calls you a God-*fearing* man, spit in his eye!"

SANTA CLAUS must have come and gone – or perhaps he booked a later reindeer flight to the Oak Bar in New York's posh Plaza Hotel. The sophisticated saloon lacked patrons *this* Christmas night. And they who sipped the soup were less than jovial. As though Santa was a guy named "Blue" who brought only presents of remorse, self-pity, and sacks of loneliness.

Rufus Manning was not among the few lone wolves positioned at the bar; he sat at a table by himself. He'd finished off one martini and was working on another. He was dead sure she was coming. A gut feeling, and every few minutes he looked confidently at his Accutron. Suddenly, the picture of perfection entered. Bundled in Russian sable down to her legs booted in calfskin that matched her gloves, her entrance gave a refreshing lift to some lonely hearts – the boys at the bar with their Sunday smiles and straining necks. He was undecided whether to flag her eye or let *her* come to him, as the captain, a distinguished-looking Latin type, whipped up an instant smile. The kind reserved for the Tommy Tippers and Lady Lookers. But she nixed his signal for the hat check girl to take her fur. She'd keep it on. Like, it's *sable*, Sally! Not to be hung on just *any* coat rack. She looked beyond the obliging captain, anxious to seat her, eyes searching for the *one* and *only* and having little difficulty in picking him out. Rufus Manning wasn't hiding. Not him, with the bright yellow sweater under a blue blazer. Not him, with those beady eyes and that shitty grin.

"Hi . . . " said Rufus, remaining seated. The lady barely nodded as the captain assisted her into a leather chair opposite him.

"Martini? Manhattan? Soda pop?" asked Rufus.

"Martini. Dry. *Very* dry. And plenty of ice," she said to the captain, then looked at Rufus, those green eyes flashing like some tigress on the hunt.

"Money sure changes things, don't it?" said Rufus, staring back at the searching eyes, rediscovering that sexy face, the "Gatsby" hairdo. "Got a name?"

"Jewell," she replied softly, curving her lips.

"Miss Jewell?"

"A ten-thousand-dollar Jewell."

"Miss Ten Thousand, Jewell? Doesn't jive, lady."

"Too expensive for you? Wasn't it you who said – 'whatever it's worth to me'?"

He was first puzzled, then shook his head in disbelief. "A couple of drinks, some dialogue, ten thousand smackers – what kind of trip are *you* on?"

She waited for the waiter to set the martini down and leave, then replied, "I thought you were rich. Or was that just a lot of b.s.?"

"Five million rich enough? Or is that the average Joe's assets?"

"Five million?" She sipped her martini between laughing lips. But her eyes were sweeping the room beyond him.

"Expecting someone? Getty or Rockefeller, maybe?"

"No . . . *him*."

Rufus followed the direction of her eyes, to the

entrance, where a powerful-looking black man had appeared. As he zeroed in on their table, Rufus sensed trouble.

"I'll be at the bar . . . Miss Jennifer," the black giant said in a peculiar, high tenor voice – quite a paradox for a man of his huge build. Two hundred and fifty or more pounds on a six foot six frame. A giant with a pipsqueak voice.

"Who was that?" Rufus asked.

"A pest," she answered.

"A pest, huh – your big league pimp?"

"Big league bodyguard. You should meet the others. On second thought, if I stay with you much longer, you probably will."

"Listen, this is getting to be like a scene out of *Foreign Intrigue*. Who are you? Some kinda princess? Ambassador's wife? Eccentric millionairess? King Kong's caretaker?"

"At least you didn't include whore."

"Black Frankenstein over there called you Jennifer, is that your name."

"That's my name."

"And Jewell?"

"I was given that one."

"By whom?"

Her finger rubbed along the edge of the glass. "Too long a story."

He glanced at the bull at the bar. "Must be a helluva long story."

"Let's talk about you. What does a Rufus Manning do for the world?"

"Rufus Manning makes pictures. *Dude*, for one, and don't tell me you never heard of it."

"*Dude*? . . . The black film?"

"Black and ballsy. Just the money was green."

She smiled. He was working on her. "You're funny. It's getting so uncommon to meet a man so vibrant, so sure of himself. Actually, that's why I came. And *nerve*. My God, you're unbelievably rude. Such gall. Are you really that crude all the time?"

"How about persistent?"

"I will admit you're refreshing . . . but don't let that lead to some silly idea I'm going to bed with you. Even if I wanted to . . . Richard would spoil it."

"And that's Richard?" Rufus asked, gawking at the huge man seated at the bar, as if he was some kind of too-tall tree.

"That's Richard, " she sadly confirmed.

With an unexpected wave of his hand, Rufus motioned him over. Jennifer looked perplexed. Again Rufus waved. This time the giant caught his signal. Slowly, he eased off the bar stool and lumbered towards them.

"You Richard?"

"That's my name."

"Yeah, well, Richard, Jennifer doesn't like you around, so fuck off."

"*Whuch* you say?"

"I said get lost. Scram!"

Scowling, Richard looked at Jennifer. "This turkey bothering you?"

"Are you still here?" said Rufus.

The giant backed off, waiting for some kind of direction, but she was too dazed to respond. "I'll be at the bar," he said, glaring at Rufus.

"In another joint," said Rufus.

"Are you mad? Are you absolutely insane?" Jennifer asked, after Richard had returned to his bar stool. "He could have torn you to pieces."

Rufus laughed, "He's lucky Mike Spenard's not here, he would have split him a new asshole."

"My God, you're not only crazy but vulgar. Does it just come naturally to you?"

The captain suddenly appeared at the table, a phone in hand. "Are you Miss Jennifer Jewell?" he asked.

"Yes."

"There is a long distance call for you. You may take it here." He readied to plug it into a jack behind their table.

"No, I'll take it someplace else . . . Where?" she asked.

"The hotel lobby, madam. The operator will connect you," he informed her crisply. Without an "excuse me" to Rufus, she slid those long miraculous legs from beneath the table and followed the captain.

The mammoth at the bar seized the opportunity and returned to Rufus's table. "You and your big mouth better behave tonight," he said in that sissy voice.

"Are you threatening me, pal?" Rufus's fangs were showing.

"You got my drift."

"Really! One phone call and you're without feet, fella," Rufus replied as the big man, looking like the Tower of Babel, stared down at him with the hate for a white slavemaster burning in his eye.

"You behave, turkey!" he again warned, backing off, leaving Rufus to stew in his own juices. Hating to be threatened by anyone, a plan quickly formed in his devious mind. "Hey, captain!" he called out, ignoring the curious onlookers who keyed on his actions as if they were viewing some kind of private picture show.

"Yes, sir." The captain moved quickly to his table.

"I'm Rufus Manning . . . we met before, right?"

"Manning? . . . " He was trying to remember, if just to be polite.

"I made the film *Dude*."

"Oh . . . yes . . . yes, of course, Mr. *Manning*."

Rufus knew that would get him. "See that gorilla over there at the bar?"

"The rather large gentleman?" the captain inquired.

"I didn't say he was a dwarf," said Rufus. "He tried to sell me grass. The pig hustled me right here, in the *Oak Room*."

"When, Mr. Manning?"

"A few minutes ago. Didn't you see the slob come over to my table? Look, Captain, I don't give a shit . . . but if it gets out that some mauler from the street is peddling dope . . . right here in the Oak Bar . . . What can I tell you?"

"But . . . isn't the gentleman somehow with your party, Mr. Manning?"

"You're kidding. The sonofabitch tried to pick up my date. Would you believe for a hundred dollar bill? Now, do I get action or what?"

" . . . I will take care of the matter immediately, Mr. Manning. Leave everything to me, please," the captain said, half convinced of Rufus's accusations. He left to confer with a waiter while Rufus grinned. His game plan was activated.

Locking eyes with the black man at the bar, Rufus raised his glass in a toasting gesture, as if to wish him the best of luck. At that moment, Jennifer Jewell returned. And the dirty glance she gave the bodyguard was a good enough clue for the observant captain to take action on Rufus's complaint.

"Order me a drink, please!" she commanded as she squeezed by him.

"*Captain*, my *captain*," Rufus called out.

"Yes, Mr. Manning. What may I do for you, *now*?"

"The lady wants another drink. And I hope that little matter is being handled."

"Shortly, Mr. Manning," he replied. "Would you like another drink, Mr. Manning?"

"Hell, yes. It's only intermission . . . but not too strong. Gotta get it up, you know." He smiled at Jennifer Jewell, but she was in orbit. That call put her somewhere around the moon, or perhaps Mercury. She didn't catch his smart-ass remark. Nor did she see the two gentlemen, accompanied by a waiter, enter the room. Rufus did. He closely watched them huddle with the captain who pointed toward the big fellow. Rufus couldn't hear what the two men were saying to the big guy, but he assumed the words were less than complimentary, for he came off the bar chair like Gargantua, hulking over them, laying some wrathful words on their comparatively puny persons.

"Looks like Richard has a problem," said a gloating Rufus, whose remark floated by Jennifer Jewell.

"Don't put your honky fingers on me," Richard squawked.

"What kinda jive talk you givin' me? *Dope*? . . . Man, *you crazy*?"

Perhaps one of the detectives had the impression Richard was a giant fairy, for he made the suicidal mistake of touching his arm. "I tole you don't touch me, turkey!" Richard yelled, spraying him with saliva, then grabbing him by the lapels and lifting him off the ground. Forehead to forehead – then a splatting sound volleyed through the Oak Bar and the detective fell backward like a broken puppet onto the floor.

His companion, the smaller man attired in a seedy suit, went for his piece, drawing on Richard, who froze. "Get a cop," he said to the captain who nudged a waiter to do so.

"Yeah, get a cop," Rufus echoed *his* sentiments while sipping on a very dry martini, as the commotion roused Jennifer Jewell from whatever thought trip she was flying.

"What's *happening*?" she asked, tugging at Rufus's coat sleeve, not believing the scene at the bar.

"He bothered me."

"Bothered *you*?"

"When I go to war . . . I *win*."

"What have you got to do with this?"

"Watch the show. It's going to get better."

"My God. What have you done?" she choked on her words.

"Man, you know you ain't got the balls to shoot dat thing," said Richard, pushing his black beads for luck, as he took a step toward the house dick, but halted rather abruptly when he saw how much the detective's hand was shaking – the hand with the pistol aimed at *his* head.

"I'll shoot, mister," the detective warned in a shaky voice, over a deadly silence. The Joes in the bar were giving them plenty of space.

The fallen detective tried a comeback but he needed more than support stockings to get his legs working again. He managed a sitting position, holding his head in his hands. Meanwhile, New York's night knockers stormed the saloon, some five of them, three in uniform and two plainclothesmen. And, with the sounds of screeching sirens, reinforcements were obviously on their way.

Cops meant confusion, and Rufus would pass up witnessing the official police business of "Spread 'em, frisk 'em, tell the bastard his rights, and book the bad boogie with the birdie's voice."

"Let's split," he said, dropping enough green onto the table to more than cover drink damages.

"*What*?" said Jennifer Jewell, riveted by the action at the bar, now milling with people.

"Let's go!" He reached for her gloved hand and dragged her past the active accuser, the captain, who was bellowing his version of the battle scene to a bored-looking detective.

"Hey! . . . What gives?" a Joe just entering the bar asked Rufus.

"Police brutality," said Rufus, brushing past him, nudging Jennifer to step lively.

"This whole thing is preposterous. We must talk," said Jennifer Jewell, trying to stall him. She'd take a stand. A firm one.

"During dinner, during dinner," said Rufus, barrelling her into the checkroom adjacent to the Oak Bar's entrance, in search of his coat.

"I'm not having dinner with you. Can you possibly understand that, crazy person?" she said, watching him hunt for his gear.

Storm coat in hand, he had not heard a word she said, or pretended so, as he slipped his arm into hers. "You like Polynesian food?" he asked, leading her away from the Oak Bar whose entrance was now lined with curiosity seekers. "Fair place downstairs," said Rufus, as they approached the stairway, where

Jennifer Jewell halted again.

"You're crazy. You're absolutely crazy!"

"Right now, hungry," he replied, the beady eyes like marbles. He started down the stairs, but she remained.

"What now?" he asked, looking back at the handsome hunk of humanity perched at the top. She looked like Wonder Woman with the Russian fur and booted legs – all she needed was the whip. But Rufus was no lowly peasant freaked on fucking her. He had her number. The only real difference between her loneliness and another chick's was the rent district, and who was paying.

"Listen, luscious lips, this trolley's travelin', so if I don't zing your heart string, catch another." He continued down the stairs without looking back. She stood there, a jilted-looking Jennifer Jewell. Just as Rufus had planned it. His hard-guy bit was nothing more than a well-timed trump. He was banking on her boredom – her loneliness on Christmas night. Jennifer Jewell hesitated a mute moment, then followed.

ALONG THE WHITE WAY, from under the neon marquee with its bold letters, THE DEVIL, John Gallolgy smiled confusedly, then lit up a small thin cigar, blowing out the pearl-gray smoke into the luminous cold night air. Waiting for Paul Bartley, he observed the faces, overhearing mixed comments from the rush of people leaving the theater. He wondered what it was coming to. Not so much the picture – it had little bearing on his mood – but the day itself. Christmas Day. Did people really observe Christ's birth. Did they merely go through the motions? *Santa's Day*, that's where it was really at. Even the "T" in Christmas was silent. What in the years to come? he thought. Would Christmas become so commercialized that toy manufacturers would heat up a line of battery-operated, walking, talking Jesus Christ dolls? It seemed all too long ago when he was growing up in Providence, enjoying Christmas day with his Irish-Yankee parents; it had been a real family get-together, complete with the singing of carols. John Gallogly sighed; such a day was fast becoming a thing of the past.

Hatless, a cigarette dangling from his lip, Paul Bartley appeared out of the crowd. "Scare 'em, baby. Halleluiah, scare 'em," he jokingly exclaimed.

"It did that, if nothing more," John Gallogly agreed.

"I wonder what we can see on Easter?"

They moved out of the crowd's way, crossing Times Square, and headed east toward Fifth Avenue. They would pass up a cab ride to the mansion, being in a walking mood.

"Get your helmet on, John, war zone ahead," Bartley joked, referring to a scattering of prostitutes stationed in doorways along their route, pitching John Does walking by. Their white collars hidden by scarfs, the two priests stepped faster, as a tall, booted Nubian hooker with grotesque hair (or wig), nimbly approached.

She flashed a mouthful of teeth. "Looking fer a good time, baby?"

An irate John Gallolgy exposed his while collar, saying, "I'm a priest."

She looked at him with indifference. "What's that to me, sugar? I've had your kind before."

"I'm sure," he answered, greatly dismayed, as

both men walked on amid the catcalls and propositions. "*Future* shock you say?" Bartley exclaimed. "Brazen lot, aren't they? It wouldn't surprise me if they were to start hanging out in front of the cathedral."

"How'd you like to hear *their* confessions. John?"

"Absolution's for all."

"Sure it is. Sin, sin, sin, then come to confession and wash it away. Come on, John, how do we continue with such bunk?"

"Rebelling again?"

"John, if I didn't have you to say things to, get it out of my system, I'd go mad. Stark raving mad."

They made a turn on Forty-eighth, having their fill of Broadway. "Confession's a joke and you know it, John."

"Without confession some people would lose all communication with God."

"Not surprising. We've brainwashed them since they were seven years old." He caught the displeased look in John Gallogly's eyes. "Forget I said it. I'm all mouth. Haven't the guts to be a revolutionist."

"Speaking of revolutionists, guess who came to mind during that picture?"

"It's not hard to guess. Ron Rebuck, I'm sure."

"You, too?"

"No. But then again I haven't been thinking about him as intensely as you have."

"Admittedly so. Can't seem to shake him. Funny, I don't even know the man, yet I've tried to picture his face a dozen times, and all I see are eyes. Deep-set eyes."

"He's getting to you more than I realized."

"This might sound crazy, but last night I felt the

strangest sensation."

"Elves? The Little People, perhaps?" Bartley kidded.

"No. It wasn't a *physical* being. Unless this Ron Rebuck has gotten me thinking about things which don't exist, I could have sworn someone, or something was in my room. A presence, Paul. A forceful presence."

"That's awful heavy. Anything further on Rebuck?"

"With the holidays, I'm sure the priest in Florida had little chance to find out anything."

"John, I'm beginning to regret my encouraging you. Any event, I guarantee this Ron Rebuck won't get his book off the ground."

"He will, Paul. Sure as hell, he will. He's coming to New York . . . and soon. I can feel it in my bones."

Paul Bartley smiled, "Just like you feel there's a hell?"

John Gallogly ignored this sly remark. They were approaching the cathedral and a new thought came to his mind. He looked at his watch; one-fifteen A.M. The big three would still be up. Archbishop McGary, second only to the Cardinal in the archdiocese; Bishop Burke, the Vicar General, a tough-nosed chief administrator; and lastly His Eminence, Cardinal Spellissy, would be gathered in conclave on Christmas night, by tradition, and reminisce over brandy. With more brandy, they would become like sharks in a feeding pattern. John Gallogly had the misfortune of attending last year's event. He still shuddered to recall the beating-down he had received. The victim of razor-sharp words from cutting wits.

Stepping into the mansion's lobby, Paul Bartley whispered, "Are they still at it?"

John Gallogly saw the streak of light coming from under the door to the Cardinal's study. "Every man for himself." He dashed toward the back stairs, leaving a flat-footed Paul Bartley far behind.

Safely reaching the second floor, he heard Bishop Burke's gravelly voice from the lobby below. "Father Bartley, how nice. Join us, join us. We've been waiting up for you."

John Gallogly shut the bedroom door behind him. Poor Paul, he thought. He'll never be the same. He went to the bed, flicked on a table light, and unfolded a pair of yellow cotton pajamas, then proceeded to undress.

New Year's Eve, but six days away, he would accompany the Cardinal to his favorite place – Bimini. Two weeks of fishing and sun. The Cardinal was big on fishing. He welcomed the thought as he glanced at the bottle of Nytol on the table, and the package next to it. Curious, he opened it. The manuscript of *The Lawyers of Hell* emerged from the package. Father Bartley must have returned it. He deliberated whether to read . . . or take a swig of Nytol, and forget Ron Rebuck. His fingers reached for the manuscript. Reluctantly, he decided to reread Rebuck's version of Genesis, for this was the heart of the man's theory.

He'd read three pages when his eyes drifted from the manuscript, his senses alerted to a sudden thinness of air. That presence, that forceful presence he had experienced only the night before, was back. He sat there as if rooted to the bed, holding onto the manuscript, with eyes darting about the half-lit room.

All at once, John Gallogly, who considered himself

a practical man, a realist who scoffed at superstition and frowned skeptically on those who didn't, felt true fear. Whatever this invisible force might be, it was moving closer.

"Who is here?" he managed to ask, through trembling lips. The force seemed to hover over him; his body stiffened. Then his eyes fixed upon the manuscript in his hands as it burst into flame.

IT WAS PAST TWO A.M. when a cab pulled up some ten feet short of the snow-banked curb. Just a block from the Plaza where the dynamic duo had kicked off an evening out. Neither felt any pain nor were they bothered by the sudden blast of cold air that flushed their faces as they tumbled tipsily out of the cab, looking like guaranteed flunkies to a balloon test.

Jennifer Jewell was jubilant. She had the look of a schoolgirl on her prom night, holding onto Rufus's arm as if they'd been long-time lovers. But now came the moment of truth. They had been delivered to their mutual address – the Central Park South building for "swells" only – and now the question was: Whose apartment? His or Hers?

"Ferget sumpthin'?" the cabbie called out from a partially opened window. Rufus was running an obstacle course, maneuvering with some fancy steps in attempting to reach the sidewalk, with Jennifer following his tracks as if he were some kind of Alpine guide.

"Roofy-woofy, I think the cab driver wants a tip."

"Tip? . . . Of course, the tip." Rufus dug into his pockets. "Right on, brother." He drew two bucks from a thick wallet. "Your tip, pal," he shouted at the cabbie. He held up the two dollars for show, then dropped the deuce on the slushy sidewalk. "No curb service – no tip service!"

"Weren't for da recession, you could shove it."

"Sure, sure," said a scornful Rufus, "g'wan, yah garbage pail!"

The cabbie hurled a few choice words upon Rufus's heritage as he climbed out and picked up the wet bucks. Rufus brushed it off like dandruff. He'd had enough aggravation, enough bullshit for one day. And with Delilah awaiting him at the building's entrance – he was *Samson*! She could clip his bush anytime. But when a gray Ford skidded to a stop, spraying him with slush, Samson looked very much the sucker. He was ready to rumble, despite the fact that there were two men hustling from the car, heading directly toward Jennifer Jewell. He took on the driver, but the shorter man, the stocky one with the vicuna coat, escaped his intercepting move.

"What's with you, shit bum?" said Rufus to the taller, thinner man, with the oddball eyes.

"Go away, Marty," said Jennifer to the shorter one, who seemed to be the leader.

"Can't, Miss Jewell. You know that."

"Just leave . . . as if you didn't see me . . . don't spoil things. Not tonight."

"I'd like to, Miss Jewell, but Sheik Ali's bread is beautiful."

"Jump ship, Marty – it's sinking."

"Who's the joker?" asked the man called Marty.

"A magician. He makes people like you disappear."

"He'll have to be Houdini to pull that off," said Marty, glancing quickly toward Rufus who was pushing his fingers into his sidekick's chest.

"*What the* – " Marty's eyes bulged, as his friend

went for thunder, hoisting a snub-nosed piece from a shoulder holster. "Jukey!" the man called Marty shouted, "stash it, fer chrisakes!"

The thin man stared at Rufus like he was something for the meat rack, then reluctantly put the pistol away.

A patrol car emerged from Central Park, and Rufus let out a whistle that could have shattered glass.
shattered glass.

"Your friend's a fool," said Marty, noticing the police car moving toward them.

"Is he?" she said. "I wonder who the police will think a fool when they find out who has the gun. But then, maybe your man has a permit . . . or does he, Marty?"

"Call 'em off."

"And Richard?" she added.

"Too late . . . it's been piped already. You don't expect *me* to foot the bail."

"Does that include your friend's bail?" she asked.

"Okay, okay . . . I'll think of something."

"I knew you would," said Jennifer, turning away from him.

"Roofy, it's all right, he's a friend," she announced in a voice loud enough for the cops to hear.

"Friends? You got some funny friends," said Rufus.

"Really, officers, there's nothing wrong. Actually, that man and I are related," she said, pointing toward Marty in the vicuna coat.

"What kinda bullshit were you peddling them?" asked Rufus, once both were away from the cops.

She smiled. He'd drop it. That is, until they reached the building's entrance where Marty and chum were standing rather glumly.

"Next time I see you – change your face!" said Rufus to the thin, weird-eyed man, then brushed past Marty, glaring, as he and the long-legged Jennifer entered the building.

*Across* the street, Mike Spenard looked out from an early model Cadillac. He'd previously called the Mannings' home in Connecticut to wish Rufus a happy birthday and was told by a curt Nancy that Rufus had returned to New York.

A wicked smile came to Spenard's face, as he watched Marty and friend get into the gray Ford and pull away.

THE ELEVATOR RIDE to the twelfth floor took the bubble out of Jennifer's champagne mood. As reality returned, she knew that this caper with Rufus must stop at her door. He'd have to piddle in another pond, for hers was filled with oil – the *Arabian* kind.

"Roofy, you've been the highlight of my life. I'll never forget you." She tenderly kissed his cheek by her apartment door.

"Forget me!"

"Don't spoil it . . . It was great fun . . . Really, Roofy." She tapped his nose with her finger.

"What is this? Remember me? I'm the *winner*."

She shook her head. That lovely, sexy face with those green eyes looking directly into his.

"Come on, at least coffee . . . a drink. A glass of milk with saltpeter in it."

"Once you're in . . . *you're* in," she mouthed the words. "You *will* behave?" she asked, almost laughing over her own absurdity.

"Won't I!" said Rufus, his reply in between a question and a suggestion, with her unable to differentiate, or not caring to.

APARTMENT TWELVE-TEN-ELEVEN was Arabian luxury supreme. Regal rugs and furniture worthy of a Shah. Eight rooms in all, and a terrace with a matchless view of Central Park. Rufus, no admirer of Arabs, nevertheless was staggered by the grandeur of it all. Big bread, he thought. But whose?

"Like it?" said Jennifer, slipping off her fur and letting it drop onto a Persian rug worth a fortune.

"The living end . . . but why so – "

"Arabic? Meet my patron saint," she murmured, pointing to a huge portrait of a youngish sheik that hung conspicuously over the fireplace.

"I *get* the picture," said Rufus. Her sugar daddy, and a fucking Arab at that. He smoldered silently.

"Liquor or coffee?" asked Jennifer.

"Coffee, can't let *it* sleep."

"My, aren't you the *cock*-y one," she replied leaving him to his heavy breathing. He watched all of her depart: the shapely shoulders, wicked waist and those long lovely legs, not to mention her fabulous high-rise front.

Rufus had no regrets, no thoughts of Nancy, no sense of guilt. Jennifer *Jewell* was exactly that. And he the jeweler, eager to work on this priceless gem. But the portrait, the fat cat with the hankie over his head, the sheik, irked him. Not so much the picture but what it represented. It was a nagging reminder that he was in the tent of an Arab who paid the mortgage.

The picture had to go, he thought. Hell, how could he, a Jew, make it, with some shish-kabab hanging so prominently on the wall. The shame on his people, his heritage!

Jennifer Jewell re-entered the spacious living room carrying a coffee tray. She placed it on a brass table standing next to a *golden* gate – the only entryway to a high circular couch of some exotic, supersoft leather. She studied Rufus as he stared at the portrait.

"Gazing at God? That's Ali Sharif," she said.

"Is *that* what it is."

"Notice the eyes? They seem to be following you wherever you go."

"Yeah, like a Peeping Tom," Rufus muttered to himself, watching her pour the coffee into two cups that looked like something out of Ali Baba.

"What did you say?"

"I said, that was quick coffee." He chucked his coat on a chair and sauntered over to the couch. "What do I say – Open sesame?"

"Watch out for the Forty Thieves," she warned as he hopped the gate like a hurdler.

"Speaking of thieves, who *were* those crumbs out on the sidewalk?"

"Just a few of *his* police dogs. He's got kennels full!" she said, glancing toward the portrait. Rufus thought he saw a dash of disgust in her eyes. "Cream?" She waited to pour.

"Black! . . . Got plenty," he bragged.

"My, aren't you the dairy," she said, handing him the cup and saucer, and settling on the sofa with a flash of silken thighs.

"Jennifer, I would like to make it with you, but that futz – that Arab's too much. You've got to do something with that picture."

She found out fast he was frank. But to make it sound like he was doing her a favor was too much. He'd reached the hurricane level of insanity on her barometer. "You're rude. Do you know that? I mean *you're rude*! . . . Rude, rude, rude . . . and you're goofy, too."

He sat silently, wondering if he'd pushed his luck too far.

"Roofy, I'm no good for you. Let's not start something we can't finish. I think you're terrific and I promise to see your next picture, but we can't get involved. Already, I've let you go too far. I don't want your broken body on my conscience."

"Who's going to break *whose* body?" he asked, putting on his war mask.

"The whole Arab world . . . that's who!"

"You're kidding! *you've got to be kidding*! I thought you knew where it's at. Haven't you heard of the Six-day War? Shit, it make all the papers . . ."

"Roofy . . . they'll ruin you. Don't you understand? *He's* an army," she pointed to the portrait, threateningly.

"Baby, he'll wish he was up against Moshe Dayan if he screws with me," Rufus retaliated, unbuttoning his blazer. He took it off and tossed it on the couch. She watched in puzzlement as he next pulled off the yellow sweater.

"Would you mind telling me what you're doing?"

"Bad? Baby, I'm the baddest."

"You're the *craziest*," she replied, as he discarded the tee shirt, and stood there – topless.

"Did I ever say my apartment was a nudist colony?"

He ignored the protest. Unbuckling his belt, his

pants came tumbling down, slipping to his ankles. He kicked them off, along with the shoes. And now for the Jockey job, the final garment left on his lean body. He shunned socks.

"You wouldn't!"

With that tricky smile and those gimlet eyes, he stood before her, looking like an ad for Fruit of the Loom. Maybe the liquor had made him loony, she thought.

"Watch this," he said, nonchalantly.

She could do little else but witness him remove his B.V.D.'s, and shoot his moon at the solemn sheik.

She quickly looked away. "Put something over it, you goofy thing!"

"I certainly will," he replied, all too eagerly.

She tried not to laugh, but the entire night had been preposterous. Why should it change? This incredible man, this dynamic man . . . she knew where the adventure would inevitably end. Face it, he had her number. In a peculiar way she admired him. He was different. Having heard the smoothest of lines from playboys all over the world, and having been, for a year, the personal property of a sheik who paid dearly, how could *this* be happening to her? Maybe the fact that he was dependent on *no one* magnetized her. Something she was not . . . and wished to be.

"Are . . . are you still here . . . crazy person?"

"Here and . . . there," he replied, floating about the sunken living room like some ballsy fairy out of *A Midsummer Night's Dream*, killing the lights, all but one – the portrait's

"Are you decent?" she asked, her hands over her eyes.

"Like a baby," he replied.

"Is your diaper on?"

"Pinned perfectly," he informed.

She braved a peek between her fingers. She couldn't believe what she saw. The face of Sheik Sharif was obscured, his majestic eyes *tented* by a pair of seedy-looking B.V.D.'s.

There was little else for her to do but laugh. "I surrender, unconditionally surrender," she declared, between laughs. "You're too much . . . you're *unbelieveably* too much."

"Then come over and smoke the peace pipe," he offered.

"*The peace pipe*! My God, you're terrible. Is there no end to your evil ways?"

His nude body extended on the plush couch, he watched her rise in the dim light.

"I'll be right back, action man, there's something I have to do."

"What? Call Cairo? Tell Big Abdul his face never looked better."

HER "BE RIGHT BACK" found him fighting off sleep. Fifteen minutes, maybe twenty, still no Jennifer and his lids were getting droopier by the second. He was fading fast, and then – Rufus Manning was missing in action. If he'd only known, he would have propped match sticks under his eyelids, for attired in a blue see-through negligee, Jennifer Jewell finally returned. She moved in the half-darkness to the couch. Placing her hands on those shapely hips, she looked down at him, in all his raunchy, naked glory. "Hey . . . action man," she whispered.

She went to her knees. Her lips pressed on his

lightly. The snoring ceased. Her fingers deftly roamed along his thighs while she purred hot breath over the hairs on his chest. He stirred. His well-endowed penis stiffened, as her fingers caressed his balls, then settled on the thick rod. Aroused, he opened his eyes to see her fabulous face bent over his crotch. Her tongue licked at his tender parts while her hand softly massaged his penis – slowly, stroking it, ever so effective. His prick primed, he then felt the magic of her mouth. A thousand feelings pulsed through him. And then, the impossible dream. His *entire* prong was drawn down her throbbing, sucking throat while his legs tightened, his whole body electrified. And then came the thunder; Mount Manning *erupted*. She took him true. His flow a flood; she drained him dry.

"How's your dairy?" she asked victoriously.

"I'm out of business," he quivered in reply.

"My, my, is *that* how you really feel?" she gloated.

"Would you really like to know?" he moaned in ecstasy.

"Why don't you tell me," she murmured.

"I feel like my feet fell off." He closed his eyes, in limpid bliss.

RON REBUCK hesitated entering his inner sanctum. Throughout the day he purposely stayed from the room and found comfort in doing so. A peace of mind he thought no longer possible. But now the hour was near. Tomorrow he would leave for New York to commence his mission for Michael, and his blood coursed with uncertainties. To be observed and guided by a supernatural force in itself was frightening. An unnatural experience his mortal being continually challenged as hazardous to his sanity.

With June asleep and Ron Junior not at home, he stood outside the door to his den, a troubled man, fearful of the presence inside the room – the invisible spiritual force, Michael, the archangel, man's champion, a member of the original souls created by God in his own image . . . or was it?

His brow was beaded with sweat, and an equally wet palm rested on the door's handle. A driven soul finally overpowered a protective body and he entered the blackened room. Hesitant, he then closed the door behind him and stood in the darkness awaiting that voice. That shallow-sounding voice. One that spoke in other worlds. One that conversed with God.

Words developed and came painfully from straining lungs. "Great angel . . . I haven't . . . haven't the will to continue."

A beam of light shot through the window. He fell back against the door, blinded, and now felt the intense pressure in the room. He struggled for breath, as from somewhere in the zone of light, the voice spoke . . . "SPEAK NOT OF BODILY FEARS. SPEAK ONLY OF CAUSE."

Ron Rebuck cowered from the powerful light. Then it dimmed, illumining the wall.

"LOOK UPON THE WALL FOR ALL YOU SHALL SEE MUST BE WASHED FROM THE MINDS OF MAN."

The Bibical feat of Moses, his staffing cane raised toward the sky and the sea parted, appeared on the wall. Ron Rebuck's hands slowly uncovered his eyes.

He was struck with awe. The colors, the dimensions, were not humanly composed. No mortal artist could ever accomplish such magnificence. Bewildered, he took in the new scene of Noah and the ark, the drowning people, then in a rapid transformation the wall became alive with a succession of Bibical events whereupon God's wrath was predominently revealed. The light vanished. The room was once again dark, and fear trickled through his veins. . . . Then the voice.

"AS YOU NOW STAND IN THE DARKNESS, SO IS MAN WHO KNOWS NOT . . . HIS TRUE GOD. YOU MUST BRING FORTH THE SPRING OF LIGHT TO THEIR MINDS. CAST OUT THE IMPLANTED VENOMOUS DEEDS MAN HAS CHARGED UPON THE LORD GOD FROM THE WRITINGS IN A BOOK CALLED HOLY. YEA, REBUCK, TESTIFY TO WHICH THE LORD GOD IS LOVE, NOT HATE. THE CONCEIVER OF BEAUTY, NOT TRAGEDY. THE CREATOR OF ETERNAL LIFE AND NOT THE FATHER OF MORTAL DEATH."

There was silence as Ron Rebuck, gasping for air, mustered all of the courage within, and cut through the tense quiet: "Great Michael . . . to correct the Bible with my book . . . to challenge centuries-old thinking . . . the opposition, great angel . . . "

" FEAR NOT MAN. YOUR EVERY ACT, EVERY WORD SHALL BE KNOWN TO ME. STAY TRUE TO YOUR DIRECTED COURSE. RETREAT FROM NONE. RID YOURSELF OF BODILY FEAR FOR IN THE WAY AHEAD THE SOULS FROM HEAVEN WHO VOWED THEIR ALLEGIENCE TO MAN'S CAUSE SHALL BE AT YOUR SIDE ALWAYS."

"Will . . . will they speak to me? Guide me?"

"CONFIDE ONLY IN THE VOICE YOU NOW

HEAR. YOU SHALL FEEL MY PRESENCE AS YOU DO NOW."

"Great Michael . . . if I should . . . fail?"

"YOU SHALL NOT FAIL." A fierceness came into the voice. "YOUR MORTAL BODY MUST UNITE WITH ITS ETERNAL SOUL IN ALL THAT YOU MUST DO. YOU HAVE BEEN CHOSEN, RON REBUCK . . . YOU CAN NEVER TURN BACK."

Ron Rebuck winced from the potent words. His mind somehow strangely thought of another. . . "What of Lucifer, great Michael?"

There was no immediate reply and Ron Rebuck felt a sudden chill of fear. In a trembling voice he again whispered, "Are you here?"

Seconds felt like minutes before the voice was to answer, "I AM HERE."

"And . . . my question? of Lucifer?"

"HE KNOWS OF YOU."

The voice seemed to weaken – becoming even more distant. A new shiver of fear ran through Ron Rebuck's entire body. The voice went on.

"LUCIFER IS AS YOU HAVE WRITTEN. YOU HAVE UNMASKED THE MANY DISGUISES MAN HAS GIVEN HIM. MORE, YOU HAVE PRESENTED HIS ARGUMENT FAIRLY AND WITHOUT PREJUDICE. THIS HAS TAKEN HIM BY SURPRISE. YET, BEWARE. HIS ENMITY FOR MAN KNOWS NO LIMITS.

On rubbery legs Ron Rebuck walked in the dark. From routine, he knew the location of his desk and made his way toward it. His hand felt for the chair; finding it, he slumped into the seat. He was a body fatigued, drawn, as the room started to vibrate, then shook, accompanied by a roaring sound as if the earth itself had trembled. Then before terror-filled eyes, lights, a multitude of lights, colors he never knew to exist, sparkled about the room. He fell from the chair, to the floor, aghast. The lights danced wildly before his eyes. Lights so pure, so brilliant, of such breathtaking beauty, he could never have imagined them. And then the lights grouped, forming a body. The brilliance of the vision forced him to cover his eyes – blinded by the supernatural event.

The roaring faded, and a sputtering, like the crackling from wood afire, infiltrated his ears. He was unwilling to look up. Unwilling to gaze upon the now burning cross.

"MAN'S FATE RESTS WITH YOU, RON REBUCK. WHERE I FAILED IN THE BODY OF CHRIST, YOU MUST NOT!"

JUNE REBUCK awakened to the smell of smoke. She reached across the queen-sized bed for her husband, but he wasn't there. Her eyes drifted in the darkness, then settled upon the luminous blue digital clock. Three-fifteen A.M. She wouldn't panic. Too many times she'd awakened in the middle of the night to something bizarre. Like finding him sitting in a chair, carrying on a conversation with the wall. But the smell of smoke was real, and the stirring from the far corner of the room revealed his presence.

"Ron," she whispered.

"Go back to sleep, June."

"What's burning?"

"Nothing to worry about."

Unwillingly, she lay back on the bed. "Nothing to worry about" – how many times she'd been told that!

Yet, like always, she'd submit. Offer no resistance, suffer in silence. But with Ron leaving on the noon plane, there were questions needing to be answered. She always felt he'd open up sooner or later. But this was a greatly changed Ron Rebuck, and she knew in her heart that the mystery could go on forever. A mystery that attacked her senses.

Being married to him was like a never-ending movie, packed with adventure and explosive situations. Always exciting, electrifying, very much living by the Roman code, "Live today, for tomorrow we die." Anything he undertook was always met head on with the same brash, dauntless confidence. Not even the monetary ups and downs could disrupt his mode of life.

But the marital movie had now turned spooky, eerie, and all because of a book. Over the years she had taught herself to be flexible to his whims. To pack and track on a moment's notice. And now to find herself unable to share her man's secret and scary obsession. How could he doubt her loyalty? That quiet inner strength he fed on. Her inspiration, like a beacon that never went out during those stormy days and nights. She had given so much – for what? To suddenly become an outsider? She deserved better.

She sat up in the bed, not to be denied. "Talk to me. For God's sake talk to me!" she cried out. But only silence prevailed.

Again, she pleaded. "I'm your wife . . . haven't I the right to know?"

" . . . Yes, June . . . you do."

She expected to hear him leave. Go to that room. Taken aback, she groped for words – and finally asked, "Why are you going away on New Year's Eve?"

"Rufus Manning might leave New York."

"Have you talked with him?"

"No . . . he won't take my calls."

"Then what makes you think he'll leave New York?"

"I said, *he might*!"

Like Ed Dowiat, she too could not understand this important need of his for Rufus Manning. "Ron, what if things don't work out? If things don't pan out the way you expect them to? What if Rufus Manning isn't interested in whatever you want him to do?"

She heard his footsteps and now felt his presence at the foot of the bed. And then his voice . . . "Rufus Manning will see the light. His greed is bottomless."

She now felt his hand moving along her leg. "Tomorrow, June, tomorrow starts the beginning of Michael's mission."

"A mission of misery, Ron?" She quickly sensed his stiffness. "I'm sorry, I didn't mean it that way. It's just . . . just that everything's so against you."

"I'd say the odds are in my favor."

Did she hear right? "Ron you've written a book, perhaps a great book, but do you honestly believe it will take the place of the Bible?"

"The words in my book have been given to me by one who *lived* with God. Not the words of men who lived in bondage, who wrote down twice-told myths to keep discipline among their fellow tribesmen."

He leaned on the bed, and she felt the warmth of his body. "What's happened to me, June, didn't just happen."

"What *has* happened, Ron?"

I told you, I've been watched since I was a child. Now I've been given my mission."

"By whom, Ron?"

He paused. But again, to her surprise, continued, "Spirits . . . angels, *souls*."

"Angels?"

"Souls without bodies . . . without gender. Souls that *know* God."

"Have you seen them?"

"If a mortal body was to see its *own* soul, the body would die. The soul's beauty would create such a depressive state in the body, it would crave death."

"Ron, the Archangel Michael, do you really talk to him?"

"If I do, would you find that unbelievable?"

She sighed and made no answer.

"June, the Bible is full of angels speaking to men. More than that, it tells of men who supposedly talked with God Himself. Do you find that believable?"

Confused, she kept silent.

"June . . . I speak to Michael."

All at once, the burden she had lived under for over a year lifted. His own admission worked through her body like a balm. Still, she could only half-believe in these wonders. "But, but the door handle . . . the wave – they weren't figments of my imagination."

"I freely accepted my mission. Michael's purpose was not forced upon me."

"But what happened on the dock . . . it was cruel."

"There are times when my body rebels and needs to be reminded of its great cause. Times that I have been tested."

The word "martyr" flashed into her mind, then exploded throughout her already worried system. "Ron

. . . hold me. Hold me tight."

She felt his strong arms slowly embrace her. Tears started to spill from her frightened eyes, for June Rebuck knew with sudden, heartbreaking certainty that her man was to die an early death.

MIKE SPENARD carefully turned the key and unlocked the apartment door. The hour was late and Rufus would be asleep, he was sure. Earlier in the evening he overheard him telling Jennifer that his daughter, Leslie, and her fiance would be coming for breakfast at eight sharp, and assumed Rufus intended to get a good night's sleep. Lately, because of Jennifer, something he hadn't been doing. But as he stepped into the living room, much to his surprise Rufus was up. A white terry cloth robe wrapped around his lean body, he sat in a leather recliner, reading.

"Where you been?" Rufus asked, not looking up.

" . . . Something I had to do."

"Moonlighting, Mike?"

Rufus didn't see the pained expression on Mike Spenard's face. "You know better, Mr. M."

"Sit down, Mike," said Rufus, yet to look at him.

Mike Spenard dutifully approached. His eyes caught the words on the title page of the black-bound manuscript. *The Lawyers of Hell*.

"You know, I've managed to get through fifty pages of this, and without a doubt Ron Rebuck's insane."

"What's that thing about, Mr. M?"

"About a whole lot of cow shit." He closed the manuscript, then tossed it at Mike Spenard. "File it under forget," said Rufus, lighting up a cigarette.

Mike Spenard put the manuscript aside. He looked at Rufus who stared at the dwindling flame of the match in the ashtray. "Something wrong, Mr. M.?"

"What *possibly* could be wrong? . . . If not for the fact that the market dropped two points, I haven't made a movie in a year, and an old friend has gone off the deep end, I'd say everything was splendid." He looked up at the diabolic face across from him. A face that had caused many a nightmare. This was the once-feared Mike Spenard whose reputation of "killer-snake" had been whispered throughout New York's boroughs. It was said, once Mike Spenard's fangs took hold, the poison was always fatal.

Rufus remembered when, as a boy living in Harlem before his father packed it in and moved to the Bronx, Mike Spenard was one of them. A thug through heredity. A kid who only knew muscle. In and out of reform school, and then the big time. Sing Sing for six. And back. The full circuit that led directly to Doomsday.

It was during the production of *Dude*, in Harlem, when things were getting hairy, especially for whiteys like himself, that he put Mike Spenard on the payroll. Four bills a week, with bonuses, and a job for life. No more stomping for shylocks, breaking backs, and sleeping with one eye open. At first Spenard balked. Cracking heads was all he knew, and the job as Rufus Manning's personal protector seemed tame. He could make a lot more as a hitter. At least that's what he thought until Rufus spelled it out for him.

A fifty-year-old with no organized mob ties, none of their high-priced lawyers, he was moving on a nowhere street. How long could he produce? Shys were looking over the younger crop – and for less money. Toughs out to make a name for themselves. He couldn't lean on the Family. He didn't have the bloodline. Son of a spic father who took off before he was born, and an Italian mother, he was a mongrel as far as the mob was concerned. He could never be a Don, sharing in the ownership of a Vegas casino or some skag distribution setup.

"The way I see it, " Rufus had said that day when Spenard groped for an answer, "you can get shot in the head, or get free lodging in the slam, or live like a human being, working for me." Mike Spenard chose the latter. To this day, he'd never regretted it.

Rufus searched those eyes. "Ever have any fun, Mike? Got any friends?"

"You're my friend."

"Besides me. How about girl friends? Come to think of it, I can't remember ever seeing you with a girl."

"Women are trouble."

"So is money. You just have to know how to use them both." He rose from the chair. "Mike, have you ever thought about your later years? What if something happens to me, what would you do?"

"Nothing *will* happen to you, Mr. M."

"Shit, we're all going to die."

"Don't talk that way, Mr. M. It's not good."

"Mike, we're almost the same age. Isn't it about time you planned for the future?"

"You're my future."

"Futures have a way of becoming pasts all too

quickly. What I'm saying is, we're getting older. Eight years, I'll be sixty. You'll be sixty-two. Can you imagine people saying, there goes big, bad Mike Spenard, Rufus Manning's bodyguard?"

He'd hoped Mike Spenard would open up. Talk about himself. Let out those deep dark secrets from the pit of his soul. But he stayed tight-lipped. Rufus tried another tack. "Mike, do you fear *anything*?"

" . . . God."

"God? . . . You're kidding. *You* fear God?" Rufus laughed, "What God, Mike?"

"The God in heaven."

"And you really believe that horseshit?"

" . . . Yes."

"You fear God. A guy who's put the hit on – how many? – and you fear God?"

Mike Spenard nodded.

"Tell me, Mike, straight stuff, how many people have you wasted? Better yet, how many did you frighten to death?"

Mike Spenard didn't answer, and gauging by the look on his face, Rufus chose not to pursue it. He'd get back to the God bit. "How can you fear God, then go out and whack someone in the head?"

"Business."

"Business?"

"That was my business. Like soldiers in war."

"Stomping on people for loan sharks isn't like war."

"What's the difference?"

"Mike . . . there's a purpose for war. Genuine purpose."

"What purpose?"

"Specific reasons. A bundle of them." He looked

at him, at Mike Spenard, "Were you in the big war?"

"Germans and Japs?"

"Yeah, the big war. Shit, it made all the papers."

"I was in the can."

"Sorry you missed it," said Rufus, "but do you get the drift of what I'm saying?"

" . . . No."

" *No*. Mike, there were justifiable reasons for that war. Hitler. Pearl Harbor. Dig?"

"What about Vietnam?"

"Vietnam was bullshit. A stupid mistake. A costly one."

"No," Mike Spenard shook his head.

"*What no*?"

"I remember seeing on the news, Cardinal Spellissy telling the soldiers they were fighting for God and country. Billy Hale, too."

Rufus grinned. Stupid Spenard wasn't all that stupid. He groped for a logical reply, then said, "You know, Mike, you just might have made your point."

Rufus rose from the chair. It was the first time they had ever conversed at length. Actually, Rufus had never thought him capable of more than a grunt. How do you carry on a conversation with a rock?

Like a dog waiting for its master, Mike Spenard watched Rufus roam about the sunken living room, engrossed in thought. Suddenly, Manning turned and said, "Okay, you say you fear God; did that ever stop you from muscling anyone? Did it ever stop you from taking someone's head off? Tell me that."

" . . . No."

"Business, right?"

"Right."

"Then tell me this, did you ever feel sorry for

anyone? Allow yourself to get personally involved?"

"Maybe once."

"What happened?"

"Crippled guy . . . club foot . . . yeah," Mike Spenard's eyes brightened as the memory returned.

"What about him?" Rufus took a seat. *This* had to be interesting.

"Played the ponies, into one of my clients for – two? . . . yeah, two G's. Deadbeat, skipped town but I found him. I always found 'em." Mike Spenard halted, as if that was the end of the story.

Rufus grew frustrated, "Go on, Mike, go on."

" . . . Could he talk. Fat little guy with the club foot." Mike Spenard laughed. A laugh that sounded like someone choking on his own tongue.

"Mike, the fucking *story*," said a demanding Rufus.

"He never stopped gabbing. Begged me to give him some time."

"Did you?"

"Yeah."

"Well, what happened for shit sakes?"

"He was a real thief. Swiped a color TV from a department store. Snatched a grand from his landlady. I didn't like that. Hocked some jewelry at a pawn shop."

"Did you get the two grand?"

"Couple hundred short."

"*Then*?"

"I came back to the Bronx."

"What about him? Did you rough him up?"

"A little. I liked him."

"What did you do to him?"

" . . . Gave him another club foot."

JOHN GALLOGLY put down the book he'd been reading. He'd try to get some rest. Since Christmas night, sleep had been hard to come by. There was that feeling of a *presence* in his room. And then, the burning of the manuscript in his hand had worked on his mind most fiendishly.

And, just when he'd convinced himself the "presence" was nothing more than an overactive priestly imagination and the burnt manuscript was caused by a lit cigar in his hand, he got an unsettling call from Monsignor O'Hara in Florida. They were dealing, so it seemed, with some kind of a nut who rigged doorhandles with electric charges, and a wife who swore she saw some kind of giant, magic wave. The good O'Hara spoke well only of Mrs. Rebuck senior, the only perfectly sane member of the family and a pillar of the parish who gave generously of her time and money.

Gallogly sighed and drew the covers up to his chin. If the worthy O'Hara knew what *he* knew he wouldn't dismiss Mr. Rebuck so lightly. Now he concentrated on the idea of sleep. He must be up early to clear his desk before heading for the airport with the Cardinal. Two weeks of fishing and sunshine in Bimini. A time to wash Ron Rebuck out of his mind. He had allowed the whole Rebuck thing to become blown up out of proportion. After all, what they had here was one lone man, armed only with an unpublished manuscript – his words against the Bible and all the mighty legions of Mother Church. Not even a contest, he kept telling himself. Yet, the picture of David challenging the giant Goliath came into his mind unbidden – and stayed there as he lay waiting, hoping, praying for sleep to come.

# 9

"WHAT KIND OF RING did you buy my daughter?" said Rufus to the thin, young man with oval-shaped, horn-rimmed glasses.

"Ring?" He wasn't sure he heard right.

"Ring. *Engagement ring,*" said Rufus, searching for it on the hand of the tall, buxom young woman, who blushed in embarrassment.

"Daddy, we don't believe in that sort of thing," she said defensively.

"What are you talking about, Leslie? Every girl gets an engagement ring." He looked at the young man, "Are you some kinda cheapie? A ring's not good enough for my daughter?"

"Mr. Manning, a ring is only a token . . . a way-back-when ritual. We decided not to make some jeweler richer. Besides, I really don't think it's any of your business. It's your daughter I'm marrying, isn't it?"

Leslie Manning feared the worst, she wanted her father's blessing, and Rufus's eyeballs seemed ready to burst right out of his head. After all, she was the love of his life, the apple of his eye.

For almost a minute, the unshaven Rufus glared fiercely at the young man. Then to the surprise of all, including the eavesdropping Mike Spenard, he broke into a wide grin. "You bet it's none of my business." He put his arm around the young man's shoulders. "Leslie, help Mike with the breakfast." Leading the young man toward the couch, he asked, "Tell me again, sonny, what is it you do?"

"I didn't say . . . but I'm at Columbia Law. Have

a year to go." Looking over his shoulder, young John Milton caught Leslie's departure, remembering her advice. "My father's as gentle as a buffalo."

LESLIE MANNING was a tall girl, almost an inch taller than her five-foot-eight mother. A large-framed young woman, she had an ample-bosomed figure of center-fold quality and a pert, happy face with glowing eyes. Daddy's investment in braces at fourteen had paid off. She was, at times, too independent, an inherited trait from both parents.

She was sociable, but not a socialite. A dungaree dolly who reveled in the "in things." After graduation from college, Leslie had left the comforts of country living, refusing to be cooped up in stale suburbia, choosing instead to catch the fast train of life that moved on the high-speed tracks of the big town. In two years she landed – and lost – six jobs. The secretary bit was a bore. She became frustrated, confused and lonely. The calls to Connecticut became frequent and her weekend stays a regular occurrence. It wasn't until her father's film hit the big money that she emerged from the pit of emptiness. Then the escapist weekends in Connecticut turned into in flings at Southampton. Then Europe for three months in the fall, armed with an American Express card, compliments of Rufus, and two thousand dollars in cash for *whatever*. She didn't want to return to the red, white and blue, but Rufus's insistent telegram brought her back in a hurry.

She picked up with the young smart set, attending all the *best* parties, mixing it up with Jewish American princesses, WASP debutantes, Irish-American writers, Italian-American journalists, sons and daughters of

New Money, feminists, rogues and scholars. It was at such an affair she met John Milton. He was an instigator personified, initiating beefs purely for the love of disputation and always the one who would tell somebody at a cocktail party they were full of shit.

Maybe it was the manner in which he'd push people to their limits, a specialty of Rufus Manning, that attracted her, for John Windham Milton, III, was by no means the perfect physical specimen. This Leslie acknowledged, but his mind was ten feet tall. She was fascinated by his brilliant rhetoric, his incredible fount of knowledge, the way he could dissect an opponent with razor-edged words, taking on all comers regardless of topic, doing a masterful job of Buckley Bull. From a flawless WASP heritage he had all credentials to some day become the president of the United States.

ALL THROUGH BREAKFAST, Rufus surprisingly remained the gentleman – until Leslie placed her coffee cup on the table where the manuscript lay. Her eyes lit on the author's name. "Ron Rebuck's book, Daddy?" She picked it up.

"His farewell to the sane world," he sourly replied.

"Love the title, *The Lawyers of Hell*," she exclaimed.

"Should have been called the *The Loony Lawyers*," said Rufus.

"A book about lawyers?" John asked.

"Would you believe, religion?"

"Big business today."

"How big?" asked Rufus. The word *big* was always close to his heart, especially when money was the noun it described.

"Well, according to James Gollin in his book *Worldly Goods*, the Catholic Church has assets of over thirty-four billion dollars in the U.S. alone. Double that world-wide."

"Who published the book, the Baptists?" Rufus laughed.

"I think Random House . . . yes, it was Random House."

Rufus's gimlet eyes studied him warily. "You seem to know 'who's who' in the spook world. Are you some kind of religious expert or what?"

"Did a research paper on tax exemptions. Religious organizations was a natural. Matter of fact, it was the best paper I've ever done."

"Tax exemptions, nice thing if you can get it," said Rufus.

"You should know something about that, Mr. Manning. Maybe not tax exemptions, per se, but surely you cheated the government out of money you made on *Dude*."

"Sure you're not with the Treasury Department, sonny?"

"Hardly," said John. He looked at Leslie who was too engrossed in the manuscript to hear. "Everyone tries to beat the government, Mr. Manning. Just that religious organizations have the inside track. Above reproach and all that jazz."

"I've always thought religion's a racket. A money scheme."

"The biggest. The all-American rip off."

Rufus lit up a cigarette, anxious to hear more. "How so?"

"I can't give you exact facts, but the government

and religion work hand in hand. Each has the other's interest at heart. Like go to church, sin no more, or burn in hell. Pay your taxes or go to jail."

"Don't make waves? Keep the sheep in line?"

"Exactly, Mr. Manning. The big stick, a hammer over your body and soul. Neither religion nor the government will tolerate a revolutionist."

Rufus grinned. "You're not bad, kid, pretty good head on those shoulders."

"Want to hear more?"

Rufus gleamed, "When it comes to rip-offs, enlighten me."

"Do you know who is organized religion's and government's common enemy?"

Rufus shrugged.

"Communism. Communism, Mr. Manning. You see, if communism was to take over this country, not only would our democratic government fall, churches would be out of business. No more tax exempt properties, and all the goodies that go with it."

Mike Spenard's words echoed in Rufus's mind, along with the picture of Cardinal Spellissy and Billy Hale praising the boys in Vietnam, telling them they were fighting for *God* and *country*.

"It's funny, Mr. Manning, the hypocrisy of it all. Christianity, their churches, the leaders, who bitterly oppose communism when all along Jesus Christ, their founder, had to be the purest communist of all."

Rufus put out the cigarette. A pleased expression shone on his face. "John, my boy, you may now call me Roof."

"Religion's become a big thing today. Quickest way to becoming a millionaire."

"How about billionaire?"

"Might take some time for that, Mr. Manning."

"Roof."

"Sorry, Roof. Yet if someone can come up with the right idea . . . religiously appealing of course . . . who knows? It's certainly possible."

Leslie Manning peered over the manuscript. She caught her father's attention. "Did Ron Rebuck really write this?"

"Who else would be that crazy," said Rufus.

"Daddy, it's good. Heavy, but real good."

"What's it about, Leslie?" John asked.

"About a couple of flaky angels and a bottle of aspirins," Rufus answered for her.

JOHN GALLOGLY passed up a drink in Eastern's V.I.P. lounge at Kennedy Airport. He looked away from the Cardinal, unwilling to meet his eyes. A nondescript group of dissident Catholics had engaged His Eminence in conversation over the abortion issue, a topic that unfailingly triggered the Cardinal's wrath. John Gallogly himself found the subject tiresome. He couldn't help but marvel at the way the Cardinal kept his cool. He was slick, no doubt about it. What a persuader, John Gallolgy thought, watching him effectively manipulate the open-mouthed group into buying his viewpoint. What an actor he could have been. Another Spencer Tracy – or perhaps Sidney Greenstreet?

Eastern's flight 101 was now ready for boarding, and the Cardinal raised his ponderous person from the lounge chair. John Gallogly took hold of the black valise, then waited for the Cardinal to give a quickie New Year's blessing to the group around him.

As they left the lounge, accompanied by an Eastern representative, and walked through the terminal en route to the departure gate, the Cardinal rasped "Idiots! Mother Church will *never* bend on that damn matter. John, if I hear one word about abortion in the next two weeks, I'll crucify the person. So help me!"

The Cardinal managed his usual smile for the various faithful who recognized him. He hoped none would ask for his blessing, or kiss his ring, but as he reached the boarding area, two priests anxiously approached. The Eastern rep selected the first-class seats, smoking area, while John Gallogly's eyes drifted. Among the scattering of people heading for the terminal, one in particular caught his attention. He was a tanned, well-dressed, black-and-gray haired man, carrying a brown overcoat and attaché case. John Gallogly wondered what profession the man was in. Then, suddenly, the man looked at him. *Those eyes*. John Gallogly felt a sudden chill. A faint smile came to man's lips as he passed by, and at that moment, John Gallogly *knew*. The man was . . . *Ron Rebuck*.

# 10

MIKE SPENARD opened the door and looked darkly at the late afternoon caller. He recognized the face of Ron Rebuck and scowled.

"Hello, Mike. Tell Roof I'm here."

"He's not in. Come back another time."

Ron Rebuck's deep-set eyes fixed Spenard like laser beams. "Don't lie to me. Go tell him I'm here."

No one other than Rufus Manning ever talked to Mike Spenard that way. "I *told* you he's not here."

" – And I know that he is."

They dueled with their eyes, until it was Mike Spenard who looked down, then away.

"Who is it?" Rufus barked out from beyond the foyer.

"An old friend," said Rebuck, brushing past the dazed bodyguard and walking into the room.

Rebuck's quick smile was met by Rufus's hard eyes and a dead-fish handshake. "What brings you to New York on New Year's Eve? Don't tell me you've come to get hassled in Times Square."

"What brings me to New York is *you*.

"Me?" Rufus strolled to the leather recliner and sat down heavily. "What in hell can I do for you, Ron?"

"First off, did you read my manuscript?"

"Fifty-some pages. I'm not much on Bibles."

"*The Lawyers of Hell* will be *the* new Bible."

Rufus turned and stared at his uninvited guest. "Are you on some new kind of drug?"

"I'm on the biggest trip of my life," said Rebuck.

"Perhaps a trip to Nowhere?" Manning came off the recliner, distrust on his face. He moved toward the bay window and looked out at the shades of night, soon to descend in final darkness upon the last day of the old year. "You know, Ron, I always thought you were a little weird. But now, you've gone way past that . . . "

He turned from the window. No longer could he cover up his suspicions. "Look, Ron, have you got some kind of conspiracy going to get me into this cockamamie scheme? Did you and Nancy get together to get me interested in your crazy book? C'mon, level. *Bottom line*."

"I need you."

"Need me? Rebuck, you don't need me. What you need is a witch doctor if you think I'd get involved with some . . . some religious bullshit." He walked over to the table and picked up Ron Rebuck's manuscript. "This is about as tempting as torture." He put the manuscript down and sat in a chair opposite him. "Ron, we've been friends a long time, and I don't pretend to understand you. I gave that up long ago. It's true I owe you . . . and I'll pay off. But if you're thinking I can help you, kick it now. Religion's not my bag. All that spiritual shit's too spooky."

"There's nothing spooky about religion once you've read my book."

"Now you sound like one of those TV soul-savers, some Georgie Garbage hollering from a pulpit."

"The Georgie Garbages of this world are what this book is *against*. This book strikes out at the Billy Hales, the Norville Rigginses, the Tex Lombards and all the other peddlers of gospel baloney."

"Fight them? With what? A book! Rebuck, they'll skin you alive. And if *they* don't, the Catholic Church boys will run you over with their Rolls Royces."

Ron Rebuck's eyes flashed. "No one is going to run me over. There is a great force behind me. A force too tremendous for anyone to stop."

From the corner of his eye Rufus saw the shadow of an eavesdropping Mike Spenard. Bolstered by his presence, he'd now come to the point and quit shadow-boxing, "Ron, I can see how you got Nancy and her leechy family lined up on your side, to work on me. But how did you get Leslie mixed up with this crazy book?"

"None of your family is involved."

Rufus Manning wasn't buying. He came directly toward Rebuck, stopping but a few feet short. "Ron, I find that impossible to believe. I find *you* impossible to believe. What I do believe is that you and my family are trying to get me admitted to some nut factory."

"That's not true."

"Your tracks are all over the place, Rebuck. You think I'm a moron? First, you start with the phone calls. Then, next thing I know, Nancy is pushing me to give you a hand, reminding me how you helped me when I was broke. Then comes the crucifix over my bed. Then the TV comes on *by itself* with the fatso Cardinal making with the hand signs. And now, just today, Leslie and her fiance do their number on me about your goddamn manuscript. The only thing that bothers me is how did you do it? Hire a magician?"

"I had nothing to do with any of those incidents."

Rufus threw up his hands in despair. "Okay, Ron. If you didn't do it, then who did?"

"Most likely it was Another."

"Another. Another *who*?"

"The Power behind the book. The great force that's behind me."

Rufus looked deep into Ron Rebuck's eyes. No

doubt about it, the poor fellow was sincere. "Damn . . . you're even madder than I thought."

"Roof, neither of us is crazy."

"Really? We'll I can't seem to shake the feeling *you* are, and you're looking for company."

"I know something you – and the rest of the world – don't know. But everyone will have the message very soon – and your help is essential in getting the message across."

"Rebuck, I don't know what you're leading up to, but it's out of my line. Look, I'm busy, up to my ass in business deals. Believe me, even if I wanted to help you make a fool out of yourself, I don't have the time."

"I happen to know you're between pictures and, other than some minor financial transactions, your time has never been freer."

"Is Hughie Gilman in on this? Did you get to my own lawyer, too?"

Rebuck, frowning, shook his head. "Roof, if you'll hear me out we can spare each other a lot of agony."

A momentarily subdued Rufus Manning sat back in the recliner and listened grimly.

"My book is being published."

"Congratulations. Who's the victim?"

Rebuck ignored the sarcasm. "McGuiness and McGuiness. The book comes out in late January. But that's only the beginning. I have a much bigger weapon in the wings. A television show, Roof, and you're the producer!"

"And what is this show *I'm* producing?"

"The Michael's Messenger Hour."

"And who's Michael? Better yet, who's the Messenger?" Rufus howled.

"If you've read the first fifty pages of my book as you said you did, you'd know that Michael is the great Archangel, man's true champion – and I'm his messenger."

Rufus Manning leapt out of the recliner, laughing. Ron Rebuck remained sitting, quiet, unperturbed. "I can see it now," Rufus shouted, "all three networks tripping over one another for the Michael's Messenger Hour." He stopped laughing and glared at Ron Rebuck. "Have you completely lost your mind?"

"The Michael's Messenger special must be aired Easter Night – prime time!" Ron Rebuck said, undaunted.

Rufus Manning turned away from him, yet Rebuck continued, "Although I'm the Messenger, the show's attraction will be another."

"Who, *God*?"

"Crack Widener."

Rufus Manning shook his head, "Enough's *enough*. I'm getting dizzy listening to you."

"Just listen," said Rebuck.

"To what – insanity? No, you listen to me. You might have a handle on the spook world, but don't tell me *my* business. You've got a better chance of getting the Pope than Crack Widener."

"I disagree."

Rufus faced him, head on. "*You* disagree . . . Ron, Crack Widener is beyond reach. He *is* superstar. TV's beneath him. He's turned down fortunes to do movies." He looked at Ron Rebuck's expressionless face. "Maybe you'll understand it this way: if you put The Beatles, The Rolling Stones, and Elton John all together, Crack Widener's still stars above them. *Rebuck*, he's out of reach. Can't you understand that?"

"Once he reads *The Lawyers of Hell*, Crack Widener, Superstar, will be more than interested."

"Read? Crack Widener doesn't read. He's got people that read to him. People that feed him, clothe him, wipe his ass, people for everything. I even think he's got people who screw for him."

"I happen to know he's frustrated. That he is fed up with organized religion, with the gurus and the various occult groups. His mind's into religion. He's primed for it, Roof, and we'll get him."

Rufus walked away, toward the window, muttering, "Aw, what's the use of my even trying to reason with you. You've already gone off the deep end."

Much to Rufus's surprise, Ron Rebuck rose from the sofa. All along Rufus had figured he would eventually have to ask him to leave. "Open your line to me, Roof; I'll be in touch."

Rufus shook his head, "Ron . . . I'm not your man for this, I'm not on your case. Can you dig what I'm saying?"

Ron Rebuck smiled. "You will be, Roof. You will be."

Mike Spenard lumbered out from hiding. He'd see Ron Rebuck to the door – the sooner the better.

Spenard held the door open; Ron Rebuck turned back briefly. "Happy New Year, Roof. To us both."

A sense of guilt swept over Rufus Manning. Ron Rebuck was a friend. An old friend. A man who'd never turned his back on Rufus in his time of need. "Are you up from Florida alone?" Rufus asked.

"Yes."

"No plans for tonight?"

"Not really."

Rufus deliberated, then said, "Hughie Gilman's

having a New Year's Eve bash. . . . Want to go?"

"It would be nice."

"Where're you staying in New York?"

"At the Elysee."

"I'll call you around eight. Give you Hughie's address on Sutton Place. Should be a good party; lots of big shots and celebrities. Maybe even some book people. Look, I'd invite you to dinner, but I've made plans."

A ghostly smile crossed Ron Rebuck's face, as if he knew Rufus's plans.

"I'll call you." said Rufus, then disappeared from the living room, leaving Ron Rebuck's departure to the care of Mike Spenard.

With Rufus out of earshot, Mike Spenard hissed, "Mr. M. don't like being spooked. You make him nervous. Stay away."

Ron Rebuck eyed the feared enforcer, and said evenly "I'm not your enemy, Mike. My concern for Roof is even greater than yours." He headed for the elevator, feeling the hit man's eyes drilling into his back.

MINUTES AFTER Ron Rebuck's departure, Jennifer Jewell breezed past Mike Spenard, entering the apartment. She kissed Rufus's cheek, murmuring, "Did a good-looking man just leave the apartment?"

"Yeah . . . why?"

"Who is he?"

"His name *was* Ron Rebuck, but I have a feeling he'll change it to Moses any day now. Why do you ask?"

"He seemed to know me."

"Know *you*?"

"We passed each other in the lobby and he said, 'Hi, Jennifer.'"

" . . . He *couldn't* know about you and me," said a puzzled Rufus. "*Mike*!" he shouted. "Did you tell Ron Rebuck anything about Jennifer?"

"I tole him nothin'."

"This is getting to be fucking ridiculous," Rufus barked.

"Roof . . . do you have to use that vulgar word?" Jennifer protested.

"That man's bad for you, Mr. M. He's trouble," growled Mike Spenard.

Rufus glared at him. "Don't let anyone in this apartment without my knowing, *ever again*."

Mike Spenard cowered under Rufus's disapproving look. His entire life was dedicated to Rufus, and failing him was a cardinal sin. That Rebuck had slipped by him like a ghost troubled him keenly. He sat, brooding, in a corner, as Jennifer settled on the couch with a swish of silken legs. Spotting the manuscript on the table next to her, she picked it up, idly studying the cover. "This Ron Rebuck's an author?"

"He's a fool," said Rufus. "A damn fool." He lit a cigarette with a shaky hand, as Jennifer started to read. "Who the hell is *he* to try and get me involved . . . Television show! *Religious* television show. Crack Widener! He's out of his tree!"

Rufus settled on the couch next to Jennifer, pondering Ron Rebuck's rude invasion of his private world. He cursed himself for asking Rebuck to Hughie Gilman's party. Jennifer turned a page, then another page, and another.

"Are you going to read that dumb thing in front of me?"

She looked up. Unwillingly, she closed the manuscript. "This is most interesting. May I borrow it? I'll finish it tonight."

"Not tonight. We're going to Hughie's bash."

"Roof . . . I'm not going."

"You're not *what*?"

"I'm not going. I've got reasons."

"Jennifer, it's a little late for games. What reasons?"

"Aly's gestapo for one. Marty Pico and his goons. I can't stand them following us wherever we go. I feel like I'm in a fishbowl. Besides, Aly is sure to call tonight."

"So what. I thought you were finished with Big Abdul. All that stuff about being a kept woman. Wanting your independence, wanting to be your own woman – was that nothing but jive?"

"You don't understand. You couldn't understand. Aly's been good to me."

"He paid for what he got."

Her body tensed. Holding the manuscript, she rose. She caught Rufus's probing eyes and laughed. A nervous laugh. "This . . . this whole thing is preposterous. You, a married man cheating on his wife, telling me, a kept woman, what I should and shouldn't do." Pressing the manuscript to her bosom she avoided his eyes. "Roof, before we start making any foolish New Year's promises, it's time we put things in the right perspective. We're nothing more than passing strangers who got together. Electricity, fireworks, but now comes the dawn."

"You'd make a helluvan actress."

She strolled to his side. She looked down at him. At that lecherous, devious grin. "Roof, you've got your own race to run and I simply can't run on that track." She moved slowly toward the windows. "You're just about the most exciting man I've ever met, but I belong to Aly Sharif and haven't the guts to break away, so let's end it before it ends us."

Rufus got up from the couch. "Jennifer, I asked you to a New Year's party and you're making it sound like till death do us part."

"Roof, I'm the property of a sheik. Aly Sharif is not a man to fool with. And besides, you're already at war with your wife, why should you ask for more trouble? There's no future for us."

"Jennifer, since we met it's been a downhill, funky ride. Don't start botching it up by making like some fortune teller. Let's the two of us bring in the New Year on a happy note, no getting sucked up by sadness."

Her chin resting on the manuscript, she gazed out the window; he'd reached her somehow where she lived. She turned and faced him. The ice in those green eyes thawed and Rufus knew she'd surrendered. "Okay, Roof, I think we'll both regret it, but I'll go to the party. But no dinner. I can't take those watchdogs any longer."

"Forget the dogs. I'll muzzle them." He looked at his watch; six-thirty P.M. "I've got some things to do, we'll eat at eight, eight-thirty."

"Roof . . . please, no dinner. Maybe your man Mike could bring us some hamburgers from McDonald's."

"Jennifer, that's what this damn country's become – one big McDonalds hamburger joint. We're going to be *original* and have *dinner*."

He half pushed her out of the apartment before she could offer any protest.

With the door closed behind Jennifer, he had a

fleeting impulse to go back and phone Nancy. She hadn't called since their spat, and that bothered him a little. Hell, she'd call soon; he pushed the idea aside and turned to Mike Spenard, who stood in the doorway of the apartment, awaiting his orders.

"Mike," said Rufus, "I've been taking it easy for the past couple of months, gotten a little lazy. But from tonight on, it's war and win. Do you read me?"

"I read you, Mr. M." Mike's eyes lit up; this was the old Rufus Manning, the hard-nosed action man.

"You keep the losers out of my way and you got yourself one hell of a pension plan . . . Marty Pico, and the rest of the sheik's hounds, I don't want to see their faces *any more*."

Mike Spenard smiled. It was a peculiar, lopsided sort of smile that led Rufus to believe the muscle man had misunderstood.

"No rough stuff, Mike. Just scare 'em. Hell, you're an expert at scaring people."

"What about this Rebuck, Mr. M.?"

"Rebuck? Hell, man, how do you scare a spook? Just leave Ron Rebuck to me. He might be off his track, but he's a friend . . . I'll straighten out Ron Rebuck myself."

# 11

HIS EYES SCANNED the high-ceilinged drawing room of Hughie Gilman's penthouse. He was aware of eyes studying him – questioning eyes – and among them, the lusty glances of certain women. The rugged, tanned face, the salt-and-pepper hair, the powerful body rippling under the dark wool suit and white turtleneck with the strange medallion hanging about his neck on a silver chain – Ron Rebuck was a dominant Presence in a room full of presences.

He'd recognized many a famous and familiar face. Including a famed ex-Congresswoman, noted for her powerful lungs and picturesque hats; a legendary jet-set couple in a foursome with their homosexual lovers; a Broadway actress without whose bouncing breasts no celebrity party was complete; a Hollywood star-stud who left his best performances in the bedroom, swarmed over by three lovelies right out of the *Playboy* centerfold. And many, many others.

Beyond them he sighted the host, Hughie Gilman, a stocky, well-kept man in his early fifties with steel-gray hair matching his aviator glasses and a pencil-thin mustache beneath his noble Roman nose. Here was a distinguished man, a successful man, but more than that, a man whose affable manner and warm smile told you that he truly cared about people.

A young woman at least six feet tall held onto his arm as if she'd never let go. Rumor had it that this tree of femininity would soon become number five on Hughie's marital record. If Hughie Gilman had one weakness, it was for long-legged girls. Each of his ex-wives was of Amazon size, with alimony to match.

Ron Rebuck had briefly met Hughie Gilman during the production of Rufus's film *Dude*. But there'd never been an opportunity to get to know the man – Rufus had seen to that. Hughie was power, and Rufus made sure that nobody got too close to the stockpile. If anyone had any influence over the headstrong, unruly Rufus, it was Hughie Gilman. Rufus depended on him greatly. And, despite the fact that Hughie had no need whatever to depend on Rufus, there was a close personal tie between the feisty producer and the genial lawyer.

A trio livened the room's mood with the latest reggae number, and with the music, the hum of voices grew louder. Minding his own business, Ron Rebuck's eyes accidentally collided with those of a man who'd been standing at the hors d'oeuvre table studying him for several minutes. The fellow seemed to have some problem with his neck, for his head was permanently tilted to the left. Now he approached Rebuck, gauging him with nervous eyes. He stuck out a hand as though it was a considerable physical effort.

"Jack Pintoff," he said.

Ron Rebuck shook the limp, fleshy hand. "Ron Rebuck."

Pintoff squinted. "Don't place the name. You a friend of Hughie's?"

"Friend of a friend."

"Who's the friend?"

"Rufus Manning."

"Rufus Manning! Didn't know he had a friend."

Ron Rebuck cracked a smile.

"You got anything left?"

"Anything left?"

"Money. Your wife, kids . . . that guy don't leave much."

Ron Rebuck sipped his drink and said nothing. The man was clearly not a Rufus Manning fan.

"I'm in advertising. Pintoff, Wales and Wyler. Wyler's dead. What's your line?"

Ron Rebuck hesitated. He always did when asked that particular question. "I'm on a mission."

The man, Jack Pintoff, tilted his head even more. Fisheyed, he looked up and said, "To where? Mars? Mercury?"

A freeze appeared in Rebuck's eyes, forcing Pintoff to look away, to think of something else to say. Small talk, whatever. He wouldn't leave. "Ever attend a party for divorcees before?"

"Didn't know this was for divorced people."

"Hughie's clients, mostly. You divorced?"

"No."

"Ever been?"

"No."

Pintoff looked at him, oddly. "For a guy with your looks, what kind of a woman could keep you at home?"

"Most likely, she's got what it takes."

"She here with you?"

"Florida, where I live."

"Miami?"

"Clearwater."

He thought for a moment. "That's on Florida's west coast, land of the living dead, isn't it?"

"I've been resurrected."

Jack Pintoff stayed on the face before him until those piercing eyes again forced him to look away. As if the eyes could see through the bone of his skull and read his mind. Jack Pintoff prided himself on being able to classify strangers with an uncanny accuracy. Was it possible that he'd just met a rarity? Had he come upon that endangered species – a man unique, doomed for martyrdom in a corrupt world? Long ago, he'd given up all hope of meeting such a mortal.

"Ron – it is Ron?" A nod confirmed it. "Is there some reason why you wish to remain anonymous?"

"To the contrary."

"Then why make a mystery out of what it is tha you really do? I mean, this mission thing. It won't go down, not with *these* people."

Rebuck was silent. He'd like nothing better than to reveal to this pack of sophisticates just what kind o mission he was engaged in. There was no better setting for a trial run. But to do so, he must deviate from his directed course. Something the angel warned him not to do.

Seeing him gazing absently into nowhere, Jack Pintoff snapped his fingers in front of the far-off eyes "Have you landed?"

"I'm sorry." Rebuck forced an apologetic smile "You were saying?"

"What do you do, Ron Rebuck? What is your pro fession?"

"Does it matter?"

Jack Pintoff examined the eyes, the face, the body in front of him. "You've got the face of an actor, the build of a ballplayer – "

"I've been both."

"Ron Rebuck, I now know what you do." He inched closer and half-whispered, "You're a hitman."

Rebuck's face beamed. "How right you are." A definite put-on, no doubt about it, thought Jack Pintoff, but he'd play along for a while. "Who's the target?"

Ron Rebuck's face grew serious. "The world – the whole world, Mr. Pintoff."

RUFUS MANNING sulked, and said little to Jennifer Jewell in the back seat of the cab. Her insistence on reading more of Ron Rebuck's manuscript had found him without dinner.

The yellow cab was nearing Sutton Place. He looked at Jennifer, then at his watch, 10:45. "We're not late . . . we're *missing*."

She blinked her eyes, and Rufus cursed, "Damn, Rebuck. The sunnuva bitch had to show up on New Year's Eve."

She looked at him, displeased. "The man could very well be the son of greatness."

He glared at her . . . "Not you, too!"

The cab's tires brushed up against the curb and Rufus was the first to depart. Fron the corner of his eye he noticed a gray Ford stopping some fifty feet beyond. He strained to see the car's occupants but the windows were clouded up with steam. He continued staring at the car, its engine idling. "The goons again, right?"

"Roof, let's go," said a pleading Jennifer.

"I told Spenard I didn't want to see those creeps following us. He must be getting old." He headed toward the car — dead-set on a collision course.

"Roof, you fool, come back," Jennifer called after him. A warning in vain. Rufus looked into the car's window, then banged on the glass. Again he rapped on the window and it slowly came down. A large black face leered up at him.

"Black Frankenstein, I thought I got rid of you."

"Stay cool, turkey," the giant Richard warned in that high-pitched voice.

From the driver's side a head popped into Rufus's view. He identified him as the man with the oddball eyes who had pulled a gun on him Christmas night. "Whacko, too," said Rufus. The man's body began to shake, his face, sick with hate, until the giant's elbow dug into his ribs, forcing him back into his seat. He then turned his attention on Rufus.

"Marty Pico pays me to watch, dig? Get traveling, turkey, before I whip up a hurricane on yah."

He leaned closer to the open window. He stared into the giant's face. "Marty Pico's a putz . . . and you got a pussy's voice . . . and ten to one you've got a small cock with marbles for balls."

The door thrust open, forcing Rufus backward. The number 911 for police emergency came quickly to Jennifer's mind, as she watched Richard climb out of the car, unfolding as if there was no end to him.

An early model limousine suddenly braked loudly next to the gray Ford.

Confused, the big guy scrambled back into the car, as a beam of a smile lit on Rufus's lips. Mike Spenard's timing could not have been better. He moved triumphantly toward the Ford, looked in, and said, "I get the feeling you dummies are in for the nightmare of your lives."

WALTER HARDY rolled his eyes, clicked his tongue and said, "My dear man, the written words in the Bible are meant for symbolic purpose, nothing more."

"What about fear purposes?" An intense Ron Rebuck asked.

Walter Hardy had had no idea that a simple introduction would lead to an open debate. Even so, *this* particular field of battle was certainly no place for it. Not at a party . . . a New Year's party. He looked over his shoulder and sadly realized the discussion had attracted a gathering. He turned to the man responsible, Jack Pintoff, and shot him a sour look, one familiar to millions of TV viewers, then gazed into the burning eyes before him. "Mr. Errr . . ."

"Rebuck. Ron Rebuck," said Jack Pintoff, whose smile broadened. From the freeze in Hardy's eyes, Jack Pintoff had succeeded in making still another shit-list.

". . . Mr. Rebuck, fear is a perfectly normal part of man's chemistry. We are not robots, incapable of feelings. What kind of a world would it be if what you term fear were somehow to vanish? I, for one, would be horrified to even think of returning to a Stone Age society where people did whatever nasty thing came to mind. The Bible, Mr. Rebuck, serves as a vital deterrent against this happening."

Ron Rebuck studied the famous face: the flippy eyes, the mouthful of teeth, the jokester's air. He looked exactly as he did on his celebrated television show, "Straight On."

"Are you saying that in order for a society to function properly, the fear of God is essential?"

"The word fear has many usages, Mr. Rebuck. It expresses one's doubts, anxieties, and much, much more."

"And you, Mr. Hardy. Are you a God-fearing man?"

"That, my dear fellow, is too vague a question. Perhaps what you are referring to is not God per se but the hereafter. The unknown. God's rightful judgment upon us all."

"Rightful? Heaven or hell, Mr. Hardy?"

A Catholic, Walter Hardy weighed answering. Christians, the intellectual ones like himself, would rather avoid the subject of an eternal hell. And with a predominantly Jewish party crowd, the less said about hell the better. "Without reading your book, Mr. Rebuck, I find myself at a loss as to exactly what point you are trying to make. Perhaps when, or, I should say, *if* your book is published, I'll have the opportunity to find out just where you're coming from."

"What about a guest appearance on your show, Walter?" said a wheeling Jack Pintoff.

A sudden toughness came into Hardy's voice. "If Mr. Rebuck's book isn't loaded with blanks and has the makings of an interesting shoot-out . . . I would, of course, consider such a possibility. . . "

Ron Rebuck cut through Hardy's smugness, "No one need solicit my appearance on Mr. Hardy's show. In time he will be compelled to face me."

More amused than angered, Walter Hardy flashed his whites and replied, "'Straight On' is a very successful show and its success largely stems from the selection of a broad spectrum of guests who have something *terribly* important to say."

"Like those numerous religious leaders who have appeared on your show?"

Walter Hardy could not readily link the connection. "Mr. Rebuck, anyone, any guest who appears on *my* show could not be a guest if their credibility was in question. It's true, there have been instances when some of my guests felt a credibility gap after *appearing* on my show."

There were some chuckles from the crowd but Ron Rebuck pursued his point. "How unfortunate that such a penetrating wit as yours, Mr. Hardy, had to be supressed in deference to Cardinal Spellissy. And Billy Hale . . . how did you control the urge to pick them apart?"

Walter Hardy's face tightened. His keen mind reviewed the past appearance of the prominent religious men Ron Rebuck had mentioned. "I fail to recall ever being suppressed. And if my memory is correct, and it usually is, the nature of the Cardinal's appearance on my show dealt exclusively with the abortion issue. Certainly that was hardly a subject for my wit."

"Do you also recall the dates that particular show aired?"

A veteran of a thousand encounters in the debating arena, Walter Hardy smelled a leading question better than any. "Are you at all familiar with the broadcasting industry, Mr. Rebuck?"

Ron Rebuck smiled. Hardy was bothered or he wouldn't be probing. "Quite familiar," he replied.

"Taping? Prints? Marketing, *syndication*?"

"I've had experience in each."

"A jack of all trades," Hardy laughed, then the famous face turned suddenly grim. "And a master of what, Mr. Rebuck?"

A force came into Ron Rebuck's eyes. "The master of my mission . . . Mister Hardy."

RUFUS MANNING looked about the crowded room and sighted Hughie Gilman. He brushed ruthlessly past knots of people in close conversation with an embarrassed Jennifer Jewell trailing behind.

"Where in hell have you been?" Hughie sharply inquired.

"Blame her," he jerked his head toward Jennifer.

Hughie's eyes glowed at the vision. An excitement rippled through his body. Swiftly he felt a squeeze on his arm – his latest statuesque beauty was feeling threatened by Jennifer's presence.

"Hughie, say hello to Jennifer," said Rufus, his eyes sweeping the room in search of Ron Rebuck.

Yanking his arm free of the clinging tower, Hughie tenderly kissed Jennifer's hand.

"Where's Rebuck?" Rufus asked, but Hughie was too engrossed with Jennifer's "jewels" to hear.

"Excuse me for a moment, Mr. Gilman," said Jennifer slipping her hand from his hold, and to the surprise of all, walking rapidly away.

"Where *you* going?" Rufus called after her. All he got for a reply was a smile as she disappeared into a horde of people.

Hughie Gilman needed answers. He handed his half-empty glass to his long-legged date. "Honey, freshen it up for me." She gave him a pouting look, and not until Jennifer was safely out of sight, did she oblige.

"*Who* is Jennifer?" an anxious Hughie inquired.

"What?"

"Jennifer, that luscious thing, who is she?"

"The property of a sheik. I stole her for a while."

"My compliments. Your stealing has improved."

"Hughie – is that Ron Rebuck over there? Talking with Walter Hardy?"

"For a gate crasher, your friend has first-class taste."

"I forgot to tell you he was coming."

"No surprise. I expected as much."

"Hughie, if Rebuck's jawing about his book to that slick crowd they'll laugh his ears off."

"Ron Rebuck's an author?"

"Wrote one of those religious jobs. Wants me to get Crack Widener for some crazy television special. He's outta his tree."

"Roofala, don't get down on religious material. It's become the *in* thing. Studio financing is most receptive to the supernatural these days. Is there a movie in it?"

"I only read fifty pages and got a hernia of the mind."

"You've become too choosy. Too selective. Get cracking on something. Anything. It's been a year since *Dude*."

"Hughie, every script I read stinks. Nothing's original."

"As your attorney and advisor, I say make a picture. Do it before the studio boys forget your name."

"Make a picture," Rufus moaned. "*It ain't easy*."

"Then write a book. Do something, bubbala."

"About what, religion?"

"Why not? But, you'd better hurry. From what I hear, the field's getting crowded."

"Listen, I better get Rebuck away from that shark before there's nothing left but bones. Come with me!"

"Can't. I'm waiting for her highness to arrive."

"Yeah, who's that?"

"Myrna Reardon, who else?"

Rufus frowned. "Is that douche bag coming?"

"Be nice."

"Why are you still kissing her ass?"

"All in the line of service to my clients."

"Not this client."

"Roofala, I hope this doesn't come as any big surprise to you, but I do have other clients. *Working* clients."

Laughter rang out from the area of the room where Ron Rebuck was located, and the subject of Myrna Reardon, gossip queen, was temporarily dropped.

"Shit, too late," said Rufus.

"From what Jack Pintoff tells me, your friend Ron Rebuck handles himself pretty well in the trenches."

"Are you daffy, Hughie? This is New York, not cockamamie Clearwater, Florida. Walter Hardy will eat Rebuck alive. And what does that crooked-neck schmuck Jack Pintoff know anyway?"

"Know how he got that bad neck?"

"Who cares?"

"Messing with Myrna Reardon, that's how."

"Hughie, yakking about a douche bag and a degenerate isn't helping Rebuck. I'll catch you later."

"Such concern. Ron Rebuck must really be a friend."

"He's a mixed-up screwball who thinks he's Moses."

"Maybe he'll change the sixth commandment. And, don't forget what I said about Myrna . . ."

Rufus flagged a finger in parting and moved toward the closely knit circle of people around Hardy and Rebuck. Looking for an opening he was surprised by all the attention given Ron Rebuck. Why would so many be interested in what he had to say? And at a party? A New Year's party? He tapped a man's shoulder causing him to turn, then wedged through the opening, inching has way to the side of a somber Jennifer Jewell. "This has gotta be like Jimmy Conners against Bobby Riggs," he whispered.

"It's thirty-love, *Ron Rebuck*," said Jennifer, her eyes fixed on the man.

Rufus gave her a puzzled look. Here was a sheik's supershack sounding like the farmer's daughter. He shrugged and took in the combatants: Ron Rebuck appeared calm, confident. Rufus was sure he was bluffing. But Walter Hardy – why, why he was biting down on his lip! And his face – was that tension he detected? Impossible. America's sharpest wit, worried? He was irritated, nothing more. And why not, a man of his prominence, a many times proven gladiator in the debating arena to be matched up against an unknown? But how the hell had he allowed himself to get trapped into it? Rufus's eye found the answer on Jack Pintoff's face. That gloating look – sickening. Rufus despised the man.

GONE SUDDENLY was the perplexed expression on Walter Hardy's face. That familiar, confident air reappeared. "Mr. Rebuck, what have you actually proven? Some dirty-tricks smear against the president elect who favored a more liberal abortion policy? Hardly. That some subversive religious powers were against him?"

"What I believe goes further. There is more at stake for those *religious powers* than the election of a president. They cannot afford to lose the abortion issue. Not in America, the last frontier of a Bible-oriented society."

"And who might *they* be, Mr. Rebuck?"

"The same *they* who used you as a tool to further their fight against abortion, Mr. Hardy. The same *they* who underwrote major advertising costs for *that* particular show. Was the papal blessing worth the covert action you lent your good name to, Mr. Hardy?"

Walter Hardy's face tightened. His rolly eyes danced with ire. It was unlike Walter Hardy. Normally, he could keep his cool under the direst circumstances. But now *he* was on the firing line. He scanned the faces of curious and interested spectators. There was no easy way out. He couldn't just up and leave. Not tactfully, without losing face. By tomorrow word would spread through the celebrity circle, blown out of proportion, that a mystery challenger had whipped him in a dogfight. His frustration mounted. There was no dossier available to him on this man. No research department to dig up facts, dark secrets, hidden skeletons. This was not "Straight On" where his TV guests sat on the hot-seat with Hardy knowing all there was to know about them. He'd now have to dig in, stand toe-to-toe, and beat him down with wit and diversion. "Mr. Rebuck, you have made it clear, with bias overtones I might add, that the subject, *they*, is none other than the Catholic Church."

"Mr. Hardy, introducing bigotry into this discussion only camouflages the facts."

"A 'fact' must be provable truth, otherwise it becomes an opinion. It's apparent, Mr. Rebuck, that you are highly opinionated." Walter Hardy flashed those great whites and added, "Tell me, Mr. Rebuck, was that Catholic experience you obviously had in your life so grievous as to leave wounds unhealed?"

Ron Rebuck eyed him with uncertainty. Walter Hardy was clever all right. A master at the switch. But he wouldn't take the bait. Instead, his smile broadened. "Mr. Hardy, I've seen your show, many times, and what you are attempting is nothing more than a familiar Walter Hardy tactic of putting your opponent on the defensive. That *you* whistled the abortion tune played by a Pied Piper Pope and *willingly* allowed a prince of the Church, Cardinal Spellissy, to cast a shadow over a man running for the presidency, is the point in question. Once again, religious interests have been served. And you, Mr. Hardy, were their stooge."

Not bad, said Rufus to himself. An approving Jennifer Jewell seconded with a smile.

Walter Hardy bobbed his head and spotted a rooter in the crowd. He winked at him, reassuringly, then rolled his eyes back on the intense face before him. "Obviously, you are not well versed in the Constitution. It so happens, Mr. Rebuck, we do live in a free society. Granted, at times I question just how free it truly is; nevertheless, I'm certain there is no law to the contrary whereupon religious leaders, for that matter, any cleric, have been deprived of the right to speak out pro or con on *any* issue. They, like any citizen of this country, enjoy the same privilege afforded them by the Bill of Rights."

"There is also another law, Mr. Hardy . . . one you so cleverly avoided to mention. It deals with the separation of Church and State. Familiar with it?"

HUGHIE GILMAN shook the attractive woman's hand and gave her handsome escort, some twenty-five years her junior, a tolerant smile.

Myrna Reardon was half smashed. Little wonder, she'd been on the sauce most of the day. Making the rounds of various *in* parties, she'd saved Hughie's shindig for last. She liked Hughie. Respected him. And never played up in print his fetish for Amazons. He was one of the few men she'd allow herself to trust. Even so, Hughie knew better than to greet her with a kiss – foregoing the common practice used by people in the entertainment world, where everyone kissed everyone. Myrna Reardon was not that sort. She'd been something of a woman's libber since way back when the term was not at all fashionable. Many took her early stand on women's equality to be rooted in a hate for men. Rumor spread she was a lesbian. The two husbands she tried out and discarded were jellyfish. She denied it all and tracked down those who initiated such rumors, making them pay dearly. Jack Pintoff was one. About to close a large advertising account with a leading food company, he somehow, at the last moment, lost the fat account to a lesser qualified agency. Abby Alden, her closest rival, a distant second at that, swore she'd been framed on a dope bust and consequently had her local weekly TV show canceled.

Not until recently did Myrna finally admit a certain dislike for men. She willingly revealed how through the years she thought herself an avenger for all women who suffered from male chauvinism.

Now in the afternoon of her career, she could look back upon her immense success. The daughter of a Brooklyn dock walloper, she hit Hollywood, became a starlet, but was soon fed up with casting couches and the gross stomachs of older men pressing against her. One such day, she drove her foot into an aging producer's maritals, and thus ended a short-lived acting career. A series of odd jobs followed; she was bent on not returning to Brooklyn, a failure. Good with words and bubbling with enthusiasm, she landed a job at a Los Angeles paper as a field reporter. A personal interview with a female star (who wished to be left alone), propelled her into bigger things, but she soon grew restless with the Hollywood beat. Waiting for Louella and Hedda to be a memory, she started her own fan magazine and worked hard on its success. It was during these years that she started to develop an investigative force. Where others relied on tipsters, she hired private eyes who furnished her with a reservoir of material that usually scooped the competition. A leading newspaper chain took notice and for twenty years now, her syndicated column "Myrna's Morning" was read daily by millions of readers.

Acclaimed Queen of Gossip, she had an open invitation to the most important events. Few at Hughie's party were not in her book.

"Hughie, what is this, a wake? Why in hell aren't those musicians playing? I've seen more action in a library." She turned to Hughie's tall story. "Hello, dearie, what basketball team do you play for?" Not waiting for an answer, she looked toward where a large crowd had formed. "What the shit's going on over there?"

"Seems Walter Hardy got his hands full."

"Hi, I'm Bill Coleman," Myrna's escort struck out his hand for Hughie to shake.

"Right now he's Just Plain Bill, but there's a chance he may land a running part in a new series," said Myrna, acidly.

"With you in his corner, how can he lose?"

"By not keeping his grubby eyes on me." A sudden meanness came into her Irish blues. "Get me a drink . . . now!" The young man flushed with embarrassment but held his ground.

"Taking another of your stands, are you?" said Myrna. The young man eyed Hughie shamefacedly, backed down and went on his errand.

"Awful hard on the boy, aren't you?"

"I'm getting soft. In the old days, I would have made him crawl on his goddamn hands and knees."

"Haven't you heard – the slaves have been freed?"

Myrna laughed, "Since when have *you* considered

a head job slavery?"

She looked up at Hughie's date, pointedly.

"Be nice, Myrna."

She gave Hughie a triumphant smile then glanced at her wristwatch. It was a diamond studded job; Hughie wondered who in the blue book gave it to her. "It's quarter till midnight, and I'll be goddamned if I'm going to bring in the New Year with this mousy crowd. Let'd go shake the bastards up."

"What about your drink? Just Plain Bill?"

"He'll sniff me out. He's good at sniffing things."

RUFUS MANNING was puzzled by Walter Hardy's permitting Ron Rebuck to make his points. Walter Hardy was calm. Too calm. In his long and illustrious career he had always dominated the speaker's spotlight. He was chief hog and gave the impression of only tolerating his opponents for the sake of debate. Rufus nudged Jennifer and whispered, "Hardy's a fox. He's letting Rebuck spiel on until he drowns in his own words."

Irritated by his unfavorable innuendos aimed at a man she was fast becoming obsessed with, she moved away, rubbing up next to a prominent stage actor who politely smiled, and gave her room. Directly across, Jack Pintoff felt someone breathing on him. He caught a scent of expensive perfume and looked over his shoulder. Myrna Reardon burned him with her eyes.

"It is *not* opinion, but fact, Mr. Hardy, that various churches membering organized religion are well represented in all levels of government. The influx of clergy holding down elected and nonelected political offices has daringly surfaced in recent years. Tell me, Mr. Hardy, will such God-fearing men and women performing dual roles vote in accord with a changing society in a bill to legalize marijuana, or will they be directed by their first priority, their ordained religious bonds?"

Hardy's lips were sealed. Not even the tips of his horse teeth were showing. And the crowd was beginning to feel an upset in the making. Even diehard Hardy fans grew concerned as Ron Rebuck continued on. "Historians, influential critics with the power of media at their disposal, like you, Mr. Hardy, are quick to remind us of this country's past mistakes, yet perennially neglect to include the sufferings caused by religious intervention. Why, Mr. Hardy? Are you and your colleagues fearful to tread on their sacred shoes? Then again, taking on those powerful religious lobbyists in Washington could find the F.C.C. breathing down your throat."

Anger was building in Hardy's eyes. Twice he'd been attacked, his character chastised. Among the multitude of people he'd dueled in debates, only a few managed to cut through that thick mick skin and wound him as Rebuck had done. His lips parted and for a second the crowd readied for an all-out Hardy assault. Instead, to the amazement of all, Hardy's lips once again locked, and Ron Rebuck drove it in deeper.

"Who can deny the religious influence that brought about Prohibition? And who, truthfully, was responsible for censorship laws? The Legion of Decency? I could go on and on – from the circumcision of a male's penis to the fight over abortion. *All* . . . motivated by religious concern." He paused, allowing the crowd and perhaps Hardy to digest what he'd said.

"Is it any wonder why young people are restless? With all the thou-shalt-nots hurled against them, how can they possibly hope to be understood by a society that allows itself to be oppressed by religious fanaticism? Aren't we already faced each day with an abundance of hypocrisy without being further burdened with religious persecution?"

Walter Hardy ended his silence and laughed. "I'm terribly sorry, but absurdity has a way of tickling my funny bone." His face hardened. "Come now, Mr. Rebuck, you speak of religious persecution as of the days of Salem and Cotton Mather are still with us."

"Only the means have changed, the persecution still goes on."

". . . *Speaking* of goddamned persecution," Myrna roared, pushing Jack Pintoff out of her way and stepping into the circle, "just who the hell are you to come off laying all that rhetoric on people at a New Year's Eve party?" She looked at a smiling Walter Hardy. "And you, Walter, taking on a *nobody*." A silence fell over the room as she stormed from the circle, with people hurriedly getting out of her way, and headed directly for the trio of musicians. "Get rid of the damn cigarettes and start working for your money. And make it loud!"

AN UP-BEAT MUSICAL number stimulated the pulse of the party and soon the room returned to a lively mood. Walter Hardy was quickly besieged by a swarm of people while Ron Rebuck stood alone. Seconds before he'd been the highlight of the evening, the object of everyone's attention, a White Knight about to slay a dragon, and now, alone, avoided. Jack Pintoff eyed him suspiciously, shrugged, then went off in search of bigger game. Only Rufus and Jennifer were left of the once crowded circle.

"He's gotta feel like horseshit," said Rufus.

"It was unfair. That . . . that obnoxious woman."

Tears had formed in her eyes and Rufus was cynical. "Carrying this Rebuck thing a little far, aren't you?"

"As far as it takes me," she replied.

"Jennifer . . . " he checked himself and went no further. The way she stared at Rebuck, like he was Christ Himself, who could reason with her? He'd try Rebuck instead; he went to the dejected man's side. "Listen, Ron . . . you were pretty good. Surprised me. But next time do yourself a favor and pick on someone not so clever . . . like a moron."

". . . He wasn't here. When I needed him, he wasn't here."

"Who wasn't here?" Rufus asked. He looked into Rebuck's eyes, glazed eyes. "Rebuck, are you getting spooky on me?"

"It was not the proper time."

"You got that right."

"Not the time. I went off my directed course. I made a foolish mistake."

"You did that, pal, but forget it. If it's any consolation, you had a couple of Irish Catholics ganging up on you. Hardy knew damn well what that douche bag was up to. They're pros. This isn't Clearwater, Florida. You need a shill, Rebuck. Someone working the crowd."

A ghost of a smile came to Rebuck's face. "If *He* had been here, you would have seen his works."

Rufus took on those strange, compelling eyes. There was no mistaking the man's sincerity, but the words made absolutely no sense to Manning. "Ron, the fact that you took on a top-seeded player like Walter Hardy and got in some aces was real. I saw it myself. But going weird, speaking of – some supernatural spook, won't cut it. Strange agents don't get invited to the matches. You got to kick all that occult stuff."

Ron Rebuck eyed him with an intensity he'd never before seen in any man. The eyes were eerie, and all at once Rufus truly wondered if he really knew this man. "Look, I can't help it but I'm a material man. I deal in real things. Crack Widener's real. And from what I've been told, he's cuckoo on religion. Which means we do have a slim chance of landing him."

"We?" Ron Rebuck smiled. "Has the Doubting Thomas turned Apostle?"

"Rebuck, make no mistake about it, I'm taking a flyer strictly for the gold. Without Widener, we go our separate ways."

Ron Rebuck was irritated. "Why Michael selected you is beyond understanding."

"Maybe

remembering something urgent he must take care of. "Stay cool. Don't start any more fires. I'll be back."

"You will not see my face again until everything has been arranged."

Rufus looked into the burning eyes, then sadly shook his head, and left.

JENNIFER, WATCHING Rufus leave, felt an odd tingle of excitement as she touched the sleeve of Ron Rebuck. Though she'd read only half of the man's book, she sensed something special about him, felt herself drawn to him, as if by a powerful magnet. It was something more than sexual attraction, though there was a bit of that, too. But mainly there was this feeling that somehow, by some mysterious process, she'd been chosen to follow him – to be a . . . well, the only word she could think of was, *disciple*.

She wanted more than anything to talk with him, to be in his presence. And now he was leaving her and walking toward the center of the room, where Walter Hardy was regaling a raucous Myrna Reardon with some tidbit of high level gossip.

From the corner of his eye, Walter Hardy spotted his recent adversary approaching, and his body tensed. He readied himself for further warfare.

"Mr. Hardy, obviously this was the wrong time and place for our debate, and I apologize. However, such a time will come, I assure you."

"Mr. Hardy won't be holding his breath," hissed Myrna Reardon.

He looked intently at her flushed face and turned away, saying, "There won't be a band to stop me next time."

For some reason she couldn't explain, Myrna was left shaken by the exchange. She said weakly to Hardy, "Brazen son-of-a-bitch. Tomorrow I'll make a point of having my investigator, Marty Pico, find out all there is to know about him."

"I'd let things be, Myrna."

"What's that supposed to mean?"

"I mean . . . I'd let it be. There's something about that fellow. I don't know what it is, but I'm damned glad you shot him down when you did."

"I've shot down bigger game with a BB gun."

"Take my advice, Myrna, the man's trouble."

"And they say *I'm* getting soft with age." Her eyes roved around the room, taking in the lively scene.

"Surveying your subjects, Queen Myrna?"

"Subjects," she uttered in dismay. "Look at 'em. Under those fancy threads they're nothing but spineless jellyfish. There's not a man in the room, other than Hughie, worth his salt."

Walter Hardy frowned, "If I didn't know you better I'd think I was included."

She shot him a vicious look. "You don't know me very well, do you?"

HUGHIE GILMAN lifted his glass and saluted a late-arriving tycoon, tall and distinguished, with silver hair. Rufus recognized him as a network chieftain.

"Got *him* in your net?"

Hughie nodded. "A cannon – like you should be."

"A cannon needs powder . . . Where's your telephone pole?"

"She retired to my *private* bathroom. Locked herself in."

"What a shame. Hope she doesn't bang her head on the fucking ceiling."

Hughie ignored the jibe as Myrna Reardon arrived, tailgated by her hopeful actor-escort. Rufus Manning beamed. She gave Rufus the once-over, then took Hughie by the arm, leading him away. "Hughie, why in the world did you invite that outsider?"

"Who?"

"The one Walter had a go with. Really, Hughie! And don't bullshit me that he's a client."

"You mean Ron Rebuck. No, he's not a client. Friend of Roo–" he quickly checked himself.

"Friend of whom?" she asked.

He couldn't dodge the question without arousing

Myrna's catlike curiosity. With the determination of a water buffalo, she'd kick him to death for an answer. From the corner of his eye, he regretfully saw Rufus approaching.

"Myrna, you know Roof, don't you?" said a jittery Gilman.

"Roof, who? Does he bark?"

"You're kidding," said Rufus.

"Manning. Rufus Manning," Hughie said quickly, with a warning glare at Rufus.

"Hell, Myrna knows who I am, don't you, Myrna?"

"Know you?" She searched her memory bank and identified the name. "Aren't you the producer, the one who exploited blacks and made some money out of it?" She looked at Hughie, "No Kubrick or Coppola, here."

"Made *some* money? When have you ever made five million?"

Hughie let out a nervous laugh, "A joker, Myrna."

"What's a matter, Myrna, your memory getting senile?" He looked at a frowning Hughie Gilman. "I met Myrna long ago. Twenty-five years, at least, when she was a starlet at Fox."

Concern showed on Myrna's face. The memory of those days, brief as they were, was grim and dark.

"Had a small ad agency on the coast then, mostly promoting independent pictures." He looked at her. "Still don't remember me, Myrna?" He went on, giving her no chance to reply. "I had some theater exhibitors in from the midwest . . . you know the kind, Hughie." Hughie Gilman wrestled with the idea of sticking his silken handkerchief down Rufus's throat. "Anyway, I hired some girls . . . for entertainment purposes? Two, or was it three, Myrna?" His eyes narrowed. "Would you believe, Hughie, I yet hear from one of those exhibitors. Swears to this day he never had a better time." With that shitty grin he met Myrna's face, flushed with anger. "Tell me, Myrna, which one of you girls did a number on all of those guys?"

Hughie Gilman groped for words of apology. But it would take more than soothing syllables to put out the fire in Myrna's eyes. The big digger for dirt found herself caught in a landslide. She'd been *had*. But by whom? DiLaurentis, Preminger, Mel Brooks? Any of which would be bad enough. Yet to be humiliated by the likes of Rufus Manning!

Rufus was enjoying her confusion, ignoring Hughie's admonishing look. Finally, Myrna sputtered, "You'd better make your next picture in the Congo, buster. You're finished in this country."

He expected more. She, a five-star newshound. Bush, he'd heard better as a kid on the Bronx blocks. He wanted to tell her to sit on it but restrained himself. "The Congo? Really, Myrna, that your best shot?" He drew closer, shoving his smirking face into hers, while Hughie turned his back in despair. "Do anything, Myrna. Write anything. Get on my ass in *any way* . . . and Abby Alden will have a picnic with the material I'll give her." His face tightened. "Who do you think you're threatening, an empty chair?"

It was no secret that Abby Alden, Myrna's younger competitor, was in the midst of a campaign to knock Myrna from her throne. She turned away from him to Hughie, who pretended to be waving at someone nearby. "Hughie, if it's the last thing I ever do, I'm going to burn this lying bastard!"

Despite Hughie's bundle of apologies, she charged

off, followed by her young escort who in passing Rufus flashed the thumbs-up sign and smiled.

A red-faced Hughie Gilman waited until Myrna was out of earshot to confront Rufus. "Now you did it. Just had to do it, didn't you? War, war, war, and for no damn reason. But you're going to lose this one, hot shot. You're finished. Do you hear? You are finished, dead in the business . . . *through*!"

"Hughie will you stop shaking. You're making me dizzy. And you're wrong. That douche bag won't do a damn thing."

"Is that what you think? You really believe that Abby Alden bit will shake her up?"

"Uh-huh. She's grinding on it right now."

Hughie shook his head, disbelieving. "Impossible, that's what you are. An impossible – at times like this, a psychopathic man." He gave him a Dutch uncle's look. "How in the world could you possibly benefit. Was it kicks? Taking a cheap shot at people with power – did it make you feel good? For God's sake, man, why did you do it?"

"On account of Ron Rebuck for one thing. He was good. Real good. Had Hardy on the ropes, punching him at will. And the crowd, intelligent people, so-called sophisticates, were magnetized with his mush. Amazing. And then *she* had to come along and bust up his act . . . You know, Hughie, I'm beginning to think Ron Rebuck isn't all that crazy."

"But *you* are. And unless you're content to be a gentleman farmer for the rest of your life, you'd better cook up a quick miracle." He looked at his wristwatch. "Ten till midnight, and you've kissed more than the old year goodbye." A serious look came into Hughie Gilman's eyes. "It saddens me to say that there is no way I can resurrect you after Myrna eats your flesh."

"Hughie, will you stop with the death chants. I've stymied that cunt and she damn well knows it. When have I ever done anything unless I was sure of the results? Forget Myrna Reardon and tell me how I can get to Crack Widener."

"I couldn't help you reach for a newspaper. Not now. You don't tangle with the likes of Myrna Reardon and ever hope to win. Sorry, Roof, friendship is one thing, but I cannot risk the chance of endangering other clients. Count me out – unless you make peace with Myrna."

"What a shame. Such a groovy pitch and you didn't take a swing. You let that bitch strike you out on what could've been the biggest home run of your life."

"Stop the con job, Roof. I've never been more serious."

"Con job? Is that what you call presenting a case before the Supreme Court of this land? A case that will be written up in all the law books for centuries to come, to be known as the attorney who defended God, and you call *that* a con job?"

"Where did you get *that* one? I thought I heard them all, but that had to be the greatest crock of shit, ever."

Rufus smiled, that evil grin. "Help me get to Crack Widener and that crock of shit, as you call it, becomes a crock of gold."

A group of early-well wishers converged on Hughie Gilman and Rufus drifted away. He looked past a galaxy of festive faces in search of Jennifer, puzzled by her and Ron Rebuck's sudden disappearance. He was intercepted by the dishonest face with the five o'clock shadow and squinty eyes. "Jack Pintoff, New York's favorite degenerate."

"Make it the world, been traveling a lot."

"Buzz off, Pintoff, I got no room for your kind of gloom."

"I saw you having words with Myrna."

"Damn, you're ugly! You know, Pintoff, you really do look like the Hunchback of Notre Dame."

"Why so hostile, Manning?"

"Why? Because if ever there was a Christ, it was a dude like you who sold him out."

"Missing something, Manning? Like your date?"

"You're moving on the wrong person, I don't have thirty silver pieces for your kind of information."

Jack Pintoff stepped aside, dodging Rufus's elbow. "Pretty girl, Manning. And your friend, Ron Rebuck, he's something else. Sure make a nice-looking couple."

Rufus gave him a murderous glare.

"You should have seen it, Manning. It was like a scene out of an old movie. She, teary-eyed, rushing out into the cold, damp night searching for her hero. But then . . . the fadeout. What do you think will happen, Manning? You're a producer. Will the ending be X-rated?" He wheezed a mocking laugh.

"Quasimodo should stay cooped up in his tower and bang only on his bell, not bait people into murder raps."

Jack Pintoff snarled at the advancing Manning. "Hit me, want to hit me, Manning?"

The fury in Rufus's eyes subsided. "Why Hughie demeans himself by continuing to represent a cockroach like you, I'll never know."

"Come on, Manning, hit me." He pointed to his chin, his eyes crazed, "Get it on, Manning. Get it *on*."

He'd drawn the attention of people close by and Rufus started to walk away. "Afraid people will see you hitting a deformed man?"

"Deranged, Pintoff, the word is *deranged*."

"Don't worry about them, Manning. They got their own hangups. Hit me, you no good son of a bitch."

". . . Pintoff, I'm not your death wish." Rufus jabbed his index finger against the man's sweaty brow. "Sick. You're a real sicky."

IT WAS A MINUTE TO MIDNIGHT and a reflective Rufus Manning was not part of the people bracing themselves for countdown. Another year, he thought. Another batch of mediocrities to gain national prominence. Another year for a Jack Pintoff to huckster consumer products via the tube, gearing his pitch for the eleven-year-old mind. Another year for young rebels to pop up. Start a few brush fires, then be relegated to oblivion by a bored and fickle society. Oh, yes, the minority groups would scream louder. Some new sex books would become best sellers. Politicians would still lie a lot. Spanish would become mandatory in public schools. Middle-income America would yet fail to unite and go on allowing itself to be squeezed by taxes. The same old rut. And then there was religion. And then there was . . . Ron Rebuck.

MIDNIGHT IN BIMINI: The soft tropical breeze, the placid sound of water lapping at a dock, fishing boats cradled in their berths, rocking gently, natives grouped on a pier, singing a song of the sea, their voices bell-like, soothing to the ear; all in all, the New Year came to this tiny sector of the world in a refreshingly tranquil mood. Without hurrah.

From a balcony of the white house overlooking the docks below, the two men clicked their drinking glasses. "May the Good God let us live to see another year," said the Cardinal, resting his great bulk on a rattan chair that creaked when he moved.

"And many more years, Your Eminence," John Gallogly added.

"You know, John, my boy, when that inevitable day comes for me to meet our Maker, I think my only regret will be missing this place."

"Bimini *has* been good for you."

"That it has. That it has." He eyed his young subordinate and said, "Tell me, what is good for you?"

"Me? . . . Oh, I really never gave it much thought. I guess my work."

"Come now, we all crave our little luxuries from life. There must be something you enjoy doing besides your work." The Cardinal's eyes twinkled. "A secret desire, scandalous adventure?"

"I could tell you about my rendezvous with a pretty woman, if you'd like."

"You? No, not you. Saint Thomas Aquinas has left too great an impression. Now tell me, what little thing do you take joy in doing?"

"Oh, I don't know, Your Eminence, chess perhaps."

"Of course. I should have remembered. The Vicar General has yet to get over the shellacking you gave him."

John Gallogly smiled modestly.

"Tell me something, John, do you now and then find yourself playing people as you do chess?"

"I don't follow, Your Eminence."

"Moves? Strategy? Checkmating the opponent at the *first* opportunity?"

For sure, the fat fox was up to something. "There's a great difference. The moves people make are not limited to a chessboard."

The Cardinal lit up a fresh cigar and blew a cloud of smoke into the clear night air. He looked at the cigar admiringly. "Fine tobacco. Wish that damn communist would have left us Cuba and taken Tampa instead. Sorry, John, what's that you were saying?"

John Gallogly smiled. "I gather His Eminence is about to enrich me with some wisdom?"

"Indeed, indeed." Spellissy paused, took another drag on the cigar then picked a piece of tobacco from the corner of his lip. "Wisdom. How difficult for one to attain." He looked at the youthful face before him. "Took a long time, years of trial and error before I came to realize the wisdom in patience. So effective, John. So terribly effective. Yes, a patient man need only watch and wait."

"You Grace, might I ask what you're driving at?"

A sudden harshness came into the Cardinal's voice. "Against my firm wishes you saw fit to explore a matter that I deemed insignificant and unworthy. And to involve Father Bartley, who already is knee deep in hot water, was a foolhardy thing to do! Did you actually believe the Vicar General wouldn't find out about that telephone call to the Monsignor in Florida?"

John Gallogly's face turned grim. All along he'd had a feeling the Cardinal knew. "Does Bishop Burke know all? Does he know of the manuscript burning in my hands?"

"And the strange invisible force you believe to have visited you. Father Bartley needed little persuasion."

"Father Bartley was acting solely on my behalf. I take full blame, and will so inform the Vicar General."

"You needn't bother. The whole matter has been dropped."

"And Father Bartley?"

"A slap on the wrist and forgiven. But the man's tenure at the diocese is coming rapidly to an end. Your friend has a reckless way of irritating people." He puffed on the cigar. "Why did he ever become a priest?" He looked at Gallogly warningly. "Promise me there'll be no more of your valuable time spent on this Rebuck fellow."

John Gallolgy rose slowly from his chair. He went to the balcony's railing, shoulders bent, mind troubled. Resting his hands on the rail, he looked out at the moonlit water. "Your Eminence, with all due respect, I cannot promise you that." He turned and faced the Cardinal, who showed surprise. "I've tried. The Lord knows I've tried. But this is no ordinary man – and no ordinary book. There are too many signs, omens – "

"*Omens*, you say?" The great tummy rolled as Spellissy laughed. John Gallogly quietly withdrew into himself. He could do little else. A Monsignor didn't provoke an argument with a member of the College of Cardinals, a prince of Mother Church.

The Cardinal shifted his vast weight, set his drink to the side, took a long puff on his cigar, then looked hard at the earnest face before him. "Since you deem it necessary to keep these fixations of yours between Father Bartley and yourself, the Vicar General investigated the matter and, as I expected, ruled out anything supernatural."

John Gallogly's lips tightened. "Your Eminence, contrary to what the Vicar General believes, I was not smoking in bed. The pages of that manuscript were not set aflame by any mortal's doing."

A threatening smile appeard on the Cardinal's chubby face, yet John Gallogly would not be intimidated. "I've tried to live by the thought that reality *must* prevail. And other than matters of great faith, things considered bizarre, so-called miraculous happenings, find me normally siding with the Doubting Thomases. With no disrespect intended, I've often questioned the powers of exorcism, the role we priests play. . . . In essence, just how much myth – even outright humbug – is involved. What I'm trying to say, Your Grace, is that I've prided myself on possessing an analytical mind that is not seduced by the occult." He paused.

"Go on, John," the Cardinal said.

" . . . Well, nothing seems to work in the case of this Ron Rebuck. I find myself unable to maintain a skeptical viewpoint and drive him from my thoughts. He continues to haunt my mind."

" . . . Sit down, John. Benefit from an old man's experience."

John Gallogly knew where this conversation would now end. As he had done with so many others – the disenchanted, the rebellious, those with their tales of woe – the Cardinal would work on his mind and leave him baahing like a tame lamb. He took a seat, his first mistake. He stood a better chance remaining erect, for the Cardinal must first relax his victims, lull them, for his magical serum to work.

"John, my boy, to be blessed with an early warning system, the gift to detect problems before they surface, is a marvelous thing. Marvelous indeed. However, sometimes blessings have a way of turning into curses. You have been a priest long enough to be familiar with how the church's machinery works. Yes, slowly, to be sure. At times, ponderously . . . but always effectively. An example, a contemporary one that comes to mind, is that devil, that communist, Rodriguez. Under our very noses he originated a base to spread his pagan germs. Mind you, John, it wan't until he showed his fangs and infested our parishioners with his virus did Mother Chruch begin to act. The point to be made here is for you to stop building fires around someone as though he was a formidable enemy. Patience, John, patience. That you are aware of this man should now suffice."

"Your Grace, I don't wish to appear ungrateful, but shouldn't one who is aware of a potential danger be readily prepared?"

"Danger, you say!" The Cardinal's eyes lost their twinkle. "Where lies the danger? In a man who wrote a manuscript that has yet to become a published book? You consider someone, who at the very most is in the hopeful stages, a danger?"

"Begging the Cardinal's indulgence, but I'm sure Karl Marx lived through a period of hopeful stages with his revolutionary writings."

"Karl Marx!" The Cardinal's face reddened. "Have you lost your senses?"

John Gallogly had to reach deep inside himself to muster the courage to continue. Taking on the Cardinal was *never* a debate. It was a war. "Your Eminence, as absurd as this may sound, I believe that once this Ron Rebuck surfaces, and with the right backers behind him, a religious revolution can spread across this country."

"That, Father Gallogly, is not only absurd . . . but asinine!"

"I'm sorry to have irritated you, but I've read this man's theory and I'm only stating how I honestly feel."

The Cardinal lifted his great weight from the chair and looked down at this defiant priest. "John, for the last time, I don't want to hear any more of this Rebuck from your lips. I urge you to clear your mind of this man. If . . . *if* he should happen to emerge as some sort of threat to Mother Church, we shall, as usual, rise to the occasion. Young man, never again underestimate the powerful institution you have vowed to uphold. You are an officer in the greatest army on earth, and from here on, act like one."

"I'm sorry, Your Grace. Truly sorry."

The Cardinal managed a smile.. The eyes were twinkling once again. "I've promised myself two weeks with nothing but fishing on my mind. And out there in the deep is the damnedest, fightingest marlin, just waiting for me." He looked at his wristwatch. "If I'm to catch that devil, I'm going to need some sleep."

John Gallogly came swiftly out of his chair. He was thankful the Cardinal had thus ended the discussion. "May I be the first to receive your blessing on this New Year?"

"That you may."

John Gallolgy went to his knees, head bowed,

eyes closed, his hands clasped together. Never before had he felt such a deep, aching need for the blessing. A sigh escaped him as he felt the heavy hand on his head and the familiar, powerful Latin words: "*In Nomini Patri, et Filio et Spirito Sancto . . .*"

FOR THE FIRST TIME in two weeks, John Gallogly felt at peace with himself. He had succeeded in relieving himself of the festering obsession by bringing it out in the open before the very man from whom he'd tried to conceal it. The Cardinal was right. He always was. The whole Rebuck matter was doubtless a tempest in a teapot. He was sure. The burning of the manuscript – perhaps he *had* been smoking. That force, that powerful force, had been nothing more than a fantasy of his weary mind. Nothing more. He would sleep soundly this night, and the hell with Ron Rebuck. In the morning when he awoke, he would do some sketches. An artist of some talent, he would get out the brushes and maybe even do some oil painting while the Cardinal searched for his marlin.

He went to the French doors of his bedroom and opened them wide, allowing the soft breeze entry, and filled his lungs with the night air. A tidy man, not one to lightly forget his early training, he impulsively tossed his short-sleeved multicolored shirt on a chair, stepped out of his trousers, and headed for the bathroom to attend to his nightly ablutions. En route, he stopped at the table where lay a couple of sketches he'd done of Ron Rebuck. Collecting them, he crumpled the papers in his hand, forming a ball, and tossed it into a straw wastepaper basket.

There was no shower in the bathroom and he ruled

out taking a bath in a tub that was obviously made for midgets. He took a yellow-handled toothbrush and a tube of toothpaste from a tan leather toiletry bag and proceeded to brush his teeth. All at once, a loud clapping sound came from the bedroom. Thunder? he thought. Not in a sky bright with stars. Wind? Curious, he came out of the bathroom and entered the living area. The thin white drapes that hung over the open French doors were still. There had been no sudden gust of wind. He looked about the room, from ceiling to floor. Nothing had fallen. And the lamp next to the bed, the only one lit, hadn't blown a bulb. He shrugged and returned to the bathroom.

Having rinsed off his toothbrush, he took a swig of water from a plastic cup, gargled, and was about to spit it out into the white basin when the bathroom's door suddenly slammed shut.

Fear pricked at his flesh. His hands gripped the basin as all at once he sensed *that presence*. That force . . . had returned. The air in the room grew thinner by the second, and he felt his breath being sucked out of his body. Beads of sweat lined his brow; he tried to cry out but he was voiceless.

The door. He must get to the door before he suffocated. Struggling with this thought, he glanced toward the mirror over the sink, and the unbelievable assailed him. . . . There was no reflection of himself.

Horrified, he was unable to tear his eyes from the reflectionless mirror. Overcome by the terror he believed to be in the room, he couldn't scream out, and was too riddled with shock to pray. Valiantly he fought off the coming blackness – as the mirror began to fog over.

Through blurred eyes he saw an outline starting to form on the clouded glass. And the, a face materialized – and eyes. *Those* eyes. *"My God in heavan protect me."* John Gallogly cried out. He shuddered violently, as a stranger's face – the face of the man he'd seen at the airport but for a fleeting moment – became his own reflection and eerily looked back at him . . .

# 13

A LIGHT DRIZZLE spattered the windshield of the old limo that rumbled over the wet and winding country road leading to the village of Lazy Hallow, a few miles away. The shades of night lifted, revealing a bleak beginning for the first day of the new year.

A perplexed Marty Pico sat between the two men in the back of the dark blue sedan wondering why he was being hassled. Why he had been snatched from a New Year's happening to be taken for a ride in the country in the wee hours of the morning. Marty Pico knew something of his abductor; the deadly one seated in the front next to the driver, with the glass partition electronically controlled, canceling conversation. He was vaguely aware of Mike Spenard's past reputation as a head hunter, but had thought he'd long retired. And his two henchmen – good God, he was being taken for a ride by some really old-time mobsters. And the driver, in that hat, was something out of the Capone era. Pico's eyes bulged as the limo pulled off the main road and entered Lazy Hollow Cemetery. He thrust his heavy body forward and hammered his stubby hands on the glass partition.

"Fer Christ's sakes . . . what gives?" he shouted at Mike Spenard in those sinister dark shades. Spenard only glanced over her shoulder.

Pico was unable to find a logical reason why anybody would go to the trouble of hiring a has-been hitter like Mike Spenard to bury him in cement. Sure, he'd made a lot of people's shit list. As a private detective, and good at his profession, this was an occupational hazard. Spying on husbands or wives, in the days before no-fault divorce, often got hairy; investigating high-powered corporate officers on the take had its moments, too. But to be dealt the death penalty didn't add up. It had to be a joke. Someone with a morbid sense of humor had cooked up this whole spiel. He anxiously made a mental list of his clientele – searching for the link that found his immediate future in the hands of a man they used to call Mad Mike. There was the stock swindler; no, he skipped to South America. The furniture tycoon and his missing teenager; no, the ten grand he paid was worth getting her back. Myrna Reardon? Hell no. He never crossed her. The Arab. Playing watchdog for a sheik. He needn't go further. "The Arab," he muttered as saliva spilled from the corner of his mouth to trickle down his chin. "The Arab," he moaned as the car braked to a halt some hundred feet behind a blue Chevy whose engine idled, its exhaust blending with the gray mist that cloaked the damp cemetery grounds.

Perspiration began to seep through the pores of his pudgy face. The finger of fear pushed on the nape of his neck, his spine shimmied with chills. He looked at the man seated to his right, the pig-faced man, and said, "Don't you think this has gone far enough?"

The man gave him a blank look as the glass partition slowly descended.

"Where's your friends, smarty Marty?" Mike Spenard rasped from the front seat.

"Listen, Mike . . . let's work this out."

"Shut up, Marty – shut up your trap," said Spenard in his deadly monotone. "Where's your friends? The big nigger with the pussy's voice . . . and the crazy with the pistol."

"I don't know. I don't know!"

"Where are they, Marty?"

"Mike, I don't know. Big Dick and Jukey didn't check in last night. I swear it!"

"Big Dick . . . hear that, Geek? He calls the spade Big Dick."

"Some joke, Mike," said the Geek whose large jowels jumped when he laughed. "Some joke, huh, Pig?" He nudged the Pig, who proceeded to cackle like a hen.

"Big Dick's a pencil," said Mike Spenard.

"A short pencil, Mike," the Geek added.

"Marty, time's money. I got to think of my retirement, so I keep the time short. Right, Geek?"

"Real short, Mike."

"Exactly. Now I had to use . . . six men . . . and uh . . . naturally myself. Plenty of money. . . . Times costs money."

"What are you getting at? For God's sake, you're driving me crazy!"

"Don't say God. This is business. No business of God's. Tell him, Geek."

"What's a matter wit you? Yah stupid. Yah want slaps?" said the Geek, grabbing the petrified Marty by his coat lapels. He was set to rough him up when a gesture from Mike Spenard spared him.

"I got no patience. Talking gives me migraines. Geek, you wanna talk?"

"I hate to talk, Mike."

"Hmmm . . . Piggy, you wanna talk?"

"I'll talk."

"So talk," said Spenard, pushing the button that raised the glass partition.

"Out!" said the Pig, pushing him, maneuvering his short, squat body over the long legs of the Geek, who appeared bored by it all.

"You like tombstones?" said the Pig, pushing him forward, ahead of him, on the narrow drive flanked by monuments to eternal rest. "I got a beaut for you to see."

Next, he noticed the two men come out of the blue Chevy – two dudes in city duds that could *hardly* pass for gave diggers.

"Jesus, Mary and Joseph," he moaned, observing the two men through blurry eyes as they moved ahead, leading the parade, a funeral procession with a new twist: the *body* was not yet a corpse. "I've had it. Holy shit, I've had it," he whimpered. "God, I'm really going to die," he groaned aloud as tears welled in his eyes.

"Almost there, shit-ass," said the Pig, as they neared a bend in the cemetery road.

"Where? Almost *where*?" he asked. His pulse was running wild, his blood pressure count zooming toward tilt.

"Big surprise," said the Pig.

" . . . Which . . . which one of you crazies is gonna kill me? Kill me in cold blood!"

"PIGGY! . . . WHAT NOW?" One of the men ahead shouted from the path leading to a mausoleum, structured in granite. A family crypt, the size of a single-car garage with the name "Ruggerio" in Romanesque lettering over the solid iron door.

"Open the goddamned thing, what else!" the Pig ordered.

"No way!" Marty screamed, falling to his knees, crying unashamedly. Out of the corner of one eye, he saw the black limo approach slowly. "You're not going to bury *me*, you crazy bastard!" he shouted at Spenard as the sedan rolled to a stop alongside him.

Mike Spenard looked out at the pathetic figure kneeling on the ground and opened the window. "Hey, Marty, you wanna catch cold?"

"You're a fiend. A lunatic!" Marty blurted out as the Pig kicked him in the shins. "You better kill me here! Right here! You crazy son of a bitch!"

"Marty, would I kill you? . . . Go with them, Marty, they got somethin' to show you. Then we'll talk," said Spenard, who closed the window, leaving Pico totally bewildered.

He struggled to his feet, brushing the Pig's hand away from him, thinking about Spenard's words. The words of a maniac, he thought. A fraction of faith, an inkling that he might not be killed, sent a cool sensation through his troubled system – suppressing the heat flashes which had erupted like volcanic blasts in his body. Marty Pico no longer prayed for a heart attack.

"Ya heard Mike. Move it, asshole," said the Pig, pushing him, as he started down the path to the tomb, where one of the men was unlocking the iron door and having difficulty in doing so. He finally found the right key, and the iron door, its hinges rusted, creaked open.

The Pig shoved him forward, a not-so-gentle thrust that made him lose his balance and fall on the wet ground less than twenty yards from a now-opened entrance – when, hands tied behind his back, his mouth gagged with adhesive, a stark-naked Richard, six foot five, and two hundred and fifty pounds of black-is-beautiful, shot out from the door, racing over cemetery plots in a zig-zag pattern that could fake the best of NFL defensive backs out of their jock straps.

"Yah dumb shits!" the Pig yelled at the two men who were too startled by the streaker to move. "Get the nigger!" he yelled over and over.

"*Pig*," the Geek shouted out from the parked limo, "let him look, then bring him to the car."

Marty Pico didn't have to be pushed; the place he feared being buried in now piqued his curiosity. Gingerly, he stepped into the tomb with the heavy breathing Pig behind him. "Jukey!" he exclaimed, not believing. His eyes focused on a man, nude, bound hand and foot with a gag in his mouth, curled up in a corner like a frightened dog.

"Ya seen him," said the Pig, his words whizzing by him like the wind, as his eyes remained glued on the poor soul freezing to death.

"How long . . . how long has he been here?" Marty asked.

The Pig took out a blackjack – the homemade kind – soaked in a chemical solution that would bring bells to the hardest of heads. "Hey . . . yah want your skull split? Let's *go*, creep!"

Once outside, Marty walked toward the limo, forgetting about Richard. He had enough troubles of his own.

"Get in," the Geek ordered, holding the rear door of the sedan; the Pig stayed outside, palming his blackjack.

"What's it going to be, Marty. Spare me details. Time's money," Mike Spenard whispered the words.

"Why the rough stuff? Did I or my people deserve all this? Could the Arab lay out that much line?"

"What Arab?" Mike asked.

"C'mon, Mike, I've already had three strokes and two nervous breakdowns. No more . . . I'll do whatever you say. Whatever!"

"How he talks . . . is he some talker, Geek?"

"Some talker, Mike."

"Hmmm . . . now listen up . . . listen good, Marty . . . no more Rufus Manning, or the next time . . . you and your amigos lay in lye. Unnerstood?"

"*Manning*? The producer? You mean the Arab, Aly Sharif . . . he didn't hire you?"

"Wud I say? Geek . . . set 'im straight." He pushed the lever for the glass partition to rise.

Marty shook his head, "How did I know this Manning guy had Mike for clout? How was I supposed to know?"

"Wha'd yah expect Mike to do, advertise it in the Yellow Pages?"

"What's this Manning got on Mike for him to do what he did?"

"Maybe he's gonna make Mike a movie star. Shoot your load."

"I've shot it. What's the commandments?"

"Just one. Stay outta Manning's face . . . and the broad who's blowing him . . . or you're dead. Clear enough for you?"

"What about my people?" Marty asked.

"The Chevy takes you and your goombas back to the city . . . couple of blankets and booze in the back seat."

"How about right now? They're freezing, for Christ's sake!"

The Geek tapped on the glass to gain Mike Spenard's attention. The partition slid back halfway.

"He gets the message, Mike."

"Get out, Marty . . . you're no longer on my time."

Marty Pico stared at the diabolical face. He would not forget this humiliation. No matter how long it took, he promised himself to get even. Rufus Manning would pay. He vowed it. "It's a cruel thing to strip a man of his dignity, Spenard."

"Stay smart, Marty . . . don't be a funny fellow," Mike Spenard warned.

"Yeah . . . Happy New Year," Marty replied, stepping from the car and hurrying to the Chevy.

"Get Piggy and let's go. I hate reunions," said Mike Spenard.

# 14

RUFUS MANNING made notes on a yellow pad while Leslie Manning and John Milton sipped their coffee.

"Daddy, where's Mike?"

"Leslie . . . two minutes and I'll be finished."

They had been watching him scribble on that pad for the last *ten* minutes and wondered for what significant purpose they had been summoned. Rufus's persistent calls had started at eight, with follow-up calls every fifteen minutes, with Rufus bitching why they hadn't left yet. It was after the last call, when he had revealed he was leaving on an afternoon flight for some two or more weeks of skiing in Montana, that Leslie had hassled John into going with her. On his first and only meeting with her father, a morning ago, Rufus had accused him of partaking in some dark mysterious plot, and called him cheap for not buying Leslie an engagement ring. What today? he wondered.

"*Done*," said Rufus, putting down the pad, lighting up a cigarette and smiling at them both. "Now, kiddies, let's get all the small talk out of the way, because I have some serious words to lay on you both." He looked at Leslie. "You were asking?"

"If you're leaving on an afternoon plane, shouldn't Mike be packing? It's after eleven."

"Mike spent the night with his ninety-year-old mother. He'll be here at noon. There's plenty of time."

"Speaking of mothers, did you call mine?"

"I did. Even invited her to go with me to Montana."

"And?"

"She'll call back and let me know. Probably has to get permission from the resident witch."

"Tired of bachelorhood, Daddy?" Leslie smiled.

"Who knows. Now, any more bullshit questions?"

John Milton laughed within. Strange how the man treated a possible reconciliation with his wife as something of a trivial nature.

"Okay, you two, open your ears, better yet, your minds, and listen to me good. Last night . . . it hit me. Like lightning. An idea that's got every color of the rainbow. Didn't sleep at all."

"You look it, Dad."

He shot her a wounded glance and continued. "Crazy as it sounds, Ron Rebuck could have the only *right* ticket on the religious train. It just might be that the rest of those religious crap shooters are using loaded dice, and Rebuck's shaking the real bones." He paused, allowing the puzzled Leslie to ask, "What happened since yesterday, Daddy, when Ron Rebuck was bonkers?"

"Yesterday's *yesterday*. I'm speaking of today, *tomorrow*. Last night at Hughie's party I saw Rebuck in action. No preliminary bout for him, he took on the champ in a nontitle fight."

"The champ, Daddy?"

"Walter Hardy. I'm sure you intellects would agree Hardy's the undisputed debating champion."

"I would, for sure," John Milton was fast to reply, obviously a Hardy fan.

"Ron Rebuck jabbed him at will, was about to knock him out when that douche bag, Myrna Reardon rang the bell."

"Ron Rebuck whipped Walter Hardy in a debate?" a disbelieving John Milton inquired.

"He didn't get the victory, Myrna Reardon saw to that, but he had Hardy out on his feet."

"He'd have to be Supermouth to do that, " John exclaimed.

"Or Super Spook," Rufus added.

"Daddy, are you cooking up some kind of plan?"

"How'd ya guess?" He smiled, wickedly.

"A religious plan? – *you*?"

"A religious *business* plan." Rufus got up from the sofa and walked slowly toward the windows. "Wasn't it John Boy who told me how big the religious business truly is?"

"Was that before or after I was allowed to call you *Roof*?"

Leslie laughed, but Rufus was all business. "The

next two weeks, how's your time at Columbia?"

"Pretty much my own, why?"

"I've got a job for you to do."

"You'll pay him, Daddy?"

"What kind of a horseshit question is that?"

"I know what you try to pay actors, remember?"

"I know. As little as I can. But John won't be acting. I need some research, and since he claims to be some kind of religious expert, he's my candidate for the job I've got in mind."

"I never said I was an expert, Mr. Manning."

"Who the fuck really is?"

"There are many theologians who will disagree with you."

"Theologians, doesn't that come from the word 'theory'?"

"I believe in this particular case you are referring to the word 'theology'."

"Daddy, what kind of research do you want John to do, and how much will you pay him?"

"Later with the pay bit. First things first. It's a double deal. I'm going to need both of you." He pointed a warning finger at Leslie. "Mention money, I'll kill you." He turned to his future son-in-law. "John, I want you to get me everything there is on Billy Hale. From his diaper days till the present."

"Mr. Manning, I don't happen to work for the *New York Times*."

"John, I'm not asking you to find out if he cheats on his wife, or what he eats, what I want to know is where he comes from. How he became a household name. Why so many people hold him in such high esteem." He locked eyes with the young man. " Too difficult for you?"

"No . . . most of it can be found in encyclopedias. And he's written a few books, though I'm not sure any are autobiographical. There must be a fair amount of material about his life. At least, magazine articles . . ."

Rufus gleamed. "Whatever you get, correlate it and put it together. And you, Leslie, I've saved the toughest for you."

"Why?"

"Because some of your old man should have rubbed off on you by now."

She settled back in her chair and braced herself for an impossible task.

"Get me a list of every TV show dealing with religion. Coast to coast."

"Daddy, that would take years to do."

"Mr. Manning, she's right. Every TV station in America starts off and ends its broadcast day with something in the religious vein. Sermonettes, the Lord's Prayer. Or something along those lines."

"Forget that garbage, concentrate on syndicated and network shows. Specials. And don't hand me any crap that they're only shown in the Bible Belt. Right here in Sophisticated City I can't turn on the damn tube without some dummy shooting off his mouth with the Holy Holies. The FCC should have the information, but if they don't, go to Hughie Gilman's office and find out from one of the attorneys if there's some kind of Religious Broadcasters' Association. The rest should be mallard consomme."

"Mallard consomme?" John asked.

"Duck soup," said Leslie.

John Milton frowned. "Mr. Manning, when I get my head into something, I like to know where it all leads. Whether my contribution is essential to the end results."

"Good point. Deserves an answer. Unfortunately I don't have one . . . not yet."

"Exploratory state, Daddy?"

"Something like that."

"This is starting to sound exciting. How about it, John?"

"I'll have to admit it does arouse my curiosity."

"Getting interested?" Rufus asked.

"That depends."

Rufus eyed him, crossly. "Spit it out, John."

"There's really nothing for me to spit out. I can only assume you're researching the bucks to be made in the religion game."

"Uh huh, and that's precisely what I told Rebuck. If I do go all the way, it's strictly for the gold."

"What did he say, Daddy?"

"What *did* he say? . . . He got pissed. Said something about that cockamamie angel he claims he talks to."

"Does this Ron Rebuck actually claim to speak with an angel?" John asked.

"Whoever believes that better get reservations for the funny farm," said Rufus, who seated himself on the sofa, next to Leslie, then to wave a finger for her to pour some coffee into his empty cup.

"Mr. Manning, concerning this research you want me to do for you . . . I'm curious. Why Billy Hale? Why not real power? The Pope? How about the Cardinal, right here in New York?"

"No way." Rufus took a fresh cup of coffee from Leslie and winked his thanks, then expressed surprise at the young man's inquiry. "Didn't you tell me the

Catholic Church has ninety billion dollars in assets?"

"I told you only what I read in James Gollin's book, *Worldly Goods*."

"In any event, ninety billion is moon money, my young friend, and if I hope to fly in that kind of orbit, then, like they say, you don't wake up a sleeping tiger."

"Daddy, are you saying that the famous Billy Hale's *not* a tiger?"

"What do you think, John?"

"A paper tiger."

"Paper tiger, *Billy Hale*? Friend of Presidents? God's greatest mouth to mankind?" she said, with a chiding smile.

"Oh, sure, he's unquestionably America's best known religious leader and he fills stadiums for his crusades, but he doesn't head up any powerful organization. He's strictly a one-man show. There you see him and there you don't."

Rufus Manning smiled. What John had said pleased him. "A tiger with no teeth, yes, John?"

"No, he's got teeth, but his bark is worse than his bite." A triumphant expression flashed on his face. "How's that for an old saying, *Mr*. Manning?"

"Good enough for you to start calling me Roof." He came off the sofa, adrenalin racing. "Billy Hale, the perfect target. Finish *him* off and we're in business."

"Finish him off? Sounds like you're going to shoot the man."

"*Rebuck*. If he's got the goods, and *we* plan carefully, blabbermouth Billy Hale . . . goes down."

"Damn it, Daddy, stop teasing us! You're sounding like someone who's about to start a religious war, and if you expect John and me to play soldiers then let us in on the battle plan."

"If, Leslie, *if* there's a shot of daylight to this deal, forget being soldiers, you'll both be part of one helluva profitable operation. A religious money-making machine."

"Ron Rebuck, Mr. Manning – I mean Roof – is he in this for the money?"

"He'll drop the bomb for nothing. He'll do anything to get on top of spooky mountain."

"Sure of him, Daddy?"

"I'll maneuver Rebuck, you people just get humping on that data I asked for."

"Still not going to tell us, are you?"

"Leslie . . . tell you what? That I'm intrigued with a far-out idea? Yes. Ron Rebuck might have something? Yes. Billy Hale's a possible target for him to take on? Perhaps . . . But there's nothing else. Not at this time."

She sat back. He was convincing enough for her to press it no further.

"Something on your mind, John?" Rufus asked of the pondering young man.

"I was thinking about Billy Hale. I hope I didn't mislead you in what I said about him. The man, after all, *is* clever. He would have to be in order to attain the prominence he's been able to enjoy throughout the years. What I'm really saying, if you're planning to pit this Ron Rebuck against him, you will need more than a bomb. Unless, of course, it's some kind of miracle bomb."

Rufus smiled. "Miracle bomb. I like it. It's got a nice sound."

Leslie interrupted his line of thought, saying, "A

super challenge, Daddy?"

"Could be . . . *the* Big Picture."

"Do you aim to make a film on this subject?" John asked, confused.

Leslie answered, "From what Daddy tells me, there's never been a movie that has made a billion dollars. At long last, I think my father has finally found a way to reach that summit."

"Would you mind backing up? I seem to have missed your point."

"My father isn't content to have made millions. He's now on the street called billions."

"I'm not that greedy; a billion will suffice."

"Can I safely assume a new religion is in the making, and Ron Rebuck's due to be its pope?"

"What took you so long, John?" Rufus kidded in asking.

"I've always been a slow study."

"Well study this: I like long shots. My film *Dude* was a long shot. Smart money wouldn't touch it. Know what they told me when I brought some of the picture's black stars with me to see them?"

"Haven't the foggiest," said John.

"Told me to get the niggers out of their fancy offices."

"Is there some significant point to all this?"

"*Dude* was a black picture, and hardly the Porgy and Bess type. Blacks weren't so beautiful, then. Studio financing wouldn't give you a quarter, and so-called smart money men thought I had brain disease. Ron Rebuck's not beautiful, *dig*?"

"I gather Ron Rebuck's book is revolutionary, and revolutionists are only beautiful when they succeed."

"Yeahhh," said Rufus.

"And Daddy's the architect, the strategist behind Ron Rebuck. It's all so exciting."

"The way this conversation's leading, it sounds like your father might be the general of a potentially violent revolution."

"What's wrong with that?" Rufus fired back. "This country needs a face lift. It's fast losing its spirit, its fighting mood. We're a nation of spectators . . . *doers* are becoming extinct. Why not a revolution?"

"But a *religious* war?"

"It's not so unique, John. Name a battle, a war going on today that's not called a holy war?"

John Milton had to think . . . The Middle East: Arab against Jew; Muslim against Christian. And Ireland: Catholic against Protestant. Rufus Manning had a point.

Their attention was diverted by Mike Spenard's arrival. From the first moment John Milton had laid eyes on the man he'd been fascinated with him. A walking portrait of menace, he'd told Leslie. She paid it little mind. Mike had been part of the family to her. Her mother, Nancy, on the other hand, despised the man. Perhaps Nancy's dislike was brought on by Mama Riley's claim that Mike Spenard was sent by the devil himself to watch over Rufus.

"This meeting is now adjourned," said Rufus. "And when I return, those reports had better be completed. Now kiddies, you've got to blow. Got a few things to do before leaving."

"Like seeing the woman in the apartment down the hall?" needled Leslie.

"As the song goes, 'It Was Just One of Those Things'."

"*Was*? Meaning it's over?"

"It never really started. And here's another oldie to hum on, 'There's No Place Like Home.'"

"Giving up bachelorhood, Daddy?"

"When I return, I'm dumping this place and going back to the house. What's more, I'm going to spray the grounds with bat poison to keep the vampire away."

"*Grandma*?" Leslie laughed. "You'll need more than bat poison, Daddy."

She kissed her father's cheek as John shook his hand, then Mike Spenard suddenly materialized at the door to see them out.

Leslie gave the sinister man a smile, then turned to her father and said, "Happy New Year, Daddy."

Fondly, Rufus blew her a kiss. John tore his eyes from Mike Spenard to echo his sentiments: "Yeah, Happy New Year, Roof. Better yet, Happy Revolution."

# 15

. . . THE EYES were brown, gold, more befitting a wild animal than a man. The nose was long, crooked, with flaring nostrils. The chin was strong, a lantern jaw. The hair, salt and pepper, predominantly the latter, was free, windblown. And the lips were wide, thin, grossly overshadowed by that lengthy nose.

An intense John Gallogly set the oil brush aside, wiped his hands on a yellow cloth, and stared at his completed work. He didn't feel the coean's breeze at his face or hear the sound of the crashing surf below. Seated on a wooden stool on the rich green Bimini lawn in front of the white house, he was totally oblivious of the magnificent view and the various activities on the docks and the fishing yachts cutting through the blue-green water that glistened under a burning afternoon sun.

He'd been touched by the supernatural. Last night's terrifying vision, the face in the mirror, the face he was trying to capture on the canvas before him, was all the proof he needed. No longer would he reject the bizarre happenings confronting him. The face, the man himself, Ron Rebuck, was truly haunting him. But why? Simply because he'd read the man's theory and considered it potentially dangerous to Mother Church? Had he come upon the blueprint for a revolution? Was Rebuck the one many believed would come and bring new light to a darkened world? Or, instead, was he, John Gallogly, the knight of warning, chosen to do battle with the devil, or being called by a saint?

CARDINAL THOMAS SPELLISSY opened his eyes. Stretched out on the bed with the great belly puffed like a pumpkin under a white tee shirt, trouserless, clad in khaki boxer shorts revealing those spindly legs, His Eminence looked very much at this moment like Humpty Dumpty—after his great fall. An attack of gastritis had put him on his back. Having to cut short his all-day fishing excursion, he was forced to give up the idea of landing that marlin and return grumpily to the white house on the hill, unbeknownst to the Monsignor.

Having taken some pills, the Cardinal had been asleep but twenty minutes when he was awakened by a voice from outdoors. He lay there, eyes opened, ears tuned, wondering if he'd dreamed it all when—again the voice.

John Gallogly's, he was now certain. Slowly, cumbersomely, he came off the bed. Curiosity drew him to the balcony. Fifty yards away, on the lawn, he made out the figure of the troubled man. John Gallogly's face was but inches from the canvas. He seemed to be talking to the painting.

"Speak, damn you, speak! Perform your miracles . . . *Now* . . . in the light of day . . . Answer me, Rebuck . . . Is it darkness you need? Damn your soul, *speak*!"

"Touched . . . the poor man's gone daft," the Cardinal sadly said to himself. His own ailment forgotten, he hurried back into the room, picked up a pair of field glasses that lay on a chair and returned to the balcony.

John Gallogly had not moved a step. A frenzied look in his eyes, his body racked with spasms, words finally burst forth from straining lungs: *"In the name of the Lord God, show yourself!"*

Suddenly, the face on the canvas began to melt. The colors merged into an orange-pinkish base and the face was no more. John Gallogly froze. Unable to speak, he could only stare at the incredible sight. A disbelieving Cardinal Spellissy held the binoculars firmly to his eyes as the impossible continued to take place. The flesh-colored base was now changing, reforming. The features of a man's face were rapidly taking shape. John Gallogly gasped as he recognized the image. *"My God, Eternal God,"* he cried, as the most familiar face—the blessed lineaments of Jesus Christ, stood fully revealed.

Cardinal Spellissy, his hand shaking, brought the glasses to his side and looked down from the balcony at the man on his knees mumbling prayers of adoration. Not one who gave much credence to things deemed supernatural, Thomas Spellissy could hardly deny what had unfolded before his very eyes.

His suspicions regarding so-called miracles went back to childhood, his years in Ireland, when he'd forever challenge the elders who'd frequently credit God or the devil for acts that were the slightest bit difficult to explain.

He'd met with the German nun who carried the stigmata of Christ's wounds and seen them bleed. He'd visited Lourdes and witnessed some of the sickly come away, seemingly healed. He'd seen tears drip from the eyes of religious icons. He'd examined the cloth supposedly used to wipe Christ's face on the road to Calvary. He'd personally witnessed the power of exorcism at work in his own diocese. He did not reject the Church's corroborated proof of the miracles performed by canonized saints. Yet Thomas Timothy Spellissy rarely spoke of these things and would avoid arguments pertaining to them.

Yet now, as he stood on the balcony, baffled by the mystical event, a memory long dormant rose from the deeps of his mind. The words of an old Italian monk on a hill in Assisi when he was a young man not more than five years into the priesthood, came back to him with new significance.

The words burned brilliantly in his mind: "YOU WILL LIVE THE DAY . . . WHEN *HE* SHALL COME."

# 16

THE SOUND of cries and shrieks came closer and closer.

The two burly men stationed outside the double doors

of superstar Crack Widener's London hotel penthouse looked up. The sound came from the bank of elevators across the corridor; the two guards stiffened visibly.

The doors of Elevator Two sprang open and out burst a screaming flock of teen-age London girls—it was easy to see why they'd once been called "birds." Actually, there were only a half dozen, but they were a determined crew, who'd somehow managed to slip through the doubled-up hotel security net on the lobby floor.

The two guards moved forward, arms linked, forcing the girls back toward the open maw of the elevator.

"Give us Crack—just a look!" screamed one.

"Give us Crack!" echoed the others.

Veterans of countless Crack Widener concerts around the globe, the men ignored their hysterical pleas, and managed to shove them gently back into the elevator. The last bird, a well-upholstered brunette, had hinted with a movement of her body as she brushed against one of the men, that there'd be something in it for him if he made her wish come true. The elevator doors sighed shut. The two security men returned to their post.

Behind the double doors, their boss, an even bigger, huskier man, stood restlessly. Clad in a garment reminiscent of the Crusades, he watched the revelry of the superstar's entourage, notorious throughout the musical world as The Dirty Thirty. Strobe lights danced across the walls and over the faces of young men and women writhing to the pounding beat of the heavy-metal rock music. Clouds of illegal smoke drifted around the dancers and floated toward the ceiling. Near the center of the room, on top of a marble-topped antique table, a black girl with serpentine body and long, racy legs did bumps and grinds to the incessant beat—totally naked.

The guardian of the entourage—Turk Savage—gazed at himself in the mirror across the room. Dimly glowing on the garment he was wearing was the Maltese Cross, emblem of the Crusades. He groaned inwardly. How'd he ever get into all this?

Turk Savage was widely reported to be the highest salaried employee of Crack Widener Industries, outside the superstar himself. His primary job was tending to the personal welfare of the human mint machine. Tycoons of the music business feared and courted him. Concert and record impresarios sought his favor. No one who wished to deal with Crack Widener—not even Widener's own brigade of lawyers, pool of tax advisors, covey of investment counselors, gaggle of music managers—none of all of these could expect an audience with Crack Widener, Superstar, until first cleared by Turk Savage.

Savage had first met Widener ten years ago, when the rock comet-to-be was a struggling singer-composer—under his true name, Stosh Widenowski—singing his original songs in a grubby St. Louis nightspot. When the owner put him on half-pay and Widenowski demanded his full salary, the owner unleashed two of his dogs of war to work the slender singer over.

Turk Savage, a part-time wrestler, was one of those dogs. Greatly impressed by the slightly built man's refusal to back down, Turk Savage laid off and left his sidekick to do the muscle work alone.

For a while Stosh peppered the much larger and stronger man with stinging jabs, but soon the muscleman's heavy artillery began to find its mark. A short, crunching right hand brought the gutsy singer to his knees, helpless. For reasons he never quite figured out, Turk Savage sucker-punched his own sidekick, taking him out with one blow, ending the fight . . . and starting a relationship that grew stronger and stronger with time.

Turk frowned at the whirling dancers. He wasn't fond of these "in house" costume parties and he couldn't wait to close this one down. Of course, he realized that public parties had become just about impossible for Crack Widener; whenever he made the scene he started a riot. At first, these private parties restricted to The Dirty Thirty and perhaps a few carefully screened guests had seemed like an answer. But then, in Rome, Crack played Nero, and he and his crew damn near burned the hotel down. Since then things hadn't gotten any better. Tonight, the theme was The Crusades, with Crack playing Richard the Lion-Hearted, and it definitely was *not* one of his Greatest Hits. Not by Turk Savage. Earlier in the evening, the Lion-Hearted one had become angry because one of his "courtiers" had blown his lines and started wielding his sword wildly, nearly decapitating the lead guitarist in his band, until Turk grabbed the sword from his hand. Crack Widener had stormed off to his room followed by four beauteous handmaidens.

TURK SAVAGE stepped from the shadows and signaled to the guard inside the double doors of the suite. Immediately, the music stopped and the lights went up. "Take it to your rooms," he said.

The mass of bodies headed for the exits, grabbing up loose bits of clothing as they went. Turk's cold gray eyes scanned the big room. They warmed a bit as they reached the black dancer. She caught his glance, paused at the door and threw him an inviting smile.

"Teasing bitch," he said, half aloud. He had a yen for her, but she was untouchable, one of four in The Dirty

Thirty stamped "Private Stock," for Widener's exclusive use. He followed her departure, then sighed. It had been a long and grueling day, starting with Crack's tantrum over the eggs not coming from a duck, later walking out of a recording session because the sound didn't measure up to his expectations. And now, King Crack was sulking in his tent, madder than ever after the sword episode.

Tomorrow, the entourage would wing it by Concorde to Washington, D.C., where Crack would fulfill a previously postponed concert commitment—a one-night stand. Then it was off to Los Angeles for a pow-wow with the brass of Silver Streak Records—a subsidiary of Crack Widener Industries. Then Australia. Crack loved Australia. Especially the girls. Half of the young women making up the female contingent of The Dirty Thirty were Aussies. Crack spent February and March of every year Down Under on the 2,000-acre C. W. Ranch, his pride and joy.

Turk Savage pressed a button on his walkie-talkie and from within the master bedroom suite a buzz sound was heard by a very small man lying on a burgundy leather couch in the anteroom outside the master bedroom. He was dressed in a jester's cap and bells. He picked up his walkie-talkie and spoke, "Everything's cool here, Turk. Crack's wide awake . . . still pissed . . . but the broads will douse his fire. They always do."

This tiny man was Crack Widener's personal secretary, but in essence he doubled as nursemaid and frequent roommate, advisor, procurer of women—and Widener's private punching bag.

The only thing they had in common was the fact that they both came from the same neighborhood turf in the St. Louis slums, and shared the memory of what it was like to be hungry and forgotten.

Constantly humiliated because of his size, he vowed to take on anyone, man or woman, who called him dwarf or midget, again. When Crack himself decided to test him, the little guy went for an ankle and bit him. He was called Impy ever since.

Now, as he lay back on the couch and gazed up at the mirrored ceiling, half-listening to Crack's latest composition coming from a stereo set, he wished Crack would get to sleep so that he could retire to his own bedroom for some much needed shut-eye of his own.

The sensuous sounds coming from the open door into Crack's bedroom didn't bother him. For him, these scenes could never be anything more than a spectator sport, for Crack Widener *never* shared. Impy had trained himself to shut his eyes and ears, and besides, by now the whole thing was old hat.

Studying his reflection in the ceiling mirror, something odd caught his eye. It was a book, on the small table next to the walkie-talkie. There'd been no book on the table moments before. He was sure. There were never any books in the suite. Crack forbade it. He lay there, wondering what he'd been smoking to create such an illusion. He looked away, but his eye was constantly drawn back to the reflection of the book. Finally, he could resist no longer; he reached over to the table and picked up the book. It had a royal purple dust jacket and the gold lettering read: *The Lawyers of Hell.*

He opened it and started to read: *"And God has existed for all eternity. And God Created Souls in His image. And one such Soul conceived the idea for man's existence."*

He continued reading, unaware that the blond-haired superstar had emerged from his oversized waterbed and vas staring at him from the doorway with wrathful eyes.

"What are you reading?" Crack Widener asked in hat familiar husky voice.

Impy was startled beyond speech, tongue-tied.

"I said, what the shit are you reading?"

"A book, Crack . . . a book."

"What kind of book?"

"Isn't it yours?" Impy asked, confused.

"A funny book?" Crack asked, ignoring his question.

"I . . . I don't think so, Crack. Religious . . . a eligious book."

"Religion's funny. Read it. *Out loud.* And you'd etter be a scream."

Impy eyed the famous face, searching for sympathy, ut the green-blue eyes held no compassion.

"C'mon in here . . . and *read*!" Widener returned to he waterbed in his room and the four lovelies arranged hemselves around him in a sort of floral design. Impy at down gingerly in a chair near the door with the book n his lap as the girls smirked at him viciously. How hey loved to see the little guy thrown into the torture hamber by King Crack!

"Get on with it, Impy. And you'd better make it good. Your number at King Crack's Court left a hell of a lot o be desired."

He wished Crack wouldn't humiliate him in front of people—make him out a total clown in the presence of the girls. After all, he was the guy charged with hiring them! He started to read, very softly.

"Louder, I can't hear you," snarled Crack, playfully jabbing one of the girls.

Distraught, he read louder, but his voice broke, rising almost an octave higher.

"You fucking dwarf, I still can't hear you."

The girls' laughter goaded him into shouting th
words: "All the Souls in Heaven stirred in anticipation
Before Almighty God, two great Souls debated over th
heralded event: the creation of man . . ."

He paused to catch his breath, as Crack thundered
"You're not *funny.* I'm not laughing."

"C'mon, Impy, make us laugh," an auburn-haire
lovely called out.

Resigned to playing the fool, he stood on the chair an
in a mocking, lisping tone, read, "And Michael, wh
championed man's creation, challenged Lucifer fo
daring to defy God's will . . ."

"Who's Michael?" asked one of the girls.

"Tell her who he is," Crack Widener said, smilin
faintly.

"Who is Michael?" Impy asked. "An angel, dear lad
. . . an angel who got tired of Lucifer fucking with him."

The girls giggled. Crack Widener only smiled as th
jester read on in his clownish voice: "And Michae
spoke to all in Heaven . . . that though Almighty Go
gave us a will that is free, it has had no significan
purpose, until this creation of man . . ." He closed th
book, leapt off the chair and said, "Which means . .
that all the angels in Heaven could jerk off to thei
hearts' content."

The girls laughed again. He went on, "You got to
picture it . . . Heaven . . . all the Angels . . . and there's
God, presiding over one big circle jerk."

The girls laughed, louder this time. And even Crac
Widener couldn't hold back a big smile.

"What about the girl angels?" one of the lovelie
inquired.

"There's only boy angels . . . *darling.*"

"He's wrong," the girl staunchly disagreed.

"Whadda you mean *I'm* wrong? What would a half-wit like you know?"

She looked at Crack, who gave her a nod to continue. She did so, revealing Bible teachings in her past. "Adam and Eve had two sons."

"Cain and Abel," another girl added.

"Yeah, and Cain knocked off Abel, so what?" said the imp, hurrying her along.

She looked at Crack with protesting eyes. "He doesn't know what I'm getting at."

Crack's face matched his voice. Hard, grim. "Let her finish, then you answer."

Satisfied, the girl went on. "How did Cain have a family? I was told he made it with an angel. A *female* angel."

Another girl, the auburn-haired one, the sexiest of the lot, fell backwards on the bed, her long, willowy legs sticking up in the air. "Wow, can you imagine Crack humping an angel?"

He turned to her indulgently—obviously she was his favorite—and gave her an affectionate slap on her tight little rump, saying, "Isn't your dear self an angel?"

She swarmed all over him, thrusting the other girls aside, her sleek body moving seductively, slithering over his. Then Crack whispered in her ear and her body became still. A tight-lipped Widener told Impy to read on.

The court jester did so, soberly: "Man shall introduce faith. Something we in heaven know nothing about. Unlike man, we have never been tested. Our wills have been used sparingly in a kingdom that knows only eternal ecstasy. Man shall not see the Face of God . . ." he looked up—pleadingly at Crack Widener. "Jesus, Crack, this is heavy stuff."

"Read!"

"Make it funny," a girl angrily demanded.

"Shut your face!" Crack turned on her. His eyes slowly shifted. *"You read it straight,"* he commanded the imp.

Surprised by Crack's sudden switch, he read on: "That man shall love The Father and obey rules without physically knowing Him, shall make man more blessed than we . . ."

The room, its glass ceiling, plaster walls, cork floor, the chairs, the tables, the bed—all shook. A slight, but definite tremor! The book in the imp's hands grew suddenly, unnaturally heavy. He looked down at the floor and felt the rumbling under his feet, then raised his startled glance. Crack sat rigid, eyes frozen. The beautiful faces about him, clouded by fright, were turning a clammy gray.

"Crack . . . what is—"

Crack placed a finger to a frightened girl's lips as the vibrations increased. Now the lights flickered on and off.

In the midst of the violent shaking, the cries and clutchings of the girls, Crack Widener sat deathly still, as if in a trance. One of the girls seized his leg in panic, her long nails driving deep into his flesh. He gave no sign, feeling nothing.

The wooden legs of the bedframe cracked and then the whole frame collapsed and the waterbed was adrift on the heaving floor, like a raft on a choppy sea. Crack Widener's eyes remained fixed on the French doors leading onto the terrace. It was as though he was waiting for something—a thing unknown.

Now a wind of hurricane force swept into the room. Furniture flew wildly about. The walls buckled and great chunks of plaster fell, leaving gaping holes. Impy, huddled in a corner, felt the book torn loose from his hands, as if the wind had fingers. The mirrored ceiling above shattered and fell, loosing a shower of wicked, glittering daggers.

A girl, blood pouring from a wound in her scalp, ran blindly from the waterbed across the floor and was flung by the wind against the remnants of the wall and fell unconscious. The girls remaining with Widener on the bed were flung about like rag dolls, but still he sat, staring fixedly ahead.

For another minute, the wind raged, tearing at the room. Only the feeble moan of someone in pain could be heard. Crack Widener lifted his bruised body from what had once been a waterbed, still gazing toward the terrace. From where he crouched, nursing a bloody hand, Impy whispered Crack's name.

THEN IT HAPPENED. Beyond the terrace windows, thrown open by the wind, a great light appeared. Crack Widener stared at its incredible, brightening beauty until it grew too powerful to look upon. He shaded his eyes. From the center of blazing light, there shot forth tongues of fire, each tongue exploding into a fiery word—words spoken by a voice to chill the heart of the bravest man:

THAT . . . MAN'S . . . SOUL . . . SHALL . . . NOT . . . KNOW . . . HIS . . . GOD . . . AS . . . DO . . . WE . . . IS . . . DANGEROUS . . . TO . . . THE . . . FATHER.

The overwhelming light vanished. Nothing remained beyond the windows, except the darkness of night.

Now Impy could hear Turk Savage and others pounding on the outer door and calling to them. But still Crack Widener stood, eyes blurred, listening. This time, the sound came faintly to his ears:

*Man's soul shall enter Heaven garlanded with praise. Man's reward from the Father shall be greater than our own . . .*

TURK SAVAGE took the fire axe from the man's hand and drove it into the heavy oaken door. With the second blow, it suddenly gave way. He charged blindly in, a .38 in one hand, the axe in the other. He tried the light switch but the room remained dark. He called Crack Widener's name, again and again.

In the darkness, over the feeble moaning of an injured girl, Impy called, "Get a doctor."

The rescue operation, once it started, was swift and efficient. Auxiliary lights lit the bedroom. Three girls were carried off to the hospital. Miraculously, no one had been fatally injured. Impy and the fourth girl were given first aid on the spot; they sat outside the shattered room, waiting for Crack Widener, who had refused all medical attention and seemed lost within himself. Cosmic.

Seated in a chair outside the bedroom, he kept repeating to himself, "I've been touched by the hand of God."

Turk Savage, who'd been engaged in battle with the hotel management, rushed into the room, to announce that the press were right on his heels. Turk took one look at the dazed Crack Widener sitting in the nude, blood trickling from his brow, and rushed to his side. He looked into strange eyes, eyes that had tripped to some far-off world.

"The bathroom, Crack. I've got to hide you in the bathroom."

Life gradually came back into the blue-green eyes. He

was back. Grasping Turk Savage's arms, he said, "God. It was God Himself. The Hand of God has touched me." He then released his grip and let Turk lead him to the bathroom and safety.

The wounded Impy, watching them leave, shook his head and said aloud to himself: "Touched by God . . . the Hand of God, he says. My ass . . . it was the Hand of The Devil!"

PAUL BARTLEY rushed headlong into John Gallogly's office. "Is that Myrna Reardon I just saw? *The* Myrna Reardon?"

"It is."

"What's she doing in a huddle with Terrible Tummy?"

"Must you constantly refer to His Eminence as Terrible Tummy?"

Bartley's eyes flashed surprise. His irreverence, if not encouraged, had always been indulged by his friend John. He eased furtively onto the small couch, clutching a small envelope in his hand. "Touchy, aren't we?"

". . . With good reason!"

Paul Bartley lit up a Winston. "How *good* a reason, John? *Good,* in the eternal sense, I mean. Ever since you got back from Bimini, you've seemed changed. What really happened down there? Did Fatso fake you out with the 'good ole boy' routine? 'Someday you'll be a bishop, my son,' and all the rest of that establishment blarney?"

"Have you something for me, Paul?"

Bartley took some newsclips from the manila envelope. "It's more of the same, John. The critics are intrigued by Ron Rebuck's theory. *Atlanta Journal:* 'A COSMIC CLEANSING OF THE MIND.' *Chicago Tribune:* 'Stimulating, significant . . .' *Los Angeles Times:* 'A new vision of Man and God and the angels . . . powerful and positive . . . a book that could change the world!' "

He looked up. "One thing's sure. All of these critics are in accord that Mr. Rebuck's book is *important.*"

"Rebuck's book is being reviewed!" Gallogly said in a half-whisper.

"Speaking to me, John?"

"To myself, Paul . . . to myself."

"Might I say you've been doing that quite frequently of late?"

"You've already said it."

"I did, didn't I? So, what's your reaction to the reviews?"

"I'll reserve judgment till the heavyweights have their say—*Commonweal, Christian Century, Commentary* . . ."

"The egghead clerics! Take 'em all together and they don't reach more than fifty thousand fuddyduds in backward collars and funny hats. The *L.A. Times* and the *Chicago Trib* reach the real people—the ones who make revolutions—and they reach them in the millions."

"Paul, let's get on with it. Got anything else, any hard news to show me?"

He took another clipping from inside his jacket pocket: "It bombed in Boston." He read from the clipping, " 'Sacrilegious slop,' says the critic Bud Burns in his headline. He goes on to say: 'Ron Rebuck, whoever Ron Rebuck *is,* would have us believe God never conceived the idea of man. That an angel . . . or soul, Michael, the same great angel we know to have driven Lucifer from Heaven, was the true conceiver, the one whose idea it was for man's existence. To our knowledge, Mr. Rebuck has no standing as a theologian, nor has he published any previous books. His thesis is sheer fantasy, offensive in tone . . . latter-day lunacy and hardly a threat to the Holy Bible.' "

He raised his eyes and looked at Gallogly. "It sure doesn't take a whole lot of smarts to realize the fix was on. Obviously Mr. Burns isn't about to rock the boat. Not unless he wants to have those influential Boston Irish, that great corps of Catholic warriors, on his ass. One thing for sure, he'd never get buried in any Catholic cemetery."

Through it all, John Gallogly hadn't cracked a smile.

Frustration showed on Paul Bartley's face. He leaned back on the couch. "Jesus, what does it take to get a laugh out of you?"

"There's nothing funny about this matter."

He studied the face. It was drawn, the eyes sunken with fatigue. "Johnny, like it or not, you look terrible. No joke, I'm seeing a man who's aged ten years."

"That bad?"

"What happened? Did someone slip old-age pills in your wine? People go to places like Bimini for relaxation, to soothe their nerves. Take it slow and easy. But you've come back a wreck."

"Sorry Paul, I didn't realize it."

"Sorry? That's the best I get? Come off it, we're supposed to be friends. And friends don't hide things from each other. . . . Something screwy's going on around here. Would you believe the vicar general hasn't chewed me out for days? Even the Cardinal realizes I'm alive. Hell, everybody knows I'm eccentric, but all this peaceful co-existence will turn me into a babbling idiot. Tell me, this sudden change toward me, are they fattening me up for the kill? Am I to be the sacrificial lamb? And you, my buddy, who hasn't smiled for days, how did you ever convince the Cardinal to go all out on this Rebuck fellow? And what kind of miracle did it take for him to permit *me* to assist you in whatever the hell you're doing? . . . Johnny . . . what's happening?"

John Gallogly's devoted secretary appeared at the door. "Excuse me, Monsignor, the Cardinal would like you to join him."

He thanked her and rose from behind the desk. "Let's go, Paul."

*"Me?"*

"No better time to find out what's going on."

CARDINAL SPELLISSY shifted his great weight and looked away from the disturbed woman seated across the desk. It wasn't his custom to grant audiences to gossip columnists, but Myrna's family were staunch supporters of the Church, and Myrna had brought in many princely contributions from the titans of show business. He eyed Myrna's male companion—a stocky man with thinning hair—with suspicion, then clasped his plump hands together, as Myrna exclaimed, "Cardinal Spellissy, am I going crazy? Could all this be really happening to me?"

He met her eyes, pleading eyes, void of their usual toughness. "My dear Myrna, I am not a psychiatrist. At least not a licensed practitioner." Dissatisfaction showed on her face. She had expected more. Much more. Spiritual guidance, at least.

He rubbed at his dimpled chin. "Music, you say?"

"From nowhere."

"Letters?"

"From no one."

"Strange writings on your walls?"

"That vanish."

"And no visions of gargoyles, or demons? Not even elves?"

"Cardinal Spellissy, are you now making fun of me?"

"A little touch of humor, dear lady. Nothing more."

JOHN GALLOGLY, followed by an uneasy Paul Bartley, entered the room. The Cardinal grunted out the introductions, neglecting to include Paul Bartley and having trouble with the name of the man with Myrna. Pico? Marty Pico.

He came from behind the desk, and signaled all to gather around the fireplace.

They sat about the open fire. That is, all save Paul Bartley. This sudden acceptance, being recognized as something more than a lamp or chair, was too much, too soon; he stood in the background.

"Father Bartley, would you mind fetching me a cigar?" the Cardinal asked.

Was he truly hearing right? Would you *mind*? Paul Bartley marveled in thought as he went about his errand.

The Cardinal squirmed in the lofty chair until finding a comfortable position. Then he addressed Myrna, "I've asked Monsignor Gallogly here to join us . . . his presence is most essential."

She gave John Gallogly a quizzical look as Paul Bartley handed the long Cuban cigar to the Cardinal. He nodded his thanks and continued, "I would like you to repeat everything you told me. Speak freely, and rest assured it shall all be treated in the strictest of confidence."

"Like confession," Paul Bartley added, softly.

"Father Bartley, there are enough statues in this room. Kindly become seated." The Cardinal then looked at John Gallogly, hopelessly.

Myrna Reardon was fast losing patience. "Cardinal Spellissy, perhaps my coming here was a mistake."

"To the contrary. To the contrary, dear lady. It's quite possible that you and Monsignor Gallogly share something in common."

"I hardly think so," Myrna replied, unbelieving.

"Well, let us be the judge of that."

"Judge? . . . Judge of what? That . . . that someone's doing their damnedest to send me to the cuckoo's nest? Can you tell me the producer's name?" She pointed a finger at Marty Pico. "He can't. And I'm paying him a fortune to find out." She stood up. "Every . . . every time I think of what's happening to me I feel like the brat in *The Exorcist.*" Her voice grew shrill. "Two shrinks, the best in Beverly Hills, a detective, and they're baffled. Can't *anyone* give me a logical explanation?"

The twinkle was gone from the Cardinal's eyes. "If you sit down and dispense with the theatrics, we just might do that!"

Instinctively she turned on him, her teeth bared, and glared into that vast moon face. No one ever spoke to her in such a fashion. Certainly not a man. But this was no ordinary man. They dueled a moment, silently, and then she withdrew. There'd be no argument. She'd been called down, recognizing that special breed of tough Irishman—her own father had been one of them.

John Gallogly cleared his throat and cut into the edgy

silence, saying, "Mr. Pico, from what I've gathered you're a detective."

"Right. Private. Got my own agency."

"Here in New York?"

"Right. Couple of blocks away." He took a card from a leather wallet and handed it to John Gallogly.

"Business good?" Paul Bartley asked.

Pico smiled. "Not bad."

The Cardinal grumbled, and that was that.

John Gallogly picked it up. "Mr. Pico, were you on the premises during these strange occurrences?"

Marty Pico looked at the subdued woman first, then softly answered, "No."

"Was anybody—other than *Miss* Reardon herself?"

Again, Pico stalled, irritating the Cardinal. "Mr. Pico, you are Myrna's investigator, are you not?"

"Huh? Sure . . . I mean yes, yes sir, I am."

"Then would you mind answering the Monsignor's questions?"

Throughout his adult life Marty Pico was awed only by power. Great power. And for him, the same Italian kid who stole wafers from the rectory at St. Finbars church in Brooklyn to be now in the presence, and in fact be talking with a powerful prince of the Catholic Church . . . he couldn't get rid of the butterflies in his paunch stomach. "Your Majesty, I mean your Cardinalship . . . my client . . . I'm not sure she'd like me to get into . . . personal things."

Myrna Reardon brightened. "What horseshit! By now, he's probably told every goomba in the city." She looked at the Monsignor, flushing slightly. "I was shacking with a young man. His name's Bill Coleman. An actor. And yes, he was there in my apartment. But he was in the other bedroom when it all happened. Does that answer your question?"

"I'll say," Paul Bartley exclaimed.

The Cardinal ignored him as John Gallogly pressed on, "Have you spoken with the man, Mr. Pico?"

"Yeah, but he didn't hear any band playing. And he didn't know nothin' about the letter."

"This letter, did you examine it?"

"He did," said Myrna, "and I was with him when he checked for fingerprints."

"Were there any?" John Gallogly asked Marty Pico, steering the line of interrogation away from Myrna.

"Sure. Myrna's, the young dude's she spoke about, and mine."

"Do you have the letter on you?"

"Myrna burned it."

"The envelope too?"

"The envelope too."

"I see." John Gallogly paused, then said, "Mr. Pico, as a detective, have you reached any conclusions?"

Marty Pico puffed up, trying to look important. "Damn right I do . . ." He blushed, "Sorry, Your Worship," he apologized to the Cardinal, who looked at him oddly, ". . . I've told Myrna who's in back of all this but she doesn't buy it."

"He's got some cockeyed notion about a producer I had words with. Such nonsense. And to think I'm paying *him* good money." She looked away, disgusted.

"Mr. Pico," said the Cardinal, "tell us more of what *you* think." He shot Myrna a warning look, "and, hopefully, *without* interruptions."

Marty Pico seemed to enjoy the spotlight. "Well, everything's got to have a beginning. No exceptions."

Paul Bartley was tempted to ask him about God, but wisely refrained.

"Well, like I say, everything has a beginning and Myrna's troubles started when she had words with this guy, Manning."

"Manning's the producer?" John Gallogly asked.

"Rufus Manning, bad dude. Made one of those black pictures. Made a bundle off it. Yeah, he's nasty."

"You speak as if you've had a run in with the man."

"Hey, Monsignor, you're all right. You should get into the investigation racket. I could use a sharp guy like you."

"Will you get on with it?" Myrna growled.

". . . To answer your question, yeah, I had the mispleasure." Marty Pico then sneered, "He had his day, but nothin' like the rumble I got in store for him."

"I don't give a crap about your problem. We're supposed to be solving mine." Myrna was now beside herself.

"Quite right, Myrna," said the Cardinal. "Mr. Pico, would you kindly get on with your conclusions?"

"Sure, sorry, I got carried away. Well anyway, this guy Manning threatened Myrna at a New Year's party. Big deal on Sutton Place. Hughie Gilman's penthouse. Familiar with the name? He's Myrna's attorney. A big league guy."

"I'm sure," said John Gallogly, wishing he'd dispense with the adjectives.

"The very next morning, Myrna started with the headaches. Get the drift?"

"I think so," said John Gallogly.

"I'm glad you do, Monsignor, for I sure as hell don't." She looked at the Cardinal. "Manning's a producer, not a magician."

"Producers hire magicians," Pico defended.

She looked at him with a sorry expression. "Pico,

you're really a putz."

"Told you she didn't buy my theory."

The Cardinal continued. "Myrna, at this New Year's party, did you happen to have unfriendly words, a quarrel with anyone else?"

She had to think. "Pintoff. Jack Pintoff."

"The advertising man?" The Cardinal was familiar with the name.

"The advertising *ass*." She frowned, searching her mind for other possibilities. "I did get sore at Walter Hardy."

"Walter was at this party?"

"Cardinal Spellissy, Walter would go anywhere as long as there's a crowd to hear him show off his authoritative intellect."

The Cardinal smiled. He knew Walter Hardy intimately. A true champ of the church. "I gather you and Walter had some differences?"

"No, not really. I did get miffed at him for taking on some unknown. How would it be if word spread Walter Hardy got licked in a debate by some total stranger?"

"Licked? Walter, licked?" The Cardinal was intrigued. "The topic, was of a political nature, of course?"

"Religious."

Paul Bartley could not be restrained. "Walter Hardy on the short end in a debate over religion? No chance."

"Believe it or not, Walter was tongue-tied until I came around to break it up."

John Gallogly's brows furrowed. "Myrna, this man who Mr. Hardy debated, what did he look like?"

"Look like? Well-built, I suppose and—the eyes, peculiar eyes. Come to think of it, Walter was actually quite leery of the man. Wanted no part of him, but his pride got the best of him. As always, he had to get into the ring and take on all comers."

The same thought lit up like a high-powered mazda lamp in the heads of the three priests simultaneously. John Gallogly was the first to give it voice: "Do you happen to know the man's name?"

"Roger . . . Raymond . . . Roland? I forget. But what I do remember is that he's a friend of that horrid producer, Manning."

Marty Pico pulled out a black notebook. "I've got his name somewhere. I got everyone's name who's connected with Manning. Let's see . . ." He flipped a half dozen pages, then stopped. "Rebuck, Ron Rebuck, that's his name."

The silence was electric. John Gallogly's eyes were locked on the Cardinal. Paul Bartley sat, lost in thought.

The Cardinal now lit his cigar and blew out the first puff in slow deliberate fashion.

A bewildered Myrna Reardon could sense the mounting tension in the room, all generated by the mere mention of that name. *Rebuck . . . was it a cabalistic word of some devil cult . . . a password to some kind of superpowered black magic?*

It was the Cardinal who broke the grim, high-tension silence.

Said he, in the famous organ-tones: "The plot thickens."

# 18

JACK PINTOFF was hypnotized by Jennifer Jewell's presence before him. He sat there, in the Polynesian fan chair in the living room of his East Side brownstone thinking how long ago it was since anything so beautiful wished to see *him*. Hunched of back, his head permanently tilted to the side, he was the Beast that gazed upon Beauty, as his swollen eyes took in the sultry face. Those magnificent eyes, so green, catlike. The full rich lips belonging to a perfectly formed mouth. And when she spoke, the glistening whiteness of her teeth, all too forbidden for the likes of himself—a face on loan from a chamber of horrors.

He'd coaxed her into shedding her boots when she'd arrived and now she crossed those long, limber, silky legs, giving him a glimpse of upper thigh. He could feel the heat rising in his body, the throbbing in his organ, the burning of his blood. This could not go on.

A thunder of reality shocked his anguished system and once again that curtained mind slammed shut—returning to its natural suspicious state. Why was she here? Truly here? A matter of the gravest importance was all she would say on the phone. What could someone so beautiful need of him? Someone he'd only seen at Hughie Gilman's party. Could she truly know of his innermost desire for the whole fucking world to go up in a ball of fire? . . . What possible gravity could stem from a book?

"Miss Jewell . . . I make it a point never to read a new book till I've checked Drew Bonds' review."

"I can assure you his review will be more than favorable."

A crafty smile came to his twisted lips. "It's most difficult to disagree with someone as lovely as you, but I know at first hand, Drew Bonds allows no one to see his critiques until the day of publication."

"Mr. Pintoff, he will give *The Lawyers of Hell* a splendid review." She was too sure. The tone of voice, so utterly positive.

"And . . . you know this for a fact?"

"Yes, I do."

"Am I to believe the irreproachable Drew Bonds has been bought?" The smile widened. "Perhaps he fell to the wishes of a Salome?"

"If Salome is his wife."

Jack Pintoff coughed in laughter. "Ah, such beauty, but truly naive. Jane Bonds happens to be a confirmed drunk. Once a beautiful woman like yourself but now a hag soon doomed by cirrhosis of the liver." He seemed to take joy in this. The next moment his puffy eyes turned suspicious. "Why have you come? Certainly not to peddle a book."

She uncrossed her legs, revealing a pair of perfect knees. "Mr. Pintoff, I'm here to recruit you."

"Recruit *me*? How marvelous. And for what, may I ask?"

"Your expertise as a star builder. The way you have taken people, complete unknowns, and made them into famous names."

"And how would a pretty thing like you know about that?"

"I've made it a point to find out. Let's not be bashful, Mr. Pintoff, it's no secret that you're the best in the business."

"*Was.* I am out of the monster-making racket these days. You see I can afford the luxury of spitting at this world without holding an umbrella." He came out of the chair, a memory at work. "You are a friend of the gutter-rat, Rufus Manning?"

She smiled, amused. "An acquaintance."

"And this Ron Rebuck, he's *also* an acquaintance?"

The face tightened, her eyes narrowed. "No, Mr. Pintoff, I'm devoted to the man."

"Devotion, such a word."

"I don't understand."

He shot her a disbelieving look. "The manner in which you left the New Year's party, touching. Reminded me of a love-struck teen-ager."

"I think you got the wrong impression."

"Did I?" He got up and moved behind her. His pudgy hands rested on the back of the chair. He said nothing.

"Mr. Pintoff, would you mind? I feel uncomfortable with someone looking over my shoulder."

He mumbled something inaudible, then slowly returned to the fan chair. "You surprise me, Miss Jewell. I've a face that hardly grows on someone. Such tolerance. Do you pity me?"

"If you read Ron Rebuck's book, you would be able to look past one's physical body and be aware of the beautiful soul that's within."

"*Words.* Words without substance. And might I add, quite unoriginal."

"Not true," she protested.

"Oh, *please*, Miss Jewell, every faked-out religious follower of someone or other talks about a soul."

"People who don't understand. Ron Rebuck does."

"Billy Hale and the rest of those clowns for Christ, they don't understand?"

"Ron Rebuck is the only living person who truly understands the soul's relationship with its body. He alone has entered the unknown and come back with the truth. He *is* Michael's Messenger."

Pintoff's ugly smile returned. The reason behind her visit was clear. "*Now* dawns the picture. My compliments to *both* of you. Apparently I was too captivated by your beauty to realize it sooner."

She looked at him questioningly as he again rose from the chair, a mind convinced, then limped toward the fireplace. "Ron Rebuck, another Elmer Gantry, and you, an even more beautiful Sister Sarah. Not very original but what is these days? Ah, yes: look out world, a new act is on the loose in search of 'In God We Trust.' " He wheezed a laugh.

Anger flared in her eyes. "You couldn't be more wrong."

He turned and snarled, "*Wrong*? Jack Pintoff is never wrong. Didn't your research tell you that?"

"My research told me Jack Pintoff was not one to duck a challenge."

"*Challenge*? You call making stars out of you and Ron Rebuck, a challenge?" He laughed, sneering, "Any half-ass agency could get the pair of you across. All you need is money."

He lifted his eyes to gaze at the rows of pictures hung above the fireplace, then glanced above them to where a large golden frame hung alone—empty. "Recognize these notables?"

His question drew her to the fireplace, where she scanned a long row of familiar people. Actors, actresses, TV personalities, all with written inscriptions of gratitude to Jack Pintoff. "Like Dante, my seven steps to hell. The first row . . . the egomaniacs. All heading for the big fall.'' He pointed to a most familiar face. ''Curt Mallory, here. Thanks to yours truly, today he gets a half million per film plus a percentage of the gross. Such is the way of the world,'' he snickered. ''Curt Mallory, the dear boy, hasn't a trace of talent. He kicked around New York, going nowhere, when this agent got the bright idea the movie world was ripe for a macho bastard.''

Jennifer Jewell smiled, recalling the nude centerfold that had propelled him to stardom. ''Did you—''

''Put him into the women's magazine without his jock? None other.'' He followed her eyes to the next level of pictures. She recognized some of the politicians. ''The fabulous fabricators,'' he announced, ''they'd think nothing of having a sexual affair with the very person they'd condemned to die.''

Her eyes looked above his gallery of glossy photos to the frame without a picture. Curious, she wanted to ask the reason but felt he would eventually come to that. Right now she became alarmed over the manner in which he was speaking of his clients. So condemning. Strange, since he'd played a crucial part in making them famous.

As he went on to describe the remaining rows, he became more and more incensed. As if he truly hated these people. Suddenly, the tone changed from hatred to excitement. ''See the man to the far corner? The picture on the top row?''

She nodded, taking in the photo of a Latin looking individual, thirtyish, with Afro hair, a lean, deadly serious face.

''Enrico Rodriguez Gonzalez,'' he said, pridefully.

''He looks familiar. But I can't associate the name.''

''Perhaps you know him as Henry Rodriguez.''

". . . Puerto Rican . . . The communist leader?"

"Himself. Now there's a man who will stop at nothing to accomplish his dream."

"What's that?" she asked, biting the bait.

"My dear, Henry Rodriguez's greatest desire is to bring the United States to its capitalistic knees."

"You're joking."

"One doesn't joke about Rodriguez. He's a born revolutionary. Another Fidel Castro with an even bigger appetite. Believes himself to be the reincarnation of Lenin. Foolish, of course."

"Especially reincarnation," she spitefully added.

"Unfortunately, his biggest handicap comes from the fact he's Latin. They're so unpredictable. At most, I give him another year before they murder him. A shame, he has such great promise."

She pointed to the mysterious empty frame, asking, "Is there some reason, some special significance to that?"

"Ah . . . you are speaking of the ultimate." The dull eyes lit up. "*That*, my ravishing beauty, is reserved for greatness. That unparalleled individual, man or woman, who shall reach the stars and bring down the very sun." He paused, as if for effect. "Untainted, fearless, such is the great destroyer."

"The great destroyer," she echoed, "how morbid." All this talk of gloom, despair. How could anyone have so much hate? She strolled back to her chair, wondering why Ron Rebuck would select this man. She wished to get on with it, bring it all to a head and leave him with his death wish for the world.

"Have I somehow offended you?" he asked, sheepishly.

"No, Mr. Pintoff. Not me . . . *yourself.*"

He left the fireplace and approached. He pulled up a footstool and sat at her feet. "Miss Jewell, obviously your research did not include any of Rufus Manning's input, for if it did you'd know that I dislike people. Dislike them immensely. Speak to me of tragedy and you shall gain my undivided attention."

"That's . . . horrible. Ugly."

"What could you know about ugly? You, the envy of women and the dreams of men."

She looked at him, at this genetically cursed man, and the challenge to convert him, to fulfill her initial act as Ron Rebuck's emissary, fueled her with new life. There would be no retreating on her part. She was utterly committed. No falling back on an Arabian sheik. Two days before she'd severed all ties with Aly Sharif, and the sheik had been more than generous in his unsolicited settlement.

Words came, flamed with determination. "What must I do to get you to read Ron Rebuck's book?"

Spawning a gruesome smile, he drew closer, placing a grimy hand on her knee. Instinctively, she withdrew her legs only to bring a scowl to his face. "Words, you're nothing but words. What happened to all that crap about my beautiful soul?"

"Mr. Pintoff–"

"Who sent you, Manning?"

"Ron Rebuck, requested–"

"*Manning*. Rufus Manning sent you. How much is he paying for you to come here and frustrate me? To leave me madder than I already am?"

"It's nothing of the kind. I came here on behalf of Ron Rebuck, to solicit your expertise."

His face tightened with fervency, the eyes flared, wildly, when the twisted mouth opened, challenging, "Prove it. Prove you're not all talk."

"Prove it? How must I prove it?"

Before her shocked eyes he dropped to the floor and reached for her. Her knees now pressed against his chest. Too stunned to react her entire body twinged as his hands touched her legs. A quivering came to her lower lip as she felt his hands moving up, under her dress, along her thigh. She squirmed in the chair but the surprisingly strong hands kept her prisoner. She made a desperate attempt to rise, but his arms locked around her legs, pinning her from the waist down. Reality ignited her defensive mechanism. She was being forcibly held against her wishes, and by whom? A man even prostitutes were reluctant to trick. Her mind flashed with lightning thoughts but uncertainty yet showed in her eyes. Her dress was now up to her waist, and his breathing was loud, interspersed with moans. He was building toward frenzy. Soon, not a thousand screaming banshees could break his hold. Swiftly, he grasped the waistband of her panty hose, then jerked it down and over her hips. She slapped him hard across the ear but this only drove him deeper into madness. What to do? He was beyond the stage of reason, and the moans were sickening.

Distraught, she made the mistake of relaxing her body as he tugged at the hose, bringing it down to her ankles. Before she could react, one leg was free of the nylon. And now he was reaching for the pink satin panties. She brought up a knee, smashing it into his face. He howled like a wounded animal, then savagely tore at her panties, shredding them apart.

Now he was fighting to pry her legs apart, as she kicked and grabbed, and yanked his kinky hair. The harder she pulled the more he howled in crazed ecstasy.

Then in an all-out effort to free herself of this clutching beast, she struck down at him with a flurry of punches and slaps upon his head and shoulders. His eyes glazed with madness, taking the blows freely without defending himself. He looked like a mad dog, saliva forming at the corners of his mouth, as he rejoiced in his pain, repeatedly calling out, "My queen, my queen!"

Sapped of strength, she could no longer fight him off. Tears came to her eyes as he drove his face toward her pubic mound. Then with a sudden jolting movement he propped her legs upright and buried his face in her silky crotch.

Twisting, squirming, she dug her nails into his back and neck. But, as before, he became even more inflamed. He opened his fly and jerked out a stiff and pulsating cock, then proceeded to ejaculate while his tenacious mouth was savagely kissing, licking, sucking. She tossed her head from side to side, her legs writhed and tightened around his neck, a spasm arched her toward the seeking mouth, as her body then surrendered to a thrusting tongue.

A BLUE LATE MODEL Chrysler Imperial with Jersey plates crawled past Jack Pintoff's brownstone, then double-parked before a church two buildings further down the street. Stepping from a doorway, the huge Richard got into the car.

Marty Pico stuck a Life Saver in his mouth, then greeted the giant with an unenthusiastic glance. "I'm busy, where is she?"

"She went into the brownstone."

Marty Pico looked over his shoulder and casually inspected the building in question. "The brownstone got a name?"

"Yeah. Dude named Pintoff."

"Pintoff? . . . Jack Pintoff?"

The giant Richard nodded, as Marty dropped another Life Saver. "Interesting . . . she splits from the Arab fortune cookie, waltzes away from Joe Movie, now hitches on to some advertising kook. Busy. Busy girl."

"What's shaking? How long I got to hang with the foxy lady?"

"Like a leech you stick with her, kapish? Eight on, eight off, you and Jukey, like revolving doors. Everything. Do you hear? Names, numbers, *everything* . . . Blow this one Richie Boy, and the *Vatican Empire* comes down on me."

"Wuch you jawing about? Man, Vatican *what*?"

"Never mind. You just keep those fucking sledge hammers in your pockets. Yah read me?"

The big guy gazed at him with contempt, but Marty wasn't intimidated by those large black scowling eyes. He grabbed onto his coat sleeve and shouted, "NO STOMPING!"

The giant shook off Marty's hand with a shrug of the arm, then started to get out of the car.

"Hey, Walio, where you goin'? . . . Hey, Richie, come on. We'll rap fer a while, all right?"

"You're busy."

"Hey, not too busy for my main man." He forced a chummy smile. "Look, I'm sorry I've been coming down hard on you, but blowing the sheik's monthly sugar puts a crunch on the overhead. Paying you, Jukey, those two *stugotts*, a secretary, the rent, phone . . . Hey, the cost of running a business these days—"

"You speaking to me, man?"

He looked beyond Marty, "See somebody else?"

"How many times I gotta hear you jiving about overhead? Save it fer those two jerk-off's you hired, don't jive me, turkey."

"You eating good?"

"Get down man, that tune's for the new recruits."

"All right. *All right.* You want it with hard nails, you got it. You worry me, Richie. Getting yourself sick over that spic, you ain't been thinking right. Thinking stupid. And stupidos get me nervous."

"I didn't see *your* dago ass get half frozen in some mother-fucking cemetery."

"What's a matter with you? You didn't see *The Godfather*? You didn't hear him say a vendetta is sweetest when it's cold?"

"Honkey flick with a bunch of wops shooting up the world. Jump a brother and we get it on when the blood's hot. The Soul way, turkey. And no intermission."

"*Jump*, that's all you know. No *smarts.* No wonder they didn't write any big book about a black Godfather. Now listen to me. Listen *good.* There's a big payday in the works. Could be I'm getting myself connected to a mint. The tax free kind. Right now Myrna Reardon's paying the freight because she's up to her ass in a ghost story, but the bottom line is what can happen through her." He beamed a smile, like a change of address. "Can you dig an office on Park?"

"Aw shit, man, you gonna feed me another one of your long shots to the stars? You got your name on the moon?"

". . . You want in or not?"

The big guy's nostrils flared. "Till the day you croak, *believe* I'm in for my piece."

"Then smarten up. Kick all that heavy talk about Mad Mike. He'll get his, the same time Manning gets his."

Big Richard weighed Marty's pledge. He'd lied to him before. Many times before. "Three weeks man, three weeks I been listening to your jive, and all I see is that motherfucker's face!"

"What, are you alone? You got some kind of private nightmare? I want Manning's ass, as bad as you got it in for Spenard, but goddamn your black skin, get it through that watermelon head . . . *not now*!!"

Marty Pico was never more sincere. He could never, even if he tried, forget the humiliation he'd endured at the cemetery. He had vowed that very day, before God and everything he deemed holy, including the good name of his late mother, that Rufus Manning would pay.

The big guy was almost believing him, when he noticed Jennifer coming out of the brownstone. "She's hit the street."

Marty Pico peered out the window to see Jennifer anxiously flagging down a cab. The big guy made a move to leave but Marty stuck out a restraining hand. "No time. She's in the cab. Get your car later. We can't afford to lose her." He started up the engine and waited until Jennifer's cab rolled by. "Yeah, sweet thing, take us to Ron Rebuck."

FROM A GRAY MORNING SKY, a light snow fell on the Shenandoah Hills. A rented yellow Pinto snailed over the treacherous mountain road. Behind the wheel, a cautious Leslie Manning cursed under her breath for letting herself be talked into something she knew would result in nothing but grief. Next to her, John Milton coolly tinkered with a tape recorder and checked out his Super Eight movie camera.

"John, this is nutsy. Crashing in on Billy Hale. What makes you think he'll see you?"

John placed the camera to his eye and kiddingly replied, "I once heard him say, 'bring me your troubled soul.' "

She didn't think him funny. Not a bit. "It's dumb. I can see us now, spending the night in some hokey jail."

She'd been complaining off and on for the last half hour—ever since they'd gassed up and John had conned the attendant into giving him directions to Billy Hale's hidden-in-the-hills estate. "Leslie, your father's paying me to do research on Billy Hale. What better way than talking to the man personally?"

"Did you ever think of phoning him? That *is* the usual procedure."

"You don't call someone like Billy Hale. You go and see him."

"Unannounced? Barge right in and violate his privacy? You call *that* the right way?"

"Leslie, there's the right way and then there's the New York way."

She gave him a dirty look and left it at that.

Reaching a hill where the road widened, John Milton took notice of an interesting road. It was paved and strangely identical in width to the one they were traveling upon. What was even more peculiar was the fact that there were no signs to reveal where it led to. Hastily, he took a piece of paper from his pocket and studied the directions given him by the gas station attendant. "We passed it. We *must* have."

"Passed what."

"The road to Billy Hale's. Stop the car."

Unwillingly she brought the vehicle to a halt—inches

from the soft muddy shoulder.

"Turn around, Leslie."

"*How?*"

"It's a Pinto, not a Mack truck."

He saw the Manning rage in her eyes. "Damn it, John. What makes you think the man at the gas station bought your story?"

"You mean we don't look like Bible students?" he grinned.

FOR BETTER THAN four miles they traveled in silence over the mystery road. It started to slick over with melting snow. They had yet to see any marker, nor was there any such road on John's map. A frustrated Leslie finally burst out, "Give it up, John. I mean it! You've got all the data my father could possibly need on Billy Hale."

Something up ahead caught his eye. "What's that? Through the trees?"

"What, John? What do you see?"

The road made a sharp bend to the left and the object came into full view. It was a cross; gray, made of concrete, towering over an iron fence that reached into the woods on both sides of the road. The moment the Pinto pulled up to the gate, John Milton bolted from the car. Camera in hand, he filmed the gate, stood on the hood, and shot more footage of the cross. Leslie watched in awe.

Out of film, John leapt from the car's hood and walked toward the gate. He pushed hard, but the gate was securely locked.

A relieved Leslie watched him return to the car—slowly—deep in thought. She waited until he took his place, then said, "Now can we go?"

He didn't answer; instead, he emptied the exposed film clip from the Super Eight, and flipped it to her.

"What am I supposed to do with this?"

"Hide it. Somewhere no one would look for it."

Totally bemused, she held the film in her hand and watched him put the Super Eight into a leather bag, then take from it a small and expensive still camera. He fiddled with the Nikon's elaborate lens, then looked up at her and smiled. "I'm going in there."

"How? Have you a tank handy? Be sensible. If this is Billy Hale's place, and not some convent or monastery, he hasn't put out any welcome sign for strangers."

"Leslie, that guy at the gas station said we'd see a big cross. This is his place all right. Billy Hale's wonderful world of humility—where he keeps his vows of poverty—erty—and I'm getting in there."

"You're crazy! You must be joking!"

"Kid you not. I'm not leaving until I at least get some pictures of what's behind that gate. I'm betting Billy's house is a lulu." He looked through the rear-view mirror. "Back it up. We've got to find a good spot to hide this thing."

"John, enough. You're making me feel like I'm part of some clandestine operation."

"Like . . . the Watergate plumbers? Or Deep Throat?" he smiled.

"Trespassing, breaking and entering—that's something to smile about?"

"Fuck it."

At first she wouldn't believe her ears. He'd rarely used that word. Often he'd remark on how uncouth her father was for his constant use of that four-letter obscenity. "*What* did you say?"

"I said fuck it. I'm tired of reading about adventures. It's time I lived one. Just because I don't look like Tarzan doesn't necessarily mean I'm at a loss for guts."

"Is that where it's at? You're doing this just to prove you have guts? That you've got more chutzpah than my father?"

"Live, Leslie, *live*. I want to live it, not read it. Your father, he does it and says the hell with any aftermath.

He's a doer, not a talker. And Ron Rebuck . . . what a trip he's on."

". . . One question. Have you given serious thought to the consequences in the event we get caught? What could happen to your future as a lawyer?"

"I'll write a book like every other asshole and make a fortune."

From the wild look in his eyes, she knew there was nothing more she could say to stop him. He'd changed. Since getting involved with her father, the damn fool had caught the adventure virus—and he had it bad! Against her better judgment she'd go along and blame Rufus Manning for whatever lay in store.

HAVING PARKED the car deep into the woods, a quarter mile from the road, they found a point where the iron fence gave way to barbed wire. Finally, they found an opening and entered the forbidden grounds. For almost forty-five minutes they tracked up and down hills, having to leap from rock to rock in the crossing of streams. From the look of the sky the light-falling snow would soon be turning into a blizzard. Still, John Milton forged ahead.

Halfway up a low-lying hill, he peered over the tips of trees ahead. His face lit up. There was smoke rising from beyond the hill. Smoke from Billy Hale's home! He was sure of it.

The gleam in his eyes fast chilled when he turned and looked down at the lagging Leslie. "Over the hill," he shouted.

"Over *your* hill," she replied.

Reluctantly, she wearily trudged after her man.

He was busily snapping pictures of what lay below when she breathlessly reached his side. "Take a look, then tell me what you think of Billy's hideout."

Her eyes took in the dense grove of snowy pines, the brook which snailed along through meadows and under small wooden bridges, the ducks waddling about the banks of a rustic pond. And there, rising in the midst of it all, fronted by a circular driveway, was a vast, rambling mansion of pale gray brick with black shutters—Billy Hale's home. Her eyes followed the smoke spiraling from two chimneys as it lazily ascended into a snow-clouded sky.

"Next stop heaven, or what?" said John.

"Beautiful. A storybook setting. Makes you think of sugar plums and candy canes and fairy tales—yet I get this strange feeling I'm looking at the estate of some powerful Mafia don."

John Milton laughed. He liked the comparison.

Leslie frowned. "It's crazy, America's best known religious leader, and here I am thinking of him as some mobster."

"What's crazy? The only difference is he uses the Bible as his cannon." He aimed the camera and clicked some more pictures. "You know, how could anyone buy Billy Hale's 'be humble' bullshit, once they've seen this place?"

BILLY HALE, attired in a cream-colored bathrobe with a gold cross stitched into the fabric, to the left of his heart, sat in the oak-paneled country kitchen, reading the *Washington Post.* Across the antique pine table, a slender, pretty woman with silver hair, his wife Doris, drank coffee from a mug embossed with a gold cross.

Billy Hale chuckled, then roared with laughter. "Seems our new Pres-ah-dent, sleeping only two nights in the White House, complains the bed is too big. I've the feeling he'll find the job much the same."

"There'll come a time when he'll be in need of your spiritual guidance."

Without looking up, Hale replied, "Let us not be bitter, Doris."

Doris Hale, usually a mild woman, could not hold

back her feelings. The words burst forth angrily, "Not being asked to give the invocation was bad enough, but to be blatantly ignored, excluded from the Inaugural completely . . . that man and his godless advisors will rue the day!"

He studied the papers with deep-set, hawklike eyes. "I do not . . . repeat, do not, wish to hear of that . . . again."

She went back to her coffee as he searched for the paper's book section. Finding it, a smile curved his full lips. "Six months, Doris, and my book yet remains among the top ten best sellers."

"Which only proves people are craving your wisdom. They're in such need, Billy."

Suddenly that world-famous smile vanished. A new book was being reviewed—by the all-powerful Drew Bonds. As he read on, that equally famous frown came to his face.

Doris Hale was concerned. "Something wrong, Billy?"

At first he didn't reply. He was totally absorbed in his reading—unable, or unwilling to believe the words on the page. "Another horse's ass writes a book on religion and Drew Bonds . . . *Drew Bonds* mind you, *raves* over it . . ."

"A Christian book, Billy?"

He ignored her question and continued reading. He then dropped the paper on the table. "I cannot believe my eyes. Read it, Doris—'Books by Bonds.' Read it aloud!"

She picked up the paper and read: " 'A cosmic belief for all . . . *The Lawyers of Hell* could very well become the foundation stone for a world-wide religion. A most—' "

"*Incredible*," Hale bellowed. "Undoubtedly another scandalous effort to fleece dollars from the confused—and *Drew Bonds* has been taken in." He rose from the table, all six-foot-four of him. "I cannot believe it. I *shall* not believe it. Drew Bonds is nobody's fool. He is not a man to be easily swayed." He started to pace the kitchen floor. "Hell, I've known Drew for better than twenty years. Good ole North Carolina boy. A man of his word. And he's *never* . . . never reviewed any of my books. For that matter *any* religious material. By the walls of Jericho, what's come over him?"

"Satan at work, Billy?"

He weighed her words. "The Bible does not exclude the possibility, Doris."

". . . Is the author's name familiar to you?"

His mind was elsewhere. He was sinking deep into thought when, suddenly, his entire body seemed to stiffen. He stood like that for a moment, then a confident smile played on his lips. "Do you remember what I said would come about during this New Year?"

She had to think. At the beginning of each New Year he issued to his millions of followers a prediction of cataclysmic events to come. These were mostly drawn from the Bible, and *no one* thought himself more in tune with Bible passages than Billy Hale. "The demons are restless, Doris. The time could be drawing near when Lucifer himself will rally his army of fallen angels for an all-out attack on man."

Doris Hale remembered when she'd last heard him say those exact words. It was four years ago in Akron, Ohio—a memorable occasion. It was one of his crusades for Christ on which he'd taken out after the Devil in everyday life in a particularly rousing style. He left the good people of Akron so fired up that they went hunting for the Adversary in every corner, and neighbor began accusing neighbor of being in cahoots with Satan. Billy had to make an emergency return appearance three days later to pacify the flock he'd turned into a pack of roaring lions.

Doris bit her lip. "Billy, are you saying this book

might be . . . a sign?"

"We'll know better after the staff has had a chance to do an in-depth study."

He sat down again at the table, perplexity creasing the craggy face. "Why would Drew Bonds suddenly—out of the blue—change his long-standing policy and review a religious book—moreover, *rave* about it?"

He leaned back. "My Almighty intuition tells me there's more to this than a mere book."

There was a long five minutes of silence as Billy Hale sat in a trance. Doris, eyes fixed on his face, shifted nervously.

Then his lips parted: "Doris, the Bible is never wrong. It has predicted a holocaust of the greatest magnitude. Could this be the time for the prophecy to unfold?"

THE SNOW WAS PERFECT — a skier's dream; and Rufus Manning set his skis in the ready position for his last run of the day. Rufus loved Big Sky Lodges, the Montana mountain owned by a syndicate of high-rolling executives. For the last five years it had been his retreat, a place where his anguished soul found a much-needed tranquillity. At Big Sky, Rufus Manning was no longer at war.

Here was God's magic: a spectacular sunset glowing beyond the mountains. He flipped down the goggles, pushed off with the poles, and he was on his way. Down the steep slope he zoomed, graceful, the upper body loose, the knees locked, as he took the turns, smoothly, so fluid. The picture of an athlete in perfect control of his body.

MIKE SPENARD looked out from the chalet perched on the slope Rufus was descending. He couldn't help overhear what Hughie Gilman was saying to someone on the phone. He'd previously summoned Hughie to Rufus's chalet and was partially aware of the reason for Nancy Manning's frantic call. Seeing Rufus draw to a stop from his flawless downhill performance, he swiftly left the chalet. Lawyers made him nervous.

"Were you watchin'?" Rufus shouted to the approaching Mike Spenard.

"Shoulda entered the Olympics."

"I'll hold my own," said Rufus, handing him the skis. "Where's Hughie, shacking with that giraffe of his?"

"In your cabin. Waiting for you, Mr. M."

"What happened, she lock him out? He's such a jerk. How I'd like to use her as a ski pole."

HUGHIE GILMAN sat by the phone, anticipating an important call, and Rufus recognized the familiar expression on his face. The one reminiscent of a principal about to discipline an unruly boy. He plopped into a chair as Mike went about his valet's chore of relieving him of the ski boots. ". . . What the fuck have I done now?"

Hughie shot a significant glance at Mike Spenard.

"Mike's all right, Hughie."

"I'm sure he is. But it so happens Mr. Spenard does not pay my fee."

Mike Spenard caught Rufus's eye message. He was gone in seconds.

"What mad force drives you?" said Gilman.

"Greed?" Rufus tried a smile.

"Craziness! . . . Sheer insanity. Commit you – that's what your wife should do."

"Mind telling me what it is I should be committed for?"

"You've done some weird things over the years, Roof. Most of them I found myself accepting as unorthodox means of accomplishing your goals . . . I'm still unable to comprehend why you took on Myrna Reardon. Why she hasn't come after you remains a mystery. But now . . . to involve your own flesh and blood . . . your own daughter . . . to have her participate in whatever scheme you're perpetrating, it's too much. I'm ready to resign as your attorney, sever our relationship."

"Leslie? What about Leslie?"

"You don't know? You didn't take the time to think of the consequences. The fact that she could be arrested never entered your mind."

"*Arrested*? What the hell are you talking about?"

"I'm talking about your daughter. Your Leslie, and her fiance, are being held for questioning in a Virginia jailhouse."

Rufus Manning sprang from the chair. "*Fuck-ups*. I'm surrounded by fuck-ups!"

Hughie Gilman laughed. "Now comes the time for placing the blame on others." He pointed a finger at him. "*You* . . . you sent those young people to Billy Hale's home. *Billy Hale*, of all people. Why, I don't want to know. The lowest, Roof . . . you've reached —"

"Goddammit Hughie, I didn't send them!"

The words rang with truth. Rufus Manning was many things, but not a liar. Hughie would sit back, hear him out.

"That crazy kid. I told him to get me information on Billy Hale, not to break into his fucking home. And Leslie, she's too bright to get sucked into such a stupid thing." His eyes fixed on Hughie. "Get her out, Hughie.

I don't give a damn what it costs, get her the hell out of there! Her boyfriend can rot. Goddamn stupid . . . What are they holding her on?"

"I said for *questioning*. Seems the Billy Hale people think they're members of some kind of cult. Devil cult, I think Nancy said."

"Devil cult? What horseshit! Were they trespassing? Breaking and entering? What? . . .

"Joe MacIntire will soon find out."

"Who's Joe MacIntire?"

"A very expensive criminal lawyer in Washington. Friend of mine." He watched Rufus pace the floor, slowly building into a tantrum, muttering curses. "Sit down! Your pacing won't make the phone ring. We're going to have a little chat, Roof."

"*Chat later.* What I want is action. We've got to spring Leslie!"

"Sit down or I'm walking out of here," Hughie threatened.

It was a threat not to be ignored. Rufus fast recognized this. Seated, he looked at Hughie with pained eyes, when the phone's ringing disrupted Hughie's line of thought.

Signaling for Rufus to remain seated, he grabbed the phone. "Hello . . . Yes, this is Mr. Gilman." He placed a hand over the receiver and whispered to Rufus, "It's MacIntire . . . Joe, what seems to be the problem down there?" For almost five minutes Hughie listened to the voice on the other end while Rufus agonized. "Thanks, Joe, I owe you," said Hughie, who hung up the receiver, then spoke softly to Rufus. "They've been released."

Relief spread on Rufus's face as Hughie continued, "It appears they were not caught on Billy Hale's immediate grounds."

"You mean they were arrested on a public road?"

"More than likely."

The blood rushed to Rufus's head. "Why that no good goddamn evangelist . . . I'll sue his religious ass off!"

"You'll do nothing of the kind. You'll sit there and damn well listen to what I have to say." He paused, purposely allowing his meaningful words to smother Rufus's budding anger. "The fact they were not caught does not mean they didn't set foot on Billy Hale's property. MacIntire's associate believes they *were* trespassing. But all that should matter to you is that they're safely on their way home."

"When I see that noodnick kid, I'm going to kick his ass."

Hughie Gilman ignored him. "Roof, I don't know why, I never do, but I believe you didn't send those kids down there. Encouraged them, I'm sure, but they should have had enough good sense not to do such a foolish thing. Which now brings me to you. . . . If you want me to represent you, counsel you — end this religious pipe dream of yours. End it now!"

"It's no pipe dream, Hughie. No pipe dream."

"And I say it is! You leave religion to the religious. They're experts. Professionals who've been at it a long time."

"Hughie, for such a bright man, the fact that Drew Bonds called Rebuck's book the basis for a universal religion, means absolutely nothing to you. You're so busy not wanting to offend anybody, you can't see a fucking mint staring you in the face."

"A mint? A mirage, you mean."

"Mirage? Is that what you think?"

"I think you've gone crazy. That's what I think."

"Crazy or clever?"

"A fox is clever. One who takes on a pack of bull elephants is mad."

"Hughie, if, yes, I said *if*, I get the right gun, those bull elephants might as well roll over."

"Crack Widener again?"

"Himself. And if you'd get off your ass and help me land him, it's a one way street to the bank."

"For the last time – Crack Widener is not among us mortals. He's a private empire. He's no Columbia, or Paramount, that has to answer to its stockholders. He's a legend, a myth. You cannot deal with legendary figures."

Rufus drew a cigarette from a half-empty pack. "I don't believe it, Hughie. I don't believe in myths. Crack Widener's human, and that means he can be had." He exhaled the smoke through his nose. "I'm going to land him, Hughie. With or without your help."

"That you should luck into a monster from the deeps, I can believe. Crack Widener? Never."

"And if I do, you'll get on my case?"

Hughie Gilman laughed, hard and long. "Roofala, I deal in facts, not wild assumptions. I don't make wagers unless the odds are stacked heavily in my favor. But in this case, this absurd nonsense of yours, if you should succeed, I'd cut my fee in half."

"Can I hold you to that?"

"Would you like I should swear on the Torah?"

MIKE SPENARD appeared at the door looking sheepish. "Mr. M., I forgot to give you a message."

"Yeah, what's that?" Rufus asked.

Spenard took out a piece of paper from his pocket,

then handed it to Rufus. "The guy said it was very important you return his call."

Rufus studied the name. Mear, Roy Mear. From Los Angeles. He looked up at Hughie. "Know a guy named Roy Mear?"

"*Roy Mear*? He called *you*?"

"Yeah, so what! Who the hell is he?"

"If it's the same Roy Mear, he happens to be chief counsel for Crack Widener Industries."

"You don't say."

"How do *you* know him?"

"I don't. Never heard of the man."

Hughie Gilman seethed with suspicion. "Roy Mear doesn't call people unless he has warranted reason. Have you been conning me?"

"I told you I don't know the man." Rufus gave the paper to Mike Spenard. "Put the call through."

Hughie Gilman followed Mike's actions with great concern. "No, it can't be," he said to himself. "Impossible."

"What's impossible?" Rufus asked, enjoying Hughie's sudden perplexity.

"Roy Mear is the Howard Hughes of the legal set. Talks to no one. Why, he hasn't attended any legal functions for years. It's impossible. It must be another Roy Mear."

"You know, Hughie, maybe I've underestimated Ron Rebuck. Maybe the creep has a direct psychic line to Widener. Shit, he's spooky enough to."

"Ridiculous," said Hughie.

"Maybe not. Maybe he's become some kind of Svengali."

"Don't be absurd. It would take God to get past Crack Widener's regiment of protectors. I don't know about Rebuck, but you and God are not on the friendliest of terms."

"Speaking of Rebuck, the son-of-a-bitch must be in hiding. He hasn't returned any of my calls for the last two weeks."

"If he's smart, he'll *stay* in hiding."

"Some dummy named Ed Dobyat, or Dowdyat, is taking all of his messages."

"I've got the man you wanted on the line, Mr. M." Mike said.

Rufus dashed to the phone. Taking it from Mike Spenard, he winked at Hughie, then spoke into the receiver: "Rufus Manning."

Hughie Gilman sat back in his chair, sure he'd be proven right. That Roy Mear was not the same Roy Mear, Crack Widener's chief counsel, but, in fact, some poor slob trying to pitch Rufus a movie deal and get himself eaten alive. But when Rufus murmured superstar Crack Widener's name into the receiver, Gilman came out of the chair like a rocket and stood by Rufus's side.

"Mr. Mear, the book is only the start of what I have in mind," said Rufus, as Hughie pressed closer to him. "Just . . . a second, Mr. Mear. So happens my attorney is right here. I'll let you talk with him."

Hughie Gilman made a grab for the phone but Rufus held it away from him. Covering the receiver, he whispered, "Crack Widener has gone ape over Rebuck's book. He wants to meet with Rebuck and me. His attorney's under the impression Rebuck won't make a move without me."

"Impression? That's the absolute fact of the matter," said a straight-faced Hughie, taking the phone from Rufus and proceeding as though it was all in a day's work.

Meanwhile, Rufus turned to Spenard. "Mike, when Hughie finishes talking, place a call to Ron Rebuck."

"Again?"

"Yes, again! Call him!" Rufus bellowed.

Hughie Gilman waved for silence. Rufus dragged Spenard out into the hall. "Call him. And keep calling till you get him. *Understand?*"

"I've called twenty times and all I get is some guy telling me Rebuck's not there and he'll give him the message."

"Then tell that shit he's screwing up a very big deal unless *I* talk with Rebuck. Call every five minutes if you have to. But get me Rebuck!"

HUGHIE GILMAN appeared at the door. "I don't believe it. Crack Widener wants to meet with you and Ron Rebuck. I just can't believe it."

With that shitty grin from ear to ear, Rufus gazed at the stunned Hughie. "Believe it, baby," he said, gleefully. "Believe the gun is loaded!"

Hughie Gilman wouldn't allow himself to be caught up in Rufus's hype. He'd believe a deal with Widener when he saw it all laid out on paper.

"The chemistry is perfect," said Rufus. "Crack Widener blows their minds with a new kinda brother love, and Rebuck slips in behind with the heavy artillery and bombards Billy Hale. Is that a team, or is that a team? The Michael's Messenger Show, Hughie, could be the greatest mission for money, *ever*."

He draped an arm around Hughie. "First, we get Rebuck on paper. For openers, fifty-fifty across the boards. The book, the show, music, merchandising, everything."

"You're so generous, Roof."

His arm slipped from Hughie's shoulder. "I don't see any halo over *your* head."

"Did it ever occur to you that Ron Rebuck doesn't need you?"

"Are you kidding? Didn't you hear Widener's attorney? He needs me, Hughie. He needs me!"

"Then why isn't the man returning your calls?"

"Because he's a spook. Because he's probably on a mountaintop talking to that cockamamie angel of his. Maybe he thinks he's Jesus and is hiking out in some desert."

"What would a Jewish boy, better yet, an atheist like you, know about Jesus?"

"Jesus and money have the same number of letters. Izzat good enough for you?"

". . . You're amazing. But a promise is a promise . . . . All right, Roof, I'll back you up. *Legally*, that is. But I get the feeling that gun you keep referring to might just blow up in your own face."

"Will you stop worrying?"

"It's my job to worry. You could be getting into something way over your head. Picking on the government you'd stand a better chance."

"Hughie, with Crack Widener in the saddle, what kind of TV audience are we talking about?"

"Gigantic. Mostly young people I'd say."

"Yeahhh. Young people who already think Billy Hale's full of shit."

Hughie looked thoughtful. "I know mine do."

"And so do mine. So do most of the young people. Hughie, the times, things are different. They're breaking away from horseshit traditional beliefs. Sophisticated, Hughie, they can't buy all that Bible bullshit anymore. The churches are in trouble. What better time for

Rebuck to do his number? That's why Billy Hale's the perfect target. He's already on the down side. And when Ron Rebuck puts him down for good, Rebuck becomes the young people's guru. Dig?"

"You have such a devious mind."

"Really? I'd say a mind for making money. Through Crack Widener, Ron Rebuck will speak to more people in one night than Christ did in a lifetime."

"What's to say he won't make a lot of enemies?"

"Hughie, Rebuck will be speaking to the young, not the shit kickers and Bible freaks. The modern minded, the revolutionary minded, not the old farts who hoard their money, waiting to die. The spenders, Hughie, the today people. Am I getting through?"

He was about to reply when Mike Spenard stuck his head in the door to say the magic words: "Ron Rebuck's on the phone."

"SUPERSTAR CRACK WIDENER to do first TV special . . ." Cardinal Spellissy read the headline haltingly, dropped the morning paper on his desk and looked quizzically at John Gallogly. "One might think His Holiness, the Pope, was to appear on American TV."

"Not to be disrespectful to His Holiness, but I'm afraid he wouldn't come close to the audience for Crack Widener."

"Do tell?" the Cardinal reddened.

"Your Eminence, if the voting age was dropped to thirteen, Crack Widener would be our next president."

The Cardinal puffed long and hard on his cigar, then rose from the swivel chair. He sauntered toward the great windows and looked out at the cold February day. "That he would strike, I was sure. But the manner . . . so clever. So damn clever." He turned and looked at his youthful subordinate. "He found his miracle, John. Television. Our Mr. Rebuck has gone directly for the jugular."

"The announcement will be formally made at the Waldorf, tonight," John informed him.

"I've seen no mention of that in any of the papers. What little bird told you that?"

"Mr. Pico. He's presently in my office conferring with Paul Bartley."

"*Is he now*?"

"The man has supplied us with some vital information, Your Eminence."

"This information, does it come unsolicited?"

"Unsolicited?"

"What I'm asking, John, is that in your vigorous efforts to find out about Ron Rebuck, have you promised the man anything?"

". . . No. No, I certainly haven't. Besides, he's being paid by Myrna Reardon."

"The man is a starling, John. A nest robber. He's after much more than Myrna's retainer. It shows in his black eyes."

"Quite possibly. However, I get the feeling he's doing this purely because of his dire hate for the producer, Rufus Manning."

"In any event . . . promise the man nothing."

"Most definitely, Your Eminence."

"Fine." Satisfied, the Cardinal went back to his desk and sat down. He paused a moment, then said, "Undoubtedly, you wish to attend this function at the Waldorf tonight. Have the opportunity to meet Rebuck, eye to eye."

"The idea did enter my mind." John Gallogly smiled.

The Cardinal's face became suddenly grave. "You know, of course, you will not be meeting with any ordinary man."

"I realize this . . . yet the fact remains, he is a man."

"Is he, John?"

John Gallogly stirred in his chair. "Am I to believe he isn't?"

The Cardinal looked at him in a fatherly fashion. "Take Father Bartley with you. And under no circumstances are you to speak with this Ron Rebuck alone. . . . Promise me that."

"Is there some reason why I shouldn't be alone with the man?"

"Trust me, John. Trust me."

A BLACK LIMOUSINE pulled up to the police barricade. A swarm of teen-agers, some with Crack Widener posters, forged bullishly toward the car but were held back by mounted police on crowd-trained Morgan steeds. Amid the chorus of ear-shattering shrieks, Turk Savage's advance security force stepped briskly from the car and moved double-time toward the Waldorf's entrance.

MARTY PICO dropped four Life Savers into his mouth and gazed about the crowded and boisterous lobby — jammed with members of the press and TV. With particular interest, he watched Turk Savage's men charge toward the two elevators that were closed off to the public, where uniformed Pinkerton guards checked credentials.

"A cinch," Marty said aloud to himself. He'd flash one of his phony press cards and . . . shazam! But what to do about the Monsignor and the other priest? Myrna Reardon had had a last minute change of mind. On being told that McGuinness and McGuinness (Ron Rebuck's publishers) were only the sponsors of record, and that in fact it was Rufus Manning who was hosting the affair, she'd called the entire event a sham and not worth her precious time.

Almost certain she'd attend, Pico had taken it upon himself to invite John Gallogly and Paul Bartley. And now he was faced with the problem of getting the priests inside the tent without Myrna's clout. He couldn't afford to lose status. A direct line to the Cardinal was worth his weight in gold, and the hefty Marty Pico had no intentions of losing weight. A confident gleam came to his round face. He'd go a "Hamilton" if necessary. Any guy from the street knows *someone's* for sale. And in the meantime when the priests came with the questions, he'd tell 'em Myrna would be late, and damn if she wasn't holding their invitations.

A gloating Rufus Manning breezed into the lobby. His estranged wife, Nancy, along with Leslie and John Milton, dragged behind. Marty Pico looked for the enforcer, Mike Spenard. It was unlike Manning to be without his protective shadow. Unless he was left watching the car. Had to be, Marty figured. How would it look for a goon like Spenard to hang out in *this* crowd? Crack Widener's gang of protectors would shoot him on sight.

A uniformed guard halted Rufus at the elevator. He checked his list of invited guests and, ironically, the host's name was missing.

Marty Pico drifted toward the crowd attracted by Rufus's loud and threatening voice. "You dumb shit! I don't have to show you *anything*. It's my party, nitwit!"

"I'm sorry, sir . . . but your name's not on the list," the man insisted.

Damned if he'd show any credentials, Rufus pushed the guard aside and entered the elevator – an action that made Marty Pico's eyes glitter with hate. Once again, he vowed to fulfill his vendetta – to get Manning, no matter how long it took. Deep in this murderous thought, he was unaware of the two priests, now at his side.

". . . Mr. Pico . . . *Mr. Pico!*"

"What? . . . Oh . . . Hello, Monsignor . . ." He managed a faint smile for Paul Bartley.

"Has Ron Rebuck arrived?" an excited John Gallogly asked.

"Monsignor, I wouldn't know the man if I fell over him. Are you sure he lives in this world?"

"I'm sure."

"Yeah . . . well, he must only come for short visits."

"Where's Myrna?" Paul Bartley asked.

"Ah . . . she'll be a little late. Got hung up with something. Asked us to wait for her."

A dubious John Gallogly was to further inquire, when Pico announced the arrival of what he termed "the players." An excitement rose in his voice. "See the broad with the sable? The one being followed by the two guys?"

John Gallogly nodded.

"Jennifer Jewell. She's been changing bed partners

the way most women change clothes."

The Biblical Mary Magdalene came swiftly to John Gallogly's mind.

"The guy on the left, the ugly one, that's Jack Pintoff. He's an open book. Every page starts off with hate. I can't get the connection between that weirdo and Jennifer."

Judas. The name, unbidden, flashed through Gallogly's mind.

At first, Marty Pico couldn't place the other man. And now that he did, he was genuinely surprised. "Hey, this is one busy lady . . . let me tell yah. . . . Know who the other dude is?"

Neither priest replied. They needn't be told anything about the man in question. For the last two years they'd suffered the Cardinal's repeated complaints about one Henry Rodriguez, the communist gadfly.

Their attention became suddenly diverted by a thunderous commotion erupting from outside the hotel.

STEPPING OUT of a Rolls Royce Silver Cloud, his face drawn, Crack Widener waved with little enthusiasm to his screaming public. Since The Incident, he'd changed. Greatly changed. Whereas he thought Ron Rebuck to be Michael's messenger, he believed himself to be touched by a higher power. He'd disbanded The Dirty Thirty. And only after a most exhaustive investigation had he kept on those he considered his twelve loyal disciples. The imp was among the twelve.

A wary Turk Savage pushed him gently ahead, away from the throng of hysterical fans who at any moment would break through the police barricade. Once inside, Turk Savage and crew formed a wedge around him, preventing the news people from getting too close. One of them had shoved a camera up against the superstar's face, then found his lip bleeding from a swift elbow he never saw.

"He's got more protectors than the President," Paul Bartley commented.

"So would you, Father, if you happened to be a walking Fort Knox," Pico replied.

Through astonished eyes Paul Bartley watched on until the superstar was herded into the elevator. "If that's the preview, I can't wait to see the rest of this show."

Marty Pico winced.

MIKE SPENARD had just re-entered the Jag when he saw the giant Richard come out from the night shadows. Instinctively, he prepared for mortal combat and came out of the vehicle from the passenger's side. They glared at each other over the car's roof. It was Richard who broke the death look and threatened, "Sucker . . . you better die of cancer before I come down on your motherfuckin' ass!"

THE ONCE CROWDED lobby was now virtually barren. The two priests were convinced Myrna was not about to *ever* show, and John Gallogly was thinking of what the wise Cardinal said about Marty Pico when a powerfully built man with blazing eyes appeared. John Gallogly stiffened. It was *he*. Ron Rebuck in the flesh. The very man who had haunted him. Tortured his mind. Who'd come near to shattering his sanity. He didn't, couldn't, notice the man and two women with him. Only Ron Rebuck occupied his mind.

The foursome moved slowly toward the elevator. Then Ron Rebuck suddenly stopped. He turned. His eyes fixed upon John Gallogly. For a time — the priest thought eternity – the two men sized each other. Then Ron Rebuck smiled. A warm, inviting, infectious smile.

John Gallogly felt a sinking sensation in his stomach as he watched Ron Rebuck whisper to the man with him, then enter the elevator with the two women. He stood, mesmerized by those eyes that eerily looked out at him – never seeing Rebuck's companion step out just as the elevator door slowly shut.

"We have company," Paul Bartley announced.

The words passed over him. It was only when the man spoke that John Gallogly returned to the present.

"My name's Ed Dowiat. Would either of you gentlemen be Monsignor Gallogly?" He ignored Marty Pico.

"This is Monsignor Gallogly," said Paul Bartley.

Ed Dowiat directed his attention to the yet dazed priest. "Monsignor, Ron Rebuck's most anxious to speak with you."

He studied the sincere face before him. "I don't know any Ron Rebuck."

Ed Dowiat smiled. "Mr. Rebuck knows of you and wishes to make your acquaintance."

"Why?"

"More than likely, he has good reason. He usually does."

"Does he?"

The smiling face turned somber. "Monsignor, if you wish to decline I'm sure Ron will understand." He made a move to leave.

"*One moment*, Mr. Dowiat." He took Paul Bartley aside. "What do you think, Paul?"

"What do I *think*? You've been eating, drinking, sleeping, thinking about the man, and now that you've got the chance to meet him, you're going to blow it?"

"You're to see him with me."

"Rebuck doesn't want to speak with me. Didn't you hear the man?"

"We shall meet him *together*." He returned to the waiting Ed Dowiat. "Father Bartley and I will meet with your Mr. Rebuck."

"Good idea, Monsignor," Marty Pico blurted. "You go ahead, I'll wait for Myrna."

"If you'll follow me . . ." said Ed Dowiat.

John Gallogly turned to the too pleased face of Marty Pico. He salted the words, "You *will* give Myrna our regrets when she arrives?"

"Huh? . . . Oh, yeah. Sure – you bet, Monsignor."

As the two priests followed Ed Dowiat, Paul Bartley snickered, "For a gumshoe, he's not very convincing."

At the elevators John Gallogly grabbed onto Paul Bartley's arm, and whispered, "Paul . . . no matter what, I want you to stay by my side. Don't ask why. *Promise* you won't leave my side."

A BEAMING RUFUS MANNING moved about the ballroom, proudly presenting a subdued Crack Widener. Nothing was too good for Crack. Hors d'oeuvres ranged from caviar to shrimp. The finest brand of whiskey. Large placards welcoming the great one were strewn about the spacious room, with its crystal chandeliers and the tall windows hung with cloth-of-gold drapes. Oddly, there was no mention of Ron Rebuck.

The original invitation list of fifty names had doubled as soon as news leaked that Crack Widener would do a TV special. And with the avalanche of media people there was little floor space without feet. A five-piece combo played Crack's songs, and whenever they paused instant violins took over – seven strolling violinists with plenty of gypsy.

All about the room, groups formed in conversation. June Rebuck and Nancy Manning found each other and were reminiscing over things past. Both Virgos, they understood each other quite well. Married to dynamic men, they had much in common – until now. And Nancy couldn't help detect the pained look in June Rebuck's eyes. The terrible secret she held within her heart. Where others saw a dove before the passing of a loved one, she had seen a black cloud – that death cloud hovering above her husband.

ABBY ALDEN was getting the brush-off from Rufus Manning and she wasn't happy. Rufus had led her to believe she would "break the story." Actually, he never did tell her *what* story.

Although she was a literary critic for a national magazine, her reviews were hardly read. Where she was gaining prominence was with her movie and TV stuff. "Four Stars" by Abby Alden speaking on the tube meant money. At least in New York. And many believed once she made the move to the coast, Myrna Reardon would be hard-pressed to hold onto the number-one gossip spot.

Abby swore to being thirty-three – but she was all of forty-five. You couldn't tell it by her legs. She could fill a Hanes ad, anytime. Unfortunately, she drank out of the wrong fountain for her face.

Noticing Drew Bonds with someone she didn't consider very important, she barged into their conversation. "Drew Doll, what's this I hear about you being on the board of some church?"

The bearded Drew Bonds made an apologetic gesture to the man he was speaking to, then set his cold gray eyes on the rude intruder. "Since when has the likes of you become interested in churches?"

"Since Crackie-Pooh's gone religious. Might turn out to be some funky fad. And you! Christ, Drew, you really laid it on with that book. You'd think it was the new Bible the way you hyped it."

"I meant every word. And I suggest you take the time to read it. Might do *you* a world of good."

"Who the hell wants to be good? . . . By the way, how's your wife?"

"She's over there, why don't you ask her?"

"She's here at the party?" She followed his pointing finger to the far corner. "I don't believe it, she's standing."

"Isn't she, though."

"I don't mean to be a smart ass, Drew baby, but everyone knows what a lush she is."

"*Was*!"

"She's not even wobbling. What happened? Did you find a magic cure-all?"

"That's right. Ron Rebuck's book."

"Are you shitting me?"

"You know, Abby, the more I converse with you, the more I believe, honestly believe, you should read *The Lawyers of Hell.* Perhaps you might find some useful mission in life . . . like being a lady."

She waited until he disappeared into the crowd, then said in a low whispy voice, "What a bloody miracle that would be."

CLOSE BY, JENNIFER JEWELL was fast becoming acquainted with Ron Rebuck's childhood by his sociable sister, Barbara Dowiat. Jennifer was particularly interested in his time spent at All Soul's —

the very place where the seed was planted, where he had first made contact with the great angel, Michael.

AT THE FAR END of the room, Ron Rebuck's name was being uttered along more contemporary lines. The dark-eyed Henry Rodriguez was absorbing Jack Pintoff's talk with keen interest, while keeping a wary eye on the scene around him.

Rufus Manning and Crack Widener, along with super body guard Turk Savage, drew near.

"Look at him," said Jack Pintoff. "The *hog!*"

"I rather enjoyed his film. Quite realistic."

"You would, Rodriguez. You Latins think like blacks."

Henry Rodriguez laughed. "And the tenacious Jew Bird feeds off us both."

RUFUS MANNING'S effervescent smile lost its carbonation when his eyes took in Jack Pintoff and the known Communist leader with him. He immediately excused himself and made tracks in their direction.

"The Barracuda comes," said Pintoff.

"Pintoff . . . I want to talk with you."

"Where's your manners, Manning? Permit me to introduce Henry Rodriguez."

Rodriguez extended his hand, but Rufus ignored it. "I said I want to speak with you!"

"The point is, do I care to speak with you?"

"Pintoff!" Rufus shouted.

"Manning!" Pintoff shouted back.

Henry Rodriguez smiled. He gave Pintoff a friendly slap on the shoulder and walked away.

A not-so-polite Rufus gripped Pintoff by the arm and hurried him off to a corner. "What the fuck are you doing showing up with a known Communist?''

"Manning, get your grimy hands off me."

"Around your neck is where they should be."

"Manning, I don't like your tone of voice."

"You don't —" Rufus gritted his teeth. The shoe-button eyes were spinning with rage. "Get him the fuck out of here!"

"Rodriguez happens to be a bona fide correspondent for a London newspaper, and has every right being here."

"Pintoff, he's a fucking Commie. There's a bunch of network brass here, you dumb shit. Queer my deal, Quasimodo, and I'll bang your ugly head on that bell tower of yours!"

"Your deal?" Pintoff gave a mocking laugh.

"Who do you think's paying for this spread?"

"Manning, your mouth, as usual, is eating at your brain. For your information, Michael's Mission's governing board must sanction all transactions, and I don't recall seeing your name on the board."

"Cockroach, what are you feeding me?"

He'd hit on something unknown to Rufus. The appointments to the Church of Michael's board of governors. He'd let Rufus stew — loving every moment.

Furious, Rufus Manning searched the room for Ron Rebuck. He was nowhere to be seen. He strode to where Jennifer Jewell and Barbara Dowiat stood. He waited a beat for Barbara Dowiat to complete what she was saying, then touched Jennifer's arm. "Where's Rebuck?"

"Roof — stop worrying, he'll be here."

He drew her away from Barbara Dowiat. "What's that weasel Pintoff telling me about — some board of directors?"

"Roof, you'll have to speak to Ron about that."

"I'm speaking to you. You're his mouthpiece, aren't you?"

"I don't know how to take that."

"Look, I don't know what kind of bullshit's going on, but *I* got Crack Widener. Not you or anyone else. And nothing's going down unless I okay it."

Jennifer Jewell laughed in his face.

"You find that funny?"

"I find *you* funny. Crack Widener wouldn't know you were alive if it wasn't for Ron Rebuck's book."

"That's what you think."

"That's what I *know.*"

"I'll tell you what you know – pillow talk. And when I find that spooky son of a bitch, Rebuck, I'm going to straighten out his head."

He walked away, leaving her close to tears. The blast about pillow talk, implying she was "making it" with Ron Rebuck, tore at her insides. Nothing could be further from the truth.

No sooner did Rufus leave Jennifer than Abby Alden nailed him.

"You've been dodging me, darling. Not nice. Makes Abby angry."

"Not now," he stormed.

"What's this not now stuff? A deal's a deal, buster."

*"What deal!* She didn't *show.* Do you see her anywhere?"

"Don't give me the tough little titty routine. Myrna Reardon or no Myrna Reardon, you'd better not roundhouse any of these reporters with special shit."

"Abby, get off my ass. Whenever anything special comes down, you'll get it."

"What kind of horseshit is that? *Whenever,* he says. You wouldn't be playing Abby like some fiddle, would you, baby doll?"

JOHN MILTON was in pursuit of a waiter when he had the misfortune to pass by the steaming Rufus Manning. He saw him waving, yet kept on walking. But when Rufus shouted his name, the commanding presence was not to be denied. The summons came as quite a surprise. Since the Billy Hale affair, Rufus hadn't spoken to him.

"John, say hello to Abby Alden. I want you to stick with her. Whatever she wants. Dig?"

"I thought you weren't speaking to me."

"I'm giving you another chance. Now do what I told you." He left before Abby could voice any objection.

She looked over the young man, inspecting him. The fact that he was so young interested her. "Hello, Sonny . . . got any hair on your . . . chest?"

ED DOWIAT ushered the two bemused priests into the semi-lit Waldorf suite. A strong, sweet odor attacked their nostrils; John Gallogly thought the fragrance was lilac. Ed Dowiat gestured for them to be seated, saying that Ron Rebuck would be with them presently, then abruptly departed the room.

Two minutes passed and the anxious Paul Bartley was about to let loose with one of his sly remarks, when a door within the suite opened. In the dim light Ron Rebuck appeared. For a moment he stood in the doorway, looking directly at John Gallogly. His approach was ghost-like, and John Gallogly could feel the strong vibrations. "I'm Ron Rebuck."

John Gallogly stared at the eyes. Those very same eyes that had caused him so many sleepless nights. Those strange animal-like pupils with their gold-flecked green magic. He was too stunned to respond and Ron Rebuck must have sensed this for he shifted his attention to an open-mouthed Paul Bartley. "Father Bartley?"

Paul Bartley nodded meekly, then stared at Ron Rebuck's outthrust hand. He cautiously grasped it, and a sudden surge of power generating from the strong hand ran up Paul Bartley's arm and radiated through his body.

Spellbound, the priests watched him walk to the farthest part of the room and seat himself in a highbacked chair. Odd that he'd select a chair so far away.

They sat in a triangle. The room's light seemed to dim even more until Ron Rebuck's face was barely visible. John Gallogly fought off becoming intimidated. This was only a man, he told himself. An unusual man, but nevertheless a man. Made of flesh and blood. Subject to pain. Capable of lust as well as love. His mind raced with questions. The burning of the manuscript in his hands. Christ's lineaments on the canvas. The reflection in the mirror. So many questions that needed explanations. Was he truly the creator, author of a book inspired by the great angel, Michael? Despite the Cardinal's warning, he was determined to find out. "Mr. Rebuck, I do not know you. We have never met. Why should a total stranger go to all this trouble just to speak with me?"

Ron Rebuck smiled. "Stranger?"

John Gallogly paused. He decided against sparring with this man, he would come right to the point: "All right, Mr. Rebuck, I won't pretend I don't know who you are. I read your manuscript long before it was published."

"I know."

John Gallogly leaned back in his chair. "Do you, Mr. Rebuck? Do you also know of the . . . the *peculiar* things that have happened – phenomena I've witnessed with my own eyes?"

Paul Bartley sat on the edge of his chair. At long last he would hear of these strange incidents that had been kept secret from him.

Ron Rebuck paused, then said, "All that happened – bizarre as it seemed to be at the time – was for a reason. Like me . . . you have been called."

"*Called,* Mr. Rebuck? Might I be so presumptuous as to ask by *whom*?"

To John Gallogly's surprise, there was no immediate reply, and it appeared none was forthcoming. Was the simple question too complex for him? Perhaps a threat to his credibility? John Gallogly felt a rush of confidence. He jumped at the opportunity to command, and was now on the offensive.

"Mr. Rebuck. you made the statement that I have been called. If such is true, I'm most curious to know who it might be that, as you say, 'called' me." Disbelief rang in his voice.

The words came back loud and clear. Words to chill their bones: "You have been called by a great power whose presence . . . is in this very room."

Ron Rebuck's revelation would not be tested nor did he offer proof as to its validity, but it weighed heavily on the two priests. Paul Bartley was speechless. He sat still, his eyes traveling about the room, searching, seeking a clue, a sign, anything . . . while John Gallogly could not bring himself to challenge Rebuck's admission of a spiritual presence. He squeezed the small crucifix concealed in his hand. A crucifix that once had been attached to his rosary beads. His hopes of interrogating this man were now dashed. Ron Rebuck had taken complete charge of the situation.

"Are you a hypocrite, John?"

"I am neither a hypocrite nor a revolutionary."

"Then what do you call a man who only a moment ago confessed he didn't believe in a Wrathful God, yet is ordained to preach that doctrine to his parishioners?"

"I do not preach or speak about a Wrathful God to anyone."

"But do you speak your heart when people are troubled and beseech you for the truth?"

"I tell them of a Loving God . . . A Compassionate God."

"Not of Hell? Of the loss of their souls? Of a Condemning God, who will cast them into eternal damnation? Do you remind them of passages from the Bible where God is portrayed a slayer . . . the great destroyer? You have never spoken of these things?"

"Mr. Rebuck, what are you driving at?"

"The truth! The truth you claim to harbor yet refuse to sail. Why, Father Gallogly, is the sea too rough? Or is it the penalty you fear? The loss of being elevated to a bishopric? To be no longer the Cardinal's protege? The fear of treading on pontifical shoes? How can a man who does not believe in a Wrathful God, yet gives lip service to the doctrines of his church, be considered anything but a hypocrite?"

"For what purpose? What would there be to gain if I openly denounced the concept of a Wrathful God? Disrupt a society that is already fast becoming atheistic, agnostic? Would it change things to the good if I were to call the Bible in error? Would peace come to the warmongers? Would man suddenly love his fellow man?"

"Yes, John. Yes!"

A startled John Gallogly glared at Paul Bartley. "Paul, you don't know what you're saying."

"I do. But I do!"

"Keep still! You're only speaking out of fear."

"John, I'm a theologian, and I have never believed in the monstrosities the Bible reveals God to have perpetrated upon man."

"Then why do you remain a priest?" Ron Rebuck asked.

There was no reply. The anger in John Gallogly's eyes was enough to silence him.

John Gallogly was now aware that Paul Bartley was fast slipping away and he wished he hadn't brought him. "Mr. Rebuck, when you previously said that someone or something besides us was present in this room, was that meant to frighten us? A scare tactic? If so, brilliantly effective. My compliments."

"*Scare tactics!* You dare to accuse me of such tactics! *You,* a member of the greatest cabal of fear experts on earth! My entire mission is to destroy fear. To rid God of the terrible stigma you and others have maligned Him with. No, it won't be I who exults in tragedies, who wrongfully uses the Name of God to grow rich."

A pale light appeared about Ron Rebuck's head. Paul Bartley blinked hard in disbelief, but the light brightened. John Gallogly now felt that familiar and powerful presence in the room. He wanted to flee but was rooted to his chair by the captivating voice. "It is not I who flies the flag of fear. They who cravenly use the Name of God to achieve personal goals. They who murder and hold hostage innocent men and women – claiming to be in communication with God."

The voice was changing. It was no longer Ron Rebuck speaking . . . but another. "Why have you prostituted the truth? Why have you not spoken out against those who war in the Name of God? Why have you not righted the wrong in a book called 'Holy'?"

Suddenly, the face was no longer that of Ron Rebuck.

The voice no longer boomed but became soft, pleading. Almost sobbing . . . "Has my body died in vain?"

Petrified, the two priests stared in awe at the face of One who died on the Cross — almost two thousand years ago.

# 23

CARDINAL TIMOTHY SPELLISSY looked out from his office window at what promised to be a beautiful spring day. Actually, spring was officially a week off, but it was safe to assume winter had come to a welcome end.

Archbishop Joseph McGary's pale blue eyes showed concern as he sipped his coffee and watched the pensive Cardinal. He'd seen a change come over the man in cent days. The hearty laugh that once boomed through the corridors had been stilled; he'd become withdrawn. At times, in the midst of conversation, he'd lose himself in thought.

Ever since the encounter with the mysterious Rebuck was revealed to him by an hysterical John Gallogly —that mind-shattering ordeal which had struck such a devastating blow to Paul Bartley's health — he had blamed himself. And now, two days before festive Saint Patrick's Day in New York, he'd initiated the Church's preliminary moves against the man John Gallogly was beginning to believe was Michael's Messenger. He'd sent off twenty copies of Ron Rebuck's book to Rome for extensive study by Vatican experts, and the "special" priest he'd called in had arrived at the chancellery and was being further briefed by the Vicar General.

The summoning of the German-born Father Augustus

did not meet with the approval of the usually reserved, quiet-spoken Archbishop McGary. "Tim . . . it appears you have made up your mind to go all the way on this thing," he said. "Heaven knows you have your reasons. But to bring in the likes of Father Augustus . . . aren't you being too hasty?"

The Cardinal turned from the window. The moon face was shadowed with fatigue, the blue eyes rimmed with red. He went to his desk, took a cigar from the gold-trimmed humidor, and turned toward the Bishop. "We've got one priest laid up in a sanitarium under psychiatric care. Another, a man with a brilliant future, is on the verge of renouncing his vows. Hell, Joe, you know how much red tape there is. If I wait any longer we'll both be dead and buried before the matter gets settled."

"But does it have to come to this? Bringing in *Father Augustus*."

"I wanted the best, and he's regarded as *the* best."

"Tim, we're talking about a man who was largely responsible for the decanonization of two saints. My God, have you thought about how John will stand up under the strain of an interrogation by the Vatican's chief devil's advocate?"

"I have, Joe. I have," the Cardinal murmured.

"From what I hear he can make you feel like you were taking a walk in Hell."

The Cardinal slumped into a chair. His fingers trembled as he lit the cigar. He blew out the smoke and gazed at the man before him. "Trust me, Joe, this examination is essential."

"Is it? For what purpose? To subject an already troubled man to such a harrowing ordeal just to prove that what happened was nothing but an . . . an —"

"Illusion?"

"Yes, an illusion. Phenomenon, if you like. These things are not that unusual."

"And what would you term the burning of the manuscript in John's hands?"

"Exactly what Bishop Burke's investigation reported it to be."

"And the face on the oil painting?"

"The *what*?"

The Cardinal quickly looked away from the searching eyes. He'd told no one of the incredible thing he'd witnessed in Bimini. Not even John Gallogly was aware that he knew.

"I've the feeling, Tim, a strong feeling, there's more to this than what you've told Bishop Burke and me." McGary leaned back in his chair. A mind, probing. "Can it be that Father Augustus's 'third degree' won't be confined to only Monsignor Gallogly?"

No reply was necessary. The answer was written on the Cardinal's face.

Somberly, Archbishop McGary got up from his chair. He placed a soft hand on the Cardinal's shoulder and said, " 'Beware the Ides of March.' "

MARTY PICO slammed down the phone and swore aloud. For better than a week he'd been unsuccessful in getting through to John Gallogly. Adding to his anxiety, Myrna Reardon had seen fit to cut off his monthly retainer, leaving a gaping hole in the overhead. His devious mind had somehow zeroed in on the party responsible for these setbacks. He cursed the name of Cardinal Spellissy hotly.

The giant Richard crossed his massive legs and laughed.

"I'm getting the cold shoulder, and you're making with the laughs?"

"I tole ya, man. I tole yer Dago ass."

"You tole me *what*?"

"All that jive. Shit about rainbows . . . a Vatican connection. Gettin' *line* from a mother-grabbin' church, ain't that some shit? The reverends take, they don't give, turkey."

At a loss for a reply, Pico angrily rose from the chair, and went to a corner of the small, shabby room where a green filing cabinet stood. He pulled out a large brown folder, then returned to his cluttered desk. A mind scheming.

Richard studied him. "You rollin' on another one of yer sucker ideas?"

Marty Pico looked up. "I'm letting the string out on this one. That piss-ant Cardinal wants to shut me out, then I gotta knock on another door."

"Shi-it," Richard said. "Sink that ship, fool. Jiving my time away talking shit! Let me take the spic out and end the mother-grabbin' thing."

"Take out the spic," Pico mimicked. "Hurt someone, that's all you know. Your head's so crazy with getting Mike Spenard, you can't see what's coming down."

"*Comin' down*? You were the one who went fishin' . . . usin' that skinny priest for bait, and got swallowed by a mother-fuckin' whale. That's what went down, turkey!"

"Know wutchu are? Do you know wutchu are? A dumb nigger . . . with a peanut for a fucking brain. If it's not in some comic book, how can I expect a moron like you to understand? Hit the street."

"Where to?"

"Get your black ass down to the studio. Check out

Crack Widener's rehearsal. Maybe Rebuck will show."

"Man, that cat ain't around, *nowhere*."

"You know that? Didley shit's what you know. Find him!"

The big guy rose from the tattered vinyl couch. "That dude Rebuck ain't human." He went to the door still protesting. "I see his ass, go after him, then the mother disappears."

"Tell me about it . . . *by phone*," said Marty, whose eyes moved to the folder's contents.

He skipped over the report on Rufus Manning, then Jennifer Jewell – and stopped at Jack Pintoff. A devious smile crossed his thick lips. He'd found the door to knock on.

FATHER AUGUSTUS said not a word. The portly red-bearded man with the darting eyes seemed content to let the Vicar General, the tough-hided Bishop Burke, question an unrattled John Gallogly.

Bishop Burke had now reached the point of interrogation that was the core of their inquiry: that night of fear at the Waldorf. It was only then that craggy Father Augustus asked his first question. "Monsignor Gallogly, what does the face of Jesus Christ look like?"

For the first time, John Gallogly looked directly into the man's eyes. He'd mentally prepared himself to meet a cold and unsympathetic man, but the eyes were warm, compassionate. Could this man truly be the Vatican's tiger? Was this the face of the feared prosecutor?

"Do you hate me?" he asked.

"Why would I hate you? Of course I don't hate you."

"I'm so glad . . . But do you feel a hostility toward me?"

"Hostility?"

"When you became aware I would be coming to this meeting, did you feel a sudden rush of resentment?"

"Not really."

"Not even a tingle of animosity?"

"Father Augustus, I was told by Cardinal Spellissy that you would be asking questions concerning what Father Bartley and I had seen. There was no feeling of hate *or* resentment toward you."

"Monsignor, do you believe in the powers of exorcism?"

John Gallogly squirmed uneasily in his chair. In his salad days, he would have parried the question deftly and easily. Today, he was tongue-tied.

"John, the question must be answered," the Cardinal said sternly.

John Gallogly bit down on his lip, and softly replied, "I believe Lucifer exists."

"My question *was*, do you believe in the powers of exorcism?"

"Frankly, no."

"Yet you do believe Lucifer *does* exist."

"I do."

"And, do you believe that, in various earthly guises, Lucifer roams this earth?"

John Gallogly hesitated, then nodded.

"Do I take that to be an affirmative reply?"

"Father Augustus, I believe it's possible that Lucifer could be on this earth, yes."

"If so, then he must be capable of great powers; don't you agree?"

"Anyone who has lived with God has greater powers than *we* who have not."

"Well stated, Monsignor. Well stated, indeed. And since we agree that Lucifer possesses such power, is it not possible for him to use it on mere mortal man?"

John Gallogly suddenly felt trapped. Effortlessly, the German priest had backed him into a tight corner. But why these questions on Lucifer? What did the powers of exorcism have to do with him? He'd testified to having seen the face of Christ, not the Devil. He tore his eyes away from this shrewd man, taking in the other faces around the conference table. His eyes met the Vicar General, who smiled a wolfish smile.

"Now let us return to my initial question. If you recall, Monsignor, I asked, what does the face of Christ look like?"

Determined he would not allow this clever man to cross him up with his own words again, Gallogly boldly replied, "What *did* the face of Christ look like?"

"*Does*. Does, Monsignor. The *did* will come in due time."

"I can only tell you what Father Bartley and I saw."

"Rest assured I shall come to that. However, my interest now lies in what you believe to be the face of Jesus Christ."

John Gallogly appeared baffled. His mind groped for a way to best describe the face of Jesus Christ. Holy pictures, paintings, statues, flashed through his consciousness. He became frustrated and angry. "I can only tell you what I saw!"

"The face of Christ?"

"Yes, Father, the face of Our Lord, Jesus Christ!"

"Now, Monsignor, calmly tell me how you could have seen the face of Christ without first being able to recognize it . . . identify it?"

"There are numerous pictures."

"Pictures?"

"Yes, pictures. Paintings, *statues*."

"Monsignor, please be more specific."

"I'm sure you are familiar with the various artists, their conceptions of Christ's face."

"Roman? Byzantine? African, Oriental? There are so many concepts of what Christ looked like. Which one did you and Father Bartley happen to see?"

"You're confusing me to such an extent that . . . I can't recall."

Like an animal on the hunt, Father Augustus seemed to be closing in, confident the prey was now his. "Monsignor, when you and Father Bartley were in the room with this man, Rebuck, how far away from him would you say you were . . . approximately?"

"He was seated at the far end of the room."

"How *far*, Monsignor?"

"I don't know. A goodly distance – it was a large room."

"Thirty feet? Forty feet?"

"It could have been."

"And the room's lighting – was it bright? Dim?"

"Dim."

"Very dim?"

"It was medium dim."

The bearded priest got up from his chair and went to the windows beyond the Cardinal's desk. He drew the drapes, throwing the room into semidarkness. "*This* dim, Monsignor?"

John Gallogly glanced about the room. "Could have been."

"Could have been, you say." Father Augustus went to the Cardinal's desk and rested his hands on the back of the leather swivel chair. "Would you say the man was this far away from you?"

"Approximately."

Father Augustus seated himself in the Cardinal's chair. His face, deep in shadows, was only half visible. "Can you see my face, Monsignor?"

". . . Yes."

"Clearly?"

Gallogly made a negative noise.

"I don't hear you, Monsignor."

"I said, *no*."

With his elbows on the desk, he clasped his hands and propped up his bearded chin. "How could you possibly see the face of Jesus Christ when in fact you were unable to clearly see this man Rebuck's face?"

"There was a light."

"Monsignor, do not contradict yourself. You previously said the room was dimly lit."

"It was not an electric light. A different kind of light."

"Different? How different?"

"Radiant . . . It glowed about his head."

"And face?"

"Yes . . . and . . . and when he spoke the face began to change."

"To that of Christ?"

"Yes, *dammit*. To that of Jesus Christ. And neither you nor any other Vatican 'Gestapo' agent will convince me differently!"

"That remark was totally uncalled for, Monsignor Gallogly," the Vicar General brayed.

The sudden outburst by the distraught John Gallogly drew a smile from the man from Rome. He came away from the Cardinal's desk, opened the drapes, and returned in a triumphant manner to the conference table. "I have no further questions for the Monsignor."

Again a silence came over the room. The interrogation was over. John Gallogly read the unspoken verdict on the faces around him, and he burned with shame, for he felt himself cast a fool. His credibility had been severely damaged by an expert. It was the Vicar General who finally broke the silence. "Thank you, Monsignor. That will be all. You're free to leave."

"Leave? Free?" he protested.

"You're excused, Monsignor." His voice was cold.

Gallogly looked at the Cardinal, eyes pleading. At first the words choked in his throat. "Is . . . this the fair treatment you promised me?"

"That will be enough!" the Vicar General warned.

John Gallogly would not be silenced. He vowed to be heard come what may. His eyes, swollen with pent-up tears, were fixed on Cardinal Spellissy. "Paul Bartley is shut up in a mental institution because he saw what I saw. Isn't that convincing enough? Shouldn't that alone have opened your eyes to the truth? But no, you saw fit to bring in a notorious devil's advocate."

The Vicar General slammed his fist down hard on the table. "I shall not listen to any more of this insubordination. You will not say another word!"

"Let the man speak," said the Cardinal.

Gallogly's voice was tremulous. "Have I ever lied to you? At any time did you find me distorting the truth, deceiving anyone?"

There was no reply.

"What could I have possibly done to deserve this? Does it please you to see me humiliated, ruthlessly grilled by an . . . an exorcist?" His glance swung from the Cardinal to the Vicar General. "Sweep it away—under the rug. It didn't happen. Don't rock the Diocese's great boat, that's all *you* seem to care about. The fact that Paul Bartley is in a sanitarium must be comforting to you. After all, who would believe the words of a crazy man? . . . Dammit, *I'm* not crazy!"

The Vicar General could only grit his teeth and look away from the tortured eyes that now fixed on the very man who had brought him to this point of sorrowful rage. But there was nothing in Father Augustus's eyes to further provoke John Gallogly's anger. There was only compassion.

The muscles in Gallogly's face tensed. As the breaking point came, he cried, "I saw the face of Christ. As God is my witness, I swear! . . . Why . . . why doesn't anyone believe me?" He buried his head in his arms and sobbed unashamedly.

Other than the sounds of the wounded man, it was quiet. Cardinal Spellissy rose from his chair like a great phoenix and came to the troubled priest. He placed a gentle hand on the grieving Monsignor's head. The words came softly . . . comfortingly. "I believe you, John. *I* believe you."

John Gallogly lifted his head and looked into the Cardinal's face.

Reaching inside his vestments, the Cardinal drew out what appeared to be a photograph and placed it before John Gallogly's bewildered eyes.

It was the face. The face he had seen on the canvas in Bimini. "Yes, John. I know!"

Father Augustus reached across the table and picked up the photograph. It was the face of Jesus Christ, taken from the original holy shroud. He studied it for a moment, then calmly placed it back on the table. He turned, and was met by an ice-cold stare. He read the challenge in the Cardinal's eyes.

# Book 2

# Michael's Messenger

# 24

OPENING IN A BLAZE of glorious color and sound, "The Michael's Messenger TV Special" traveled over the airwaves Easter night into millions upon millions of homes.

Crack Widener, in powder-blue denim, backed up by a line of long-legged dancing beauties in red briefs, belted out "Michael's Man" to a pounding, hard-rock beat. The live audience, mostly young people, was carried away by Widener's hypnotic voice, first soothing, then coaxing, then roaring out his message. On the last note, the crowd went wild, surging forward toward the stage – barely restrained by a triple-strength security team.

The stage lights dimmed and now a solitary spotlight shone on a single, rugged face. The mobile cameras came in close, and Ron Rebuck spoke:

"A lot of people have said a lot of terrible things about Someone – Someone they couldn't possibly know.

"They have charged this Someone with barbaric and monstrous acts – far beyond the worst deeds ever done by Man. . . . And in so doing, they have called this Someone . . . the greatest mass murderer of all time.

"Who am I talking about? Who is this Someone? . . . My friends, the name is God."

Now Ron Rebuck's face was cloaked in darkness. Center stage lit up to reveal a huge lectern and, resting on it, a gigantic Book, bound in red leather.

Ron Rebuck stepped into a spotlight and pointed at the book. "It's all in there . . . in *that* book. The one called good. The one called holy."

The stage went dark, and seconds later, on a giant screen, a familiar scene appeared: an artist's conception of the Flood with Noah's Ark in the foreground. There were horrifying vignettes of men and beasts drowning – a whole world destroyed, save for Noah and his small band of shipmates. Then the screen switched to another scene of Biblical slaughter: the waters of the Red Sea, which had parted for Moses and the Chosen, closing over the multitudes who pursued them.

The screen went dark and Ron Rebuck stood on center stage, next to the lectern holding the giant Bible. His eyes were aflame. "I ask you, would the God of all creation do these things? Would a Loving God commit random slaughter of the creatures He had made?"

He pointed to the Bible. "The True Testament, they call it . . . the unchallengeable and unimpeachable Word. The evangelists will tell you that God Himself inspired its writing. They, and most other religious tycoons dare you to contradict them and warn you of dire consequences should you try.

"True, they also tell you the Bible speaks of hope and charity. All of that is good and I do not deny it or challenge it.

"Yet, in their very next breath, they speak of a savage Scripture – of sinners in the hands of a vengeful and angry God."

He walked away from the lectern, the spotlight following, while all around him was darkness. "Are we to believe that a forgiving, compassionate, Loving God, who conceived our existence, would then murder us?

"Why would the Supreme Being, whose all-encompassing knowledge made Him totally aware of Man's weakness prior to the Creation, ever conceive us? Are we to believe in a sadistic God, reveling in our sorrows and agonies?"

His voice lowered to a conversational tone. "Good evening, my name is Ron Rebuck, and tonight I bring to you Michael's Message. Tonight we begin our crusade against the wrathmongers, the peddlers of fear. The ministers of myth, and the preachers of poison. Tonight we shall begin to explore the motives of these self-proclaimed Guides of God, exposing the awful harm they have wreaked. Tonight, we bring you the Message of the great Archangel Michael — and commence to penetrate the absurdity of a Wrathful God!" His face faded into darkness. Within seconds, Crack Widener and his bandsmen and dancers were on the stage. The superstar charged into his second song, to a pulsing upbeat tempo: "Don't Blame it on the Lord."

A VISIBLY SHAKEN June Rebuck came out of the bedroom. She'd been watching her husband on the triple Sony TV setup until she could no longer bear it.

Josephine Rebuck sat alone in the living room, pretending to read a book; she'd refused to watch her son on television. She caught a glimpse of June going into the bathroom, pale and near tears. She dropped the book and went to the closed door, rapping lightly. She could hear the sobbing from inside.

"June," the matriarch of the Rebuck clan called softly. After a moment the door opened, and the frightened woman with tears dripping from large eyes collapsed into her arms.

CRACK WIDENER completed his second song and now

Ron Rebuck was back on stage, standing alone before a blue-green curtain. The crowd listened in wide-eyed silence, awed and at the same time turned on by this strange, intense-eyed man.

He waited for absolute silence and then began: "From the Bible comes many a revered name — men of honor and truth. These men, we are told, were in direct contact with God. There were those who conversed with God and those who were tested by God. These Biblical names echo today from church pulpits throughout our land.

"These are the saintly, the learned, the prophets, the apostles and the disciples from long ago. From Moses' Genesis to John's Revelations, their holy names glow in the Book of Scripture. Yet, strangely, not one of these great heroes of the Bible ever spoke out and denounced the existence of a Wrathful God . . . *Not one*!"

The curtain slowly rose and Ron Rebuck strolled toward a dim-lit corner of the stage. "To best illustrate the absurdity of a Supreme God . . . Who, we are asked to believe, conceived our very existence, knowing beforehand what we shall do before we do it, then *condemn* us come Judgment . . . you see what is meant to resemble a courtroom." Overhead lights beamed down on a staged set. "However, this is no ordinary courtroom, but one God, Himself, presides over."

Two figures stood before an elevated bench. Off to the side, another. A gold-clad figure was seated behind the bench. All were robed and hooded, and their faces veiled. Ron Rebuck spoke on, "The examination before Judgment is about to begin. The prosecution and the defense stand before the Supreme Judge. The clerk is about to summon the soul of man."

Ron Rebuck now gestured toward the stage. "The

figure in the purple robe is counsel for the defense, man's champion – Michael. The figure in black, the father of mortal death, is the prosecutor – Lucifer. Standing to the side, robed in silver, is God's Herald – Gabriel.

"Finally, and with no blasphemy intended, seated in the judge's chair, robed in gold – The Lord God.

"The soul of man standing trial represents the evilest of all men . . . I shall play his role."

"THE SOUL OF PETER BRIAN, *come forth*!" Gabriel commanded.

Portraying the fictitious soul of a fictitious man, Ron Rebuck went toward the bench where he was flanked by prosecutor and defense counsel, as all stood before the impersonated Presence of God.

"Will the clerk read the charges?" asked the judge.

"The defendant is accused of every sin and crime known to Man," said Gabriel, going on to read a lengthy list that included murder, blasphemy, arson, rape – a breaking of each and every one of the Ten Commandments.

"How does the soul of Peter Brian plead?" asked the judge.

"I am neither guilty nor innocent," said the accused.

Lucifer laughed contemptuously. Then, in a somber voice, he addressed the Supreme Judge. "My Lord, of all the souls that have come before your exalted Presence, this one is the most guilty of all. There can be no valid defense made in this soul's behalf. He has admitted to his crimes, and we have countless witnesses who might be called. I, therefore, move for a summary judgment against this soul and claim custody of this soul in the Limbo I govern."

"I object!" Michael exclaimed. "The soul of man is entitled to a fair and unbiased hearing. This is stated in the 'Articles of Man.' "

"A fruitless exercise, Michael." Lucifer turned to the accused soul of man. "You have been observed by a legion of souls in my force. Your every despicable deed has been lodged in the book of records. How can you plead anything but guilty?"

"I am neither guilty nor innocent."

"You are as corrupt as the body you came from."

"If I am corrupt, it is not I who am responsible."

Lucifer pointed threateningly at the soul of man. "Your insolence will not be tolerated in this great court. You are not on earth where you and the body you rotted in did as you pleased." He drew closer to the bench, then addressed the Lord. "Again, I move for a summary judgment and claim custody of this soul in the Limbo I govern."

"The *Purgatory* you govern," said Michael. "Great Father, Lucifer is attempting to intimidate this soul, and I object to his unwarranted threats. I ask that he be restrained from any further abuse of this soul."

"Abuse? Hah," Lucifer sounded. "Go on, go on, Michael, proceed with your futile defense."

Ignoring Lucifer's words, Michael spoke to man's soul.

"You have made the statement you are neither guilty nor innocent. Speak freely of this."

"The responsibility of any acts, as damnable as they were, cannot be blamed on the Body that now decays in the Earth nor on the living soul that I am."

Lucifer roared, "This soul shows total disregard for this Court. In the presence of the Almighty, it has the audacity to perjure itself further."

"Continue," said Michael to the soul of Peter Brian.

"Whatever I am, I'm the result of an imposition. As was the body I once inhabited."

"An imposition? Do you truly feel the creation of your soul was forced upon you?"

"And the Body that died, as well."

"Whom do you blame?"

"Whoever created me."

"The Supreme Being you now stand before is the Creator of all. Have you not learned of this on Earth?"

"I've learned many things on Earth. Mostly, of the Hell Man's body and soul are subjected to."

"And *you* have perpetrated every damnable act known to Man," said Lucifer.

Michael turned to his great adversary. "This hearing is for the express purpose of determining where this soul shall await final judgment. I charge you, Lucifer, to abide by the laws of procedure during this hearing."

"Pursue, Michael. Pursue your path of folly."

Angered over Lucifer's continued interruptions, Michael dispensed with preliminaries and got to the heart of his defense. "Do you seek separate hearings for body and soul?"

"I object," Lucifer shouted. "Michael is leading this soul into answering a question that is inadmissable. The body is dead. The soul shall bear the full guilt of the body it once possessed."

"There is nothing in the Articles of Man to exclude me from introducing the question of Man's body into this hearing."

Lucifer's voice spilled over with hate. "There . . . there beside you stands a tainted soul . . . a soul as corrupt and wicked as the body it dwelt in. Never did it influence the body toward a path of righteousness. Never did it challenge evil. Never did it encourage the body to destroy itself. I dare this man's soul to deny the charges."

"I seek only the reason, the motive behind my creation," said the soul of Man. Neither counsel would respond and the silence lingered. At long last the figure robed in gold spoke:

"Man's soul asks of thee . . ."

THE CHANCELLERY'S darkened library was silent. A threatening silence. Cardinal Spellissy tore his eyes away from the television screen and looked past the shadowy shapes of the priests seated about, searching for John Gallogly.

Engrossed to the point of obsession, John Gallogly was not aware of the Cardinal's stare. But another was: Father Augustus smiled . . . darkly.

BILLY HALE sizzled. Seated in his specially designed chair, made of oak, with a cross intricately carved into the backrest in eighteen karat gold, he glared at the TV set. Heavy brows knitted in anger. "The gall . . . the absolute gall of that man."

Her eyes glued to the set, Doris Hale was too intrigued to comment.

"Doris . . . I believe this man is a rabble-rouser."

"He's said nothing derogatory, Billy."

"He's called the Bible – the Holy Bible, mind you – a pack of lies!"

"Not really. He differs only where it portrays a wrathful God."

"*Only*? Woman, he's calling Moses, John, Paul – even Christ himself – liars. They all told us of God's wrath."

He gave her a reproving stare, then looked up at the cross-shaped clock that rested over the fireplace. It read: 8:20 P.M.

"In ten minutes my Easter Show will be on the air. Turn to that channel. I've seen all that I care to see of this Ron Rebuck."

Doris looked at him pleadingly. "Billy, wouldn't it be wise to hear what this Ron Rebuck has to say?"

"Doris, the man is a troublemaker. And I don't wish to discuss it any further. Now please do what I asked."

Obediently, she reached for the remote control. She pressed down.

It clicked to snow. She pressed again. Snow, and the sound of a station that had gone off the air. Again and again, she pressed down on the button. More of the same.

"What's wrong, Doris, has the TV gone on the blink?"

He came out of the chair and went to the large color set that was built into the paneled wall. Manually he turned the dial. "What . . . I say, what in blazes is going on?" For a full minute he went from channel to channel, but only "The Michael Messenger Show" appeared. He stepped back from the set. "Four out of five stations off the air? How can this be?"

"SPEAK ON YOUR OWN behalf," said Michael. "Speak freely before your Maker."

Undaunted, the soul of Peter Brian moved away from the arch enemies and approached the Divine Being. "I have heard of the various purported reasons for my creation. And despite Michael's noble intentions, his valiant effort in championing Man's cause, I am convinced my soul and every soul that comes from Man, represents an imposition of the greatest magnitude.

"I have been repeatedly told of Man's free will. I have been told that Man was not created to be a puppet. That Man was given a will that is free, to choose right from wrong. But Man's 'free will' comes only *after* the fact. Neither I nor the body I inhabited ever asked to be created. We had no choice in our creation nor in our roles on earth. Our existence was forced upon us without our original consent.

"In essence, Man's so-called *will* has already been willed."

"Do you dare to question the will of God?" Lucifer thundered.

"I dare to question a God who conceived the idea for my existence if . . . I repeat, *if* I am to be punished."

"You have freely sinned and the eternal punishment I seek for you is justified."

"Justified? Who besides you, Lucifer, shall find me guilty?"

"The Lord God, come final judgment, who shall rightfully condemn your soul to everlasting damnation."

"Rightfully condemn? You speak of this as justification? I see it as a crime more grievous than anything man on earth could ever possibly commit. That a Supreme God would punish an existence He alone created, knowing from the start the final results!"

Before Lucifer could reply, the Lord spoke, "Do you truly condemn your God?"

"I condemn the God that manifests Himself in many pages of a book called the Holy Bible. A God who created, then killed, His own creation. Are you that God?"

There was a silence, then the Great Judge continued,

"Am I that God, Michael? . . . Am I that God, Lucifer? Come forth. Join the soul of Man before me."

Dutifully, they came and stood next to Peter Brian's soul. The Lord waited a moment, then spoke on: "Man's soul has said it was your God whose plan it was for Man's existence. A plan that was a grave imposition upon Man's body and soul, for Man had no choice in their creation. Man's soul says that its will is not truly free. That it comes only after the fact.

"Man's soul has also introduced into this court a book called Holy. And in parts of this I am portrayed as the Great Destroyer. In this book, it is revealed that I have condoned the spilling of Man's blood and the agony of men's souls, in the wars on earth that have been fought in My name. I am revealed to be the Father of Man's bodily death. In this same book it is foretold that in Man's time on earth, I am to destroy the earth, raise the dead, summon all of the souls and bodies of Man before me, then to cast those I judge to be guilty into eternal damnation. . . . Am I this God?"

Prosecution and Defense Counsel bowed their hooded heads, but Peter Brian stood tall.

"From this book and through the tongues of Man, past and present, Man is ignorant of the true face of his God. And what of those who use the illusion of a Wrathful God to benefit their own cause? . . . Am I deserving of this? Is your God to be continually grieved by the lies, the fallacies, Man lives under? Look up at me, Michael; look upon your God, Lucifer. Your declaration of war upon each other finds Man placed in helpless jeopardy.

"Oh, sons of mine, any agony Man endures is not of your God's choosing but of your own. Who does this man's soul charge for his existence? You, Michael, who planned it? You, Lucifer, the true father of Man's bodily death? Or shall Man blame your God, who allowed all?"

"... YEAH!" CHANTED Rufus Manning jubilantly, clicking his fingers. Hughie Gilman shot him a dubious glance, then settled back to watch as the big, soaring sound and sight of Crack Widener filled the screen in front of them.

"Hughie, I can feel it. A ten million dollar take. Maybe double. And that's only the beginning!"

"Then what?"

"Whatta you mean *then what*? Merchandising, T-shirts, bracelets, medallions, necklaces, statues, membership cards, the whole enchilada. Michael's *everything*! Factories, we'll need a slew of factories . . . And he says, 'Then what?' "

"You make it sound so . . . unholy."

"Will you listen to the saint! Hey, I'm in this strictly for the dough and I never told you or anyone else otherwise. And you, Mr. Morals, I don't see you giving back your piece of pudding on the deal I made with those dummies."

"You raped them, Roof."

"Twenty-five percent across the board is raping them? I call it taking advantage of my good-heartedness."

"You gunsel! How do you figure to be entitled to *anything*? Ron Rebuck wrote the book. He founded the church. Jennifer Jewell came up with the money for the TV special – how, I'll never know. She also got Jack Pintoff to handle all the advertising on the cuff. And Crack Widener, besides donating half of everything he makes on the music, is doing the show for nothing. Just what *is* your contribution?"

"You know, Hughie, for such a smart man, you're really a dummy. I'm *The Bank*, baby. Rebuck can't afford to ask for money. He'd be like the rest of those religious bunko artists. He needs me. This way, his hands stay clean and mine get filthy with green."

"Roof, the more I think about this Ron Rebuck, the more convinced I am that you've got a tiger by the tail."

"As long as the tiger shits money, who cares?"

"I don't know. It's too smooth, too easy. I get the feeling that in the long haul it'll be you who's being used. Take my advice – call it a gut intuition – get out of it. Really, Roof, I'm not joking."

"You know what your problem is, Hughie? You've been living high off the hog too long. There's no challenge left in you."

"What's to prove? Long ago, I gave up the idea of rivaling Rockefeller. It so happens my father didn't start me off with a few million."

"Know what my father left me? A pastrami on rye."

At the sound of a phone, Hughie Gilman sprang from his chair. "I'll take it in the other room. And don't listen in on the extension!"

He was almost out of the room when Rufus yelled, "Forgetting something, counselor?"

Puzzled, Gilman looked back at the evil grin. "What?"

"This," said Rufus, shooting him a bird.

HUGHIE RUSHED BACK into the room, stopped, looked at Rufus, who was settled back in his chair, blissfully grooving on Crack Widener, who was now bowing to tumultuous applause.

"Roof, switch the channel!" he said excitedly.

"What did you say?"

"I said turn to another channel."

"Are you nuts?"

"Roof, if you don't, *I* will."

"Hughie, Rebuck's about to come on. This is the part of the show where they get the big religious come-on."

"What if I told you that your show is the only thing on television?"

"I'd say you were full of shit."

"Turn to the other channels and let's see just how full of shit I am."

Curiosity aroused, Rufus rose and turned the knob from one channel to another and another, until he'd hit them all. Nothing! Not even a test pattern. He tried it again, and again drew a total blank. He looked at Gilman, too baffled to speak.

"Coast to coast, it's the same thing. That was Bendix—Bendix from the network on the phone. He's as puzzled as you look. What's more, there's not a single radio program on the air, either."

"Hughie . . . that's . . . that's nutsy."

Gilman shook his head. "Not nutsy, Roof . . . *spooky*."

DRESSED IN A BLACK SUIT with a metallic blue shirt open at the neck to reveal a Michael's medallion, Ron Rebuck stepped onstage to spontaneous applause. He made a faint motion with one hand and the studio audience became deathly still.

"To the Christian world," he began, "Easter is the commemoration of a man who died on a cross and three days later rose from the dead."

The stage went dark. And from the darkness came a barely audible sound, which rose subtly in volume until "Hallelujah, Hallelujah" boomed out from an invisible choir. A wide beam of light revealed onstage a re-enactment of Christ's rising from the dead.

Ron Rebuck, standing in a small spotlight to one side of the scene, directed the audience toward the actors, dressed in mourning clothes, congregated around the vacant tomb.

"He has risen as He said He would," a woman joyfully exclaimed.

"He is truly the Son of God," a man cried out.

Ron Rebuck turned from the biblical scene. The sound of the "Hallelujah's" from the choir faded to a murmur. "Did the body of this man truly achieve victory over Death? Who was this man called Christ?"

From out of the shadows a figure with a long and flowing beard came forth. He held in his hand the Hebrew Bible. "I am Malachi, the messenger of Yahweh. From Moses, the father of all prophets, comes the law of Yahweh: 'You shall not have other gods before me.' "

Another stepped from the shadows, a man attired in the style of the ancient Greeks. He, too, carried a book in his hand. In bold letters, the title read "The New Testament." He said, "I am Luke, and in this holy book lies the gospel. He that died on the Cross and has risen is truly the Son of God."

"I hear the words of myth and nothing more," said Malachi. "He that died on the Cross was not the Son of God, nor of Yahweh . . . but only a man."

Luke answered: "Great prophet, you who remain covered in mystery, you who wrote the last book of the Testament you carry: the prophet of the coming of the Son of God you foretold came in the person of John the Baptist. With his powerful voice, John announced the coming of the Lord. 'Glory be the Son of God, Jesus

Christ, who died and has risen!' "

Malachi laughed a mocking laugh. "The gospel *you* have written in the book you clutch to your heart is the gospel told by a man who never met this Christ, never witnessed his crucifixion nor his rising from the dead. This is the gospel of *one* whose knowledge has been passed to him by others."

Malachi continued: "Moreover, he that is called Paul – the apostle Paul, known as Saul of Tarsus, who called you the beloved physician, is another like yourself, who never met this man called Christ, yet fills your Bible with his revelations and writings. Who is to believe the words of Saul of Tarsus, whose hands are stained with the blood of many?"

Luke drew himself up and answered: "The very book you hold, Malachi, tells us of those who murdered many, yet changed their terrible ways when the light of God touched their hearts. Yet, tell me, great prophet, why is there no clear record of your name? Why have you written a book under a disguise – the disguise of God's messenger?"

"It is not I who must explain myself and my identity. It is *you*. Unlike you and Paul, who passed along the word of others, I have delivered the message from Yahweh – the *only* God. An all-knowing God, who need not come into this world in the guise of a man to die on the cross. I say to you there is *no* son of god called Christ. There is *no* trinity. You and the other architects of the Bible you hold in your hand have conceived the existence of a false God, and have willfully violated the great Commandment given to Moses: 'I am the Lord thy God, thou shalt not have any false gods before me.' "

The pageant of prophets faded into darkness. Ron

Rebuck's face, his tricolored eyes blazing, now appeared in a beam of light. "Jesus Christ came into this world like us all, through mankind's greatest miracle: childbirth. Jesus Christ was different from all other human beings because he was born without an *original* soul!"

Ron Rebuck's face slowly dissolved as lightning, followed by claps of thunder, flashed with terrifying reality. A gentle rain commenced to fall as the scene of Christ's crucifixion materialized. A great light glittered at the foot of the cross, and from this light a voice pleaded: "Denounce man, Michael. Denounce the unworthy existence you have foolishly championed. I implore you to bring about the end of this bitter war between us."

From within the body on the cross, nearing death, came the final refusal: "You shall not know glory this day on earth. You have lost, Lucifer."

The voice from within the glittering light no longer pleaded but thundered: "Why should you, the man Jesus, be falsely encouraged by a soul that tastes not water – experiences not death. I command you to denounce the soul of Michael within you, and all the souls that await in limbo shall honor your name. Denounce Michael and your death shall not have been in vain."

The rain subsided. The agonized face of Christ looked upward, silhouetted against a strange purple sky. As the lightning flashed again and the thunder raged in the distance, a thin river of blood trickled from Christ's mouth, and there came the groans of approaching death.

Unheard by Man, Michael's voice trumpeted forth from the body it would shortly leave: "By the death of this glorious Body, Man's salvation has been achieved. Man's soul shall enter Heaven garlanded with praise. Come judgment, Man's reward shall be greater than that of all the angels."

JACK PINTOFF looked away from the TV set, past the face of Marty Pico, and rested his black eyes on Henry Rodriguez. They exchanged knowing smiles as Pintoff left his chair and took a photo from a large stack on a side table. As the communist leader watched, he went to the fireplace and proceeded to insert the photograph of Ron Rebuck into the frame – reserved for The Great Destroyer.

RON REBUCK was now moving into the final segment of "The Michael's Messenger Show" and the audience sat on the edges of their seats, waiting for whatever would come next.

"Medical science, physiology, psychology . . . these disciplines tell us how our minds and bodies work. Yet theology stumbles in the dark when it tries to explain our soul. *Soul.* To many, it's just a word. To others, a myth, a figment of man's fantastic imagination. Technology has come very far and very fast, but the would-be technologists of the soul – the reverends and religious scholars – know little of the soul.

"Oh, they're quick to explain how the soul leaves the body upon the body's death. They're adept at citing the Bible wherever it speaks of the soul. But they fail to understand, much less explain, the soul's independence of the body in which it dwells."

Ron Rebuck's face shone with uncanny brilliance. "There is no greater battle than the one that goes on within you. Two separate and independent forces in a perpetual struggle. Your mortal body, created through the evolution of lower animals, is constantly in conflict with an eternal soul made in the image of God. The war between body and soul rages on without ceasing until your body perishes. What I ask now is: Why? Why must mortal body and immortal soul forever war with each other?"

There was a clashing of cymbals and a roll of drums and a towering wooden structure appeared behind Ron Rebuck. Suddenly, huge letters were burned into the wood. The drums and cymbals ceased. The letters, blazoned in silver, read: THE LAWYERS OF HELL.

Ron Rebuck stepped closer to the tall structure. "Within this book lies the truth about man's life and death – and about man's immortal soul. This truth, like all truth, is dangerous. It will rock the great established religions of our world.

"I speak of those who launch the frail theological ships that cruise through the minds of men. That vast fleet whose leader is Admiral Fear. There is no admiral of agony on the vessel I sail. For the flag I hoist is not the skull-and-bones, not the blood-stained colors of a Wrathful God. Help me, sail with me on the perilous course, to sink those ships of fear."

The volume of the electric guitars and drums built in the background as Rebuck's face streamed with sweat. "I am a messenger of the great Archangel Michael, who calls out to every man, woman and child to help destroy the myth of a vengeful God. Help me vanquish those who have built mighty religions on foundations of fear.

"If they came out and told you there was no Wrathful God, no eternal Hell, who would support their monuments, their vast properties, their tax-free churches, farms and mansions? I say to you, the next time a priest, minister, faith-healing fool or religious faker speaks of some tragic event as being an act of God, tell 'em to preach their poison elsewhere. Don't let them chain your soul by whipping the body with words of fear."

He now extended his arms, his voice trembling with

emotion. "Become my army . . . join my cause!" He cried the words out over the choir and the wailing guitars. "Condemn those who war in the name of God. I beg of you to let your soul live harmoniously with your body. For then, you shall truly find peace on earth.

"Fear not the death of your body, for it releases an eternal soul. . . . I beseech you to *stand up for your soul* and your body will live and rejoice as never before!"

Crack Widener and the entire musical cast invaded the stage as Widener's throbbing, hypnotic voice brought down the house with his final song: "Stand Up For Your Soul."

HUGHIE GILMAN was at a loss for words, overwhelmed. He couldn't find a way to properly praise what he'd just seen. Rufus Manning's eyes were still fastened on the screen as Gilman finally managed to speak.

"Roof . . . that was the damnedest thing I've ever seen! Dazzling, magnificent! The entire thing . . . Rebuck, Widener, the music, the words . . . incredible!"

"Hughie–"

"The sound and those lights . . . Roof, how did you blend in those fantastic colors?"

"Hughie–"

"And that Crucifixion scene–totally unbelievable!"

"Hughie, listen . . ."

Now Gilman saw that Rufus Manning's face was ashen, pale as a ghost.

"Roof, what is it?"

"Hughie–that Crucifixion scene . . . I swear, *there never was a Crucifixion scene*!"

THE OLD MAN stared at the set. So totally exhumed by the Michael's Messenger special was he, the announcement for the following television show fell upon deaf ears. Ron Rebuck's potent words worked heavily on his mind, like the ghostly sound of a bell, ringing over and over, calling hime, compelling. . .

The crazed eyes under heavy lids slowly shifted. The far-off, almost frenzied glare vanished, as his eyes now rested on the woman seated in the reclining chair. She was fast asleep, thatched blanket over her legs.

His eyes now traveled from the old woman to the row of photos on a shelf. Pictures of his children and their children which held the highest place of honor in his tiny three-room flat.

With great effort, he then raised his tired and pain-filled body and went to the shelf. His eyes grew damp as he looked at each and every photo; then he came upon the black and white picture of himself and the woman asleep in the chair. The wedding photo, when he was young and strong, fired up with life, and she was so beautiful. The wedding photo, taken over fifty years ago.

He brushed away the tears with the sleeve of his bathrobe and turned toward his partner in life. At first, he stared down at her. The memories of their life together paraded through his tortured mind.

A victorious soul now won out over a frightened body, as the uncontrollable urge would not be stymied. He kissed her gently on the cheek. The words "I love you" came sobbingly in a whisper.

Standing erect, he now gazed at the window. For a monent the body rallied against its unyielding soul. Then, on unwilling legs, he went to the window to look out at the street twelve stories below.

Minutes later, the old woman in the chair stirred as she felt a sudden draft. Her eyes opened and fixed upon the open window that allowed the cold night air to chill her bones.

"Morris," she uttered. "Morris," she again called out through trembling lips as the shrieking sound of a siren from the street below now filled her ears.

# 25

RON REBUCK set off a bomb heard around the world. His revelation of the new Church of Michael, his denunciation of the Bible, found the Right Reverends Billy Hale, Norville Riggins and other noted Bible champions reluctant to publicly take on this strange man who called them all a pack of liars.

What produced a greater impact was the inexplicable fact that for two full hours only "The Michael's Messenger Show" had been on the air, while all the rest of American television and radio had been silenced. This incredible phenomenon was on the lips of people in all walks of life, from the big cities to the remotest hinterlands.

"A MIRACLE. GOD'S MIRACLE," said Crack Widener to the herd of reporters who tracked him down in the lobby of a New York hotel. Turk Savage and the wall of bodyguards around the superstar moved with great difficulty toward the elevators and were finally stopped short by the persistent newshounds. Savage tried to fend off the array of microphones being shoved at Crack's face, then reluctantly surrendered.

"All right, one at a time," he shouted.

Over the babble of voices, the pushing and shoving, a

woman reporter asked, "Do you really believe it was a miracle, Crack?"

"A great miracle," he answered.

"What about Ron Rebuck," said another. "Is he this what's-his-name's messenger?"

He gave the man a disapproving look, saying, "He is the archangel Michael's true messenger."

A large, ruddy-faced man asked, "Whose messenger are you?" Crack Widener paused. His face lit up with pride: "*God's*."

WATCHING THE TV news coverage on the set in Hughie Gilman's office, John Milton and Leslie Manning exchanged dubious expressions.

An unshaven Rufus Manning, seated behind Hughie's desk, had just finished a heated telephone conversation and was lost in thought when Hughie Gilman strode into the room. He waved Rufus out of his chair, then pressed down on the intercom. "Hold all calls. I mean *all* calls."

Still ignoring Rufus, he placed the various newspapers Rufus had scattered about his desk into an orderly pile, folded his hands, then fixed the people in the room with a stern eye.

John Milton made a move to leave but Hughie motioned for him to remain. Next, he took on the beady eyes of Rufus Manning. "Before I say what I have to say, out with it!"

"I just got off the phone with Nancy and she tells me there's a bunch of men snooping around my house."

"Not surprising," said Hughie.

"What kind of crappy remark is that? Nancy thinks they're FBI."

"When they come knocking at her door and flash

their badges, she'll really know, won't she?"

"What are you telling me?"

"You'll shut up and listen?"

"I'm paying for it, aren't I?"

"Not today, Roof. What I've got to say to you today is free of charge."

Rufus plopped into a chair and eyed him with uncertainty. Anything free, including advice, made him nervous.

"I have just witnessed top-level executives, powerful decision makers, groping in the dark. I've heard theories about what happened last night that the farthest-out science fiction writers couldn't repudiate. It seems the whole country is baffled."

He turned to Rufus. "This morning I took it upon myself to announce immediate termination of your deal with Ron Rebuck."

"You did *what*?" Rufus shouted.

"I told Dan Runkel at the network you were through. There'd be no more specials produced by you. And that's exactly what you are going to tell the press."

"Hughie, where are you coming from—Mars?"

"Ron Rebuck's trouble! I want you to stay oceans—not lakes—but *oceans* away from him."

"Hughie, you need sleep. You're not thinking straight."

"Don't tell me what I need! It's you who's in need."

"Okay, Hughie, the bottom line. Give me the bottom line," Rufus's voice trembled with anger.

"Ron Rebuck has apparently set off every nut case in America."

"What's that supposed to mean?"

"Don't you read the papers?"

"You mean the stuff about people jumping off

buildings?"

"You call it *stuff*? My God, man, an epidemic is in the making."

"Bullshit, Hughie. A few nuts do themselves in and Rebuck gets blamed for it."

"A *few*? For your information, wisenheimer, less than six hours after Rebuck's show there were more suicides in the greater New York area than the total reported for the last five months."

"Hughie, you're making it sound like Rebuck's telling people to kill themselves."

"I'm not making it sound that way! It *is* that way!"

"Horseshit," said Rufus, as he looked for support from the young people. A frown came to his face when he got none.

"Roof," said Hughie, "Dan Runkel's up to his neck in problems. He's getting flak from everyone. Two calls from the President of the United States, not to exclude the director of the FBI, the chairman of the FCC, and he swears the CIA boys are hiding in his closets."

"What the hell has a network president got to do with me?"

"WE. You and me, Roof. *We* sold him on the special—"

"Bullshit!" Rufus roared, coming out of his chair. "His goddamn network sold two hours of prime time. Nothing more. He didn't do a lick. The church paid all costs of production, advertising, *everything*. Runkel begged youfor the show."

"Are you finished?" Hughie asked.

"Facts, Hughie. When we gave him the show, letting him ace the other networks with Crack Widener, Dan Runkel was the big man. Or have you forgotten all the fucking bows he took?"

"What does it take to penetrate that mind of yours?"

"A lot more than feeling sorry for Dan Runkel because some heavyweights are on his ass, let me tell yah!"

"Then chew on the word conspiracy."

"*Conspiracy*?" John and Leslie voiced the word simultaneously.

"That's what I said."

"Against whom? What . . . Where?" an amused Rufus asked.

"Against the FCC . . . United States of America," said Gilman. "If your mind wasn't so obsessed with money, you would recognize the serious problem that now exists."

"Hughie, I recognize that you are attempting to shatter my right to the all-American dream of greed."

Anger flared in Gilman's eyes. "Now you listen to me and listen good! Someone or some*thing* tampered with the airwaves over this country and by doing so it has become a federal matter. *Federal*, do you understand? And from the reports I'm getting, the government's security agencies are seeing *red*." He got up from the chair and came around the desk to take on Rufus face-to-face. "Why do you think strange people are snooping around your home? Because you happen to be the producer of the biggest broadcasting mystery of all time. *You* are a suspect. Suspect–do you comprehend the meaning of the word?"

"You're outta your skull, Hughie."

"Anyone, and I mean anyone, connected with Ron Rebuck, no matter how slight the association, is considered a suspect. *Suspect.* Myself included."

He pointed a shaky finger at the phone on his desk. "Ten to one–a hundred to one–the damn thing's bugged."

"I don't believe you, Hughie. You're talking like Nixon's back in the White House."

"J. Edgar Hoover's dead, Mr. Gilman," Leslie added.

Hughie Gilman turned toward a thoughtful John Milton. "Don't *you* have anything to say?" he asked sarcastically.

"Only that I happen to agree with you."

"You *do*?" Hughie pointed a finger at Rufus. "Tell *him*!"

"Yeah, tell me, John," said Rufus, welcoming another viewpoint.

". . . Well, the way I see it, Ron Rebuck defended God, condemned the religious wrathmongers, but made the fatal mistake of performing a miracle."

"John, surely you don't believe Ron Rebuck performs miracles?"

"Prove he can't, Leslie. The experts are saying 'no comment.' Which means they don't know. Besides, you realize there's quite a parallel to all of this."

No one asked what it was, and John continued, "It's believed Jesus Christ performed miracles, and it got *him* crucified."

There was silence as the ghost of a wicked smile played on Rufus's lips.

"Not bad," said Rufus. "Jesus Christ and Ron Rebuck. Not bad at all."

"You're *not*," said Hughie, reading his thoughts. He went back to his desk shaking his head in dismay, followed by those beady eyes. "For God's sake, man, must I draw you a picture?"

"Not if it's got a yellow streak in it."

"Roof, there's a bomb about to blow up in Rebuck's face, and you are in range. Didn't anything I said get through?"

"Sure . . . the words of a frightened man."

"A wise man," Hughie countered. "One who for some crazy reason cares about you *and* your family. Roof, look at me, I'm begging you to get out of this before you get hurt."

"Hughie, don't think I'm ungrateful for your concern, but Ron Rebuck hasn't done a damn thing wrong. He's broken no laws. I can't explain how the crucifixion scene got on the viewing tape, and I'm as confused as everyone else as to how the special was the only thing that went over the airwaves, but I refuse to get a hernia of the mind thinking about it any longer. The shit about the man being a threat to the government—that'll never wash and *you* know it."

Rufus paused to light a cigarette, then resumed, "Oh, he's a threat, all right. To every religion, church, who made fortunes out of fleecing the public. And now, now that it appears Rebuck is going to shake their tax free money trees, they're running to big brother government.

"You know what I think, Hughie? I think Ron Rebuck caught the entire religious industry with their pants down. Why, Hughie, why haven't the big boys in religion taken on this Reverend Moon guy? It's okay for him to steal kids from their parents, okay for him to own an ammunition factory in Korea—making bullets to kill people—but not one of those religious leaders have come out against him. And do you know why? Because he preaches out of the same Bible, uses the same words, only with a different slant. Who are they shittin', Hughie? For them to attack Moon, they cut their own throats. But Rebuck's another story. He's stuck 'em in the ass, and they're making tracks for Washington."

"Roof, for argument's sake, let's say I agree with you."

"*Say*? No, Hughie, you either agree or you don't."

"Even if I do, it doesn't change a damn thing. Until someone comes up with the right answers, the Feds will have Ron Rebuck under a microscope."

"Aren't you overlooking something, counselor?"

"If I am, now's the time to remind me."

Rufus looked over at John Milton. "Read him the tote sheet."

From a vest pocket John Milton took out a piece of paper, then proceeded to read its contents: "Ron Rebuck's book has sold out in the greater metropolitan area. McGuinness and McGuinness predict the same nationwide. Widener Industries *grossly* underestimated the potential sales of the album and are being swamped with orders."

"And that," said Rufus, "doesn't include what's happening with merchandising sales, or membership in the Church of Michael."

He leaned over Hughie's desk. "The *people*, baby. The *people* are speaking. Rebuck's a solid hit."

Hughie Gilman leaned back in his chair, impressed. He looked into those hawklike eyes. "God knows I tried. But you're going to bang for that billion, even if it destroys you."

"Counselor, let me worry about who's going to destroy whom. As long as the press stays free, the government can't afford to fuck with Rebuck. He's selling papers, baby."

He moved away from the desk, then stopped, having more to say. "And, Hughie, the President of the United States most likely called Runkel because his minister probably blew his ears off reading him the Bible."

"Where are you going?"

"To get myself acquainted with some of the loot."

"Roof."

"Yeah?"

"Never mind."

Hughie Gilman's personal secretary popped her head into the room. "Mr. Gilman, there's a gang of reporters in the reception area."

"Who do they want to see?"

"I think Mr. Manning."

He dismissed her with a cordial wave, then came out of his chair. "That *free* press you spoke of . . . awaits you."

"What are you going to tell them?" Leslie asked.

"Tell them? The truth, Leslie . . . the *gospel* truth."

JOHN GALLOGLY stood at the doorway to his office and watched the Vicar General lead a group of priests down the hall. Not one of them looked his way in passing. He could understand why the Vicar General shunned him. Ever since their confrontation, neither had said a word to each other.

For the last three days priests from around the Catholic globe were arriving at the chancellery. Strange men, humorless, all possessing that cold, deadly look in their eyes. Men from the same mold as Father Augustus.

The Cardinal had not taken him into his confidence, nor had he been asked to participate in the frequent lengthy conferences the Cardinal had with Father Augustus.

His initial dislike for Father Augustus had now grown into hate. And this sudden fall from the Cardinal's favor—he could only believe Father Augustus was behind it.

And now, the urgent gathering of mysterious priests—what was it Paul Bartley called this breed of men, Ghoul Chasers?

MARTY PICO hurriedly stepped into the courtyard that led out of the chancellery.

"*Pico*!"

Instinctively, he turned. "Hey . . . what's happening, Monsignor Gallogly?" he said with false joviality.

"What are you doing here?"

"Confession." He smiled.

"What are you doing here, Pico?"

"Hey, I left some things and came to pick 'em up, all right?"

"You're lying."

"Am I?"

"You didn't leave anything, Pico. You brought something. What, and to whom?"

Pico started to turn away. "Coming on awful heavy, ain't you, Monsignor?"

"You lying bastard, tell me the truth!"

Startled, Pico noted the flaming eyes of the priest.

"*Heav . . eee*," he repeated over and over, backing away.

A frustrated John Gallogly remained following him with his eyes.

Slowly, Gallogly made his way back to the building. Approaching the courtyard, he looked up—toward the second story where he recognized the face in the window looking down at him. The bearded face of Father Augustus . . .

# 26

IT STARTED WITH a demonstration. A peaceful demonstration. A busload of divinity students from a nearby
Bible college parked in front of the Rebucks' home.
When they sang in force, "Onward Christian Soldiers,"
it was then for the first time that June Rebuck felt the
crunch of opposition to her husband's crusade.

As a young girl growing up in West Virginia, she
could never forget the countless times she'd fervently
sung this particular song when attending those *mus*
church services. And now, the words "Onward Christian soldiers marching off to war" had a very differen
meaning to her. The war was against her very husband.

There had been other incidents. An oddball had come
dressed in a long Biblical robe, staff in hand, and had
shouted out bits of scripture damning her husband to
burn in eternal Hell.

June Rebuck gradually resigned herself to accep
these protests, but the calls, those threatening calls from
persons anonymous, vowing to do bodily harm to her
husband, were becoming too much to bear. Twice she'd
changed the phone number, requesting it to be unlisted
but still the calls came.

Her only consolation was that she'd soon be leaving
for New York to join her husband.

The last time she'd talked directly to him was on the
night of the special, a week ago. Since then the only
communication she'd had with him went through Ed

Dowiat or Jennifer Jewell. She was a trifle hurt that this woman had become her own husband's closest confidant. "Security reasons," she was informed.

What bothered her the most was the drastic change that had come over her son, Ron Rebuck, Jr. Gone was the boyish smile, that carefree attitude. He walked about as if the weight on his father's shoulders was on his own as well. She could see how he was becoming more like him every day. But what gave her chills was the amount of time he'd spend in his father's den. Hour after hour he'd remain in that room, that very room she had so much reason to hate.

June Rebuck could now see how her once close-knit family was slowly coming apart, and she cursed the day her husband was called by the angel Michael.

Watching late-night television, June Rebuck sat up in the bed. For the first time in a week, a day had passed without being plagued with threatening calls. Greatly relieved, she'd decided to leave the phone on the hook for the remainder of the night.

Tom Snyder was questioning his guest, a Bible scholar, about her husband's philosophies, when her attention was suddenly diverted by a noise from outside. A rapping or scratching that seemed to be coming from the front door. Or was it? She couldn't readily identify its origin.

The doors were bolted, the windows locked, only Ronnie's whereabouts remained in doubt. Was he home or out for one of his midnight walks on the beach?

She turned off the TV and sat quietly, her ears tuned, and the sound returned. This time it was louder. Someone was at her front door and for certain it wasn't Ronnie. She wouldn't panic. Having prepared for every possibility, she reached for the phone on the small table next to the bed and dialed the police.

The receiver pressed to her ear, she waited, wondering why they didn't answer. She was about to redial when it suddenly, fearfully dawned on her that the phone was, in fact, dead.

She slipped out of bed, trembling. On shaky legs, she left the bedroom and went down the darkened corridor. Nearing the kitchen, she halted, staring at the front door. Outside she could hear men's laughter, then a man's muffled voice.

"Who's there?" she asked in a voice just above a whisper. "Who's out there?"

The sounds behind the door ceased. Silence. She heard only her own rapid, frightened breathing. Desperately, she fought off hysteria and forced her immobile body to move.

She went past the door and into the kitchen. She inched closer to the window. Through terror-stricken eyes she saw the face of a demon staring back at her.

RON REBUCK, JR. wiped the sand from his bare feet and got into the green TR7. His nightly walk on the beach had been longer than usual and he thought of his mother, all alone in the house.

He sped away from the beach and onto the causeway. A two-minute stretch before making the turnoff for Island Isles.

There was a confident, determined glow about his face. He'd thought it all out and, no matter what, nothing could prevent him from joining his father. His mind was so engrossed with this thought that he didn't realize he was being followed—trailed by a dark blue van that stayed an inconspicuous distance behind.

Turning onto his street with the house in view, he at

first couldn't believe his eyes. Two men, their faces covered with rubber masks, resembling gargoyles, were throwing objects at the windows while another watched and laughed from a blue and white pickup truck parked on the lawn.

He could hear the faint yet frantic cries of his mother from within the house. Blinded with rage, he ran the Triumph onto the lawn with its high beams zeroed in on the truck.

"Haul ass!" shouted the man in the pickup.

The kitchen light went on. Then the porch light over the front door—where a red cross had been freshly painted. The door opened a crack and June Rebuck appeared.

"Get away from them! Call the police!" she screamed.

"Mother, get in the house!" he shouted back. Then he moved quickly to intercept one of the masked men—blocking his path to the truck.

The pickup's driver stuck his masked head out the window. "Git it on, Mack, before I run over the sunuvabitch!"

"The boy wants some of my ass."

"Kick it and let's go," the driver hastily replied.

The young Rebuck stayed his ground as the heavily built man taunted him.

"C'mon, boy. C'mon an' git it."

Young Rebuck faked a move and succeeded in drawing the man closer; then with the devil's face within striking distance, he unloaded a short right that landed on the rubbery nose of the devil-face and crunched human cartilage beneath.

Dazed by the swiftness of the blow, the man reeled backward, but the young Rebuck was upon him. Another right sent him crashing to the ground. Incensed, young Rebuck sprang on top of him and tore the rubber mask from his head. He looked down at the beefy face of a man in his late twenties, whose sideburns grew all the way to his chin. A trickle of blood seeped from the nostrils. Enraged, he drove his fists into the bleeding face.

He didn't hear his mother's cry of warning. Nor did he hear the sickening thud from the butt of a shotgun that came down on his skull.

AT DAWN, SHERIFF'S deputies found an abandoned blue and white pickup in a ditch off a secluded country road near Lakeland, Florida. Later that very morning, a caretaker of a church-owned cemetery discovered the bodies of three men. Torn rubber masks lay beside them. Their hands were tied and lashed to tombstones. Their throats had been slit.

THE NATION HAD YET to digest the apparent similarity between Christ and Ron Rebuck, a similarity having mainly to do with miracles being nurtured by a promotion-minded Rufus Manning, when news bulletins telling of the assault upon Ron Rebuck's son flashed over radio and television.

One early report had the young Rebuck's condition near death. Another claimed he was comatose and had suffered severe brain damage. The neurosurgeon whose patient Ron was, one Troy Pittman, dispelled these rumors when he revealed his medical report to the throng of reporters who converged upon the Clearwater Hospital.

The young Rebuck had suffered a concussion; the lacerations to his head took thirty stitches. He would remain in the hospital for further observation but was *not* on anyone's critical list.

JOHN GALLOGLY blamed them all—each and every religious denomination that clung to the belief in A God of Wrath—for what happened to Ron Rebuck's son. Sadly, he blamed his own beloved Church. And as soon as he could get his things together, his days as a Catholic priest would be over.

He took the picture of his mother and father from atop the bureau and carefully placed it in his metal footlocker. He had only a few more articles to pack when there came a light rapping on the bedroom door. Thinking it was one of the maintenance men to help him with his luggage, he went to the door and opened it.

Cardinal Spellissy brushed past him and into the room. "Going somewhere, John?"

"I would think it's obvious."

"Might I ask where?"

"It's all in the letter."

The Cardinal followed the direction of his eyes to where an envelope lay on a small table. He ambled toward it and casually picked it up.

In no hurry to read its contents, Spellissy put the envelope back on the table, saying, "Sometimes people, intelligent people, write things they wished they hadn't."

"If that was for my benefit, I can assure you I'm not one of those people."

"Bit snappy, aren't you, son?"

John Gallogly stopped what he was doing, stayed

from the Cardinal's digging eyes. "Cardinal Spellissy, I was hoping my departure would be an amicable one without a sermon or chastisement."

The Cardinal strolled toward the bed and balanced his great bulk on its edge.

"My visit does not include a sermon. However, before you abandon the great vocation you chose, I suggest you weigh carefully what I have to say."

For the first time since Spellissy entered the room, John met the Cardinal's eyes. He wanted to tell him he needn't bother, but the almost mystical glow radiating about the Cardinal's round face stopped him.

"John, I have been neglectful in not telling you this sooner, but few could have stood up under the excruciating ordeal you've been through. Most men would have broken."

"You mean, like Paul Bartley?"

"Father Bartley did not possess your faith or your strength. He was vulnerable. That is why he fell prey to this Rebuck's witchery."

John Gallogly tossed the blue shirt he was holding into an open suitcase.

"Cardinal Spellissy, I think you have it turned around. The finger of guilt points at *us*. Organized religion. *We* are the ones who prospered through the use of witchcraft. Cardinal, we *pioneered* the practice!"

The Cardinal leaned back on the bed. His smile clouded over; he'd now forego the gentle approach.

"Damn it, John, if you think I am going to sit by and allow you to denounce your sacred vows, toss away a brilliant future, all because you have been taken in—"

"Taken in! By *whom*? Surely you're not referring to Ron Rebuck."

"*But I am*. And before you turn your back on Mother

Church you shall damn well listen!"

"*To what?* To what, Cardinal Spellissy? For months I *have* listened, been patient. What did it get me? I've been treated like an outcast—ignored by my superiors . . . including Your Eminence. Spied on day and night by a face I've grown to despise."

"There were reasons," said the Cardinal. "We had good reasons."

"*We*? Does that 'we' mean Father Augustus?"

"Being a trifle unfair, aren't you? But then people like Augustus who seek out the truth, well, they never are too popular, are they?"

"He's a destroyer, Cardinal. One who takes great pleasure in his work."

"I did not come here to talk about Father Augustus."

"Then what about the likes of Marty Pico? His frequent visits to the chancellery? A man that you, yourself, warned me to stay away from."

"Mr. Pico has volunteered his services to the Church he belongs to. The Roman Catholic Church of which you are an officer."

John Gallogly laughed bitterly. "Pico has never volunteered for anything in his life. What was it you called him, 'one of the dogs of the world'?"

"You are making things complicated, John."

"Your Eminence, for better than a week my entire life has been complicated."

The Cardinal leaned forward, resting the pudgy hands on his knees.

"Tell me one time I ever led you astray? One time when I did not have a pretty good and powerful reason for what I did?"

To this, John Gallogly had no rebuttal.

"John, all I ask is for you to be patient a while longer."

". . . I'm sorry, I can't. It's only because of my feelings for you that I haven't left sooner. But the power that compels me, drives me, can no longer be denied."

The Cardinal looked deeply into the face of the young Monsignor. "Tell me, John, this force, this driving compulsion of yours, might it not be directed by a false power?"

Slowly the picture of it all came clear. The reason why he'd not been privy to what went on in those long meetings between the Cardinal and Father Augustus now stood revealed. "Destroy Ron Rebuck's credibility, is that the plan? Is that why the chancellery has become filled with witch-doctors?

"But why smear Rebuck's religious philosophy; wouldn't it be simpler to attack him in a more conventional way? Like having him examined by the IRS? Or have Marty Pico set him up on some morals charge? Weren't those some of the methods used on *Henry Rodriguez*?"

The Cardinal stiffened. The thrust of Gallogly's words cut deep.

"But then, there's even a quicker way. All you would have to do is contact one of our charitable Mafia friends. The ones who donate so heavily for the building of churches. I'm sure they wouldn't think twice about killing Ron Rebuck. Sort of a spiritual contract, you might call it. But, of course, it would have to be a cleaner job than the one done on Ron Rebuck's son . . . wouldn't it?"

"How . . . how dare you speak of Mother Church in such a vein?"

"I'm speaking of a small number of powerful individuals in the Church. Men who can swing political elections. Men with the kind of power I have seen *you* wield."

His face knotted with anger, Spellissy rose from the bed. "I have been vested with the power to do battle upon Mother Church's enemies. And so I shall until the final breath has left me!"

"In whose name, Your Eminence, the Church's or God's?"

"There can be no separation!"

"Hogwash! The Church's enemies are just that. The God Ron Rebuck so courageously revealed has no enemies."

The Cardinal stormed to the door, unwilling to hear any more from a man he once regarded as a son. But his hand paused on the door's handle. Without turning back he said, "Are you possessed by so great a force that you must say the terrible things you have said?"

"My soul is free, Cardinal, no longer chained by bodily fears."

"And now you are going to join this man who set your soul free."

"I am. Maybe I can undo some of the wrongs I condoned in the years I spent in the service of a church I now deplore."

The Cardinal turned swiftly from the door. "You fool! You are being had, but you are too blinded to realize it. Have you given thought to why Rebuck wants you? Why *you*, and not me?"

"It's obvious why not you."

"The only thing obvious, young man, is that I am more than Rebuck can chew. But in you, he's found a plum. Someone to discredit Mother Church with. Someone to give him a much-needed credibility. You have been victimized by his magic and if I did not think so, you could go to the devil for all I care. And if you walk out on Mother Church, join this man, that is *exactly* where you are heading."

"The words of a wounded man, Cardinal Spellissy. Father Augustus and his pack of vultures will have to come up with better material than that."

Without warning the Cardinal came up to him, and in one swift movement of his arm, there came the clapping sound of meat against meat . . .

More shocked than hurt, John Gallogly brought a soothing hand to his already-reddened face.

"Was that done in the Name of God . . . or the Church?"

A rush of embarrassment rinsed the fury from the Cardinal's face. He couldn't find appropriate words of apology. He released his eyes from the anguished man. There was little more he could say. The round shoulders slumped even more as he walked to the door; words came chokingly.

"I will be in my office. I shall pray you drop in."

With that, he opened the door and was about to depart when John Gallogly's voice, shaking with emotion, made it seem all so final.

"Goodbye, Your Eminence . . . God bless you."

# 28

TWO GIRLS in minidresses and four-inch heels emerged disheveled from Jack Pintoff's bedroom. The younger one, not over fifteen, stuck close to the older, black-haired girl.

Marty Pico looked up from the lounge chair where he was sitting.

The older girl greeted him bitterly. "Your friend's a psycho."

"Hey, what can I tell yah?" Marty replied as he took a bill out of a leather wallet.

She hawked the hundred in his hand and grimly snapped, "Double that, Charlie."

"Double your ass!"

She put a protecting hand on the shoulder of the youngster standing at her side, staring blankly. "Your friend's screwed up this kid's head so bad it'll take a month before she's any good to me."

"Yeah, tell me all about it—*next Wednesday.* You want the bread or not?"

She snatched the bill from his hand. "My pimp's gonna come down heavy on you, Fatso."

"What pimp? *You're* the lousy pimp. Get lost before I punch holes in yer face." She continued her bitching all the way out the front door, but he paid no heed and sauntered back to the living room, stopping short when he saw Jack Pintoff's twisted face at the bedroom door.

Through drooling lips he blew Marty Pico a kiss. "So sweet, so succulent. My compliments, Mr. Pico, your selections have greatly improved."

Disturbed by his innuendo, Marty Pico followed him into the king-size living room. "I think it's time we got a few things straightened out."

"Such as, Mr. Pico, such as?"

"The bit about the broads. The sign on my office door says 'detective,' but you read it 'pimp.' "

"Mr. Pico, in one way or another we are all pimps."

He sprawled out on the twenty-foot beige couch. His sexual appetite sated, a debate with Marty Pico was light dessert.

"What's on your mind, Mr. Pico? Spare me none of the details."

Pico eyed the grotesque figure distastefully.

"The freaky things you do to broads . . . they talk, you know?"

"To whom, Mr. Pico?"

"To a whole lot of ears. And some of 'em are bulls. Like, I don't want my license yanked."

"Hookers, Mr. Pico. Hookers."

Marty Pico took a seat opposite him. "You're not hip to what's happenin' on the street, are yah?"

"The street," Pintoff laughed. "The street is a garbage pile of puny lives."

He sat up, eyes flashing. "You're playing in the big game now, Mr. Pico, not where dog eats dog, but where giants slay giants."

"Talking money," said Pico, "you'll have to bump the retainer another two bills. The overhead's killin' me."

"Mr. Pico, are you trying to fleece me?"

"Some fleecing! I'm spending twice, three times as much time with you as any other client."

"Clients, Mr. Pico? I happen to know that in your blind greed you've neglected your business. And if it weren't for my retainer you would be out working the streets with a tin cup. So let's dispense with the fabrications, shall we?"

"Look, *guy,* I ain't alone. Got a junior partner the size of a mountain who's already bustin' my balls. And when I tell him the business is a little short, he sticks his black eyeballs down my throat wantin' to know why."

"Shoot him!"

". . . Wud you say?"

"Shoot him. You have a gun. And, I presume, a license to carry it. Kill him, Mr. Pico. Using your vernacular—waste him!"

Pico got up, saying, "Listen, maybe I should split. I

mean you're a bedbug and I don't feature where you're comin' from."

"Sit down! You have not been excused."

"Not *what*?"

"Excused. Given permission to leave."

He looked down at the ugly face, meeting the narrow, slitted eyes. Pico slowly unbuttoned his jacket to reveal the butt end of a pistol. Tapping it, he said, "This piece says I'm leavin'. "

"You will leave when I tell you. If that pistol is meant to frighten me, it doesn't."

"Pal, I gunna make like an Indian. And like Indians never fucked with crazies."

"Where are you going, Mr. Pico?"

"To put a lotta daylight between you and me. You're too much of a nightmare for me to hack."

From the door, he turned and said, "Forget the retainer. Forget me. And you can forget the C-note I laid out for the broads."

"Mr. Pico, before you depart, I think I should warn you that your life is in great danger."

"Why, you little cock-knocker, are you threatening me?"

"No, Mr. Pico, not I."

Pico strode swiftly back to the couch. His eyes blazed at Jack Pintoff. "Talk!"

"Before I do, Mr. Pico, you will sit down and calm yourself. We shall approach this in a businesslike manner."

"Just forget the bullshit and get to the point."

"I'll ignore that remark. But I warn you, Mr. Pico, I shall not tolerate another like it."

Marty Pico gritted his teeth and sat down.

Jack Pintoff continued, "The day you came to me

with such a flimsy con was the day we became involved. The fact that we shared a common hate for Rufus Manning interested me. And when you boasted of having access to the chancellery, and the Cardinal himself, my interest mounted."

He then rose from the couch, circled a wary Marty Pico and seated himself in a lounge chair across from him.

"In essence, Mr. Pico, when you so hungrily took the retainer, you then committed yourself . . . body and soul."

"That's what you think!"

"Know, Mr. Pico, know."

"Yeah, well maybe you know what you're talking about, but I sure as shit don't."

"The *war,* Mr. Pico. You are a participant in the greatest of all conflicts."

"You better stop sniffin' whatever you're sniffin' 'cause the only war I got brewing is the one I'm gonna lay on you if I don't hear the name of the dude threatening me."

"Mr. Pico, only you have the distinction of being able to cross the lines of both camps."

"Camps, my ass! And if you don't start makin' sense I'm gunna camp a loaded piece at your ugly face."

The phone rang. Pintoff quickly picked it up, pressed a button and a voice came over the loudspeaker. Pico immediately recognized the voice of Ed Dowiat, Ron Rebuck's close advisor.

"Mr. Pintoff, I just wanted to remind you as one of our three advisors, that we have a board meeting on Friday morning—10:30."

"You can count on me . . . By the way, Mr. Dowiat, I hear the board—and the Church of Michael—has a distinguished recruit from the *other side*—"

"Yes, Mr. Pintoff, Monsignor Gallogly is a full-fledged member of the Mission's board. Ron's delighted."

"A great coup, Mr. Dowiat. My compliments."

"By the way, wasn't that terrible, what happened?"

"Ah, I don't believe I understand you."

"You don't know?"

"Know what, Mr. Dowiat?"

"Apparently you haven't been watching television. They found the men who assaulted young Rebuck."

"Indeed?"

"I should have said . . . their bodies."

"They met with foul play, Mr. Dowiat?"

" 'Fraid so. Ron's really shook up about it. Found 'em with their throats cut, the story goes."

"Where? Where did this happen?"

"Florida. Near Lakeland. In a cemetery, no less."

Marty Pico's eyes widened. The image of Mike Spenard flashed through his mind as Dowiat spoke.

"Ron's gone to Florida. I'm not expecting him to attend the board meeting on Friday. Oh, by the way, we'll be bringing up the subject of bodyguards. The Rebuck family is going to need them. I'm counting on you to help us on this matter."

"Be assured, Mr. Dowiat. Be assured."

"Thanks. See you Friday, then."

"Yes, Friday. Goodbye, Mr. Dowiat."

A knowing smile came to Pintoff's lips as he placed the receiver back on its hook. "The religious revolution's first turncoat, and a monsignor, at that!"

Pico didn't hear; he had something else on his mind. "There's only one dude who gets his kicks in cemeteries, Pintoff, and he ain't in your collection of pictures."

"Who, Mr. Pico, who?"

"That maniac . . . Mike Spenard."

"You think he killed those men?"

"I'd bet my life on it."

"Then you're also accusing Rufus Manning."

"Bet your ass I am. Spenard doesn't take a leak unless Manning tells him. Yeah, Manning gave that butcher the orders for the hit all right."

"Mr. Pico, I have no love for Manning, but do you really believe he'd send his goon out to commit cold-blooded murder?"

"Hey, he had that snake take me for a ride for a lot less reason."

"Oh, yes. The ride was to a cemetery, wasn't it, Mr. Pico?"

"Yeah, a cemetery," said Pico, frowning at the memory.

Jack Pintoff let him agonize a while longer, then said, "Mr. Pico, if it's any consolation to you, the murderer of those men in Florida was not this Spenard."

Marty Pico eyed him suspiciously.

"Smile, Mr. Pico. Your vendetta against Manning will end in glory, but, right now, fortune awaits you. How many bodyguards would you say it will take to protect Rebuck and his family?"

"Around the clock?"

"Of course."

"An army."

"Whatever the numbers, Mr. Pico, they'll be hired through your detective agency."

"Are you kidding? I'd have to infiltrate Burns or Pinkerton."

"No, Mr. Pico, you won't be troubled with the actual hiring."

"The riddles again, right?"

Jack Pintoff came back to the couch and stretched out. "Mr. Pico, I think it time you know I am not your true benefactor, merely an intermediary."

"That's not what the checks say."

"Mr. Pico, the connection you've made at the chancellery is most vital to your true benefactor. Do what you're told and you shall come out of this war unscarred – and a rich man. Cross him, and you shall leave this life."

"Pintoff, how do I know you're not jerking me off?"

"You don't. However, if you're the detective you claim to be, I'm sure his identity will come to you."

Marty Pico's eyes shifted to the gallery above the fireplace.

"A clue, Mr. Pico?"

He stared at the portrait of Henry Rodriguez, then turned to the twisted face he despised.

"If I'm thinkin' who I'm thinkin' . . . *forget it*!"

"Mr. Pico, all your life you have lived with the motto 'buyer beware.' You sold your services like a whore on the street. You fleeced the sheik, and countless others. But it's different now, isn't it, Mr. Pico? It's beware *of* the buyer. And, Mr. Pico, you have good reason to sweat."

"Cool it, Pintoff. You don't have to draw me a picture."

"Good night, Mr. Pico. And stay by your phone."

Subdued, Marty Pico went to the door, then suddenly turned. "You know, I don't know who I hate more– you or Manning."

Jack Pintoff waited for the front door to slam shut, then approached his gallery.

He studied the photograph of Henry Rodriguez.

"You've got your war, Henry. How much blood shall you spill?"

His laugh echoed eerily in the vast room, like the howl of a jackal.

AT A PHONE in the farthest corner of the chancellery's library, Bishop Burke, the Vicar General, spoke in a whisper to a late-hour caller.

Seated at the head of the conference table, the Cardinal listened to Father Augustus, now and then pausing to glare at the front-page news picture of Ron Rebuck and John Gallogly, locked in brotherly embrace. He couldn't bring himself to read the story.

Father Augustus droned out his concluding statement. "The slaying of these men is only the beginning of things to come. If I understand correctly, a Biblical prophecy of earth-shaking force will soon come to pass."

Cardinal Spellissy searched the faces of the priests seated around the conference table—theologians, members of Father Augustus's Vatican team, and the Cardinal's oldest and most trusted friend, Archbishop Joe McGary.

"Thank you, Father Augustus. Most enlightening. And a bit terrifying, I might say. However, I for one cannot put much stock in the supernatural being responsible for the actual killing of those men. People are murdered by people. Not by angels." His hand rubbed that great belly. "Oh, I know the Bible tells us of angels who've slain men, but we're not living in Biblical times. No, gentlemen, the killer or killers are of flesh and blood."

"Tim," said the Archbishop, "you don't believe Ron Rebuck is in back of all this, do you?"

"I think he is as surprised and shocked as anyone else."

"Your Eminence," said the Vicar General, returning to the table, "I wouldn't be too quick to rule out Rebuck's involvement. That was Mr. Pico who called just now. Seems he knows who the killer is."

"Has he called the police with this information?"

"I told him to," the Vicar General replied. "Swears it's Rufus Manning's man-of-all-work, the fellow named Mike Spenard."

For better than a minute, the Cardinal remained silent, then to the Vicar General's dismay, he said, "Let's go over Mr. Pico's written report, once again."

"Cardinal," the Vicar General protested, "we've been through it a dozen times. Just *what* are you searching for?"

"A link, Bishop. A positive link."

The Vicar General gave him a questioning look, then opened a legal-sized folder before him. He was about to read from its contents when the Cardinal interrupted.

"Skip Ron Rebuck. After all, Father Augustus has been commissioned by Rome to investigate the man." He turned to the bearded priest. "I'm sure whatever information we might need, you will provide."

Father Augustus's smile was noncommittal.

"You may also skip Ed Dowiat."

"That leaves only Crack Widener and Jennifer Jewell," the Vicar General said.

"The woman first, if you don't mind."

The Vicar General thumbed through the report until he came upon the name of Jennifer Jewell. He read:

"Born, Jennifer Desmond, in Dallas, Texas. Age, twenty-six. Married at nineteen to one Reese Hubbard. Divorced at twenty-one. Reason, mental cruelty.

Occupation, model. Bathing suits in particular. Went to Europe where she was employed by an English sportswear firm. Was followed around the Continent by one Sheik Ali Sharif. Became Sheik's mistress—"

The Cardinal broke in, "What does Pico have to say about her tenure with the sheik?"

"It's not in this report, but he did tell me the separation was most friendly. Economically speaking, as well. . . . Now that I recall, he did mention a tape he had in his possession. Something to do with a conversation between the sheik and the woman."

Archbishop McGary read "blackmail" in the Cardinal's mind, as the Vicar General went on to the report on Crack Widener.

"Thus, the so-called Church of Michael's governing board," he said with a sigh of relief.

"And now the advisors, please," the Cardinal said firmly.

Wearily, he flipped the pages and read the intelligence summaries on Drew Bonds and Rufus Manning. He then closed the folder and pushed it away from him.

"No others?" the Cardinal asked.

"Not in Mr. Pico's report."

The Cardinal leaned back in the chair, puzzlement evident on his face. "I could have sworn there was another advisor." He thought about it a moment, then dismissed it from his mind and rose from his chair. "Gentlemen, 'tis my guess whoever is guiding Rebuck intends to make him out to be a modern-day Jesus Christ. And while Father Augustus goes about his business, finding out just who this supernatural guide truly is, we shall concentrate our efforts in a less spectacular arena.

"What we have, gentlemen, is Edward Dowiat, in the

role of Peter. Perhaps not a strong one, but nevertheless, Ron Rebuck's 'rock.' Jennifer Jewell, however, seems to be a powerful and influential Mary Magdelene." He gazed around the table. "What we must find, gentlemen, is Ron Rebuck's Judas."

"Begging your pardon, Cardinal," said the Vicar General, "but if this report is as credible as I'm inclined to believe, and with this new information from Mr. Pico, it seems obvious that Rufus Manning is the Judas."

"Tell me, Bishop, for what significant purpose would Manning betray the man who's making him rich?"

"Are you saying Mr. Pico's all wet about this Spenard fellow?"

"Bishop, I am not saying anything of the kind. The police will determine just how wet Mr. Pico is or isn't."

He stood behind his chair, grasping its backrest firmly in his hands. "The hour's late, and unless someone has anything further to say, I suggest we adjourn for the night."

The Vicar General, bidding a cool-sounding goodnight, was the first to leave the room.

The Cardinal motioned for the Archbishop to remain behind, then waited for the room to clear.

Archbishop McGary studied the face he'd known for better than forty years. The expression was one of deep concern.

"Tim, you're worried sick over this Rebuck, aren't you?"

"I am, Joe. I damn well am."

He moved away from the chair and began to pace the floor. "The man has moved farther, faster, than I ever anticipated."

The Archbishop stirred and said, "I would only be fooling myself not to admit Rebuck is the most spectacular religious star to come along in ages. But I think of him as a meteorite. And meteorites do have a way of burning themselves out, don't they?"

The Cardinal returned to the chair. He slapped its backrest lightly, and said, "My first mistake."

"How's that?"

"When John first brought the man's name to my attention, I wrote him off as a flash in the pan. I was wrong. Dead wrong!"

He slowly walked to the opposite end of the conference table.

"Rebuck is now at the threshold. What's more, the Vatican is within range of his guns."

He turned to look at row on row of books ranged around the huge room. Pointing to them he said, "The greatest theological minds the world has known—silenced by one man and his book."

"Speaking of being silenced," said the Archbishop, "it's surprising Billy Hale and Norville Riggins have kept quiet this long."

"What can they say? What can they possibly do to combat Rebuck? His theory not only provides a comforting universal belief, but absolves the Almighty of all wrath. They are stumped, and Rebuck damn well knows it."

The Cardinal slumped into the head chair. "Joe, Rebuck will run over Billy Hale and the rest of those evangelists without breaking stride. He's already taken out after that Reverend Earth – who knows who'll be next on his hit parade. And *we* cannot afford to let him go any further. We do, and he's at the Vatican's door."

"What about Father Augustus? Has he come up with anything?"

"If he has, he's keeping it to himself." The Cardinal

paused. A scowl came to his face. "The man has the personality of a polar bear."

"Seems I've heard someone else say the same thing—John Gallogly, wasn't it?"

The Cardinal's scowl turned to a look of pain.

"Tim, don't you go blaming yourself. John was vulnerable."

A priest stuck his head into the room. Seeing the Cardinal, he quickly went to his side.

"Excuse me, Your Eminence, this was lying under your office door."

He handed him a manila envelope and left.

The Cardinal opened the envelope and took from it a piece of yellow paper. Each letter in the message had been cut out of a newspaper and pasted to the paper. It read: THREE FOR ONE!

The Cardinal slammed his fist down hard on the table.

Archbishop McGary got up and rushed to his side. He took the paper from the Cardinal's hand.

" 'Three for one'—What does it mean, Tim?"

"It means that if I have to arm every priest in the diocese I will damn well do so." He heaved himself to his feet. "What I feared the most has happened. The Devil's among Rebuck's movement."

"Tim, what in God's name are you talking about?"

". . . Henry Rodriguez just left us his calling card."

TWO YOUNG MEN and a woman crawled along the wet grounds toward the high fence—away from the compound they were fleeing—away from the Divine Church and its world-renowned leader, Reverend Earth, the Asiatic who had left his native land to invade this country and somehow recruit two million followers. But now things had changed. The young rebels and the disenchanted, those who joined the Church in a quest for a truth beyond the materialism of American lives, were leaving Reverend Earth's Divine Church in droves. Ron Rebuck's message had broken through the brain-washing machinery of the hypnotic Reverend Earth, and his Church itself was now on shaky foundations.

For better than six years, Reverend Earth had done what he pleased. His minions had even gone as far as to kidnap young men and women, cause them to sever all ties with their grieving families and become totally committed to his Church. He feared not the great leaders of organized religion in the country. He knew all too well that were they to come out and publicly attack him, they would in essence be attacking themselves. After all, they both read and taught out of the same book – the Holy Bible. Moreover, well-placed cash "research grants" by his Divine Foundation had won him high-placed friends in Washington.

But now all his power was for naught. Ron Rebuck read out of his own book and was giving Reverend Earth financial fits. He'd all but lost his airport trade. The young devotees who solicited for his Divine Church had abandoned their posts and left the field to the panhandlers of Hare Krishna.

Tonight, Reverend Earth himself had come to his training center in an effort to soothe the rebellious souls in his church.

In an auditorium at the main building, through an interpreter, he openly condemned Ron Rebuck before his wavering trainees. He called him a heretic, a blasphemer, but was vocally attacked by a rebellious youth from the audience when he went so far as to call Ron Rebuck an agent of Satan.

The wide, almond-shaped eyes fixed on his challenger like a laser beam. The tall, portly, round-faced Divine Church leader was an awesome presence. At his signal, two instructors came to the speaker's side in an effort to silence hime, having to physically subdue him as he spat out hateful words at the mighty Reverend Earth himself.

If this untimely interruption wasn't enough, Reverend Earth was never to finish his damning spiel against Ron Rebuck. He was once again interrupted by the loud and vicious barking of the attack dogs who patrolled the grounds behind the high steel fence that circled the compound.

The sound of the dogs could only mean one thing to the young people who jammed the small auditorium. Another attempt to escape had been foiled. It showed in their eyes as many now glared at the man they'd once worshipped with all their hearts. Since Ron Rebuck's message had filtered into their minds the training center had become a prison. Their outside contacts with the rest of the world had been cut off by a tight screen of security. Finally, this very night, a revolt was in the making.

With lightning efficiency, the band of instructors went to the doors and stood before the trainees menacingly. Under their robes, hands rested on concealed weapons.

Reverend Earth, surrounded by bodyguards, hurriedly left the stage and went out of the auditorium intending to personally chastise whoever had dared to leave. The dogs doubtless had the escapees at bay. He briskly made his way through the grounds and approached the fence.

Strangely, the howling of the dogs had abruptly ceased. And, as the leader and his guards reached the fence, the escaping trainees were nowhere to be seen.

Speaking in his native tongue, an angered Reverend

Earth signaled the advance guards to go on through the gate – harshly reprimanding them for their failure – demanding the capture of the escapees.

At the bank of a stream that bordered the property, the guards stared in awe at the sight of the attack dogs lying motionless. Vainly, they examined the carcasses for whatever had felled them. They looked for wounds, but there were none. Unless they had been somehow drugged or poisoned, there was no explaining their death. Confused, they looked at each other in disbelief when a rustling noise from across the stream caught their attention. The two young men and the girl had risen from the shadowy ground, revealing themselves in the moonlight as they clambered up the steeply sloping hill. The two guards gave chase, wading through the stream to the base of the hill. As Reverend Earth stood at the edge of the stream, watching them give pursuit, from the shadows at the top of the hill a man revealed himself.

Halfway up the sloping terrain the guards froze, as they saw the figure looking down at them – like a giant cat – the eyes gleaming strangely in the night. The two men stood stock-still, fearing to take another step.

Reverend Earth did not have to be told the identity of this strange man. He knew instinctively it was Ron Rebuck. For a moment, he gazed at the man on the hill with bitter hatred. Then his eyes drifted to the sight of the lifeless dogs. He spoke in a whisper to his interpreter, his chief aide, at his side.

The aide, a small, wiry, yellow-skinned man, called out to the two guards, ordering them back, as Reverend Earth fixed vengeful eyes on the man on the hill.

"Are you this Rebuck?" the aide shouted.

"I am." The voice was deep, resonant, chilling.

"Reverend Earth demands the return of those lured from his sanctuary."

"They have been released from your bondage. As will all who wish to leave," the voice seemed to carom off the hill.

"This is private property, owned by the Divine Church. *You* are a trespasser.

"*You* are the trespasser!" Ron Rebuck roared. "*You* who mesmerized the minds of the troubled young. You who have trespassed into the lives of families and stolen their children."

The interpreter looked back at Reverend Earth, seeking guidance. A smile, more of a snarl, curled the Reverend's lips. The large almond eyes shifted from the accuser on the hill to his aide. He nodded, and the aide was quick to comprehend.

Leaving Reverend Earth's side, the aide snapped his fingers and a guard with a rifle stepped forth. Relieving him of the weapon, he released the safety, looked back at Reverend Earth in case he should change his mind, then sighted in on the man on the hill. He smiled faintly at the target he could not miss.

For the last time he looked at Reverend Earth, who merely nodded. The interpreter then aimed the muzzle directly at Ron Rebuck. As his finger applied pressure to the trigger, the ground he stood on gave way . . . swallowing him whole.

Reverend Earth looked down in horror, as the man on the hill disappeared into the night.

# 29

BEHIND THE WHEEL, the F.M. radio blaring out Crack Widener's music, Rufus Manning drove with lordly abandon; he thought himself the duke of all drivers—supreme master of the roadways. But Mike Spenard's feet played hell on the floorboard. If he had *any* fear, it was of Rufus's driving.

Spotting a traffic jam ahead, Rufus swung the Jag off the Henry Hudson Parkway and onto the Seventy-third Street ramp. He reluctantly stopped for a light, then stepped on the accelerator and crossed the white line, cutting off the lead car as he grudgingly braked for another traffic light.

"You crazy bastard!" a man yelled from the cut-off vehicle.

"Fuck off," said Rufus as he bolted away with the light still red.

In the next ten minutes he cut off five cars, a bus, played chicken with a cab and won, came inches from running over three pedestrians, until finally the Jag pulled up in front of an old warehouse building on Ninth Avenue.

The news came on the car's radio; Rufus cocked his ear, while Mike Spenard looked out across the street where a green station wagon was parked.

The commentator spoke of a three-alarm fire in Manhattan, then went into what Rufus was eager to hear.

". . . According to the network's president, Dan Runkel, a multi-TV contract has been agreed upon between the network and producer Rufus Manning. Asked why the network did an about-face—when less than a week ago the same network said it would not be televising any future Michael's Messenger shows—Mr. Runkel revealed that the tremendous flood of favorable mail had influenced the reversal. The network, after all, was in the business of televising what the public wants."

"You bet your ass," said Rufus, turning it off. "The will of the people, baby," he said to Mike Spenard, who kept looking suspiciously at the parked car across the street.

Rufus followed his line of sight.

"Is that black Godzilla?"

Spenard said not a word.

"Pico's ape. What's he doing here? . . . Mike, what's *he* doing here?"

"I been seeing a lot of him lately, Mr. M."

"Why? . . . What goes with you and King Kong?"

Again Spenard said not a word, and his silence irked Rufus.

"Mike, what do you know that I don't? And don't bullshit me."

"It's personal."

Rufus took a quick look at the face across the way, then turned back to Mike Spenard. That relentlessly inquiring mind was at work.

"A couple of days ago, the cops were eager to know of your whereabouts for a twenty-four-hour period. Now Pico's muscle man is following you around. What gives, Mike? And make it short, I'm in a hurry."

"Nuthin', Mr. M. Nuthin' I can't handle."

Rufus's suspicions grew. "Nothing you can't handle, is that what you said?"

"Mr. M. . . . there's no problem."

"Really? Then how come I get the feeling there is? Tell me why all of a sudden I see your old-age pension sprouting wings?"

"You shouldn't keep saying that to me."

*"To remind you,"* Rufus shouted. "Anything, anything happens to me, where are you? Back busting heads for shylocks? You're too old."

"Mr. M—"

"Get me through this one and you can reminisce over the good old days without ever having to scratch again. But no fucking secrets!"

Rufus tore his eyes away from the wrathful face and looked at his watch. He was already forty-five minutes late for the board of governors' meeting.

"Take the car to the garage on Fifty-seventh. Get a cab back and meet me on the tenth floor."

He got out of the car as Mike Spenard slipped over to the driver's side. Then Rufus stuck his head through the open car window, his face only inches from Spenard. "I want to know!" he shouted, pointing to Big Richard in the green station wagon. "I want to know what *his* problem is. What Pico has to do with it. And how Pico knew where this meeting was, when I didn't know until two hours ago. Get lost!" Then he made a run for the building's entrance.

Mike Spenard put the Jag in gear and slowly crept away from the curb. Carefully he inched up next to the green station wagon and studied a grinning Richard, sitting on the passenger side. Switchblade in hand, the giant black mimicked the cutting of his throat from ear to ear.

Mike Spenard watched in silence, then spit out the window. The saliva spattered over the black face as he sped away.

JOHN MILTON AND LESLIE anxiously approached Rufus as he entered the lobby of the old building.

"Daddy, we couldn't get upstairs."

Rufus motioned for them to follow as he charged toward the elevator. The door closed just as a gang of reporters with "Press" badges, and TV cameramen swarmed in on them.

At the tenth floor, Rufus made his way through the gang of bodyguards but was stopped cold at the conference room door by an Oriental of Sumo-wrestler proportions.

From the corner of his eye, he saw Turk Savage smiling over his discomfort.

"Will you tell this asshole to let me in?"

"He don't belong to me," said Savage.

"What the hell are you talking about?"

"He's not mine . . . he's *Rebuck's*."

The door cracked open and Ed Dowiat appeared. "I might have known you were in back of all the commotion. A little late, aren't you, Manning?"

"Dowiat, you got ten seconds to get this Jap fireplug out of my way or I'm blowing this joint."

Ed Dowiat signaled the Oriental to step aside and let Rufus pass, but John and Leslie were held at bay.

"Sorry, Manning, but only you."

"Why am I talking to a flunky? Get Rebuck out here!"

"Get? You don't *get* Ron Rebuck."

"Get . . . or I go."

Ed Dowiat hesitated, then reluctantly let the two young people pass through.

THE ROOM WAS DARK, save for the beam of light coming from a projector aimed at a small portable screen. Rufus stood in the back while John and Leslie seated themselves on metal chairs. He looked about the room, to identify its occupants. In the dim light he saw a strangely mixed group: Crack Widener, Drew Bonds, Jennifer Jewell, Jack Pintoff, and the new recruit, ex-Monsignor Gallogly.

But where was Rebuck? He looked to and fro. Sensing a presence behind him, he then turned. There, in the darkest corner of the room, he saw those eyes. Those intense, wild-animal eyes—fixed directly on him.

Rufus turned to the screen where Billy Hale, the Superman of the scriptures, was flailing his arms and wailing out Biblical chapter and verse. Then came Norville Riggins. There were others, slightly less famous syndicated saviors from Ohio and Oklahoma. Then, the bathing beauty who'd once paraded her ass before twenty million horny men, and now was praising God for showing her the golden way. And then Reverend Moon with his English interpreter, and band of religious brigands.

The final segment revealed a crew-cut Doctor of Divinity, sporting a toothy grin, and peddling some eight-year-old boy as Evangelism's prodigy.

"Geethuth told me," the child lisped.

"Now, remember, all you wonderful people," the Doctor intoned, "remember that little Billy will be at that big revival meeting. So make sure you are there to hear Billy speak of the Lord."

"My record will be on thale too."

"Yes, good people, make sure you get an autographed record of Billy singing 'The Way of the Lord'!"

The lights came on, and Jack Pintoff turned off the projector.

"I don't know what your intentions are," said Rufus,

"but if what I just saw is supposed to be the format of any of the shows I'm producing, *forget it.*"

"I think that's a matter for the Board of Governors," said Ed Dowiat.

Rufus flared, but Jennifer quickly intervened. "Roof, no one was trying to exclude you. It just happens you're almost an hour late."

"Well I'm here *now.*"

"Yes, we know," said Pintoff, sarcastically.

Shaking with rage, Rufus pointed threateningly at the leering Jack Pintoff. "One more word . . . just one—"

*"Roof,"* Ron Rebuck sounded, "what is it you want to say?"

"I got plenty to say."

"Could you be brief and to the point?" Ron Rebuck requested.

*"Brief?"*

"God's work must be done," Crack Widener heatedly proclaimed.

For the first time, Rufus noticed the recording giant's apparel. He was clad in a long white Biblical robe. Rufus gazed at him in utter disbelief.

He finally tore his eyes from the bizarre figure of Crack Widener and said, "It so happens that *I* negotiated the TV deal with the network, and if you read page nine, paragraph six, it specifically defines the role of the producer. If that's not good enough, I happen to have a signed contract with you people. One made in perpetuity, wherein *I* am the producer, with veto powers equal to that of Ron Rebuck. Now, the way I see it, if you people are contemplating doing any shows without me, then I'll have to show you just how an injunction truly works."

"Get off it, Manning," said an irate Ed Dowiat.

"You've already skimmed twenty-five percent from whatever the Mission makes."

"Yeahhh," said Rufus, "and I'm going to keep on skimming, baby."

Drew Bonds rose from his seat. "Excuse me," he said softly, and left the room.

Swiftly, Ron Rebuck came forward. He placed a restraining hand on the enraged Crack Widener, and faced Rufus Manning.

"Roof, as long as you live up to your commitments to the Mission, you have nothing to fear. You're a businessman and you made a good deal. Now, just what type of format do you have in mind for the next special?"

Rufus Manning looked deeply into those eyes. A sudden chill swept through his body. "Damn . . . you *are* scary."

MIKE SPENARD was the target of many a suspicious eye. Waiting for Rufus to come out of the meeting, Turk Savage's men and the squadron of Rebuck bodyguards eyeballed him with grave mistrust.

Suddenly, the door burst open; Crack Widener, his robe flying, was the first to emerge from the room. Jack Pintoff, with Rufus Manning behind him, exited next, and as Pintoff watched the ritual of the superstar being escorted into the elevator by a wall of muscle, Rufus Manning came up from in back of him, snatched his arm, and hustled him into the men's room.

Mike Spenard stared off any would-be intruders from the gang of guards, then stationed himself outside the bathroom door.

Inside the latrine, Rufus released his grip and shoved the much smaller man, who lost his footing and slipped to the floor.

"Answers, baby!"

"Go to hell, Manning, you son of a bitch!"

Grabbing him by the shirt, Rufus picked him off the loor, keeping one hand free. "The *bodyguards,* who ɩired them? *Pico,* what's your connection with him? *Vhat's your game?*"

"You can suck your mother's tit!"

Blow after blow fell upon the face and neck of the ınyielding Pintoff. Blood flowed from his nose and rickled down his lips, as he cursed his attacker.

ED DOWIAT, sent by Ron Rebuck to find Manning, was lirected to the men's room by one of the bodyguards. Ie came upon the sentry, Mike Spenard. "Is Manning n there?"

"Who wants to know?"

"I don't think that's any of your business."

"He ain't in there," said Spenard.

Ed Dowiat could hear the groans of pain coming from he bathroom. "Get out of the way!"

Mike Spenard sneered and stood immovable.

Ed Dowiat moved to push the enforcer away from the loor. With lightning speed, Spenard grabbed him by the ɔack of the collar and sent him crashing into the wall.

Dazed, Ed Dowiat managed to call out for assistance. Three men, including the massive Oriental, rushed to ɩis side.

"Remove that man. Any way you can!"

Mike Spenard, his back pressed to the door, faced the three men like a hissing snake. Routine, one of them took out a snub-nosed revolver and shoved it at the enforcer's face.

"Turn around and spread 'em," the man with the gun ordered.

With one man kicking his legs apart, the other friske
him. Rufus forbade him to carry a gun, and he wa
clean, but the order didn't include a knife. A six-inc
switchblade that was relieved from his person.

As both men stepped back, the Oriental lowered hi
head and charged—driving the bald head crashingly int
Mike Spenard's back.

As if struck by an express train, Spenard gasped an
slumped senseless to his knees.

The Oriental then spun him around. Holding th
defenseless man by the shoulders, he came up with
knee that smashed into the groggy face.

Ed Dowiat winced as he looked down at the broke
heap of humanity. Then he entered the men's room.

The continual flushing of a toilet brought him to on
of the open stalls.

"*What the* . . ." Dowiat's eyes widened in shock.

There before him, Rufus Manning had Jack Pintoff'
entire head stuck down the toilet bowl . . . attemptin
valiantly to flush him down the drain.

# 30

THE RON REBUCK—Crack Widener combination sailed
through the second TV special without incident. This
time there were no miracles.

Laden with fresh material, Ron Rebuck hammered
away at the hellfire-and-brimstone preachers, and the
biased politicians with religious axes to grind. He did a
humorous spoof on the faith healers, yet, to Rufus's

dismay, when he spoke of the evangelists, he refrained from attacking Billy Hale by name.

The special was almost as potent as the first. If there was a flaw, it lay in Crack Widener's performance. The critics agreed, he was a little *too* spiritual in the singing of his songs.

The ratings showed "The Michael's Messenger Special" destroying its opposition. Despite this, the network surprisingly announced cancelation of all future Michael specials—a decision that fed the fires of an all-out controversy.

RUFUS MANNING looked out from his chalet-office, the latest addition to his Connecticut manor. His eyes roamed about the spacious grounds, at the house on the hill, at the Olympic-sized swimming pool below, at the Har-Tru tennis court, and finally, at the men working on the foundation of his soon-to-be constructed bubble-top indoor tennis court, complete with all the goodies of a swank men's health club.

Hughie Gilman sat off in a corner of the plush interior of Rufus's automated office-hideaway, studying a legal document.

"That no good sonuvabitch," Rufus cursed, "I'll fix his *goy* ass." He turned from the window to Hughie. "I thought you told me Dan Runkel was a stand-up guy."

"I also warned you in the beginning that the network had an escape clause."

"C'mon, Hughie, for two shows the network approves everything and now, all of a sudden, it's too controversial?"

"Roofala, all of the networks have the same Catch-22!"

"It's a fucking conspiracy and you know it!"

Hughie Gilman put the legal document down on the table next to him. "Strange as it seems, I believe you're right."

Rufus moved away from the window toward Gilman. "What about the other networks? Would I be wasting my time?"

"Your phone's not ringing."

He let Rufus think about it for a moment, then said, "Roof, if there is a conspiracy against Ron Rebuck, it's . . . it's coming out of Washington."

"Not the fucking government again, Hughie."

"Religious interests just happen to be well represented. Their lobbyists are the most powerful in Washington, D.C."

He watched Rufus sit down, then continued. "I've known Dan Runkel a long time. He's not the kind of man who buckles under ordinary pressure."

"What you're saying, counselor, is that Billy Hale, or *someone* in religion, has clout in high places."

"The knock-out kind."

Rufus sprang to his feet. "Knock-out, my ass! You're talking as if Rebuck and Widener are a couple of stumblebums. They're heavyweights, baby. You know how many followers have paid five bucks apiece to join Rebuck's cause? Better than six million."

"And you don't get a nickel out of it. And without a slice of the church money, you'll never make that billion you keep dreaming about! So why don't you take what you've got and the hell with Rebuck and the rest of them?"

"Hughie, I got the hottest duo in the country . . . maybe in the world. Rebuck's face is on every magazine you see on the stands. I got a pair of household names. Secretariat and Forego in the same stable."

"And without TV they don't have a track to run on."

"What am I . . . an empty chair? You're talking to an expert in the TV business. Hell, I sold enough shit to television, I could write a textbook about it."

"An author you're not."

Rufus started to pace the floor and Hughie sat back in his chair. He knew Rufus would soon reveal his plan.

Rufus didn't disappoint him. "The three networks can only own five stations apiece, right?" he asked.

"So what else is new?"

"The rest of their line-ups consist of affiliates. And affiliates don't have to air programs the network wants them to."

"Which means you're about to form your own network."

"You got it, baby."

"I am not your baby. I'm your lawyer. And my advice is for you to take the money you've made, and run like a thief."

"Your advice," Rufus moaned. "Ever since I started this deal, you have yet to be right. Pretty soon you'll be catching up to Jimmy the Greek."

"Roof, you are the king of greed—that's an unquestioned fact. But your obsession about making a billion dollars leads me to believe that behind this greed lies a strain of insanity."

"Are you telling me I'm bugs?"

"You're eccentric, utterly charming when you so desire, yet you'll turn on people without the slightest provocation. To analyze your character is utterly impossible."

"If I'm what you say I am, why do you stick with me?"

"Because I find you a most fascinating animal. You

are a master of the unexpected. And some of your moves, the methods you use to achieve results, are truly genius. What amazes me to this very day is how you convinced the author of your film *Dude* that his written words were really your own."

"I gave the bastard credit on the screen."

"You gave him that . . . but not the money."

"Hughie, is this another of your sermons?"

"My last."

Gilman rose from his chair. "Roof, I will assist you in putting together your network. I will continue to represent you until I can no longer go against my conscience."

"You make it sound like I'm doing something crooked. Like I'm a destroyer."

"But you are."

Rufus's eyes glittered with anger. "Who, who in the fuck am I destroying?"

". . . Yourself."

THREE DAYS LATER, at Hughie Gilman's New York office, Rufus Manning presented his new plan to the leaders of Michael's Mission.

Jennifer Jewell listened with a faint smile; John Gallogly, somberly. Hughie Gilman sat quietly behind his desk as Rufus concluded his spiel.

"I am not at all surprised," said Jennifer. "Ron told us you would work things out. But are you certain of the TV stations?"

"Jennifer, just today, I landed the flagship station Channel 5 in New York. Before the end of the next week I'll have sixty major markets covered. At air time, we'll be in every market in America."

"Including the Bible Belt?" asked John Gallogly.

Rufus grinned. "I gotta believe when it comes down where a TV station has the chance to make money or ive in to pressure from some religious quack, the oney will win every time."

Rufus got up from his chair, winked at Hughie, and aid, "Which now leads me to what *I* expect to get out f all this."

"For a moment you had me fooled," said Jennifer. "I as almost believing you were doing it from the oodness of your heart."

Hughie Gilman fought off a burst of laughter, as ufus zeroed in on the picture of feminine excellence. Iis eyes were drawn to that magic mouth. "I hope ou're not trying to convert me?"

"Convert, *you*?" She laughed. "How could anyone et past your gluttony for gold?"

"They can't," Hughie whispered to himself.

John Gallogly shifted in his chair impatiently. "Mr. Ianning, I'm speaking at a function in less than an our; could we possibly get on with it?"

"Glad to. I simply need ammo, and you people have he arsenal."

"Such as?" Jennifer grew dubious.

"Relax, I'm not looking to tap the sacred loot from our precious Mission. But I have to give the stations 'm pitching enough juice to make it worth their while."

"Orange or prune?" said Jennifer.

". . . Is she quick?" Rufus said to Hughie who ignored is left-handed compliment and made a judicial gesture or him to continue.

"There's no way I can give the stations a piece of the nusic."

"Especially since you don't have the rights," said Iughie, sternly.

"What about merchandising?" Jennifer was quick t remind.

"That presents another problem. You see th distributors I already have are a bunch of hungr wolves. They'd never buy the idea of sharin distribution with the stations."

Hughie Gilman dropped the pencil in his hand. H had to look away. Rufus was lying through his teeth The Michael's jewelry, statues, dolls, T-shirts, bumpe stickers and so on were, in fact, manufactured an distributed through dummy corporations, owned ex clusively by Rufus Manning.

"That leaves only the book," said Rufus.

*"The Lawyers of Hell?"* Jennifer's voice was sharp "You know that McGuinness and McGuinness are th publishers."

"Hard cover only," said Rufus. "The soft-cove rights have not been assigned to *any* publisher."

"I gather you want these rights?" Jennifer said.

"You guessed it."

John Gallogly could be silent no longer. "Mr Manning, *The Lawyers of Hell* has sold over thre million copies in the hard-cover edition. But of cours you would know that since you receive twenty-fiv percent of the Mission's royalties. What are you offerin for the paperback rights?"

"One dollar."

Jennifer Jewell kept her composure. "You are to generous, Roof. It must pain you to part with such a sum."

"I'll get over it."

She gave him a venomous glare, then turned t Hughie Gilman. "If you will draw up an agreement, th Mission will study it."

"Hold on," said Rufus. "There're a few more points."

"Haven't you asked for enough of the pie?" Jennifer hissed.

He ignored her. "Since I'm now in the publishing business, I'll be in need of future books. What better follow-up than the autobiography of Ron Rebuck?"

"You'll have to speak to Ron directly about that."

"No, Jennifer, *you* will speak to him." He let her stew, then went on: "I also want a firm option on one other book. Sort of as a protective measure. You see, ladies like yourself who become associated with famous men, well, sometimes they write very *interesting* memoirs. *Juicy* ones."

"Roof, you're pushing it a little too far."

"Am I, Jennifer?" he said with that shitty grin.

"Is there anything *else* you want?"

"Just one more thing. I want full authority over the format of all future TV shows."

She turned to John Gallogly. "That falls in your department, John."

"What kind of format do you have in mind, Mr. Manning?"

"I want Rebuck to forget any ideas of picking on the Pope, and bang on Billy Hale."

"Mr. Manning, that's the second or third time you've spoken about Billy Hale today. Why are you so obsessed with the man?"

"I've got my reasons."

"Are you under the impression Billy Hale was the one who used pressure to force Michael's show off the network? Because if you are, you're grossly mistaken."

"Really?"

"Yes, *really.* A much more powerful man than Billy

Hale struck that blow."

"You wouldn't be referring to your ex-boss, Cardina Spellissy, would you?"

"I'm referring to the most powerful religious figure ir America. And, Mr. Manning, you will find him ar overwhelming opponent. A match for Ron Rebuck, bu I do believe somewhat out of your league."

Jennifer Jewell and Hughie Gilman broke into smiles Both relished the ex-Monsignor's cutting-down o Rufus.

"We all have the right to our own opinion," said a red-faced Rufus. "Nevertheless, the format will con centrate on Billy Hale. I'll tell Rebuck when the time comes for him to take on the Goliath in Rome."

Abruptly Jennifer got up from her seat. "Thank you Mr. Gilman, you have been most kind. We shall let you know of our decision after we've read the agreemen you're going to draw up."

John Gallogly bid the lawyer farewell, but there were no parting words for Rufus, as he and Jennifer left the office.

Hughie Gilman waited until he was sure they'd lef the reception area, then looked upon Rufus with dire contempt. "You . . . you shark!"

"The great white one, Hughie Baby."

"Do you know what I hope? I hope they turn you down *flat.*"

"They won't, bubbalah. I got all the trump cards and Jennifer knows it." He moved to a chair closer to Hughie and plopped his feet onto the desk. "The challenge match, Hughie! I'll bill it as the religious championship of the world. Rebuck will knock Hale out in the first round . . . but what a fucking payday!"

Hughie Gilman waited for him to calm down, then said, "I'd like you to answer one question, truthfully."

"Yeah, what's that?"

"For argument's sake, let's say you achieve your goal. You make that billion. Then what?"

"What do you mean?"

"Then . . . *what*?"

Rufus looked quizzically at the gray eyes that seemed already to know the answer. He groped for a logical reply, but failed to find it.

"I thought so," Gilman said.

Disregarding the remark, Rufus took his feet off the desk and stood. "While you make like a shrink, I gotta get humping on that network."

Hughie's intercom rang, and he motioned for Rufus to remain.

"Yes, Mary, what is it?"

"A Mr. Whitcomb is calling."

*"Who?"*

"Mr. Rex Whitcomb, from Washington. He's president of the American Religious Broadcasters' Association."

A worried expression came to Hughie Gilman's face. "Have him hold." He looked up at Rufus. "Know who he is?"

"I heard."

"The odds against you getting that network have now doubled. You're in over your head."

"Showers of power?" Rufus asked.

"A hurricane," said Hughie.

Rufus smiled. "I like long shots, remember?" He then made a dash for the door, saying, "Get those contracts drawn up."

"Roof! Whitcomb's no lightweight. He's got plenty of Washington pull."

Rufus stopped by the door. "Does he? Well, I got some pull of my own . . . *Angel pull,* baby."

# 31

THE MICHAEL'S MESSENGER HOUR blazed across the nation on July Fourth with its own special fireworks. The TV special, produced live from New York, was a cinch to bring about the challenge match Rufus Manning dreamed about. He was sure.

He made a believer out of John Gallogly when he put together a network that included the majority of TV stations in the so-called Bible Belt. Even Ed Dowiat, much to Jack Pintoff's surprise, endorsed his promotional ideas for launching this particular program. Rufus ballyhooed it to the rooftops as "The Declaration of Religious Independence."

Ron Rebuck took it from there when he called for *all* people to join a universal belief, free of fear and the eternal damnation of one's soul, and to rebel against the stigmas passed down through the ages by the Bible's teachings: the concept of original sin, the great insult to womanhood in the greatest miracle of all, the resurrection of the bodily dead, the nonsensical notion of the Trinity, and lastly, the God of Hate, destruction and death.

But as Rufus saw nothing but golden sunshine ahead, others heard the rumbling in the clouds. The smart boys, experts in political science, who'd been observing Ron Rebuck's movement, thought Rufus's much-publicized declaration of "religious independence" a declaration of war.

With the nation's larger cities screaming bankruptcy, and the national rate of unemployment having soared to record heights, some of these political analysts went so far as to predict Rebuck's movement would set off a time bomb in a nation where violence lay just beneath the surface. They warned that Ron Rebuck's dramatic appeals for man's soul to be free could, in fact, turn the meek—the sheep—into undisciplined beasts.

RUFUS MANNING entered the offices the New York Flagship TV Station had assigned to his production, bubbling with excitement. The smile turned to a frown when he saw his two overworked and underpaid assistants feverishly taking telephone calls.

"What the hell's going on here?"

Leslie waved for quiet.

He stormed from the room, went to the reception area, told the operators to hold all calls for Manning Productions, and returned to the production office.

Leslie was free now and the look on her face told him there was trouble.

"Daddy . . . they were killed."

He looked at her oddly, then went to his desk without a word. He waited for John Milton to complete his phone conversation and asked, "What's she talking about?"

"Two television stations were bombed. People were killed."

*"So?"*

"Daddy, the stations were ones you didn't sell. The ones in the Bible Belt. Mr. Gilman wants you to call him right away."

"Why? What does he want?"

"I don't know."

"So get him on the phone!" He turned to John. "Is that what all the calls were about?"

"No. Turk Savage called."

"What's *his* problem?"

"Seems Crack Widener was baptizing people in Central Park . . . in the nude."

"What a flake *he's* become."

"He demands you let Crack Widener out of his contract."

"No big deal. But does Crack want out, or is it Turk Savage who wants him out?"

"I wouldn't know."

Rufus spun around to face his daughter. "Leslie, what's holding Hughie?"

She said a few words to someone on the phone, then hung up. "Mr. Gilman's on his way over here, and he wants you to stay put."

Rufus looked at his watch. "I better get to that story conference." He looked at John. "Where?"

"Green Room . . . Stage Two."

"Who's representing the Rebuck people?"

"Mr. Gallogly."

Rufus grinned, deviously. "I got him eating out of my hand," he said as he walked out.

INSIDE THE ANTEROOM of Stage C, John Gallogly was chatting with a gum-popping production secretary, when Rufus entered.

He ignored the production girl and stuck out a hand to John Gallogly.

"How does it feel to be on the winning side?"

John Gallogly eyed him peculiarly. "I don't think I follow."

"Are you kidding?" said Rufus, slumping onto a small green couch. "One more special with Ron Rebuck kicking Hale's teeth in, and it's Telstar, baby. We go world-wide."

"Mr. Manning, I nver thought of my joining Ron Rebuck's mission as being on a side–rather, a cause."

"Side, cause, what's the difference? When I get finished, Rebuck will be the king of the whole religious world."

"When you get finished with *what,* Mr. Manning?"

Rufus gave him a look. Then he became conscious of the girl's loud cracking of her gum. "Will you give your fucking jaws a rest!"

She stared at him sulkily.

"Miss– whatever your name, take a walk, will ya?"

"My name's Geraldine," she tossed back, on her way out.

For a moment, Rufus had to collect his thoughts, then said, "I think it's about time you and I get to understand each other."

"Mr. Manning, I understand you quite well."

"Well, if you do, then you'd realize what we got here."

"Mr. Manning, your intentions, your interests, do not happen to coincide with the Mission's. The fact that you provided Ron with a vehicle, a springboard, is one thing–"

"The only thing! Without national television, Rebuck's out of action and you fucking well know it. Get down, baby. I got the avenue you people need to travel on, so why don't you get off that high-flying cloud, and talk *shop.*"

John Gallogly eyed Rufus closely as he continued, "The challenge match with Hale means as much to you people as it does to me."

"Does it?"

"You bet your sanctimonious ass. After Hale goes down, Rebuck then gets what he really wants."

"Which is?"

"The Pope's ass, baby."

"Is that what you think, Mr. Manning?"

"I don't think; I know! Shit, he's given more hints than a prostitute. The latest show, what did he say?"

"Might you be referring to his remark about the Pope's infallibility?"

"Yeah, when he called it an intoxication for idiots." He now sat up on the couch, somewhat puzzled by John Gallogly's deadpan expression. "Listen, you were a priest a long time. You lived a sheltered life, right?"

"Being a priest did not necessarily mean I lived a sheltered life, Mr. Manning."

"C'mon, you never had to make a buck . . . worry about where the next meal was coming from. Sure, people called you 'Father,' but what the hell would you know about raising a family? What I'm saying is that we're bedfellows. I do my number, you people do yours, and everybody—"

"Lives happily ever after, Mr. Manning?"

"You got it. A storybook ending."

HUGHIE GILMAN burst through the door. He seemed glad that a member of Michael's Mission was present. "I have some news for both of you!" He turned his attention to John Gallogly. "I just received word—the producers of 'National Spotlight' have invited Ron Rebuck to appear on their show."

Before Rufus could voice an objection, he added, "They also want Billy Hale on the same show."

Rufus Manning's eyes shone as John Gallogly took in the news calmly.

"I'm sure the show is prestigious enough for Mr. Rebuck," said Gilman, "but then again, the panel of interviewers usually acts like a pack of prosecuting attorneys.''

''Are you kidding, Hughie? Rebuck will drown 'em all,'' said Rufus.

''Has Mr. Hale accepted?'' John Gallogly asked.

''I haven't the foggiest. All I know is that the show's producers are most anxious to have both Rebuck and Hale on at the same time.''

John Gallogly switched his eyes from Hughie Gilman to a thoughtful Rufus Manning.

''This is the challenge match you wanted, Mr. Manning.''

Hughie Gilman looked at Rufus with surprise. ''You're not sore, Roof!''

''Why, because the 'National Spotlight' people picked up on my idea? Hell, no! I was hoping something like this would happen all along.''

John Gallogly got up from his chair. ''Mr. Gilman, I'll call you the moment I can get in touch with Ron Rebuck.''

Rufus Manning escorted him to the door. ''Tell me something. Where do you people hide Rebuck?''

''Hide?''

''He's not in Florida. Neither is his family. You got him on some cloud?''

John Gallogly finally broke into a smile. ''Let's just say he's much closer to the clouds than you or I.''

BILLY HALE'S refusal to appear on the celebrated ''National Spotlight'' show was the lead story on the national TV news.

When asked the main reason for turning down an opportunity to face Ron Rebuck, hale avoided any personal attacks upon the man who gave him nightmares, and blamed the show's panel of pagan interviewers. Hale called them a trio of Mammon worshippers, knee-jerk liberals who'd meet a true man of God for only the sake of mockery and controversy.

RUFUS MANNING scoffed at what he considered to be a feeble cop-out. In between his calling Hale "chicken-shit," he revealed to John and Leslie, and the ever-present Mike Spenard—who were all seated about Rufus's chalet—what he thought were the true reasons for Hale's backing down.

He scornfully pointed out that the mighty evangelist would be naked and lost without his supporting cast—the Gospel Singers, beauty pageant winners, and the God-fearing guest celebrities to testify as to the wonderful way they truly found God. And even worse, Rufus was to reason, Billy wouldn't be able to bring his Bible, since "National Spotlight" required its guests to leave their books and props at home.

John Milton waited for him to stop cursing, then said, "I think it goes deeper. If you ask me, I think Billy Hale is being manipulated."

"Manipulated?" Rufus asked.

"Either that or someone's got his head screwed up."

John Milton's warning came forcefully to Rufus's mind. "You're not talking about that fat Cardinal?"

"There's nothing fat about the Cardinal's mind," John staunchly replied.

Rufus sprang from his chair. "Mike, get the car ready to roll!"

Like a shot, Mike Spenard disappeared from the room.

"I want you people to stay here and hang by the phones."

"Daddy . . . for how long?"

"Until I get a chance to speak with Ron Rebuck."

"But, Daddy, the 'National Spotlight' show isn't till tomorrow afternoon."

Rufus moved from behind the desk. "Leslie, I got to catch up with him before he goes on that show, or kiss the challenge match goodbye."

"How do you catch a ghost?" John asked.

Rufus bristled. "I could be losing millions, and *you're* making with the funnies!"

"I didn't mean it to be funny."

"He's right, Daddy. No one knows of Ron Rebuck's whereabouts."

Rufus heard Mike Spenard beeping the car's horn. "I'll get to him if I have to wait on the TV station's doorsteps," he vowed. "See yah."

He bolted out of the room and bounded down the circular stairs.

Leslie followed, but gave up the pursuit as a lost cause. From the top of the stairs she shouted after him, "Even criminals get time off for good behavior!"

From the chalet's window, John Milton watched Rufus and Mike Spenard speed away in the Jaguar. A forlorn Leslie came to his side.

"He's just *got* to hire some people," Leslie moaned.

"Your old man doesn't trust people."

"Well, that's just *too* bad. I don't know how you feel, but I'm nobody's peon. *Including* my father's."

"Is that your soul talking, Leslie?"

"Whatever it is . . . I've had it!"

He walked away from the window and settled behind Rufus's desk. "I think your father's headed for a bad fall."

"Don't worry about my father. He's like a roller coaster."

"Something tells me he will regret the day he became involved with Ron Rebuck."

"What are you driving at, John?"

"The mood, the pulse of the country, it's scary. Like everyone is waiting for the bomb to fall . . . I'm beginning to believe Ron Rebuck is the most dangerous man in the world. . . ."

RON REBUCK fielded the questions of the National Spotlight panel with remarkable ease. The trio of award-winning journalists, and the moderator of the prestigious television show, failed to unnerve him and were unable to trip him with their probing questions.

The commercial break over, the moderator, Emmy-winner Max Kaiser, resumed speaking:

"We only have enough time for one more round of questions. Mr. Levine, will you begin, please?"

"Mr. Rebuck, charitable institutions come under the tax exemption laws. In recent times it has come to the public's attention that some of these institutions, mostly religious, have been found to engage in certain irregular practices with the monies they receive. With almost ten million members donating five dollars apiece to *your* mission, how is this money being used?"

"The membership money donated to Michael's Mission is given back to each and every member in the form of services."

"These services, Mr. Rebuck, are they spiritual?"

"Mr. Levine, the membership forms for Michael's Mission are not laden with Shakespearean jargon. Each sentence is simple and clear. If you were to read the membership form, you'd find the services consist of: insurance, medical costs, legal fees, and other welfare benefits that are available to every member.

"Within the year we hope to have twenty missions operational. Each mission will be headed by a messenger, who shall handle his own administration.

"We are not a religious organization that takes money from the public to line its own pockets. I'm especially referring to those with great real estate holdings, wealthy portfolios of stocks and bonds, and other vast holdings that I consider to be fraudulent ventures and at the public's expense."

"Thank you, Mr. Rebuck. Your question, Mr. Bracken?" the moderator moved it along.

"Mr. Rebuck, on a personal vein, isn't it true Crack Widener is currently undergoing observation for some mental disorder? And why did Drew Bonds resign as an advisor to your mission?"

"Mr. Widener is suffering from mental fatigue. As for Mr. Bonds, his reasons for leaving the Mission's advisory board are of a personal nature, and I suggest you ask Mr. Bonds himself."

"Mr. Coates, your question, please."

"My question will have a few babies."

"Small babies, I hope, Mr. Coates," said the moderator, smiling.

"Mr. Rebuck, according to FBI statistics, crime has taken a sharp turn upward since you have emerged on the national scene. The FBI predicts this surging rate of crime will soon reach crisis proportions. What do you say to the analysts who believe *you* are responsible for the violence that is sweeping the country?"

"I have never asked or suggested that anyone commit crimes against society."

"But haven't you brought about a danger to society when you profess the belief that there exists a state of civil war between body and soul?"

"The civil war you're referring to originated long before my lifetime."

"Mr. Rebuck, when you tell people that the soul lives in a state of conflict with the body, and that the soul continually seeks the body's death, are you not, in fact, advocating suicide?"

"Mr. Coates, I can only answer your questions by saying that a movement, any controversial movement, provides an umbrella for people with other motives. I'm sure the violence that followed Dr. Martin Luther King was neither instituted nor condoned by him.

"I certainly do not advocate any violent revolution. I wish only to expose those religious leaders who have presented to people all over the world the portrait of a Wrathful God. The goal of my entire mission is for mankind to live in a society free of religious intervention, harassment, and the persecution that now exists."

He paused, then said, "In reply to your last question . . . honesty and integrity of one's own self are the basic requirements of martyrdom."

"Mr. Rebuck, that sounds like a parable."

"Thank you, Mr. Coates," the moderator quickly cut him off. He then turned his attention to Ron Rebuck. "Mr. Rebuck, due to the intense differences that exist between you and Reverend Hale, do you wish to make a comment as to Reverend Hale's refusal to appear on this show?"

"It doesn't surprise me. I've repeatedly challenged Mr. Hale to debate me, and he's repeatedly refused. The fact he is unwilling to appear with me on an impartial television show such as this one only proves Mr. Hale is fearful of the results."

"FEARFUL! I'LL SHOW the son of a bitch who's fearful," Billy Hale thundered.

Rex Whitcomb, the powerful religious lobbyist, once a preacher himself, a homer, with the kind of face easily forgotten, adjusted his horn-rimmed glasses. "He'll cut his *own* throat, Billy."

"Will he? But in the mean time, he's making a laughing stock out of me before the world."

The older man, whose Bethesda, Maryland home Billy Hale was staying in, went to the anguished evangelist's side, placing a consoling hand on his shoulder. He then toyed with the American flag pin in his lapel.

"What is it they say, 'The Lord moves in strange ways'?"

"Not fast enough to suit me!" Billy exclaimed. He came out of his chair, the famous eyes burning. "Don't we have enough muscle to get this man off television?"

"Billy, the President is up to his ears with other serious problems. Besides, he's made it perfectly clear he will not intervene."

"Damn it, Rex, Rebuck must be stopped!"

"He'll be stopped, Billy. The man will be stopped!"

"*When* . . . and by the grace of God . . . *how*?"

# 32

A CARAVAN of limousines, escorted by four police cruisers with flashing lights, drew up to the gate of Billy Hale's estate in the shadow of the towering cross. Half a dozen guards of Hale's security force, carrying shotguns and sidearms, took over, checking the occupants of each car before guiding them inside the evangelist's sprawling grounds.

Two red and white Jeeps led the visitors over the wooden bridge spanning the large pond where a scattering of ducks swam serenely. Beyond, several armed men with leashed dogs could be seen patrolling the grounds. The road led them onto the circular driveway of Billy Hale's gray brick mansion, where the distinguished visitors were rapidly ushered inside.

The first meeting of Religion, Incorporated, was about to begin.

THEY MET IN A ROOM Billy Hale called "Daniel's Den" —an oval-shaped room with stained-glass windows. Numerous busts of Biblical figures—Daniel, Moses, John, James, Luke and Paul, among others— were stationed at intervals around the vast inlaid mahogany conference table.

From his place at the head of the table, Billy Hale was only half-listening to the speaker, religious lobbyist and Washington insider Rex Whitcomb. Rather, he was surveying the opposite end of the table, where the Roman Catholic contingent was seated. He studied the familiar face of Cardinal Spellissy, and then glanced suspiciously at the bearded priest to whom he'd just been introduced. Father Augustus caught his glance and smiled back politely.

Next, Hale scanned the others at the table, taking inventory of his fellow evangelists.

There was Norville Riggins, whom many believed to be the uncrowned king of all evangelists, studying the Biblical busts with keen interest. His black hair had grown thin, and his craggy face was wrinkled, but the tent-show spellbinder who took the boondocks of America by storm back in the forties and fifties could still rouse 'em. The difference was that now he had a numbered Swiss bank account and his suits were made by a Savile row tailor.

Next to Riggins was Tommy Sunday, the lean and lanky savior from the southwest, with a face like old saddle leather, who banged his Biblical drum with such fervor during his services that some of his followers believed he actually levitated a couple of feet off the ground. Tommy had laid his Stetson on the table, and was toying restlessly with its wide brim as he listened to Rex Whitcomb.

Then Billy Hale took in the portly form of Wallace Langley, undisputed champion of the faith healers, whose healing powers could do nothing for his own falling hair, now hidden by an expensive toupe. Langley was giving only half an ear to the speaker; his main focus of attention was aimed at the Cardinal. He didn't mind sharing a brotherhood in Christ with the boys from Rome, but when the Catholic Church branched out from Lourdes and invaded the American faith-healing market, it didn't include a brotherhood of greed.

Next and last, seated next to the speaker, Whitcomb, came Harley Lombard, the crew-cut fifty-year-old with the baby face, whose ministry was the biggest and most lucrative in the midwest, and who seemed to be the only one among his peers who was interested in what Rex Whitcomb had to say.

All of these men were evangelists, true, Billy Hale reflected, but each had more than that in common. Every single one of them had become powerful and prosperous through the medium of television. And now, a new gun in town, Ron Rebuck, with his new *sacrilegious* pitch, was beating them at their own game, and their once-impregnable ministries were in deep financial trouble.

"Gentlemen," Rex Whitcomb was saying, "with the exception of His Eminence, Cardinal Spellissy, I've spoken to each of you during the past two months about the situation in Washington. Unfortunately, it remains the same. Congress will not interfere unless the federal authorities investigating this man Rebuck and his movement can prove beyond a doubt that his cult represents a clear and present danger to the country. Moreover, the President, mindful of Watergate and the Ellsberg case, no doubt, has made it clear that he won't tolerate any move to silence Rebuck. . . . It's our war, gentlemen."

"Then let's git at it," said Tommy Sunday.

"Just what are you suggesting?" said Billy Hale.

"I'm not suggesting, I'm demanding. We got to blow that demon right out of his saddle."

"What with? A bolt of lightning from heaven? Let's not be absurd."

"Absurd, hell. Where I come from we take the Bible seriously when it speaks of 'an eye for an eye, a tooth for a tooth.' We don't need a crystal ball to see who's behind Rebuck. It's the damn Commies and the government won't admit it. I'll tell you all one thing: there won't be any bombing of TV stations or long-hair hippie riots in my neck of the woods."

Nearly everyone at the table smiled indulgently at Sunday's ranting, but Harley Lombard picked up on one key point: "Who's to say Rebuck isn't part of a Communist takeover scheme?"

"Why, because he's drawn from the agnostic and atheist ranks?" said Norville Riggins.

"They don't believe in God—they're damn Commies," roared Tommy Sunday.

Rex Whitcomb interposed. "According to FBI reports, neither the Communist nor the Socialist Party has any link with Rebuck." He pulled a newspaper clipping from his pocket. "With your permission, I'd like to read what yesterday's *Times* editorial had to say about Ron Rebuck.

"The headline reads, 'The Sheep Are In Revolt.' It goes on to say: 'This strange man, Rebuck, with his spiritual shepherd's staff, has invaded the great barns of the religious Establishment and freed the sheep from their pens . . .

" 'The shepherd Rebuck reaches everywhere. His new, radical gospel has reached the mansions of the wealthy, the ranch houses of the middle class, the tenements of the ghetto minorities. The flower children of the sixties have found a new cause, and young and old alike are flocking to him.

" 'He is beginning to achieve where so many others have failed. His sparking of the soul has aroused the silent majority. The usual trodded upon, God-fearing people of America are finding a new dimension to their lives. Through Rebuck's message, they are slowly beginning to realize—life is more than birth, marriage, the raising of a family, and then to die. . . . Ron Rebuck has introduced them to their soul.' "

He paused to adjust his horn-rimmed glasses, then went on: " 'It is the supreme irony that Ron Rebuck, who some believe has written the only book that truly defends God, may in fact bring about utter chaos in our already wounded land. For his sheep, once freed, no longer behave like sheep. . . .' "

Whitcomb now scanned the faces around the table. "I know for a fact that certain people in the very highest places in Congress and the executive branch are hoping and praying that one of you, perhaps Billy, will come out and challenge this Ron Rebuck before his cancer spreads any further. I'm sure all of you read the papers. Just yesterday, in one middle-sized city, two politicians were assaulted, eight food outlets were bombed and six churches and one synagogue were destroyed. The time for action has come!"

Billy Hale rose from his chair. "Can anyone here give me one good reason why I shouldn't debate this man publicly, over nationwide television?"

There was a pause. Then Wallace Langley stirred in his chair.

"Billy, you're taking this personally and I don't blame you. He's zeroed in on you, chosen you as his primary target. But when he speaks about you, he's attacking us all. And I'm not sure debating this man is really the answer."

"That's fine for you to say, but not any of you hear the names I'm being called. Billy Bandit. Hale's Horseshit. Have any of *you* received a dozen chickens lately?"

Tommy Sunday smiled, and Billy fumed.

"There's nothing funny about this, Tommy!"

Norville Riggins turned toward the Cardinal. "Your Eminence, Billy tells me it was your idea to convene this meeting. Yet you haven't said a word. I'd be *most* interested in hearing what you have to say."

The Cardinal drew on his cigar, releasing the smoke in an ominous cloud. "First of all, none of you should debate Rebuck."

Billy Hale glared at the rotund man. "And you, Your Eminence, does that include you?"

"It does."

"Are you saying that a Prince of the ancient and

mighty Roman Catholic Church, an esteemed member of the College of Cardinals, fears this man?"

"I don't fear the man, but The One he represents."

Tommy Sunday, red with anger, turned to the Cardinal for the first time. "I know who he represents and so does everyone except the goddamn government. And if the lot of you are scared to shoot it out with this Commie, I will."

"If you do, Reverend Sunday," said Spellissy, "the man will, to use your own jargon, shoot you down."

Billy Hale shook his head. "Cardinal Spellissy, that's pure nonsense."

"Is it now? Is it really? Have you taken the time to think how in hell you are going to combat the man's theory of a Loving God? An Unwrathful God? A Neutral God? Face it, the God we all perpetrate to exist *is* wrathful. The God we ask our people to believe in, to worship, to love and obey, is precisely what Rebuck is against."

"Cardinal Spellissy, that is highly debatable."

"Is it, Bill? Think about it."

A silence seeped through the room as theological minds grinded over the Cardinal's statement until frustration confronted the issue. These were intelligent men, with soaring egos, yet they could never have achieved such rich and revered status without bending, without allowing reality to prevail.

Wallace Langley disrupted the uneasy silence and said, "What we need is some time to collectively work out a plan. A formidable plan to rid ourselves of this man."

"I don't have time," Billy shouted out. "My computer reads 'tilt.' My monthly mailings are at an all-time low." He looked scornfully at the Cardinal. "Unfortunately, unlike our distinguished Catholic colleague, I haven't any Vatican treasury to tap."

The Cardinal couldn't keep a straight face as he met the disbelieving eyes of his fellow priest. He wondered just how much money Billy and the rest of these purists had stashed away in some Swiss bank accounts.

"We are all feeling the pinch," said Norville Riggins. "Some of us more than others."

"And I'm that 'some' you're referring to, Norville," moaned Wallace Langley. "I can no longer afford television time."

"You're not alone, pardner," Tommy Sunday voiced, in his Western twang. "I had to cut my advertisin' budget in half."

"What about you, Harley?" asked Wallace Langley.

"I hate to admit it but I'm losing my followers by the droves."

Billy Hale shook his head in disgust. "I never imagined the day when the most influential religious leaders in America would become stymied by a lone man."

Norville Riggins said, "Cardinal Spellissy, I can hardly believe that a man of your importance would travel so far merely to gab and swap grievances. If you're against Billy debating Rebuck, you must have some plan in mind."

"Rest assured," said the Cardinal, smiling, "Father Augustus and I didn't make the trip from New York merely to enjoy the spectacular mountain scenery. To be very frank, it would be against my church's best interest. Present company included, against all of our interests—spiritually and monetarily. No offense intended, but I happen to know Rebuck considers you people nothing more than appetizers. The Catholic Church is the main course he's after."

The Cardinal shifted his great weight in the chair. "Again, no offense intended, yet we Catholics have endured much longer, and unlike you Evangelists, who rely on dramatics for effect, we are more subtle in how we state passages from the Bible."

"I've always said you Catholics let us do *your* dirty work for you," said a meaningful Tommy Sunday.

A slight smile came to the Cardinal's lips, but the twinkle was missing in the blue eys. "Let's not turn this into a Belfast of our own. There's much, much more at stake than any of you realize."

Billy Hale brought a hand to his chin. A finger rubbed along the bottom lip. He responded to Norville Riggins's disapproving look with indifference.

"Gentlemen," said the Cardinal, "we've come to meet with you for the sole purpose of stopping Ron Rebuck before he destroys every religious belief we hold dear."

He gazed out through the stained-glass windows. "Does this sound far-fetched? Perhaps, but I'm not one to make rash statements. And I tell you now that Ron Rebuck is the messenger of doom."

He looked directly at Billy Hale. "I realize how difficult it has been for you, Billy, to bear the full force of his onslaught. But I'm sure you realize that it's only because you are the household name among us."

He then looked away from Billy, at the others. "I don't mean to deflate anyone's ego, but Billy's name is like speaking about apple pie."

"And the Pope's like speaking about an international pizza," said Wallace Langley, sourly.

"I have never heard the Pope being referred to as a pizza, but if you are wondering why Rebuck chose

Billy, and not the Pope, it's because he must get by Billy before making an attack upon Rome. And gentlemen, Father Augustus and I are here to make sure that will never happen."

"Your Eminence," said an impatient Norville Riggins, "you said you had a plan?"

"I have. But I can't claim it as original. It comes directly from the Holy Bible."

Silence fell. Each of these men considered himself to be an authority on the Good Book, yet each one was unmistakably stumped.

Seeing their embarrassment, the Cardinal swiftly rose from his chair. The crafty old warhorse had them in the palm of his hand.

"The Bible gives each of us something different, in its endless richness and diversity. We have been lucky to hit upon what we believe is the answer to our mutual dilemma. But it could just as well have come to any one of you.

"Please bear with me for a bit of background before I get to the *piece de resistance*. . . . Gentlemen, long before Ron Rebuck came out of obscurity, I was warned of the man and his then-unpublished manuscript by someone who was very dear to me. I refer to Monsignor Gallogly, who, as you doubtless know, has left the Church and become a key figure in Rebuck's movement."

He cleared his throat to conceal the unbidden emotion, and continued. "After I personally witnessed what I can only describe as a supernatural event, I requested that His Holiness send me an experienced investigator. His Holiness sent me his best . . ." He looked benignly down on Father Augustus. "While Father Augustus went about his business, tracking down the source and nature of these happenings, I concentrated my efforts on one Henry Rodriguez. To those of you not familiar with the name, Rodriguez has been a thorn in my side for the last ten years. That the FBI was unaware of any true Communist connection within Rebuck's following doesn't surprise me. I doubt that Rodriguez is a card-carrying member of the Party for public exposure could interfere with his ultimate purpose."

He paused, enjoying the air of anticipation among the men around the table.

"Since his arrest during the Martin Luther King civil rights march on Birmingham, Henry Rodriguez has never seen the inside of a jail. Unlike other subversives, he avoids political disturbances. He reserves his poison for the religious establishment. He believes that once organized religion falls, the government itself will crumble. He is the uninvited, behind-the-scenes leader of the violent wing of Rebuck's movement. And gentlemen, make no mistake about it; each and every one of our names is on his death list."

"And Rebuck's name, too?" said Billy Hale. "When he and his instant Church have served their usefulness for Rodriguez and his comrades, he'll be eliminated?"

"True," Spellissy said, "but meanwhile the Church of Michael has given Rodriguez a perfect vehicle to create violence and chaos, while taking none of the blame. He is the one responsible for the vicious murders of the three men who fought with Rebuck's son—and for the bombings where so many were killed and injured."

"What makes you so sure?" Billy Hale asked.

"We have our informants, and they come from—every stratum of society. The activities of Henry Rodriguez have been triple-checked and verified. We are one of the oldest institutions in the world—and we've learned to be very thorough."

"So, unbeknownst to Rebuck, this fellow Rodriguez is his enforcer?" asked Hale.

"All opposition to Rebuck is stifled violently—and it isn't the hand of God, for sure," said Spellissy.

"Myrna Reardon—the columnist—she wrote that series exposing Rebuck's producer, that Manning character and the woman, Jennifer Jewell? And she died under odd circumstances," said Billy Hale.

"Billy, she was called a suicide but I'm convinced she was murdered. And I feel personally responsible. It was I who supplied her with the material for those articles."

The Cardinal examined the famous face known on five continents—the determined chin, the hawk's eyes, heavy-lidded, darting with intelligence. He'd always been fascinated, even a trifle jealous of Billy Hale. As a young auxiliary bishop in Brooklyn, he remembered when Billy barnstormed out of the West, packing ballparks with his gift of Biblical gab, magnetizing skeptics and turning them into believers. He'd thought then: *if the Protestants could ever unite, Billy Hale would be their first pope.* Now, he looked at him again, years later, with renewed admiration.

"I mention Myrna Reardon because there's great danger in what I'm about to recommend to you. But it is the *only* way that Ron Rebuck can be brought down—the only way to destroy Rodriguez."

Billy Hale never flinched. "Proceed, Your Eminence."

After a whispered conference between the Cardinal and Father Augustus, the room was cleared of aides and other support people. "This material is of the utmost confidentiality," explained the Cardinal.

At his signal, Father Augustus spoke: "The clerical investigator of the supernatural—exorcist, if you will—must work with a totally open mind, free of all religious prejudice. In the case of Ron Rebuck, I followed these basic rules to the letter. I must say that *in appearance* he came closer in word and deed to our Lord, Jesus Christ than any who have ever walked the earth. He preaches love, forgives sinners, condemns war. And, like Christ, he has, seemingly, performed miracles."

Gloom descended over the conference table. Billy Hale slumped down in his chair. Where, in all this, was the ammunition to shoot down Rebuck?

"I'd reached a complete impasse, when His Eminence insisted that I concentrate my sole efforts on seeking out Ron Rebuck's Judas. It was—"

Abruptly the bearded priest stiffened. His eyes bulged and his face turned pale. He remained motionless, corpselike, for what seemed an eternity. Then, suddenly, his great, shaggy head swiveled toward the stained-glass windows, and back again to the Cardinal.

The Cardinal seemed to receive some wordless message from the priest. He drew a deep breath and then exhaled slowly.

"What is it, Your Eminence? What's the matter?" asked Billy Hale.

In a grim voice he replied, "We have a visitor . . ."

The room became deathly still.

Father Augustus finally regained his composure and reached down to the black satchel at his feet. From it he withdrew certain religious articles—a black stole, a book, and a bottle of holy water. He lifted the stole, kissed it, then carefully, ceremoniously draped it around his neck.

The Cardinal's voice was low, yet firm and reassuring.

"Gentlemen, remain seated. Do not move. I shall come to the point as rapidly as I possibly can, but in Heaven's name, do not panic. No matter what, do not *panic*."

Harley Lombard's eyes roamed nervously about the room. Norville Riggins sat, totally numb, as though pole-axed. Rex Whitcomb, twice felled by heart attacks, took out a nitroglycerine ampule from a gold case and held it ready in a shaking hand. Wallace Langley fixed his timorous gaze on Tommy Sunday, who seemed to be reaching for a nonexistent sixgun. Billy Hale stared straight ahead at the stony face of Thomas Timothy Spellissy.

"When Father Augustus tracked down Ron Rebuck's Judas, one who has been supplying Rodriguez with vital information, and this Judas's identity became known to us, we then knew that Rebuck's path was marked with false signs. Signs that could only have been conceived by the Master of Deceit!"

The air in the room became thinner. A cold sweat appeared on Rex Whitcomb's brow. His face was clammy and he was having trouble breathing.

The Cardinal knew that there was little time left. "In reading Ron Rebuck's book, all of us were blinded to a most vital passage. It is the one in which he explains that a living man cannot see a soul, for he would die from its overwhelming beauty. By his very own testimony, therefore, Rebuck cannot see the great angel who speaks to him. He cannot know the true identity of that angel."

The men in the room listened intently, curiosity overcoming fear.

"Brothers in Christ, it is clear from all the evidence that Ron Rebuck does not confer, is not possessed, by the great Archangel Michael. No, unknowingly, he is being guided by the Master of all evil, the Lord of Lies."

As he spoke, Spellissy was hurled to the floor, his chair shattered beneath him.

They watched through unbelieving eyes as the Cardinal struggled to his feet, while Father Augustus commenced to chant in Latin.

Gasping for breath, the Cardinal shouted out, "The Bible, the Holy Bible warns us—"

The stained-glass window burst open. A moaning sound rose to a deafening pitch.

"HE SHALL COME."

The door to the room was ablaze, as well as the area beneath the windows that had been so mysteriously fung open.

"HE SHALL SWAY THE MASSES—"

There was a thunderous pounding on the walls. The floor rocked beneath their feet.

"HE SHALL PERFORM MIRACLES—"

Now the eyes in the busts on the table came alive, rolling wildly.

"THE BIBLE WARNS US TO BEWARE . . ."

The murmuring became more pronounced and Father Augustus could make out the word "liar," spoken in Hebrew, Aramaic and Greek.

"HE IS NOT GREAT MICHAEL'S MESSENGER—" the Cardinal shouted.

The heads of the prophets spun, dervishlike.

"HE IS THE MESSENGER OF THE KING OF HELL."

The bust nearest to Spellissy, that of John the Baptist, spat full in his face; he was drenched in blood.

Rex Whitcomb stared unbelievingly at the face of Daniel approaching him, feces spilling from its ears, nose and mouth. He clutched at his chest, his face turned purple. He then let out one last breath and fell dead on the mahogany table.

Billy Hale made a frantic move toward the stricken man, but was intercepted by the bust of Moses, suddenly within inches of his face.

"Kiss me, Billy, kiss me," it screamed, over and over.

He sat, rooted in horror, as a long penislike object shot out of the mouth and thrust itself against his lips.

Now the heads swarmed toward the Cardinal, who was slumped against the table. Father Augustus stood boldly between him and these hellish spectres, praying loudly.

Tongues became fangs, razor sharp, striking out at the priest, cutting him deeply about the face and neck. He fell backward into the Cardinal's arms, groaning in pain.

The Cardinal gazed numbly past the ghoulish faces, and saw a towering shadowy figure—a figure without a face.

All at once, in the darkened cavity of the head there appeared a face—the face of his beloved Pope.

With all of the strength left in him, Spellissy cried out: "Begone, Deceiver! It is Rebuck who serves you. HE IS THE ANTICHRIST!"

# Book 3
# Blood Harvest

# 33

UNDER AN ORANGE MOON on a late autumn night, the Hollywood Bowl was packed to overflowing with humanity.

Norville Riggins, Harley Lombard, Wallace Langley and Tommy Sunday were on stage with Billy Hale to launch what Billy had named "A Night of Light." The six P.M. (Pacific Coast Time) special was being nationally televised under the combined sponsorship of these famed evangelists' organizations, with a substantial contribution from the Roman Catholic Church.

The audience swarmed with young people—a far greater proportion than was usual at Billy Hale's crusades. Reminiscent of the young men and women attired in red, white and blue who waved their banners during that particular Republican convention, chanting out "Nixon's the One." Security forces were everywhere. Uniformed policemen patrolled the aisles, while plainclothes detectives sat in the audience. A riot control squad was stationed at the ready in a van outside the main entrance.

The show of strength wasn't lost on the throng of peaceful demonstrators, many with long hair, the men with beards, the women barefoot with flowers in their hair. They carried posters denouncing Billy Hale, and chanted "Hale's a hypocrite." One large, unwieldy poster depicted a huge, fearsome face emerging from the clouds with fire blazing from the nostrils, with a vivid crimson caption: "Billy Hale's God."

Absent from the stage was the usual cluster of celebrities from the world of sport and entertainment, who praised God for their success. This time, there was only the group of famed evangelists and Eulalia Johnson, the great gospel singer, who first did her famous version of "Amazing Grace" and then led the audience in the rousing old standby, "Bringing in the Sheaves."

Tommy Sunday, Wallace Langley and Harley Lombard each did his turn in his own special style, each denouncing the devil with foot-stomping vigor. Then the mighty Norville Riggins stepped forward to thunderous applause to set the mood for Billy Hale's eagerly awaited warning to the world. At last, Hale himself came forward.

The cheering and stamping subsided. Billy Hale looked out soberly over the massed faces. His usual smile of greeting wasn't there, nor was his famous opening salutation, "Everything's wonderful when you know Jesus."

"My fellow Christians," he began grimly, "prepare for a war! A war against an enemy whose sole purpose is to steal your very soul. . . . Yes, my friends, the Book of all Books, the words of the great prophets, the holy testimonies of the Apostles, the sacred sermons of Jesus Himself have been put in jeopardy by a man who disguises himself as 'Michael's Messenger.' "

Billy Hale shook his head dolefully. "His message is not from the Archangel Michael. His message comes, rather, from the dark haunts of the greatest of all deceivers. The Lord of all Evil has sent his Apostles of Hell to walk this earth in search of susceptible souls."

The great mass of people sat motionless as Billy Hale thrust his Bible aloft.

"That such a man would appear shouldn't surprise anyone who reads his Bible carefully. John warns of his coming. Paul reveals that such a man will spread universal evil among God's children. The Good Book tells us of one who shall twist the minds of those weak in faith with *apparently* logical explanations of the great mysteries of Christ. I say to you that this man is now among us—Christ's enemy, Lucifer's delegate, who uses the medium of television to plant his deadly seeds of destruction in the minds of man."

Again, he paused and seemed to search out every eye in the vast stadium. "Is it coincidence that, since this man entered our lives, suicides have risen to an all-time high? Is it coincidence that congregations in our Christian churches have dwindled to an all-time low? How is it that many of our young people for the first time publicly ridicule the Holy Bible, even spit upon the Book of Books, the true guide to your salvation and mine?"

Billy Hale smiled a canny smile. "Ah, but this man is clever. He does not present himself as an atheist. No, he says there is a God. But what kind of God does he speak of? He tells us of a God who is indifferent. A Father who cares nothing for his children. A God without love or hate. A God who says the existence of man is a mistake made by someone else. A God who has denied the very creation he alone could have conceived."

Now he stared forward at the crowd, his mouth curled in something that resembled a sneer. "I say to you that this man, who goes under the name of Ron Rebuck, is not a messenger of the great angel Michael, but a disciple sent by the Devil himself. I say to you: return to your churches! Read your Bible! Cast out this enemy of us all! Destroy his dangerous decrees before he delivers your soul unto eternal damnation. In the Name of God and His great son, Jesus Christ, strike out with your spiritual swords at this man—for his works have been made by the King of Despair. Christians in Christ, heed me now—the Anti-Christ seeks your souls!"

So mesmerized was the crowd by Billy Hale's revelation that for nearly a minute they sat locked in absolute silence. It was only when the thin, shrill voice of one woman pierced the stillness with "Hallelujah," that the spell was broken.

As a great roar rose from the crowd, Norville Riggins sprang from his chair and rushed to embrace a drained, shaken Billy Hale, tears welling from his eyes.

In a choked voice, the gospel singer commenced to sing "Onward Christian Soldiers." The evangelists on stage quickly joined in, waving their arms to lead the audience.

It was a moving spectacle—people, old and young alike, joining hands, rising and singing as one, their faces beaming. The song rose in the night air, electric with the feeling of Christian unity. Billy Hale, so overcome, wept unashamedly.

And then it happened, suddenly, so unexpectedly. First there was a whistling sound, then, a split second later, the devastating concussion and a gigantic blaze of white-hot light.

An antipersonnel missile, a mortar shell, had landed on the stage where Tommy Sunday had been waving his Stetson, where Wallace Langley and gospel singer Eulalia Johnson had stood, arms interlocked and raised in triumph. Then they were gone.

The blast spat out fragments of human bodies. Tommy Sunday's head sailed over the first five rows of seats and fell into the arms of a young man who stared at the macabre thing he was holding, then fainted dead away.

A sobbing Norville Riggins crawled about the stage on hands and knees, his face covered with blood, crying out, "My God, I'm blind."

Close by, Billy Hale lay helplessly on his back. He had tried to get up three times and each time had failed. His left leg, bloody and mangled, lay under him, twisted at a grotesque angle.

Harley Lombard, unhurt, stood motionless, frozen in shock.

# 34

FIVE DAYS HAD PASSED since the night of horror at the Hollywood Bowl. The word "Antichrist" echoed from pulpits world-wide. Stones and refuse were hurled at the boarded-up windows of Michael's Missions. Public sentiment against the Church of Michael mounted daily and members were defecting in legions.

From a California hospital, where surgeons debated whether or not to amputate Billy Hale's leg, the evangelist further assailed the man he'd publicly identified as the Antichrist.

Norville Riggins, who'd lost one eye, not only blamed Ron Rebuck for what had happened at the Bowl, but for all recent landslides, floods, earthquakes and other natural disasters. The eulogies for the late Tommy Sunday and Wallace Langley pictured them as martyrs whose noble lives had been snuffed out by the dark doings of the Devil's ambassador. Harley Lombard, evangelist spokesman in the absence of Billy Hale, called on all decent people, Christian and non-Christian, to join him in driving the Antichrist Rebuck from the face of the earth.

At long last, a weary and troubled John Gallogly, speaking in behalf of the Church of Michael, announced that Rebuck's rebuttal to Billy Hale's libelous charges would be made at a press conference at the end of the week. Too late for the wary Turk Savage.

THE SLEEK SILVER Rolls Royce sped through the night, followed by a Chrysler limousine full of security men. Inside the Rolls, watched over by the loyal Turk Savage, a demented Crack Widener squirmed in his seat, muttering incoherently. Suddenly, he turned to Turk and gestured frantically: "Turn back! Turn back! Michael's Messenger needs me!"

"Crack," said the quick-thinking Turk Savage, "*God* needs you in Australia—remember?"

Gradually, Widener, soothed by the words, leaned back and closed his eyes. Turk Savage sighed with relief as he watched the tension pass out of Crack's body. He felt for the handcuffs attached to his belt and prayed that he wouldn't have to use them. He prayed, too, that the trip to the airport, where Widener's 707 awaited them, would be mercifully quick.

ED DOWIAT stared out the rear window of his limousine. He had suddenly realized he'd been traveling far longer than it took to reach his destination—Jennifer Jewell's Central Park South apartment. He looked suspiciously at the man beside him—his bodyguard, the massive Oriental. The man's tiny eyes appeared to be closed and his expression was serene.

The limousine pulled off the street and into a garage,

then down a narrow ramp. Ed Dowiat's suspicions suddenly turned to fear as the car pulled up in a darkened area. The chauffeur blew the horn once, cut the engine, then got out and stood by the car's open door. Ed Dowiat now heard the sound of footsteps.

A tallish, slender man entered the car and the chauffeur closed the door behind him. Dowiat knew the face—lean and menacing—but the name escaped him.

"Mr. Dowiat," the man said in a faintly accented voice, "I wish we could have met under better circumstances."

All of a sudden, Dowiat placed the man. "You're . . . aren't you Henry Rodriguez?"

"I am, Mr. Dowiat."

"What do you want with me? Why am I here?"

"You have been chosen, Mr. Dowiat."

"Chosen? Chosen for what?"

". . . To die, Mr. Dowiat . . ."

Ed Dowiat's face turned ashen white. His eyes darted about, looking for an escape; his lips moved, but no words came. He made a futile lunge toward the door, but the massive Oriental pinned him back against the seat with one powerful arm.

"Why? Why are you doing this to me? What have I ever done to you?" His voice trembled.

In the tone of a corporate executive explaining the firing of an employee, Rodriguez replied: "The decision wasn't made in haste, Mr. Dowiat. Yes, the Church people were aroused, but all I heard were words. Threatening words—five stinking days of them. But not one deed. Not one of those Christian yellow-bellies could produce a single violent attack on your cause. . . . So, you see, Mr. Dowiat, I must act for them."

"My children . . . my wife," Dowiat sobbed

unashamedly.

"Yes, your children. They will always remember their father as a great martyr. What better inheritance, what better glory can any man leave his loved ones?"

"Please . . ." Dowiat started to beg, then stopped. For a moment, he thought he saw a hint of mercy in Rodriguez' eye. Perhaps, after all, his life would be spared—news would come that one of Michael's Missions had been bombed, or an abortive assassination attempt had been made on Ron Rebuck's life. But his soul knew better, as it prepared his body for an unwelcome death.

"I'm sorry, amigo, truly sorry." With that, Henry Rodriguez got out of the car and disappeared into the dimness.

The Oriental's eyes popped open. He took a pair of skin-tight gloves from his coat pocket.

Ed Dowiat watched in quiet horror. He'd often wondered how death would feel. The pain of a heart attack . . . the seconds before drowning.

His body now jerked with spasms. Tears streamed down his cheeks. Like an animal waiting to be devoured by a stronger beast, he closed his eyes. Strangely, he thought himself to be sitting in a dentist's chair, about to have a bad tooth extracted. Then he felt the powerful hands locking around his neck. He emitted a gurgling sound. Then — oblivion.

THREE DAYS LATER, on Thanksgiving Eve, Ron Rebuck's press conference in New York drew a swarm of newspaper, magazine and TV reporters, with pooled TV coverage by the networks. Rebuck's opening statement expressed sorrow for the tragedy at the Hollywood Bowl and reasserted the belief that no true follower of the Church of Michael could have had anything to do with this or any other act of violence.

Jennifer Jewell and John Gallogly watched from inside the control booth as the journalists commenced to fire their questions at Rebuck, swift and hard as a flight of steel-tipped arrows. John Gallogly found it impossible to remain attentive. He hadn't slept a wink in the two nights since Ed Dowiat's disappearance.

He looked at Jennifer. Jennifer, who seemed so unaffected, so totally divorced from Ed Dowiat's strange disappearance. He wondered how a woman as beautiful as she could walk away from the worldly pleasures bestowed on her by a wealthy sheik, and then become so feverishly dedicated to Ron Rebuck.

He wondered further, as she sat there, hanging on Ron Rebuck's every word, if she too spoke to great Michael; for more than ever she'd become Ron Rebuck's confidante, ministering to his every need.

She must have sensed him staring at her, for she turned, suddenly. Their eyes collided. John Gallogly's built-in radar signaled a warning. Then she smiled, and he dismissed the warning as false.

A woman reporter was questioning Ron Rebuck. "Mr. Rebuck, you have been called the Antichrist. *Are you?*"

His face was grim. "I have been attacked because I dare to defy certain words and ideas in a boor of curious authorship, written by all-too-mortal men. My opponents could find no other way to discredit me . . ."

A gruff-voiced newsman, known as an s.o.b. among his colleagues, broke in, reading from the Bible: *"The son of perdition will be revealed and the Lord Jesus Christ will destroy him with the breath of his mouth . . ."* He flipped over some pages and then read on: *"The Lawless one . . . will appear as part of the workings of Satan, and shall have the powers of wonder at the disposal of falsehood."*

The newsman closed the Book and looked up. "That last quotation was from Paul. . . . Mr. Rebuck, since Jesus Christ hasn't destroyed you—at least not yet—I take that first quotation with a grain of salt. But, in view of the frightening things that have been happening in your wake, wouldn't you say that Paul's description of the Lawless one fits you quite well?"

"I am not the son of perdition, but one who has openly challenged those who use scripture as a weapon of fear, and so defame God. As for your question about 'the Lawless one,' consider the source of your quotation. Paul in his earlier life was Saul, the Butcher of Tarsus, a destroyer of men, a tainted source."

Another questioner asked, "Billy Hale has urged everyone to read the Book of Revelations, so that we shall know the enemy. What do you think of Revelations?"

"Unadultered horror, composed by the Edgar Allen Poe of his day."

The moderator began to signal the end of the press conference when an attractive young girl reporter rose with one last question.

"Mr. Rebuck, in your book, *The Lawyers of Hell,* you have portrayed Lucifer—also known as Satan or the Devil—as a being unlike the monster we've all been brought up to believe in. You've treated him with a certain respect, and you've shown him as having valid reasons to oppose the existence of man." She hesitated for a moment to give her key question greater impact.

"Since you do not *see* the angel, or soul, who speaks to you—for if you did it would contradict what you have written—couldn't you, in fact, be speaking with, or for, the Devil?"

In the control booth, John Gallogly winced. He knew where *this* loaded question came from. Beyond a doubt, Cardinal Spellissy had primed this young ingenue.

For the first time since he'd come upon the American scene, Ron Rebuck struggled visibly for a reply, but recovered swiftly. "Judge me for what I am, what I say, whom I defend. Judge me by my works and then you'll know that it's not *I* who's being used by Lucifer—but those who condemn me."

Just as the conference ended, an inspector and two uniformed cops entered the control booth and solemnly conferred with Jennifer Jewell and John Gallogly. Instantly, Ron Rebuck headed for the booth, where he was given the bizarre news. The dismembered body of a man the police believed to be Ed Dowiat had been found stuffed inside a gunnysack, with the words "An eye for an eye, a tooth for a tooth" written in blood on the outside of the sack.

Surrounded by guards, the Oriental among them, Jennifer guided the grief-stricken Ron Rebuck out of the studio, leaving John Gallogly to attend to the gruesome ordeal of identifying the body.

"WHY & WHY?" Ron Rebuck asked himself over and over again. Jennifer Jewell stood at the window of the luxury apartment that, along with the building itself, had been the sheik's parting gift. She gazed into the night for several minutes before she turned to look at the anguished man who was sitting with his face buried in his hands. Then she quietly left the room.

She could hear his sorrowing words as she shed her street clothes and sat clad only in panties and bra before her elaborate dressing table. She looked at her image in the oval mirror, but not in the manner of a woman searching for flaws. Rather, as a woman full of confidence, a woman in command.

She rose from her chair, an image of beauty. Her long willowly legs, firm curving hips and magnificent protruding ass, slender waist, high, perfect, thrusting breasts formed a portrait of any man's desire.

She slipped into a blue satin negligee, slit wickedly all the way up the front, stepped into fluffy blue slippers, and walked sinuously toward the living room door, where she paused briefly.

Ron Rebuck raised his eyes and met hers.

"Why? Why did he have to die?"

She moved to the couch and sat quietly beside him. The slit in the negligee opened to reveal a long, sensuous curve of silky thigh.

His eyes roamed about the room until they rested on the portrait that hung over the fireplace. The gilded frame that had once held the portrait of an Arabian prince now held his own.

Jennifer's arm slid along the couch behind him. She inched closer and, as she did, the negligee opened even wider. Her fingers touched his upper back, then moved to his neck, which she massaged gently.

She rested her head gnetly on his shoulder and breathed in his man-smell. Her face flushed and her breath came faster as desire overtook her. Moving closer, she put her other hand on his leg and felt the energy pulsing through that powerful body.

Suddenly, he leaned forward and her arm fell aside, limply.

"June . . . Ron, Jr.?" he asked.

"Everything's fine. They've been contacted."

"My sister?"

"She and your mother will arrive from the mission in the morning."

"My God . . ." he said with a sigh.

"Relax. Try to relax," she said softly.

He leaned back on the couch. Her face close to his. Her fingers began to rub his thigh; slowly, seductively, her fingers moved up to his genitals—where her hand was gripped and overpowered by his.

"Jennifer, how could anyone have contacted June and Ron, Jr. when only Michael and I know where they are?" His face clouded with suspicion.

"Ron, you told me. Don't you remember?"

He looked at her doubtingly.

"Even I? You're distrustful even of *me*?"

All uncertainty left his eyes. He kissed her cheek. She was, after all, his most valued, loving and loyal disciple. If he doubted her, then he must doubt himself.

There were a few minutes of complete quiet. They sat, side by side, not touching each other. She was wondering what was going on inside this extraordinary man, but she knew enough to stay silent.

Finally, he strode.

"Jennifer . . . who am I?"

The dead-serious look on his face told her that she must answer.

"You're . . . Michael's messenger."

"Am I?"

"Of course you are, Ron. What are you saying?"

"I don't know."

"Ron, you have been chosen. Miraculously chosen by Michael. Great Michael!"

"—Or great Lucifer."

"You mustn't talk that way. You're letting them wear

you down with this nonsense about the Antichrist. They're only trying to confuse you."

"Jennifer, I speak of love, but I bring about hate and murder. I speak of free souls, yet I bring new disasters to a torubled society."

He rose swiftly from the couch and moved toward the door.

"Where are you going?"

"To where it all began. . . ."

# 35

FOR SEVEN DAYS, there came to pass—a blood harvest.

The brutal murder of Ed Dowiat, coming on the heels of the deaths of the evangelists, set in motion a multitude of violent acts. Henry Rodriguez' murder machine struck at will, leaving the remains to the scavengers. The poor, the embittered—that "third wave" which follows in the wake of any war or civil disturbance.

A Southern millionaire, a deacon in his church and a deeply respected force in his community, tired of promiscuous police protection, organized a group called Crusaders for Christ, typical of the vigilante groups that were springing up in the Bible Belt to combat Rebuck's Church of Michael.

The Crusaders for Christ invaded Michael's Missions in the South and Southwest, dragging out the young men and women who were the true core of Rebuck's following. Taken to isolated spots and tied to trees, their cries of innocence went unheard, as whips lashed across their naked backs, and those who judged them read fiery passages from the Bible.

Not long after the Crusaders began their night rides, a task force of Henry Rodriguez' well-trained guerrillas snatched the deacon from his bed and hung him from a lamppost in the middle of town, for all the local folk to view. . . .

Congress was up in arms. Because the role of Rodriguez in fomenting trouble could not be proven, they blamed it all on Ron Rebuck. The senior congressman from New York City called on the Attorney General with the demands that he halt this madness before the whole nation came apart at the seams. A delegation of leading senators went to the President, asking for immediate action.

JACK PINTOFF, following these violent events with great interest, now tossed aside the *Times* to answer the buzz from the lobby of his brownstone townhouse. His contorted face shone with lust as he recognized the female voice at the other end of the line.

"Come up, my darling, come up," he said, gleefully pressing the door-opening switch.

She was almost an hour early. He was thinking he'd have to be lightning-swift in his preparation for an afternoon of sexual kinkiness and perversion when the phone rang, interrupting his frantic activity.

The sound of the voice on the line made his black eyes blaze with fury. "I told you before, I don't know any Marty Pico!"

He slammed down the receiver and cursed aloud just as the elevator bell rang shrilly, announcing his guest and sending a tremor of anticipation through his twisted body.

He rushed to open the elevator door, peering through the brass-barred gate for a glimpse at a face to make him drool.

MARTY PICO ducked Richard's scowling eyes and checked out Jack Pintoff's townhouse, just across the street.

"How do you know the turkey's home?"

Marty Pico looked at his watch. "He's in there."

"Two hours ago the bastard hung up on me. His phone's been off the hook ever since. You know what that tells me? He's in the kip with some sixteen-year-old broad."

"You know that . . . I mean, you *know* that?"

A big paw suddenly landed on Pico's shoulder. Before he knew it, he'd been spun around, full circle. He looked into that mean black face and blinked.

"There's only one motha-fuckin' thing I ain't forgettin'. You reading me, Italian boy?"

"Save the muscle, will ya," said Pico, trying to push the massive hand off him. "Save it for Pintoff."

The giant eased off. The angry face broke into a grin of disbelief. "Fool! That dude's not going to spit up two hundred G's."

"He will, I guarantee it, Richie. He's got a fetish about knives. Once you threaten to cut his ass, he'll shake loose with the bread. And in cash."

He shook his tremendous head. "Man, you've run out of rainbows. You better be right this time."

"Yeah, yeah. Just give me the keys."

The keys Pico had had specially made to crash Pintoff's brownstone worked as he expected, and despite Marty's warning that the elevator was electronically controlled, the giant Richard bitched about having to walk up three flights.

Now, inside Pintoff's living quarters, Marty Pico sniffed; he smelled a faint trace of perfume.

"The bedroom," he pointed.

Reaching the master bedroom door, he looked over his shoulder and whispered, "Hope the bastard hasn't come off."

His hand rested lightly on the door handle. He glanced once more at Richard's bored-looking face, then yanked hard on the handle and bolted inside.

His eyes were riveted on the gargantuan bed. Only the sound of the unshockable Richard's breath being sucked was heard, as he realized what lay in the bed.

Jack Pintoff's eyes were permanently fixed on the mirrored ceiling. Rivers of blood had run from his nose and mouth down over his chin and onto the sheet which was drawn up to his chest. The grotesque twist of the head was even more bizarre in death.

Pico pulled down the bloody sheet, revealing the deep gashes in Pintoff's stomach. Part of the man's intestines protruded from one gaping wound.

One hand, crimped into a fist, was at the crotch. Driven by curiosity, Pico pried the hand open. Gripped in it was Jack Pintoff's severed tongue.

Pico backed away from the bed, nauseated and confused. Then a new jolt of terror struck as a powerful arm clamped around his neck. "How's that dead motha-fucker gonna pay two hundred G's? Tell me, turkey? You tell me *how*!" Richard growled.

"I . . . can't . . . breathe," he said, struggling for air.

The huge man applied more pressure, then released him and shoved him forward. Pico fell against the bed, but kept his balance. Again, the huge hand grabbed him and forced him to look down at the gory corpse. "There's your rainbow, *sucker*!"

". . . All right, all right," said a breathless Pico, "we hit Manning and Spenard."

"WORLD WAR III," said Rufus Manning as he put the newspaper down on the kitchen table and reached for his orange juice.

"And you're not part of it," Nancy Manning said happily.

"Run, Rebuck, run. Right off the big cliff," said Rufus, lighting up a cigarette.

"Roof, let's not talk about Ron Rebuck. We've got a beautiful life ahead of us . . . A whole month in Switzerland, skiing to our hearts' content. We—" She noticed the gloominess to his face. "Roof, it's over. You've got to stop thinking about it."

"Nancy, one year ago today I signed the contract with the network. I'm the guy who shot him to the moon. Remember?"

"Roof, it's his trip. It always was Ron's trip."

"Yeah, I know. But I can't help feeling sorry for him. They've made him into some kind of ghoul. A doctor Frankenstein."

"I feel sorry for June Rebuck. She must be going through hell. I'm almost tempted to call her. Do you suppose she's in Florida?"

"Who knows?"

"Do you think she's with Ron?"

"And where in hell is that? He could be in any *one* of his Missions. But I get the feeling God Himself doesn't know where Ron Rebuck's hiding out. I hope he's got a very deep foxhole."

Unwilling to let her happy mood escape, she kissed him on the cheek and got up to leave the room, then remembered something. "Roof, did you get the plane tickets?"

"Mike's getting them when he picks up Leslie and John at the railroad station."

Her eyes glowed. "Your daughter; our Leslie, married in Europe . . . Roof, isn't it just wonderful?"

"Yeah, wonderful." He rose from the table. "Nancy, I'm paying off those security guards and letting them go."

"Roof, are you sure that's a wise thing to do?"

"We're leaving tomorrow and if I don't dismiss them today, I get stuck for another week."

Nancy followed him out of the kitchen to his den. A look of concern crossed her face as she saw him take a bill out of his desk drawer and begin writing a check.

"Roof, keep them. Please. I'd feel much safer."

"Nancy, they're a pain in the ass. Besides, Mike's all the security we need for one night."

She still wasn't convinced. "Roof, make it an early Christmas present, but keep them."

"A Christmas *what*?"

She saw the beginning of the familiar upward spiral of the eyeballs. "Oh no, not this year!" She blew him a kiss and beat a hasty retreat.

He smiled. A full smile. For the first time in his stormy life, he was out of the fray. True, his goal of a billion dollars had fallen considerably short, yet even this failed to disturb his calm. He'd beaten the odds, hit the long shot; Rufus Manning was finally at peace with the world.

But at the very moment he sat savoring his contentment, men were on their way to kill him.

NIGHT MOVED IN, swiftly. A sky clear of clouds, the temperature in the high forties, only the hint of a breeze, a quarter moon dimly lighting Rugus Manning's grounds.

The two men emerged from the shadowy woods and

crept toward the balloon-like structure of the indoor tennis court.

Inside the big bubble, dressed in a green warm-up suit, Rufus Manning was furiously engaged in a tennis match—and John Milton was giving him fits. He shellacked him in the first set and was about to blank him in the second when Rufus faked a cramp and called it a "no contest."

"You didn't win," said Rufus, limping toward the young man.

"Of course I won. You couldn't go on."

"We resume play in Europe," said Rufus, slapping his hand. "Go take your shower. I think I'll practice my serve. It needs a little work."

"A *little*?" said John, grinning mischievously.

Rufus motioned for Mike Spenard to go with him and had turned away to collect a basket of tennis balls when he saw his protector, lingering.

"Mike, will you blow!"

Spenard still hesitated, then grudgingly followed John Milton through the passageway that led to the dressing room and showers.

Absorbed in practicing his lack-luster serve and cursing the inventor of the game, Rufus wasn't aware of someone jimmying the outside lock. Moments later, he didn't see or hear the main door behind him crack open. But as he concentrated on placing the ball at a particular spot, he suddenly heard the shuffling of feet—and froze.

"Don't move, Manning. You do, and you'll never return *my* serve."

He turned on the unwelcome sight of Marty Pico and massive friend.

"A Jimmy Connors you ain't. We've been watchin' through the window. You really stink, Manning."

The big black ignored Pico's commentary and pointed to the area where Mike Spenard and John Milton had entered. "What's behind there, honky?"

"Better tell him, Manning, before he swallows you whole."

Rufus stayed silent and met the giant's threatening approach with a snarl, until the sound of John Milton's loud whistling from the shower area brought the big black to an abrupt halt.

His nostrils widening, he turned and moved toward the passageway like a big cat smelling its prey.

"Bad timing, Manning," said Marty Pico, slipping the .38 out from the shoulder holster. "How do you like the odds, Manning? Me with a piece and you with a tennis racquet?"

He moved closer so that the two stood less than a few yards away, with only the net between them.

"Must be nice. Big fuckin' house, swimmin' pool, good-lookin' wife—would you believe *two* tennis courts? The one outside by the pool ain't good enough. Naw, you gotta have one inside a blimp." The gap in his front teeth showed in a snarl of envy.

"Where I was growin' up in Brooklyn," Pico went on, "anyone caught playin' tennis would get lumped on the head with a lead pipe."

"Pico, you never grew up. You've *always* been a load of shit."

"Manning, I got the piece. *You* give with the sweatin'."

"I wouldn't give you the sweat off my balls."

Marty Pico eyed him, curiously, dumbly. All along he'd pictured Rufus to be on his knees, begging, pleading. Instead, Rufus treated the whole thing with an incredulous calm.

"Manning, this ain't no cap pistol I'm holdin'."

"Get down, Pico, the only thing you're shooting off is your big mouth. I got you figured. You're no killer. You're dealing."

Marty Pico's eyes flashed with surprise. "You gotta crystal ball or sumpthin'?"

"Don't need one. You face is lit up like a neon sign."

"Pretty smart, Manning, a real shrewdie. Now I know how you faked out all those millions. Whud you make on that black flick?"

"You can't count that high."

Remembering his vendetta, Pico said bitterly, "How I'd love to drop you where you stand! I've dreamed about wastin' you a thousand different ways. I even swore on my mother's grave to chop you up. But Richie wouldn't go along with me on snatchin' the Cardinal, so you're the last shot I got at my rainbow."

"I'm touched, Pico. I got tears in my eyes and I know I'm going to cry like Niagra Falls when you get to the money bit."

"One million bucks! One million soldiers, that you greased outta Rebuck's church. And you can forget the spiel about where you'd get that kinda loot in a hurry. One of your *ex*-security guards had a mouth like Western Union. Told how you gotta couple of million in cash stashed away in some underground vault."

"Aren't you forgetting something, Pico; like a joker in your deck?"

"You mean Richie?" Marty Pico checked the rounds in his pistol. "We *deal,* Manning, I don't give a shit who comes through that hallway—your killer or mine."

INSIDE THE DRESSING room, Mike Spenard peered through the narrow, eye-level window in the door to the showers and sauna. John Milton had turned off the spigot and was reaching for a large yellow towel.

"Gotta check on Mr. M.," Spenard growled through the closed door.

"Okay, Mike," John said, drying himself.

Mike Spenard opened his jacket, took the .44 Magnum from its wide hip holster and went to the dressing room door, planning to check out the weapon as he made his way along the narrow passageway leading to the playing court. But as he opened the door, a huge, hammerlike fist smashed into his nose with bone-shattering impact. The gun flew from his hand as he staggered backward, falling against the paneled wall, then sliding to the tiled floor in a senseless heap.

Richie picked the weapon up off the floor and placed it on a card table as Spenard dragged himself to his knees and looked through a haze of blood at the towering black.

Stunned, John Milton looked through the small shower room window, heard the clicking sound and saw the wicked switchblade materialize in the big bearlike paw. Terrified, he locked the door and met the olive-black eyes that turned upon him. He quickly stepped away from the window, shaking.

Hulking over his helpless victim, Richard first tore the jacket and shirt from his body. Then taking hold of Spenard's hair, he waved the gleaming blade before expressionless eyes.

With the skill of a matador, he flicked his wrist and the blade sliced through the lobe of Spenard's left ear.

In his odd, high-pitched voice, Richard laughed at the sight of blood gushing from the wound.

"WHAT'S IT gonna be, Manning?"

"You want to deal, Pico, you first better capture your headhunter. Because if anything happens to Mike or the kid, you can stick the deal up your greasy ass."

Rufus's words tore at his mind. The fact he'd deal was comforting, but to stop the likes of Richard from tearing Spenard apart was easier said than done. Marty Pico stood there confused, seeing with frustration.

Suddenly, Rufus Manning's face turned gray. He stiffened. His hands tore at his chest. Letting out a loud groan, he fell face down onto the court.

Bewildered at first, Marty Pico then scrambled around the net and knelt at the fallen man's side.

"You're bullshittin', Manning! Get up, you lyin' sunuvabitch!"

He reached down and felt Rufus's pulse. Bitterly he realized the futility of attempting to converse with a comatose man. His quest for that golden rainbow once again queered, he turned his maddened thoughts elsewhere and left the critically ill man's side.

Entering the passageway, Pico stopped before the dressing room door, then charged through in gangbuster style.

What he saw made him wince.

Mike Spenard was hunched in a corner like a dying dog. An ear hung by a thread, his chest criss-crossed with bloody gashes, his face barely visible through a crimson shroud.

"Jesus, Mary and Joseph, finish him off," Marty pleaded. Then, looking about, asked, "Where's the kid?"

"In the shower, man, in the shower." Richard's high-pitched voice sounded annoyed.

Pico gazed pityingly through the small window at John Milton, then turned on his heel and headed for the exit, with final words for the frenzied butcher, "We gotta get the hell outta here."

"The kid. Take him out!" the giant thundered.

"No way, Richie. He's *your* witness."

With Pico gone, the big black looked down at the man who'd humiliated him—the man he'd vowed to kill—now completely at his mercy. This was the honky who'd buried him in the mausoleum on that bitter cold night, who laughed at his nudity—who stripped him of all dignity . . .

Holding him by the throat, he dragged the hapless Spenard to his feet and pinned him to the wall.

"I'm gonna squeeze your head till your brains come outta yer ears . . ."

John Milton turned away from the sight in horror, looking for an avenue of help, even praying to Ron Rebuck's Michael. There seemed no way out. He'd soon be butchered by a man who'd *have* to kill him. Still, he despearately looked about him for some implement with which to defend himself.

Something drew him to the sauna. Told him to look inside. The fireaxe Rufus had insisted upon having there filled his tormented eyes. He reached out and seized it, ripping it from its plastic cradle; then moved cautiously toward the windowed door.

Through blurred eyes, the tortured Mike Spenard saw the shower-room door open. But his eyes shut and he let out a chilling cry as he felt something cracking in his face.

Sensing a presence behind him, the giant Richard slowly released his death grip and spun around. At that very moment, John Milton drove the fireaxe deep into his chest.

MARTY PICO stood over Rufus's body—sure he was dead. He didn't notice the towel-clad John Milton standing shakily at the passageway entrance. He'd expected to see only his black sidekick emerge from the dressing rom, and had already holstered his gun.

Marty Pico finally saw his true rainbow approach, but not the bullet from a .44 Magnum that blew him dead away . . .

FOR TWO DAYS Rufus Manning battled for his life in a Connecticut hospital. Outside the intensive-care wing a vigil was kept by the grieving Nancy Manning, with John and Leslie, and the heir-apparent who'd found time to leave the ski lodge in Vermont, Stewart Manning.

Hughie Gilman, who'd taken the first plane out of California when he heard the news, had just arrived. He was consoling Nancy Manning when a nurse reminded them of the doctor's explicit orders, then escorted Hughie Gilman to the cubicle where Rufus was isolated.

"Only a few minutes," she whispered in departure.

Gilman moved slowly toward the motionless Rufus Manning. See Rufus on his back, staring up at the ceiling with glazed eyes, was a sight Hughie'd never imagined.

"Hello, Roof," he voiced, looking down at the pale and partially paralyzed face.

With great effort, the eyes left the ceiling and fixed on him.

"Roof, Nancy wanted me to tell you that Mike will be all right. He's too tough to die, just like his boss."

Hughie searched for a coherent sign, but the beady eyes, once electrically alive, looked damp and dreary.

"Roof, is there anything I can do for you?"

The lips slowly parted. The speech was sparse, and came with great effort. "Rebuck . . . Rebuck," he said again.

"No one has seen or heard from him. Seems he's dropped off the face of the earth."

"Hughie–do–you–think–he–was–full–of–shit?"

"It's not important, Roof. What matters is for you to get well."

"Hughie–God–is–"

"There's a God? Is that what you're saying?"

Hughie saw what appeared to be a nod, and replied, "Yes, Roof, there's a God."

"Hughie–it's–it's goning to take–someone–someone bigger than God–to light my candle."

Tears swelled in Gilman's eyes. "Roof, you need your rest," he said chokingly.

He started for the door, when Rufus's coarse voice called out his name. He anxiously returned to the side of the bed.

"Yes, Roof, what is it?"

" 'Member–'member all those–sermons–you gave me?"

"How could I forget?" he replied fondly.

"I–I gotta big one–for you."

Hughie thought he saw the beginning of that all too familiar shitty smile that always preceded a Rufus Manning plan.

"The–the sheet–pull it–down."

Hughie Gilman first hesitated, then carefully pulled back the sheet. He shook his head, disbelieving what he saw. The middle finger of Rufus's right hand was–indeed–shooting him a bird!

"Roofala, Roofala," he sobbed, as he placed a tender hand over the thrusted finger and felt Rufus's laughter from within.

AT 4:05 A.M. RUFUS MANNING expired. The cause of death—ventricular fibrillation, due to extensive myocardial infarction. But what the death certificate didn't say was that Rufus Manning came into this world and left it in the same manner: with his finger held high in the air. . . .

# 36

THE PHONE rang insistently in Cardinal Spellissy's study. It had been ringing almost steadily since word had come that the President of the United States had declared a moratorium on all religious radio and television shows until the current epidemic of violence subsided. In the anteroom to his office, a flock of reporters clamored for interviews, even though he'd refused to issue a statement.

Actually, ever since the slaughter at the Hollywood Bowl, when he publicly expressed his deepest sorrows, the Cardinal had remained mute. Not once did he mention the name Ron Rebuck. And as for Rebuck's being the Antichrist, the word throughout the great diocese was mum. The priests in their respective parishes paid as little attention to the Antichrist theme as they did to exorcism.

The Vicar General, Bishop Burke, plowed through the mass of reporters and stuck his bulldog head inside the Cardinal's office.

"Cardinal, Harley Lombard is calling for the fifth time. I do believe you should talk to him."

"You talk to him."

"He only wishes to speak with you."

Earlier, he'd refused calls from Norville Riggins and Billy Hale himself. Wearily, the Cardinal reached over and picked up the phone.

"Hello, Harley," he said to the agitated voice on the line. "What can I do for you this fine day?"

"First of all, you could have returned our calls. But more important, you must give us your support in fighting this—this moratorium the President just hit us with!"

"Indeed! And what sort of support do you want from me?"

"We want you to accompany Norville, Billy, and I to Washington, and have the President reverse this disastrous hiatus he's called for."

"Harley, I don't think all our considerable clout could swing that."

"Cardinal, we *must* try."

"Harley, the way I see it, this moratorium comes as a blessing in disguise."

"You call the cancellation of our Christmas specials a blessing? Cardinal Spellissy, it's a catatrophe!"

"Harley, I'm referring to our war against Lucifer and his emissary, Rebuck. Surely, you haven't forgotten the war at hand?"

There was a slight pause on the other end. "Cardinal, we can fight Lucifer and Rebuck much better with our specials."

"I'm sorry, Harley, I will have to disagree. Keeping Ron Rebuck off the airwaves will bring about strangulation to his whole movement. It shall then die for lack of financial oxygen."

"Cardinal, I don't think you quite understand. *We* cannot afford to lose our Christmas specials. And—and what about your famous Mass? Are you going to sit back and allow it to be cancelled?"

"Harley, we all must be willing to make some sacrifices if we are to achieve total victory."

"How nobly stated, Cardinal. Your Roman Catholic Church is sitting on billions, but we *depend* on our TV and radio crusades for all our support."

"I'm sorry, Harley, I'm not about to go tilting at windmills."

"Cardinal Spellissy, are you telling me that you, you who planned the strategy of the Antichrist campaign and allowed Billy Hale to take all the heat, will not go to Washington and help us fight for our survival?"

"Harley, if you recall, I did not force Billy to do anything. He bravely, and of his own accord, chose to slay the dragon."

"My God, man, as a result of *your* plan two great men are dead, another half blinded and another about to lose a leg."

"You have my deepest sympathy, Harley, as do all our martyrs. But I *must* decline."

"You—you manipulate us behind the scenes, sit back, away from the bloody front, and now turn your back in our time of need. Cardinal Spellissy, you are a pig of a man!"

The phone at the other end slammed down. Thomas Timothy Spellissy sat for a moment, a look of concern on his round face as he brooded over Harley Lombard's strong accusations. That he was directly responsible for the deaths at the Hollywood Bowl, he considered ridiculous. But the fact that he alone had been the architect of the plan to brand Rebuck the Antichrist, couldn't be dodged. And that he had left Hale and the others to execute the plan could not be denied. True, he could have sat back and waited until Mother Church exhausted all other avenues before authorization came for him to attack Rebuck as the true Antichrist. That would have taken time, perhaps months of deliberation, before such a Vatican declaration was ever made. But time was what he didn't have. Rebuck was virtually unopposed in his march, and had to be stopped. His conscience was clear. He did what he had to do.

As he sat back in the swivel chair, a new thought troubled his mind: where was Father Augustus?

ARCHBISHOP McGARY entered the room and hurried to his side. "Tim, someone would like to see you."

He looked up into the pale blue eyes of his trusted old friend. "And who might that be?"

"John," he whispered. "John Gallogly."

The Cardinal's eyebrows rose; his eyes brightened. "Where? Where is he?"

"In the Cathedral, third row. It was his own idea."

"And a good idea it was," said the Cardinal, rising from his chair.

At the door, he turned to McGary. "Keep those press wolves at bay. If they see me with John, His Holiness will be reading about it in Rome for his breakfast."

"Sure you don't need anyone to come along? An observer?"

"I'm sure." He patted his good friend on the shoulder and entered the great Cathedral at the main entrance to avoid the reporters.

The Cathedral was sparse of people. A handful of parents and children and a scattering of elderly ladies—that was all. He walked down the farthest aisle, hoping not to be noticed. He nodded at a couple of biddies who, wide-eyed, recognized him.

John Gallogly heard the footsteps, those familiar

footsteps. He turned and looked at the man he once idolized—and still loved. Slowly, with great effort, he rose to his feet and faced him squarely.

He tried to hold himself in rigid control, but it was too much to bear. His eyes commenced to fill with tears and sobbing, he fell into the Cardinal's outstretched arms. The prodigal son had returned.

Thomas Spellissy patted him gently and led him into the pew. Neither spoke. No words were necessary.

From the Cathedral loft, the choir was commencing Christmas rehearsal. "Hark, the Herald Angels Sing" echoed thunderously from the great vaulted ceiling. John Gallogly left his seat and went to the communion rail. He knelt in worship as Cardinal Spellissy looked benignly on. As the man he loved like a son silently renewed his vows, Spellissy rose from the pew, tears trickling down his cherubic cheeks.

John Gallogly rejoined him. Together, they genuflected, then made their way down the aisle. The gigantic organ pipes blending with the song-filled voices made their hearts swell, their bodies tingle. "Hark, the Herald Angels sing—Glory to the newborn King!"

Halfway on, an old woman with a black shawl over her head knelt in the middle of the aisle, blocking their way. The Cardinal extended his hand and she kissed his ring with a strange ferocity. Retrieving his hand, he walked past her toward John Gallogly who waited for him a few yards ahead.

The deadly shape of a .45 revolver took aim. There was a flash of fire as the bullet entered the base of the Cardinal's skull, exiting through the orbit. His head and neck jerked violently forward and in one horrible moment John Gallogly saw a gaping hole where an eye once had been. Then the body was flung forward with such force that it somersaulted over a pew.

Screams came from the choir loft. The old woman stood, the gun still smoking in her gloved hand. Smiling, she moved quickly toward John Gallogly. Behind the mask of powder and wrinkles were the eyes of a young woman. Gallogly's radar flashed the same warning as once before; but this time he knew it wasn't false.

Suddenly, before he knew what was happening, the woman had shoved the gun into his nerveless hand, then pointed the finger of guilt at him. She was almost out the exit before he gathered his wits to give chase. He was stopped in his tracks short of the door by the choristers who had descended from the loft and were now milling about, staring at him with suspicion in their eyes.

John Gallogly ran toward the rear of the Cathedral, passing the bloodied corpse of the Cardinal, bits of brain tissue oozing from the gaping hole in his head. He went past the maze of faces, blindly, instinctively heading toward his old office.

BEHIND A LOCKED DOOR, in the room where he's first heard the name Ron Rebuck, where he and Paul Bartley had spent hours discussing Rebuck's *The Laywers of Hell,* John Gallogly stood, deaf to the voices beyond the door, begging him to come out.

He raised the gun that had killed Cardinal Thomas Spellissy, placed its muzzle against his temple and closed his sorrowing eyes for the last time.

Soon, John Gallogly's soul would know—the great master.

# 37

IN HIDING from the world, a bearded Ron Rebuck walked through the backwoods in an isolated portion of the hilly acreage once owned by the priests of All Souls, now converted into a monastery by the monks of the Eastern Order of St. Francis.

The night of December 23rd was brisk and nippy. The first major snowfall of the year had been predicted for this upper New York State region. Rebuck was unaware that Christmas was at hand as he made his way among the tall evergreens and great oaks. For a month to the day, he'd roamed these hills in search of a Truth he must know. Now, without watch or calendar, he'd lost all idea of time; only the light of day and the black of night had meaning for him.

During the day he kept himself hidden away. Late at night, and only then, he'd appear to the good and kindly monks who provided him with warm clothes, food and other necessities by standing on a hill in a clearing, from where he looked down at the old brick building in which he'd slept so many nights as a boy.

Usually, once the monks brought the provisions to him, he carried the food to the backwoods and was not seen again. Tonight, though, he remained on the hill longer than usual. The monks, peering out of the monastery windows, could see a man in monk's attire outlined against the skyline, standing on the hill, motionless. This was the man once whispered to be the Antichrist. And though they didn't come right out and say it, they wondered if this man wandering about their hills was truly Lucifer's demon.

PROVISIONS IN HAND, he moved through the night, wondering when the great angel would speak to him. The patter of animal feet, the screech of an owl, any of nature's weird noises, might be a sign of the angel's coming. Many a time, these sounds had played tricks on his mind.

For forty days and forty nights he'd not heard the voice of the great angel, nor felt the presence of its great soul. He'd grown hoarse beseeching the angel to speak to him. The people in the monastery mistook his cries in the night for that of a wolf.

In an old cow shed—Rebuck couldn't help thinking of it as a manger of the sort that had sheltered the infant Jesus—he slept during the day. At night, he stalked the grounds, often cursing the angel who'd broken the promise made to him.

A light snow began to fall as he was sitting on the edge of a cliff near the half-ruined shed. He was weeping in deep despair when, from a distance, lights flickered like a cluster of giant fireflies. He brushed aside the tears and stared in disbelief at the dancing lights. Was this merely another figment of his imagination? An illusion of a troubled mind?

Now a droning sound, humming through the trees, filled his ears. Charged with hope, he got up from his perch and followed the sound as it grew louder and louder.

It led him to a clearing in the woods, where he stopped, trembling, as a great flash of light illumined the whole area. In the midst of the column of blinding light was the *statue*—the very figure he'd marveled at as a boy in the dormitory of All Souls—but vastly larger and suffused with light. The Archangel Michael stood with his sword upraised over the figure of Lucifer, just as he remembered it.

In a quivering voice, he asked, "Who are you?"

He waited for an answer that seemed as though it would never come. Then, abruptly, the angelic figures changed places; now Lucifer, sword lifted, held the upper hand.

"Who *are* you?" he repeated, his voice now strong and clear.

The figures reverted to their original positions.

Ron Rebuck would not be denied. Again, he challenged the vision of light before him. "Who in the name of God are you?"

There were no words, but a violent reaction. In rapid succession the angelic figures spun around, exchanging places faster than the eye could follow.

Then the figures stopped spinning, and Lucifer resumed his usual position. The lights diminished. Just as Rebuck began to think the strange apparition was about to disappear, a voice from another world boomed: "SPEAK OF CAUSE, NOT BODILY NEED."

"I speak of *truth*," Rebuck shouted.

There was no reply, yet Rebuck pursued his questioning. "Are you the heavenly Prince I vowed to serve, or are you the King of all deceivers?"

"I AM HE WHO WORSHIPS THE LORD GOD. I AM THE DEFENDER OF GREAT HEAVEN."

"It is Lucifer who claims to be the defender of Heaven. Are you he?"

There was no immediate reply, yet Rebuck continued. "Whom do you defend Heaven from? The Soul of Man?"

"YOU HAVE LEARNED WELL, REBUCK. YOUR GREAT MISSION HAS BEEN ACCOMPLISHED. THOSE IN LIMBO HAIL YOUR

MORTAL NAME."

"If you are Michael, then why have you forsaken me?"

There was no response; Rebuck asked again: "Why have you allowed the bloodshed that has followed in my wake?"

"THE DEATH OF MAN'S BODY IS SACRED ONLY TO THE BODY. HAVE YOU NOT SPOKEN OF THIS IN YOUR VALIANT EFFORTS TO FREE MAN'S SOUL?"

"I have spoken of the independence of the soul from the body, yet never have I advocated the rueful destruction of the body."

"TELL ME, MAN, DOES YOUR BODY NOW BECOME MUTINOUS TO ITS SOUL? DOES IT REBEL FROM THE GREAT CAUSE YOU HAVE CHAMPIONED?"

"What cause, Great Angel, that of Michael's, or that of Lucifer's?"

"DOES IT TRULY MATTER? HAVE YOU NOT CAST THE FATHER IN A LOVING LIGHT? HAVE YOU NOT FOUGHT OUT AGAINST THEY WHO SPEAK AND PREACH OF HIS WRATHFUL IMAGE? AGAINST THEY WHO KNOW NOT THEIR GOD?"

"If you are Michael, then all that I have done is sacred to my body and soul. If you are Lucifer, the father of death, the mortal body that I am curses your name."

"AND WHAT OF THE SOUL?"

"My soul and body alike seek your true identity. Why do you now persecute me? Why did you lead me to believe you are great Michael, and now wish to remain anonymous?"

"TRUE, REBUCK, YOU HAVE BESTOWED

GREAT GLORY ON THE FATHER, YET YOU ARE NOT EXCLUDED FROM THE GREAT TEST OF FAITH THAT ALL MEN MUST ENDURE."

Ron Rebuck bowed his head. He could no longer speak.

"STAND PROUD, REBUCK, YOUR WORKS HAVE NOT BEEN IN VAIN. BUT NOW, THE TIME HAS COME THAT I MUST CHOOSE ANOTHER–ONE YOUNGER OF BODY, WHO SHALL CARRY ON YOUR GREAT MISSION. IN THIS WORLD YOU SHALL NOT AGAIN HEAR MY VOICE. I SAY TO YOU–BEWARE THIS NIGHT–FOR ONE WHO THIRSTS FOR YOUR BLOOD NOW LURKS ABOUT THESE VERY GROUNDS."

The radiant lights vanished. The waning snow turned to a light rain. The presence Ron Rebuck lived with, that unyielding obsession, seeped rapidly from his body. He now longed for his wife and son. With a rejuvenation he never felt possible–to live like an ordinary man, no longer to be burdened with his message for the world–he proceeded to run. And run he did.

Through the woods, he sprinted. His face dawned with content. But his thought of going to the monastery to thank the monks for their hospitality and to return to the confines of his mission place where his wife and son would be waiting, were never to materialize.

As he was about to leap over a ditch, something below made him halt. He looked down and saw the body of a man in priests' attire whose stomach had been brutally mutilated. Father Augustus had finally met up with the Judas he'd tracked.

He sensed a presence from across the ditch and looked

up to see eyes glowing in the woods. A figure moved out from the blackness and came slowly toward him. The face, below the eyes, was muffled in a black veil. The figure now halted directly across from him and he could see it was a woman.

He looked down at the body in the ditch, then stared into the depths of Jennifer Jewell's eyes.

"How many more have you slaughtered? How many have you killed in the name of Lucifer?"

She was silent, deadly silent. The face had lost its beauty, as now she returned his probing look with that of a demonic glare.

Grimly, he asked, "Are you my executioner—my Judas?"

Four men, their faces hidden, moved out from the night shadows. Ron Rebuck had his answer.

# Epilogue

AT THE APPROACH of dawn, a drizzle of rain fell on the hills. The morning dew secreted its ghostly vapor as it rose from the ground. A gray mist drifted under the overcast sky. There was no sign of the snow forecast for Christmas day.

Two monks walked through the woods in quiet meditation. They became distracted by the sound of crows causing a commotion beyond the next ridge. Curious, the monks walked over the top of the ridge, sending the crows flapping their black wings, cawing and flying off in every direction.

Through a cluster of trees and with the mist adding its eerie effect, they now looked upon the grotesque sight of a man crucified upside down. The monks stood transfixed in horror.

AT 7:00 A.M., the first bulletins telling of Ron Rebuck's death flashed over TV and radio.

At 7:15 Jennifer Jewell had made the transportation arrangements for the Rebuck family to depart from the First Michael's Mission in the Pennsylvania Poconos.

At 7:45, reporters, cameramen and other media personnel from New York City and parts elsewhere joined the local reporters who had first spread the news.

At 8:00 sharp, Henry Rodriguez took a sip of his morning coffee at the Brazilian plantation he was visiting.

At 9:25, the Governor put the nearest National Guard units on standby.

At 9:35, angry radicals in St. Louis didn't know who to blame.

At 10:00, in a mental institution not far away, Paul Bartley heard the news and thought Ron Rebuck was a football player.

At 11:05, the hired-out Sabre Star carrying the Rebuck family touched down at an airport ten minutes away.

At 11:07, Mike Spenard drove Nancy Manning to Christmas Mass.

At 11:10, Mr. and Mrs. John Milton watched their TV for the latest coverage of the tragedy.

At 11:15, Billy Hale prayed for Ron Rebuck's soul.

At 11:22, a blue and white police car entered the monastery gate and stopped at a bend in the road where numerous police vehicles and station wagons bearing the code letters of various TV and radio stations were parked.

JUNE REBUCK, Ron Rebuck, Jr. and Mrs. Rebuck, Sr., along with Jennifer Jewell, stepped out of the police car and were quickly escorted by a cadre of police to a waiting "Cheyenne" Jeep that would take them into the woods to the site of the crucifixion.

Shortly thereafter, the three Rebucks and Jennifer Jewell got out of the Jeep and made their way a short distance on foot to the scene of the tradegy.

From the corner of her eye, Josephine Rebuck saw here dead son; she crumpled into a trooper's arms. A lone monk watched and wept.

June Rebuck refused to look up; she kept her eyes fixed on the ground. The sheriff, who was standing by, realizing the futility of any effort to persuade her to withdraw and spare herself the horrendous sight, physically pushed reporters out of the way as he led her along the trail of sorrow.

At the foot of the cross, her eyes still on the ground, her arms firmly around her son's, she suddenly felt the jolting vibration of his body. Ron Rebuck, Jr. had seen his father and was weeping bitterly. "Take me to him, Ronnie . . . Take me to your father," she pleaded.

The deputies standing nearby caught the signal from the sheriff for them to withdraw. It was a courtesy that would enable Ron Rebuck's wife and son to be alone in their grief.

As Ron, Jr.'s sobbing intensified, June Rebuck finally looked up. Her body quaked. She turned ashen-pale, as though the bood in her veins had stopped flowing. Feeling her falling, her son tightened his grip around her waist, but she tore loose from her son's hold and fell to her knees, her head close to the face of the man who'd been her partner in life . . . the face of the man she loved and lived for. She gently wiped away the blood from his nose and that which had caked around his mouth. Then she kissed her dead husband's cold face, over and over, whispering words from a broken heart.

Ron Rebuck, Jr., stared at the man, the pathetic figure of his father—his arms and legs extended, his hands and feet nailed to the rough wood with railroad spikes. The rain, the rain, like a million tears, dripped on the nude body.

The pupils in Ron Rebuck, Jr.'s eyes gleamed—a familiar gleam, reminiscent of his father's. With Jennifer Jewell now at his side, he saw for the first time the torn sheet that hung loosely above the cross, its crude letters painted in red that spelled out the words: THE ANTICHRIST.